Elizabeth Strout is the Pulitzer Prize-winning author of *Olive Kitteridge*, the Man Booker Prize for Fiction and Baileys Women's Prize longlisted *My Name is Lucy Barton*; *The Burgess Boys*, a *New York Times* bestseller; *Abide With Me* and *Amy & Isabelle*, which won the *Los Angeles Times* Art Seidenbaum Award for First Fiction and the *Chicago Tribune* Heartland Prize and was shortlisted for the Orange Prize and the PEN/Faulkner Award. She lives in New York City and Portland, Maine.

ELIZABETH STROUT

Olive Kitteridge

SCRIBNER

LONDON NEW YORK TORONTO SYDNEY NEW DELHI

First published in Great Britain by Pocket Books, an imprint of
Simon & Schuster UK Ltd, 2008
This edition published by Scribner, 2016
A CBS COMPANY

3 5 7 9 10 8 6 4 2

Simon & Schuster UK Ltd
1st Floor
222 Gray's Inn Road
London WC1X 8HB

www.simonandschuster.co.uk

Simon & Schuster Australia, Sydney
Simon & Schuster India, New Delhi

A CIP catalogue record for this book
is available from the British Library.

PB ISBN: 978-1-47116-886-4
EBOOK ISBN: 978-1-4711-2865-3

Printed and bound by CPI Group (UK) Ltd, Croydon CR0 4YY

Simon & Schuster UK Ltd are committed to sourcing paper that is made from wood grown in
sustainable forests and support the Forest Stewardship Council, the leading international forest
certification organisation. Our books displaying the FSC logo are printed on FSC certified paper.

For my mother
who can make life magical
and is the best storyteller I know

Contents

OLIVE KITTERIDGE

Pharmacy

For many years Henry Kitteridge was a pharmacist in the next town over, driving every morning on snowy roads, or rainy roads, or summertime roads, when the wild raspberries shot their new growth in brambles along the last section of town before he turned off to where the wider road led to the pharmacy. Retired now, he still wakes early and remembers how mornings used to be his favorite, as though the world were his secret, tires rumbling softly beneath him and the light emerging through the early fog, the brief sight of the bay off to his right, then the pines, tall and slender, and almost always he rode with the window partly open because he loved the smell of the pines and the heavy salt air, and in the winter he loved the smell of the cold.

The pharmacy was a small two-story building attached to another building that housed separately a hardware store and a small grocery. Each morning Henry parked in the back by the large metal bins, and then entered the pharmacy's back door, and went about switching on the lights, turning up the thermostat, or, if it was summer, getting the fans going. He would open the safe, put money in the register, unlock the front door, wash his hands, put on his white lab coat. The ritual was pleasing, as though the old store—with its shelves of toothpaste, vitamins, cosmetics, hair adornments, even sewing needles and greeting cards, as well as red rubber hot water bottles, enema pumps—was a person altogether steady and steadfast. And any unpleasantness that may have occurred back in his home, any uneasiness at the way his wife often left their bed to wander through their home in the night's dark hours—all this receded like a shoreline as he walked through the safety of his pharmacy. Standing in the back, with the drawers and rows of pills, Henry was cheerful when the phone began to ring, cheerful when Mrs. Merriman came for her blood pressure medicine, or old Cliff Mott arrived for his digitalis, cheerful when he prepared the Valium for Rachel Jones, whose husband ran off the night their baby was born. It was Henry's nature to listen, and many times during the week he would say, "Gosh, I'm awful sorry to hear that," or "Say, isn't that something?"

Inwardly, he suffered the quiet trepidations of a man who had witnessed twice in childhood the nervous breakdowns of a mother who had otherwise cared for him with stridency. And so if, as rarely happened, a customer was distressed over a price, or irritated by the quality of an Ace bandage or ice pack, Henry did what he could to rectify things quickly. For many years Mrs. Granger worked for him; her husband was a lobster fisherman, and she seemed to carry with her the cold breeze of the open water, not so eager to please a wary customer. He had to listen with half an ear as he filled prescriptions, to make sure she was not at the cash register dismissing a complaint. More than once he was reminded of that same sensation in watching to see that his wife, Olive, did not bear down too hard on Christopher over a homework assignment or a chore left undone; that sense of his attention hovering—the need to keep everyone content. When he heard a briskness in Mrs. Granger's voice, he would step down from his back post, moving toward the center of the store to talk with the customer himself. Otherwise, Mrs. Granger did her job well. He appreciated that she was not chatty, kept perfect inventory, and almost never called in sick. That she died in her sleep one night astonished him, and left him with some feeling of responsibility, as though he had missed, working alongside her for years, whatever symptom might have shown itself that he, handling his pills and syrups and syringes, could have fixed.

"Mousy," his wife said, when he hired the new girl. "Looks just like a mouse."

Denise Thibodeau had round cheeks, and small eyes that peeped through her brown-framed glasses. "But a nice mouse," Henry said. "A cute one."

"No one's cute who can't stand up straight," Olive said. It was true that Denise's narrow shoulders sloped forward, as though apologizing for something. She was twenty-two, just out of the state university of Vermont. Her husband was also named Henry, and Henry Kitteridge, meeting Henry Thibodeau for the first time, was taken with what he saw as an unself-conscious excellence. The young man was vigorous and sturdy-featured with a light in his eye that seemed to lend a flickering resplendence to his decent, ordinary face. He was a plumber, working in a business owned by his uncle. He and Denise had been married one year.

"Not keen on it," Olive said, when he suggested they have the young couple to dinner. Henry let it drop. This was a time when his son—not yet showing the physical signs of adolescence—had become suddenly and strenuously sullen, his mood like a poison shot through the air, and Olive seemed as changed and changeable as Christopher, the two having fast and furious fights that became just as suddenly some blanket of silent intimacy where Henry, clueless, stupefied, would find himself to be the odd man out.

But standing in the back parking lot at the end of a late summer day, while he spoke with Denise and Henry Thibodeau, and the sun tucked itself behind the spruce trees, Henry Kitteridge felt such a longing to be in the presence of this young couple, their faces turned to him with a diffident but eager interest as he recalled his own days at the university many years ago, that he said, "Now, say. Olive and I would like you to come for supper soon."

He drove home, past the tall pines, past the glimpse of the bay, and thought of the Thibodeaus driving the other way, to their trailer on the outskirts of town. He pictured the trailer, cozy and picked up—for Denise was neat in her habits—and imagined them sharing the news of their day. Denise might say, "He's an easy boss." And Henry might say, "Oh, I like the guy a lot."

He pulled into his driveway, which was not a driveway so much as a patch of lawn on top of the hill, and saw Olive in the garden. "Hello, Olive," he said, walking to her. He wanted to put his arms around her, but she had a darkness that seemed to stand beside her like an acquaintance that would not go away. He told her the Thibodeaus were coming for supper. "It's only right," he said.

Olive wiped sweat from her upper lip, turned to rip up a clump of onion grass. "Then that's that, Mr. President," she said. "Give your order to the cook."

On Friday night the couple followed him home, and the young Henry shook Olive's hand. "Nice place here," he said. "With that view of the water. Mr. Kitteridge says you two built this yourselves."

"Indeed, we did."

Christopher sat sideways at the table, slumped in adolescent gracelessness, and did not respond when Henry Thibodeau asked him if he played any sports at school. Henry Kitteridge felt an unexpected fury sprout inside him; he wanted to shout at the boy, whose poor manners, he felt, revealed something unpleasant not expected to be found in the Kitteridge home.

"When you work in a pharmacy," Olive told Denise, setting before her a plate of baked beans, "you learn the secrets of everyone in town." Olive sat down across from her, pushed forward a bottle of ketchup. "Have to know to keep your mouth shut. But seems like you know how to do that."

"Denise understands," Henry Kitteridge said.

Denise's husband said, "Oh, sure. You couldn't find someone more trustworthy than Denise."

"I believe you," Henry said, passing the man a basket of rolls. "And please. Call me Henry. One of my favorite names," he added. Denise laughed quietly; she liked him, he could see this.

Christopher slumped farther into his seat.

Henry Thibodeau's parents lived on a farm inland, and so the two Henrys discussed crops, and pole beans, and the corn not being as sweet this summer from the lack of rain, and how to get a good asparagus bed.

"Oh, for God's *sake*," said Olive, when, in passing the ketchup to the young man, Henry Kitteridge knocked it over, and ketchup lurched out like thickened blood across the oak table. Trying to pick up the bottle, he caused it to roll unsteadily, and ketchup ended up on his fingertips, then on his white shirt.

"Leave it," Olive commanded, standing up. "Just leave it alone, Henry. For God's sake." And Henry Thibodeau, perhaps at the sound of his own name being spoken sharply, sat back, looking stricken.

"Gosh, what a mess I've made," Henry Kitteridge said.

For dessert they were each handed a blue bowl with a scoop of vanilla ice cream sliding in its center. "Vanilla's my favorite," Denise said.

"Is it," said Olive.

"Mine, too," Henry Kitteridge said.

As autumn came, the mornings darker, and the pharmacy getting only a short sliver of the direct sun before it passed over the building and left the store lit by its own overhead lights, Henry stood in the back filling the small plastic bottles, answering the telephone, while Denise stayed up front near the cash register. At lunchtime, she unwrapped a sandwich she brought from home, and ate it in the back where the storage was, and then he would eat his lunch, and sometimes when there was no one in the store, they would linger with a cup of coffee bought from the grocer next door. Denise seemed a naturally quiet girl, but she was given to spurts of sudden talkativeness. "My mother's had MS for years, you know, so starting way back we all learned to help out.

All three of my brothers are different. Don't you think it's funny when it happens that way?" The oldest brother, Denise said, straightening a bottle of shampoo, had been her father's favorite until he'd married a girl her father didn't like. Her own in-laws were wonderful, she said. She'd had a boyfriend before Henry, a Protestant, and his parents had not been so kind to her. "It wouldn't have worked out," she said, tucking a strand of hair behind her ear.

"Well, Henry's a terrific young man," Henry answered.

She nodded, smiling through her glasses like a thirteen-year-old girl. Again, he pictured her trailer, the two of them like overgrown puppies tumbling together; he could not have said why this gave him the particular kind of happiness it did, like liquid gold being poured through him.

She was as efficient as Mrs. Granger had been, but more relaxed. "Right beneath the vitamins in the second aisle," she would tell a customer. "Here, I'll show you." Once, she told Henry she sometimes let a person wander around the store before asking if she could help them. "That way, see, they might find something they didn't know they needed. And your sales will go up." A block of winter sun was splayed across the glass of the cosmetics shelf; a strip of wooden floor shone like honey.

He raised his eyebrows appreciatively. "Lucky for me, Denise, when you came through that door." She pushed up her glasses with the back of her hand, then ran the duster over the ointment jars.

Jerry McCarthy, the boy who delivered the pharmaceuticals once a week from Portland—or more often if needed—would sometimes have his lunch in the back room. He was eighteen, right out of high school; a big, fat kid with a smooth face, who perspired so much that splotches of his shirt would be wet, at times even down over his breasts, so the poor fellow looked to be lactating. Seated on a crate, his big knees practically to his ears, he'd eat a sandwich that had spilling from it mayonnaisey clumps of egg salad or tuna fish, landing on his shirt.

More than once Henry saw Denise hand him a paper towel. "That happens to me," Henry heard her say one day. "Whenever I eat a sandwich that isn't just cold cuts, I end up a mess." It couldn't have been true. The girl was neat as a pin, if plain as a plate.

"Good afternoon," she'd say when the telephone rang. "This is the Village Pharmacy. How can I help you today?" Like a girl playing grown-up.

And then: On a Monday morning when the air in the pharmacy held a sharp chill, he went about opening up the store, saying, "How was your weekend, Denise?" Olive had refused to go to church the day before, and Henry, uncharacteristically, had spoken to her sharply. "Is it too much to ask," he had found himself saying, as he stood in the kitchen in his undershorts, ironing his trousers. "A man's wife accompanying him to church?" Going without her seemed a public exposure of familial failure.

"Yes, it most certainly is too goddamn much to ask!" Olive had almost spit, her fury's door flung open. "You have no idea how tired I am, teaching all day, going to foolish meetings where the goddamn principal is a moron! Shopping. Cooking. Ironing. Laundry. Doing Christopher's homework with him! And *you*—" She had grabbed on to the back of a dining room chair, and her dark hair, still uncombed from its night's disarrangement, had fallen across her eyes. "*You*, Mr. Head Deacon Claptrap Nice Guy, expect me to give up my Sunday mornings and go sit among a bunch of snot-wots!" Very suddenly she had sat down in the chair. "Well, I'm sick and tired of it," she'd said, calmly. "Sick to death."

A darkness had rumbled through him; his soul was suffocating in tar. The next morning, Olive spoke to him conversationally. "Jim's car smelled like upchuck last week. Hope he's cleaned it out." Jim O'Casey taught with Olive, and for years took both Christopher and Olive to school.

"Hope so," said Henry, and in that way their fight was done.

"Oh, I had a wonderful weekend," said Denise, her small eyes behind her glasses looking at him with an eagerness that was so childlike it could have cracked his heart in two. "We went to Henry's folks and dug potatoes at night. Henry put the headlights on from the car and we dug potatoes. Finding the potatoes in that cold soil—like an Easter egg hunt!"

He stopped unpacking a shipment of penicillin, and stepped down to talk to her. There were no customers yet, and below the front window the radiator hissed. He said, "Isn't that lovely, Denise."

She nodded, touching the top of the vitamin shelf beside her. A small motion of fear seemed to pass over her face. "I got cold and went and sat in the car and watched Henry digging potatoes, and I thought: It's too good to be true."

He wondered what in her young life had made her not trust happiness; perhaps her mother's illness. He said, "You enjoy it, Denise. You have many years of happiness ahead." Or maybe, he thought, returning to the boxes, it was part of being Catholic—you were made to feel guilty about everything.

The year that followed—was it the happiest year of his own life? He often thought so, even knowing that such a thing was foolish to claim about any year of one's life; but in his memory, that particular year held the sweetness of a time that contained no thoughts of a beginning and no thoughts of an end, and when he drove to the pharmacy in the early morning darkness of winter, then later in the breaking light of spring, the full-throated summer opening before him, it was the small pleasures of his work that seemed in their simplicities to fill him to the brim. When Henry Thibodeau drove into the gravelly lot, Henry Kitteridge often went to hold the door open for Denise, calling out, "Hello there, Henry," and Henry Thibodeau would stick his head through the open car window and call back, "Hello there, Henry," with a big grin on a face lit with decency and humor. Sometimes there was just a salute. "Henry!" And the other Henry would return, "Henry!" They got a kick out of this, and Denise, like a football tossed gently between them, would duck into the store.

When she took off her mittens, her hands were as thin as a child's, yet when she touched the buttons on the cash register, or slid something into a white bag, they assumed the various shapes of a graceful grown woman's hands, hands—thought Henry—that would touch her husband lovingly, that would, with the quiet authority of a woman, someday pin a baby's diaper, smooth a fevered forehead, tuck a gift from the tooth fairy under a pillow.

Watching her, as she poked her glasses back up onto her nose while reading over the list of inventory, Henry thought she was the stuff of America, for this was back when the hippie business was beginning, and reading in *Newsweek* about the marijuana and "free love" could cause an unease in Henry that one look at Denise dispelled. "We're going to hell like the Romans," Olive said triumphantly. "America's a big cheese gone rotten." But Henry would not stop believing that the temperate prevailed, and in his pharmacy, every day he worked beside a girl whose only dream was to someday make a family with her husband. "I don't care about Women's Lib," she told Henry. "I want to have a house and make beds." Still, if he'd had a daughter (he would have loved a daughter), he would have cautioned her against it. He would have said: Fine, make beds, but find a way to keep using your head. But Denise was not his daughter, and he told her it was noble to be a homemaker—vaguely aware of the freedom that accompanied caring for someone with whom you shared no blood.

He loved her guilelessness, he loved the purity of her dreams, but this did not mean of course that he was in love with her. The natural reticence of her in fact caused him to desire Olive with a new wave of power. Olive's sharp opinions, her full breasts, her stormy moods and sudden, deep laughter unfolded within him a new level of aching eroticism, and sometimes when he was heaving in the dark of night, it was not Denise who came to mind but, oddly, her strong, young husband—the fierceness of the young man as he gave way to the animalism of possession—and there would be for Henry Kitteridge a flash of incredible frenzy as though in the act of loving his wife he was joined with all men in loving the world of women, who contained the dark, mossy secret of the earth deep within them.

"Goodness," Olive said, when he moved off her.

———

In college, Henry Thibodeau had played football, just as Henry Kitteridge had. "Wasn't it great?" the young Henry asked him one day. He had arrived early to pick Denise up, and had come into the store. "Hearing the people yelling from the stands? Seeing that pass come right at you and knowing you're going to catch it? Oh boy, I loved that." He grinned, his clear face seeming to give off a refracted light. "Loved it."

"I suspect I wasn't nearly as good as you," said Henry Kitteridge. He had been good at the running, the ducking, but he had not been aggressive enough to be a really good player. It shamed him to remember that he had felt fear at every game. He'd been glad enough when his grades slipped and he had to give it up.

"Ah, I wasn't that good," said Henry Thibodeau, rubbing a big hand over his head. "I just liked it."

"He was good," said Denise, getting her coat on. "He was really good. The cheerleaders had a cheer just for him." Shyly, with pride, she said, "Let's *go,* Thibodeau, let's *go.*"

Heading for the door, Henry Thibodeau said, "Say, we're going to have you and Olive for dinner soon."

"Oh, now—you're not to worry."

Denise had written Olive a thank-you note in her neat, small handwriting. Olive had scanned it, flipped it across the table to Henry. "Handwriting's just as cautious as she is," Olive had said. "She is the *plainest* child I have ever seen. With her pale coloring, why does she wear gray and beige?"

"I don't know," he said, agreeably, as though he had wondered himself. He had not wondered.

"A simpleton," Olive said.

But Denise was not a simpleton. She was quick with numbers, and remembered everything she was told by Henry about the pharmaceuticals he sold. She had majored in animal sciences at the university, and was conversant with molecular structures. Sometimes on her break she would sit on a crate in the back room with the Merck Manual on her lap. Her child-face, made serious by her glasses, would be intent on the page, her knees poked up, her shoulders slumped forward.

Cute, would go through his mind as he glanced through the doorway on his way by. He might say, "Okay, then, Denise?"

"Oh, yeah, I'm fine."

His smile would linger as he arranged his bottles, typed up labels. Denise's nature attached itself to his as easily as aspirin attached itself to the enzyme COX-2; Henry moved through his day pain free. The sweet hissing of the radiators, the tinkle of the bell when someone came through the door, the creaking of the wooden floors, the ka-*ching* of the register: He sometimes thought in those days that the pharmacy was like a healthy autonomic nervous system in a workable, quiet state.

Evenings, adrenaline poured through him. "All I do is cook and clean and pick up after people," Olive might shout, slamming a bowl of beef stew before him. "People just waiting for me to serve them, with their faces hanging out." Alarm made his arms tingle.

"Perhaps you need to help out more around the house," he told Christopher.

"How dare you tell him what to do? You don't even pay enough attention to know what he's going through in social studies class!" Olive shouted this at him while Christopher remained silent, a smirk on his face. "Why, Jim O'Casey is more sympathetic to the kid than you are," Olive said. She slapped a napkin down hard against the table.

"Jim teaches at the school, for crying out loud, and sees you and Chris every day. What *is* the matter with social studies class?"

"Only that the goddamn teacher is a moron, which Jim understands instinctively," Olive said. "You see Christopher every day, too. But you don't know anything because you're safe in your little world with Plain Jane."

"She's a good worker," Henry answered. But in the morning the blackness of Olive's mood was often gone, and Henry would be able to drive to work with a renewal of the hope that had seemed evanescent the night before. In the pharmacy there was goodwill toward men.

Denise asked Jerry McCarthy if he planned on going to college. "I dunno. Don't think so." The boy's face colored—perhaps he had a little crush on Denise, or perhaps he felt like a child in her presence, a boy still living at home, with his chubby wrists and belly.

"Take a night course," Denise said, brightly. "You can sign up right after Christmas. Just one course. You should do that." Denise nodded, and looked at Henry, who nodded back.

"It's true, Jerry," Henry said, who had never given a great deal of thought to the boy. "What is it that interests you?"

The boy shrugged his big shoulders.

"Something must interest you."

"This stuff." The boy gestured toward the boxes of packed pills he had recently brought through the back door.

And so, amazingly, he had signed up for a science course, and when he received an A that spring, Denise said, "Stay right there." She returned from the grocery store with a little boxed cake, and said, "Henry, if the phone doesn't ring, we're going to celebrate."

Pushing cake into his mouth, Jerry told Denise he had gone to mass the Sunday before to pray he did well on the exam.

This was the kind of thing that surprised Henry about Catholics. He almost said, God didn't get an A for you, Jerry; you got it for yourself, but Denise was saying, "Do you go every Sunday?"

The boy looked embarrassed, sucked frosting from his finger. "I will now," he said, and Denise laughed, and Jerry did, too, his face pink and glowing.

Autumn now, November, and so many years later that when Henry runs a comb through his hair on this Sunday morning, he has to pluck some strands of gray from the black plastic teeth before slipping the comb back into his pocket. He gets a fire going in the stove for Olive before he goes off to church. "Bring home the gossip," Olive says to him, tugging at her sweater while she peers into a large pot where apples are burbling in a stew. She is making applesauce from the season's last apples, and the smell reaches him briefly—sweet, familiar, it tugs at some ancient longing—before he goes out the door in his tweed jacket and tie.

"Do my best," he says. No one seems to wear a suit to church anymore.

In fact, only a handful of the congregation goes to church regularly anymore. This saddens Henry, and worries him. They have been through two ministers in the last five years, neither one bringing much inspiration to the pulpit. The current fellow, a man with a beard, and who doesn't wear a robe, Henry suspects won't last long. He is young with a growing family, and will have to move on. What worries Henry about the paucity of the congregation is that perhaps others have felt what he increasingly tries to deny—that this weekly gathering provides no real sense of comfort. When they bow their heads or sing a hymn, there is no sense anymore—for Henry—that God's presence is blessing them. Olive herself has become an unapologetic atheist. He does not know when this happened. It was not true when they were first married; they had talked of animal dissections in their college biology class, how the system of respiration alone was miraculous, a *creation* by a splendid power.

He drives over the dirt road, turning onto the paved road that will take him into town. Only a few leaves of deep red remain on the otherwise bare limbs of the maples; the oak leaves are russet and wrinkled; briefly through the trees is the glimpse of the bay, flat and steel-gray today with the overcast November sky.

He passes by where the pharmacy used to be. In its place now is a large chain drugstore with huge glass sliding doors, covering the ground where both the old pharmacy and grocery store stood, large enough so that the back parking lot where Henry would linger with Denise by the dumpster at day's end before getting into their separate cars—all this is now taken over by a store that sells not only drugs, but huge rolls of paper towels and boxes of all sizes of garbage bags. Even plates and mugs can be bought there, spatulas, cat food. The trees off to the side have been cut down to make a parking lot. You get used to things, he thinks, without getting used to things.

It seems a very long time ago that Denise stood shivering in the winter cold before finally getting into her car. How young she was! How painful to remember the bewilderment on her young face; and yet he can still remember how he could make her smile. Now, so far away in Texas—so far away it's a different country—she is the age he was then. She had dropped a red mitten one night; he had bent to get it, held the cuff open and watched while she'd slipped her small hand in.

The white church sits near the bare maple trees. He knows why he is thinking of Denise with this keenness. Her birthday card to him did not arrive last week, as it has, always on time, for the last twenty years. She writes him a note with the card. Sometimes a line or two stands out, as in the one last year when she mentioned that Paul, a freshman in high school, had become obese. Her word. "Paul has developed a full-blown problem now—at three hundred pounds, he is obese." She does not mention what she or her husband will do about this, if in fact they can "do" anything. The twin girls, younger, are both athletic and starting to get phone calls from boys "which horrifies me," Denise wrote. She never signs the card "love," just her name in her small neat hand, "Denise."

In the gravel lot by the church, Daisy Foster has just stepped from her car, and her mouth opens in a mock look of surprise and pleasure, but the pleasure is real, he knows—Daisy is always glad to see him. Daisy's husband died two years ago, a retired policeman who smoked himself to death, twenty-five years older than Daisy; she remains ever lovely, ever gracious with her kind blue eyes. What will become of her, Henry doesn't know. It seems to Henry, as he takes his seat in his usual middle pew, that women are far braver than men. The possibility of

Olive's dying and leaving him alone gives him glimpses of horror he can't abide.

And then his mind moves back to the pharmacy that is no longer there.

"Henry's going hunting this weekend," Denise said one morning in November. "Do you hunt, Henry?" She was getting the cash drawer ready and didn't look up at him.

"Used to," Henry answered. "Too old for it now." The one time in his youth when he had shot a doe, he'd been sickened by the way the sweet, startled animal's head had swayed back and forth before its thin legs had folded and it had fallen to the forest floor. "Oh, you're a softie," Olive had said.

"Henry goes with Tony Kuzio." Denise slipped the cash drawer into the register, and stepped around to arrange the breath mints and gum that were neatly laid out by the front counter. "His best friend since he was five."

"And what does Tony do now?"

"Tony's married with two little kids. He works for Midcoast Power, and fights with his wife." Denise looked over at Henry. "Don't say that I said so."

"No."

"She's tense a lot, and yells. Boy, I wouldn't want to live like that."

"No, it'd be no way to live."

The telephone rang and Denise, turning on her toe playfully, went to answer it. "The Village Pharmacy. Good morning. How may I help you?" A pause. "Oh, yes, we have multivitamins with no iron. . . . You're very welcome."

On lunch break, Denise told the hefty, baby-faced Jerry, "My husband talked about Tony the whole time we were going out. The scrapes they'd get into when they were kids. Once, they went off and didn't get back till way after dark, and Tony's mother said to him, 'I was so worried, Tony. I could kill you.' " Denise picked lint off the sleeve of her gray sweater. "I always thought that was funny. Worrying that your child might be dead and then saying you'll kill him."

"You wait," Henry Kitteridge said, stepping around the boxes Jerry had brought into the back room. "From their very first fever, you never stop worrying."

"I *can't* wait," Denise said, and for the first time it occurred to Henry that soon she would have children and not work for him anymore.

Unexpectedly Jerry spoke. "Do you like him? Tony? You two get along?"

"I do like him," Denise said. "Thank goodness. I was scared enough to meet him. Do you have a best friend from childhood?"

"I guess," Jerry said, color rising in his fat, smooth cheeks. "But we kind of went our separate ways."

"My best friend," said Denise, "when we got to junior high school, she got kind of fast. Do you want another soda?"

A Saturday at home: Lunch was crabmeat sandwiches, grilled with cheese. Christopher was putting one into his mouth, but the telephone rang, and Olive went to answer it. Christopher, without being asked, waited, the sandwich held in his hand. Henry's mind seemed to take a picture of that moment, his son's instinctive deference at the very same time they heard Olive's voice in the next room. "Oh, you poor child," she said, in a voice Henry would always remember—filled with such dismay that all her outer Olive-ness seemed stripped away. "You poor, poor child."

And then Henry rose and went into the other room, and he didn't remember much, only the tiny voice of Denise, and then speaking for a few moments to her father-in-law.

The funeral was held in the Church of the Holy Mother of Contrition, three hours away in Henry Thibodeau's hometown. The church was large and dark with its huge stained-glass windows, the priest up front in a layered white robe, swinging incense back and forth; Denise already seated in the front near her parents and sisters by the time Olive and Henry arrived. The casket was closed, and had been closed at the wake the evening before. The church was almost full. Henry, seated next to Olive toward the back, recognized no one, until a silent large presence made him look up, and there was Jerry McCarthy. Henry and Olive moved over to make room for him.

Jerry whispered, "I read about it in the paper," and Henry briefly rested a hand on the boy's fat knee.

The service went on and on; there were readings from the Bible, and other readings, and then an elaborate getting ready for Communion. The priest took cloths and unfolded them and draped them over a table, and then people were leaving their seats aisle by aisle to go up and kneel and open their mouths for a wafer, all sipping from the same large silver goblet, while Henry and Olive stayed where they were. In spite of the sense of unreality that had descended over Henry, he was struck with the unhygienic nature of all these people sipping from the same cup, and struck—with cynicism—at how the priest, after everyone else was done, tilted his beaky head back and drank whatever drops were left.

Six young men carried the casket down the center aisle. Olive nudged Henry with her elbow, and Henry nodded. One of the pallbearers—one of the last ones—had a face that was so white and stunned that Henry was afraid he would drop the casket. This was Tony Kuzio, who, thinking Henry Thibodeau was a deer in the early morning darkness just a few days ago, had pulled the trigger of his rifle and killed his best friend.

Who was to help her? Her father lived far upstate in Vermont with a wife who was an invalid, her brothers and their wives lived hours away, her in-laws were immobilized by grief. She stayed with her in-laws for two weeks, and when she came back to work, she told Henry she couldn't stay with them much longer; they were kind, but she could hear her mother-in-law weeping all night, and it gave her the willies; she needed to be alone so she could cry by herself.

"Of course you do, Denise."

"But I can't go back to the trailer."

"No."

That night he sat up in bed, his chin resting on both hands. "Olive," he said, "the girl is utterly helpless. Why, she can't drive a car, and she's never written a check."

"How can it be," said Olive, "that you grow up in Vermont and can't even drive a car?"

"I don't know," Henry acknowledged. "I had no idea she couldn't drive a car."

"Well, I can see why Henry married her. I wasn't sure at first. But when I got a look at his mother at the funeral—ah, poor thing. But she didn't seem to have a bit of oomph to her."

"Well, she's about broken with grief."

"I understand that," Olive said patiently. "I'm simply telling you he married his mother. Men do." After a pause. "Except for you."

"She's going to have to learn to drive," Henry said. "That's the first thing. And she needs a place to live."

"Sign her up for driving school."

Instead, he took her in his car along the back dirt roads. The snow had arrived, but on the roads that led down to the water, the fishermen's trucks had flattened it. "That's right. Slowly up on the clutch." The car bucked like a wild horse, and Henry put his hand against the dashboard.

"Oh, I'm sorry," Denise whispered.

"No, no. You're doing fine."

"I'm just scared. Gosh."

"Because it's brand-new. But, Denise, *nitwits* can drive cars."

She looked at him, a sudden giggle coming from her, and he laughed himself then, without wanting to, while her giggle grew, spilling out so that tears came to her eyes, and she had to stop the car and take the white handkerchief he offered. She took her glasses off and he looked out the window the other way while she used the handkerchief. Snow had made the woods alongside the road seem like a picture in black and white. Even the evergreens seemed dark, spreading their boughs above the black trunks.

"Okay," said Denise. She started the car again; again he was thrown forward. If she burned out the clutch, Olive would be furious.

"That's perfectly all right," he told Denise. "Practice makes perfect, that's all."

In a few weeks, he drove her to Augusta, where she passed the driving test, and then he went with her to buy a car. She had money for this. Henry Thibodeau, it turned out, had had a good life insurance policy, so at least there was that. Now Henry Kitteridge helped her get the car insurance, explained how to make the payments. Earlier, he had taken her to the bank, and for the first time in her life she had a checking account. He had shown her how to write a check.

He was appalled when she mentioned at work one day the amount of money she had sent the Church of the Holy Mother of Contrition, to ensure that candles were lit for Henry every week, a mass said for him each month. He said, "Well, that's nice, Denise." She had lost weight, and when, at the end of the day, he stood in the darkened parking lot, watching from beneath one of the lights on the side of the building, he was struck by the image of her anxious head peering over the steering wheel; and as he got into his own car, a sadness shuddered through him that he could not shake all night.

"What in hell ails you?" Olive said.

"Denise," he answered. "She's helpless."

"People are never as helpless as you think they are," Olive answered. She added, clamping a cover over a pot on the stove, "God, I was afraid of this."

"Afraid of what?"

"Just take the damn dog out," Olive said. "And sit yourself down to supper."

An apartment was found in a small new complex outside of town.

Denise's father-in-law and Henry helped her move her few things in. The place was on the ground floor and didn't get much light. "Well, it's clean," Henry said to Denise, watching her open the refrigerator door, the way she stared at the complete emptiness of its new insides. She only nodded, closing the door. Quietly, she said, "I've never lived alone before."

In the pharmacy he saw that she walked around in a state of unreality; he found his own life felt unbearable in a way he would never have expected. The force of this made no sense. But it alarmed him; mistakes could be made. He forgot to tell Cliff Mott to eat a banana for potassium, now that they'd added a diuretic with his digitalis. The Tibbets woman had a bad night with erythromycin; had he not told her to take it with food? He worked slowly, counting pills sometimes two or three times before he slipped them into their bottles, checking carefully the prescriptions he typed. At home, he looked at Olive wide-eyed when she spoke, so she would see she had his attention. But she did not have his attention. Olive was a frightening stranger; his son often seemed to be smirking at him. "Take the garbage out!" Henry shouted one night, after opening the cupboard beneath the kitchen sink, seeing a bag full of eggshells and dog hairs and balled-up waxed paper. "It's the only thing we ask you to do, and you can't even manage that!"

"Stop shouting," Olive told him. "Do you think that makes you a man? How absolutely pathetic."

Spring came. Daylight lengthened, melted the remaining snows so the roads were wet. Forsythias bloomed clouds of yellow into the chilly air, then rhododendrons screeched their red heads at the world. He pictured everything through Denise's eyes, and thought the beauty must be an assault. Passing by the Caldwells' farm, he saw a handwritten sign, FREE KITTENS, and he arrived at the pharmacy the next day with a kitty-litter box, cat food, and a small black kitten, whose feet were white, as though it had walked through a bowl of whipped cream.

"Oh, Henry," Denise cried, taking the kitten from him, tucking it to her chest.

He felt immensely pleased.

Because it was such a young thing, Slippers spent the days at the pharmacy, where Jerry McCarthy was forced to hold it in his fat hand, against his sweat-stained shirt, saying to Denise, "Oh, yuh. Awful cute. That's nice," before Denise freed him of this little furry encumbrance, taking Slippers back, nuzzling her face against his, while Jerry watched, his thick, shiny lips slightly parted. Jerry had taken two more classes at the university, and had once again received A's in both. Henry and Denise congratulated him with the air of distracted parents; no cake this time.

She had spells of manic loquaciousness, followed by days of silence. Sometimes she stepped out the back door of the pharmacy, and returned with swollen eyes. "Go home early, if you need to," he told her. But she looked at him with panic. "No. Oh, gosh, no. I want to be right here."

It was a warm summer that year. He remembers her standing by the fan near the window, her thin hair flying behind her in little undulating waves, while she gazed through her glasses at the windowsill. Standing there for minutes at a time. She went, for a week, to see one of her brothers. Took another week to see her parents. "This is where I want to be," she said, when she came back.

"Where's she going to find another husband in this tiny town?" Olive asked.

"I don't know. I've wondered," Henry admitted.

"Someone else would go off and join the Foreign Legion, but she's not the type."

"No. She's not the type."

Autumn arrived, and he dreaded it. On the anniversary of Henry Thibodeau's death, Denise went to mass with her in-laws. He was relieved when that day was over, when a week went by, and another, although the holidays loomed, and he felt trepidation, as though he were carrying something that could not be set down. When the phone rang during supper one night, he went to get it with a sense of foreboding. He heard Denise make small screaming sounds—Slippers had gotten out of the house without her seeing, and planning to drive to the grocery store just now, she had run over the cat.

"Go," Olive said. "For God's sake. Go over and comfort your girlfriend."

"Stop it, Olive," Henry said. "That's unnecessary. She's a young widow who ran over her cat. Where in God's name is your compassion?" He was trembling.

"She wouldn't have run over any goddamn cat if you hadn't given it to her."

He brought with him a Valium. That night he sat on her couch, helpless while she wept. The urge to put his arm around her small shoulders was very strong, but he sat holding his hands together in his lap. A small lamp shone from the kitchen table. She blew her nose on his white handkerchief, and said, "Oh, Henry. Henry." He was not sure which Henry she meant. She looked up at him, her small eyes almost swollen shut; she had taken her glasses off to press the handkerchief to them. "I talk to you in my head all the time," she said. She put her glasses back on. "Sorry," she whispered.

"For what?"

"For talking to you in my head all the time."

"No, no."

He put her to bed like a child. Dutifully she went into the bathroom and changed into her pajamas, then lay in the bed with the quilt to her chin. He sat on the edge of the bed, smoothing her hair until the Valium took over. Her eyelids drooped, and she turned her head to the side, murmuring something he couldn't make out. As he drove home slowly along the narrow roads, the darkness seemed alive and sinister as it pressed against the car windows. He pictured moving far upstate, living in a small house with Denise. He could find work somewhere up north; she could have a child. A little girl who would adore him; girls adored their fathers.

"Well, widow-comforter, how is she?" Olive spoke in the dark from the bed.

"Struggling," he said.

"Who isn't."

The next morning he and Denise worked in an intimate silence. If she was up at the cash register and he was behind his counter, he could still feel the invisible presence of her against him, as though she had become Slippers, or he had—their inner selves brushing up against the other. At the end of the day, he said, "I will take care of you," his voice thick with emotion.

She stood before him, and nodded. He zipped her coat for her.

To this day he does not know what he was thinking. In fact, much of it he can't seem to remember. That Tony Kuzio paid her some visits. That she told Tony he must stay married, because if he divorced, he would never be able to marry in the church again. The piercing of jealousy and rage he felt to think of Tony sitting in Denise's little place late at night, begging her forgiveness. The feeling that he was drowning in cobwebs whose sticky maze was spinning about him. That he wanted Denise to continue to love him. And she did. He saw it in her eyes when she dropped a red mitten and he picked it up and held it open for her. *I talk to you in my head all the time.* The pain was sharp, exquisite, unbearable.

"Denise," he said one evening as they closed up the store. "You need some friends."

Her face flushed deeply. She put her coat on with a roughness to her gestures. "I have friends," she said, breathlessly.

"Of course you do. But here in town." He waited by the door until she got her purse from out back. "You might go square dancing at the Grange Hall. Olive and I used to go. It's a nice group of people."

She stepped past him, her face moist, the top of her hair passing by his eyes. "Or maybe you think that's square," he said in the parking lot, lamely.

"I am square," she said, quietly.

"Yes," he said, just as quietly. "I am too." As he drove home in the dark, he pictured being the one to take Denise to a Grange Hall dance. "Spin your partner, and promenade . . . ," her face breaking into a smile, her foot tapping, her small hands on her hips. No—it was not bearable, and he was really frightened now by the sudden emergence of anger he had inspired in her. He could do nothing for her. He could not take her in his arms, kiss her damp forehead, sleep beside her while she wore those little-girl flannel pajamas she'd worn the night Slippers died. To leave Olive was as unthinkable as sawing off his leg. In any event, Denise would not want a divorced Protestant; nor would he be able to abide her Catholicism.

They spoke to each other little as the days went by. He felt coming from her now an unrelenting coldness that was accusatory. What had he led her to expect? And yet when she mentioned a visit from Tony Kuzio, or made an elliptical reference to seeing a movie in Portland, an answering coldness arose in him. He had to grit his teeth not to say, "Too square to go square dancing, then?" How he hated that the words *lovers' quarrel* went through his head.

And then just as suddenly she'd say—ostensibly to Jerry McCarthy, who listened those days with a new comportment to his bulky self, but really she was speaking to Henry (he could see this in the way she glanced at him, holding her small hands together nervously)—"My mother, when I was very little, and before she got sick, would make special cookies for Christmas. We'd paint them with frosting and sprinkles. Oh, I think it was the most fun I ever had sometimes"—her voice wavering while her eyes blinked behind her glasses. And he would understand then that the death of her husband had caused her to feel the death of her girlhood as well; she was mourning the loss of the only *herself* she had ever known—gone now, to this new, bewildered young widow. His eyes, catching hers, softened.

Back and forth this cycle went. For the first time in his life as a pharmacist, he allowed himself a sleeping tablet, slipping one each day into the pocket of his trousers. "All set, Denise?" he'd say when it was time to close. Either she'd silently go get her coat, or she'd say, looking at him with gentleness, "All set, Henry. One more day."

Daisy Foster, standing now to sing a hymn, turns her head and smiles at him. He nods back and opens the hymnal. "A mighty fortress is our God, a bulwark never failing." The words, the sound of the few people singing, make him both hopeful and deeply sad. "You can learn to love someone," he had told Denise, when she'd come to him in the back of the store that spring day. Now, as he places the hymnal back in the holder in front of him, sits once more on the small pew, he thinks of the last time he saw her. They had come north to visit Jerry's parents, and they stopped by the house with the baby, Paul. What Henry remembers is this: Jerry saying something sarcastic about Denise falling asleep each night on the couch, sometimes staying there the whole night through. Denise turning away, looking out over the bay, her shoulders slumped, her small breasts just slightly pushing out against her thin turtleneck sweater, but she had a belly, as though a basketball had been cut in half and she'd swallowed it. No longer the girl she had been—no girl stayed a girl—but a mother, tired, and her round cheeks had deflated as her belly had expanded, so that already there was a look of the gravity of life weighing her down. It was at that point Jerry said sharply, "Denise, stand up straight. Put your shoulders back." He looked at Henry, shaking his head. "How many times do I keep telling her that?"

"Have some chowder," Henry said. "Olive made it last night." But they had to get going, and when they left, he said nothing about their visit, and neither did Olive, surprisingly. He would not have thought Jerry would grow into that sort of man, large, clean-looking—thanks to the ministrations of Denise—not even so much fat anymore, just a big man earning a big salary, speaking to his wife in a way Olive had sometimes spoken to Henry. He did not see her again, although she must have been in the region. In her birthday notes, she reported the death of her mother, then, a few years later, her father. Of course she would have driven north to go to the funerals. Did she think of him? Did she and Jerry stop and visit the grave of Henry Thibodeau?

"You're looking fresh as a daisy," he tells Daisy Foster in the parking lot outside the church. It is their joke; he has said it to her for years.

"How's Olive?" Daisy's blue eyes are still large and lovely, her smile ever present.

"Olive's fine. Home keeping the fires burning. And what's new with you?"

"I have a beau." She says this quietly, putting a hand to her mouth.

"Do you? Daisy, that's wonderful."

"Sells insurance in Heathwick during the day, and takes me dancing on Friday nights."

"Oh, that's wonderful," Henry says again. "You'll have to bring him around for supper."

"Why do you need everyone married?" Christopher has said to him angrily, when Henry has asked about his son's life. "Why can't you just leave people alone?"

He doesn't want people alone.

At home, Olive nods to the table, where a card from Denise lies next to an African violet. "Came yesterday," Olive says. "I forgot."

Henry sits down heavily and opens it with his pen, finds his glasses, peers at it. Her note is longer than usual. She had a scare late in the summer. Pericardial effusion, which turned out to be nothing. "It changed me," she wrote, "as experiences do. It put all my priorities straight, and I have lived every day since then with the deepest gratitude for my family. Nothing matters except family and friends," she wrote, in her neat, small hand. "And I have been blessed with both."

The card, for the first time ever, was signed, "Love."

"How is she?" asks Olive, running water into the sink. Henry stares out at the bay, at the skinny spruce trees along the edge of the cove, and it seems beautiful to him, God's magnificence there in the quiet stateliness of the coastline and the slightly rocking water.

"She's fine," he answers. Not at the moment, but soon, he will walk over to Olive and put his hand on her arm. Olive, who has lived through her own sorrows. For he understood long ago—after Jim O'Casey's car went off the road, and Olive spent weeks going straight to bed after supper, sobbing harshly into a pillow—Henry understood then that Olive had loved Jim O'Casey, had possibly been loved by him, though Henry never asked her and she never told, just as he did not tell her of the gripping, sickening need he felt for Denise until the day she came to him to report Jerry's proposal, and he said: "Go."

He puts the card on the windowsill. He has wondered what it has felt like for her to write the words *Dear Henry.* Has she known other Henrys since then? He has no way of knowing. Nor does he know what happened to Tony Kuzio, or whether candles are still being lit for Henry Thibodeau in church.

Henry stands up, Daisy Foster fleeting through his mind, her smile as she spoke of going dancing. The relief that he just felt over Denise's note, that she is glad for the life that unfolded before her, gives way suddenly, queerly, into an odd sense of loss, as if something significant has been taken from him. "Olive," he says.

She must not hear him because of the water running into the sink. She is not as tall as she used to be, and is broader across her back. The water stops. "Olive," he says, and she turns. "You're not going to leave me, are you?"

"Oh, for God's sake, Henry. You could make a woman sick." She wipes her hands quickly on a towel.

He nods. How could he ever tell her—he could not—that all these years of feeling guilty about Denise have carried with them the kernel of still having her? He cannot even bear this thought, and in a moment it will be gone, dismissed as not true. For who could bear to think of himself this way, as a man deflated by the good fortune of others? No, such a thing is ludicrous.

"Daisy has a fellow," he says. "We need to have them over soon."

Incoming Tide

The bay had small whitecaps and the tide was coming in, so the smaller rocks could be heard moving as the water shifted them. Also there was the twanging sound of the cables hitting the masts of the sailboats moored. A few seagulls gave squawking cries as they dove down to pick up the fish heads and tails and shining insides that the boy was tossing from the dock as he cleaned the mackerel. All this Kevin saw as he sat in his car with the windows partly open. The car was parked on the grassy area, not far from the marina. Two trucks were parked farther over, on the gravel by the dock.

How much time went by, Kevin didn't know.

At one point, the marina's screen door opened wheezily and slammed shut, and Kevin watched as a man moved in slow steps in his dark rubber boots, tossing a coil of heavy rope into the back of the truck. If the man noticed Kevin, he gave no sign, even when he backed up his truck and turned his head in Kevin's direction. There was no reason they would recognize each other. Kevin had not been to this town since he was a child; thirteen, when he moved away with his father and brother. He was as much a stranger up here now as any tourist might be, and yet gazing back at the sun-sliced bay, he noted how familiar it felt; he had not expected that. The salt air filled his nose, the wild rugosa bushes with their white blossoms brought him a vague confusion; a sense of sad ignorance seemed cloaked in their benign white petals.

Patty Howe poured coffee into two white mugs, placed them on the counter, said quietly, "You're *wel*come," and moved back to arrange the corn muffins that had just been passed through the opening from the kitchen. She had seen the man sitting in the car—he'd been there well over an hour—but people did that sometimes, drove out from town just to gaze at the water. Still, there was something about him that was troubling her. "They're perfect," she said to the cook, because the tops of the muffins were crispy at the edges, yellow as rising suns. The fact that their newly baked scent did not touch off a queasiness in her, as they had two times in the past year, made her sad; a soft dismalness settled over her. The doctor had said to them, For three months you are not to even think of it.

The screen door opened, banged shut. Through the large window, Patty saw that the man in the car still sat looking at the water, and as Patty poured coffee for an elderly couple that had seated themselves slowly into a booth, as she asked how they were this nice morning, she suddenly knew who the man was, and something passed over her, like a shadow crossing in front of the sun. "There you go," she said to the couple, and didn't glance out the window again.

"Say, why doesn't Kevin come over here instead," Patty's mother had suggested, when Patty had been so small her head had only reached the kitchen counter, shaking it *No, no, no,* she didn't want to go there. She'd been scared of him; in kindergarten he had sucked on his wrist so hard it was always a brilliant disk of a bruise, and his mother—tall, dark-haired, deep-voiced—had scared her, too. Now, as Patty put the corn muffins onto a plate, she thought that her mother's response had been graceful, brilliant almost. Kevin had come to her house instead, and he'd patiently swung a jump rope whose other end was tied around a tree, while Patty had jumped and jumped. On her way home from work today, Patty would stop by her mother's house. You'll never guess who I saw, she'd say.

The boy on the dock stood up, holding a yellow pail in one hand, a knife in the other. A seagull swooped in and the boy waved his arm with the knife. Kevin watched as the boy turned to come up the ramp, but a man was sauntering down onto the wharf. "Son, put the knife in the pail," the man called out, and the boy did that, carefully, and then grabbed the rail and climbed up the ramp to meet his father. He was still young enough that he took the man's hand. Together they peered into the pail, and then they got into the truck and drove off.

Kevin, watching all this from his car, thought, *Good,* and what he meant was that he had felt no emotion watching this, the man and the son.

"A lot of people don't have families," Dr. Goldstein had said, scratching his white beard, then unabashedly brushing away anything that had fallen onto his chest. "But they still have homes." Folding his hands, calmly, across his big stomach.

On his way here to the marina, Kevin had driven past his childhood home. The road was still dirt, with deep ruts, but there were a few new homes tucked back into the woods. Tree trunks should have doubled in girth, and perhaps they had, but the woods remained as he remembered them, thick and tangled and rough, an uneven patch of sky showing through as he turned up the hill to where his house was. It was the shed that made him certain he'd not taken a wrong turn—the deep red shed beside the house, and, right next to that, the granite rock that had been large enough that Kevin used to think of it as a mountain, as he climbed it in his little-boy sneakers. The rock was still there—and the house, but it had been renovated; a wraparound front porch added, and the old kitchen gone. Of course: they'd have wanted the kitchen gone. A sense of umbrage pricked him, then left. He slowed the car, peering carefully for any signs of children. He saw no bicycles, no swing set, no tree house, no basketball hoop—just a hanging pink impatiens plant by the front door.

Relief came, arriving as a sensation beneath his ribs, like a gentle lapping of the water's edge at low tide, a comforting quiescence. In the back of the car was a blanket, and he would still use it, even if there were no children in the house. Right now the blanket was wrapped around the rifle, but when he returned (soon, while this relief still touched, quietly, the inner blankness he had felt on the long ride up), he would lie down on the pine needles and put the blanket over him. If it was the man of the house who found him—so what? The woman who had hung the pink impatiens? She wouldn't look for long. But to have a child—no, Kevin could not abide the thought of any child discovering what he had discovered; that his mother's need to devour her life had been so huge and urgent as to spray remnants of corporeality across the kitchen cupboards. Never mind, his mind said to him quietly, as he drove on past. Never mind. The woods were there, and that's all he wanted, to lie on the pine needles, touch the thin, ripping bark of a cedar tree, have the hackmatack needles above his head, the wild lilies of the valley with their green, open leaves near him. The hidden white starflowers, the wild violets; his mother had shown him all these.

The extra noise of the clanking sailboat masts made him realize the wind had picked up. The seagulls had stopped their squawking now that the fish entrails were gone. A fat gull that had been standing on the rail of the ramp not far from him took off—its wings flapping only twice before the breeze carried it along. Hollow-boned; Kevin had seen gull bones as a child, out on Puckerbrush Island. He had shouted with panic when his brother had collected some to take back to the house. Leave them where they are, Kevin had shouted.

"States and traits," Dr. Goldstein had said. "Traits don't change, states of mind do."

Two cars drove in and parked near the marina. He hadn't thought there would be so much activity here on a weekday, but it was almost July, and people had their boats to sail; he watched a couple, not much older than he was, take a big basket down the ramp, which already, with the tide coming in, was not so steep. And then the screen door of the diner opened and a woman came out, wearing a skirt that went well over her knees, as well as an apron—she could have stepped out of a different century. She had a metal pail in her hand, and as she moved toward the dock, he watched her shoulders, the long back, her thin hips as she moved—she was lovely, the way a sapling might be as the afternoon sun moved over it. A yearning stirred in him that was not sexual but a kind of reaching toward her simplicity of form. He looked away, and his body jumped a little to see a woman staring through the passenger window, her face close, staring straight at him.

Mrs. Kitteridge. Holy shit. She looked exactly the same as she had in the classroom in seventh grade, that forthright, high-cheekboned expression; her hair was still dark. He had liked her; not everyone had. He would have waved her away now, or started the car, but the memory of respect held him back. She rapped her hand on the glass, and after hesitating, he leaned and unrolled the window the rest of the way.

"Kevin Coulson. Hello."

He nodded.

"You going to invite me to sit in your car?"

His hands made fists in his lap. He started to shake his head. "No, I'm only—"

But she had already let herself in—a big woman, taking up the whole bucket seat, her knees close to the dashboard. She hauled a big black handbag across her lap. "What brings you here?" she asked.

He looked out toward the water. The young woman was moving back up from the dock; the seagulls were screeching furiously behind her, beating their large wings and darting down; she'd have been throwing out clamshells, most likely.

"Visiting?" Mrs. Kitteridge prompted. "From New York City? Isn't that where you live now?"

"Jesus," Kevin said quietly. "Does everybody know everything?"

"Oh, sure," she said comfortably. "What else is there to do?"

She had her face turned to him, but he didn't want to meet her eyes. The wind on the bay seemed to be picking up more. He put his hands into his pockets, so as not to suck on his knuckles.

"Get a lot of tourists now," Mrs. Kitteridge said. "Crawling all over the place this time of year."

He made a sound in his throat, acknowledging not the fact—what did he care?—but that she had spoken to him. He watched the slim woman with the pail, her head tilted down as she went back inside, closing the screen door carefully. "That's Patty Howe," Mrs. Kitteridge said. "Remember her? Patty Crane. She married the older Howe boy. Nice girl. She keeps having miscarriages and it makes her sad."

Olive Kitteridge sighed, rearranged her feet, pushed the lever— much to Kevin's surprise—to make herself more comfortable, moving the seat back. "I suspect they'll get her fixed up one of these days, and then she'll be pregnant with triplets."

Kevin took his hands from his pockets, cracked his knuckles. "Patty was nice," he said. "I had forgotten about Patty."

"She's still nice. That's what I said. What are you doing in New York?"

"Oh." He raised a hand, saw the reddened marks that spotted them, crossed his arms. "I'm in training. I got my medical degree four years ago."

"Say, that's impressive. What kind of doctor are you training to be?"

He looked at the dashboard, couldn't believe he hadn't noticed the filth of it. There in the sunlight it seemed to be telling her he was a slob, pathetic, not a shred of dignity. He took in a breath and said, "Psychiatry."

He expected her to say "Ahhh . . ." and when she said nothing, he glanced at her, and found that she was giving a simple matter-of-fact nod.

"It's beautiful here," he said, squinting back toward the bay. The remark held gratitude for what he felt was her discretion, and it was true, as well, for the bay—which he seemed to view from behind a large pane of glass, larger than the windshield—and which did have, he understood, a kind of splendor, the twanging, rocking sailboats, the whipped water, the wild rugosa. How much better to be a fisherman, to spend one's day in the midst of this. He thought of the PET scans he had studied, always looking for his mother, hands in his pockets, nodding as the radiologists spoke, and sometimes tears twinkling behind his lids—the enlargement of the amygdala, the increase in the white-matter lesions, the severe depletion in the number of glial cells. The brains of the bipolar.

"But I'm not going to be a psychiatrist," he said.

The wind was really picking up now, making the ramp to the float bob up and down. "I imagine you get a lot of wicky-wackies in that business," Mrs. Kitteridge said, adjusting her feet, making a scraping sound as she moved them across the grit of the car floor.

"Some."

He had gone to medical school thinking he'd become a pediatrician, as his mother had been, but he had been drawn to psychiatry, in spite of his recognition that those who became psychiatrists did so as a result of their own messed-up childhoods, always looking, looking, looking for the answer in the writings of Freud, Horney, Reich, of why they were the anal, narcissistic, self-absorbed freaks that they were, and yet at the same time denying it, of course—what bullshit he had witnessed among his colleagues, his professors! His own interest had become narrowed to victims of torture, but that had also led him to despair, and when he had finally come under the care of Murray Goldstein, Ph.D., M.D., and had told the man his plans to work at the Hague with those whose feet had been beaten raw, whose bodies and minds lay in ruinous disorder, Dr. Goldstein had said, "What are you, crazy?"

He'd been attracted to crazy. Clara—what a name—Clara Pilkington appeared to be the sanest person he'd ever met. And wasn't that something? She ought to have been wearing a billboard around her neck: COMPLETELY CRAZY CLARA.

"You know the old saying, I'm sure," Mrs. Kitteridge said. "Psychiatrists are nutty, cardiologists are hard-hearted—"

He turned to look at her. "And pediatricians?"

"Tyrants," Mrs. Kitteridge acknowledged. She gave one shrug to her shoulder.

Kevin nodded. "Yeah," he said softly.

After a moment, Mrs. Kitteridge said, "Well, your mother may not have been able to help it."

He was surprised. His urge to suck on his knuckles was like an agonizing itch, and he ran his hands back and forth over his knees, found the hole in his jeans. "I think my mother was bipolar," he said. "Never diagnosed, though."

"I see." Mrs. Kitteridge nodded. "She could've been helped today. My father wasn't bipolar. He was depressed. And he never talked. Maybe they could've helped him today."

Kevin was silent. And maybe they couldn't, he thought.

"My son. He's got the depression."

Kevin looked at her. Small drops of perspiration had appeared in the pockets beneath her eyes. He saw that she did, in fact, look much older. Of course she wouldn't look the same as she had back then—the seventh-grade math teacher that kids were scared of. He'd been scared of her, even while liking her.

"What's he do?" Kevin asked.

"A podiatrist."

He felt the stain of some sadness make its way from her to him. Gusts of wind were now swooping in all directions, so that the bay looked like a blue and white crazily frosted cake, peaks rising one way, then another. Poplar leaves beside the marina were fluttering upward, their branches all bent to one side.

"I've thought of you, Kevin Coulson," she said. "I have."

He closed his eyes. He could hear as she shifted her weight beside him, heard the gravel again on the rubber mat as her foot scraped over it. He was going to say *I don't want you thinking about me*, when she said, "I liked your mother."

He opened his eyes. Patty Howe had stepped back out of the restaurant; she was walking toward the path in front of the place, and a nervousness touched his chest; it was sheer rock in front there, if he remembered right, a straight drop down. But she would know that.

"I know you did," Kevin said, turning to the big, intelligent face of Mrs. Kitteridge. "She liked you."

Olive Kitteridge nodded. "Smart. She was a smart woman."

He wondered how long this would have to go on. And yet it meant something to him, that she had known his mother. In New York no one knew.

"Don't know if you know this or not, but that was the case with my father."

"What was?" He frowned, passed his index knuckle briefly through his mouth.

"Suicide."

He wanted her to leave; it was time for her to leave.

"Are you married?"

He shook his head.

"No, my son isn't either. Drives my poor husband nuts. Henry wants everyone married, everyone happy. I say, for God's sake, let him take his time. Up here the pickings can be slim. Down there in New York, I suppose you—"

"I'm not in New York."

"Excuse me?"

"I'm not—I'm not in New York anymore."

He could hear that she was about to ask something; he thought he could almost feel her desire to turn around and look at the backseat, see what was in his car. If she did, he would have to say he needed to go, ask her to leave. He watched from the corner of his eye, but she was still looking straight ahead.

Patty Howe, he saw, had shears in her hand. With her skirt blowing about her, she was standing by the rugosa, cutting some of the white blossoms. He kept his eye on Patty, the choppy bay spread out behind her. "How'd he do it?" He rubbed his hand over his thigh.

"My father? Shot himself."

The moored sailboats now were heaving their bows high, then swooping back down as though pulled by an angry underwater creature. The white blossoms of the wild rugosa bent, straightened, bent again, the scraggly leaves around them bobbing as though they too were an ocean. He saw Patty Howe step back from them, and give her hand a shake, as though she had been pricked by the thorns.

"No note," Mrs. Kitteridge said. "Oh, Mother had such a hard time with that no-note business. She thought the least he could've done was leave a note, the way he did if he'd walked to the grocery store. Mother would say, 'He was always considerate enough to leave me a note when he went anywhere.' But he hadn't really gone anywhere. He was there in the kitchen, poor thing."

"Do these boats ever get loose?" Kevin pictured his own childhood kitchen. He knew that a .22 caliber bullet could travel for one mile, go through nine inches of ordinary board. But after the roof of a mouth, the roof of a house—after that, how far did it go?

"Oh, sometimes. Not so much as you'd think, given how fierce these squalls can be. But every so often one does, you know—causes a ruckus. They have to go after it, hope it doesn't smash up on the rocks."

"Then the marina gets sued for malpractice?" He said this to divert her.

"I don't know," Mrs. Kitteridge said, "how they handle that kind of thing. Different insurance arrangements, I guess. Acts of negligence or acts of God."

At the very moment Kevin became aware of liking the sound of her voice, he felt adrenaline pour through him, the familiar, awful intensity, the indefatigable system that wanted to endure. He squinted hard toward the ocean. Great gray clouds were blowing in, and yet the sun, as though in contest, streamed yellow rays beneath them so that parts of the water sparkled with frenzied gaiety.

"Unusual for a woman to use a gun," Mrs. Kitteridge said, musingly.

He looked at her; she did not return the look, just gazed out at the swirling incoming tide. "Well, my mother was an unusual woman," he said grimly.

"Yes," Mrs. Kitteridge said. "She was."

When Patty Howe had gotten done with her shift, taken her apron off, and gone to hang it in the back room, she had seen through the dusty window the yellow daylilies that grew in the small patch of lawn on the far side of the marina. She pictured them in a jar next to her bed. "I'm disappointed too," her husband had said, the second time, adding, "but I know it must feel like it happens just to you." Her eyes moistened now, remembering this; a great swelling of love filled her. The lilies would not be missed. No one went to the far side of the marina, partly because the path that ran right in front was so narrow, the drop-off so steep. For insurance purposes the place had recently posted a KEEP OUT sign, and there was even talk of fencing it off before some small child, unwatched, scrambled off into the brush there. But Patty would just snip a few lilies and get going. She found the shears in a drawer and went out to get her bouquet, noticing when she stepped out that Mrs. Kitteridge had joined Kevin Coulson in the car, and it gave her a feeling of safety, having Mrs. Kitteridge with him. She couldn't have said why, and didn't dwell on it. The wind had picked up amazingly. She'd hurry and get her flowers, wrap them in a wet paper towel, and stop off by her mother's on the way home. She bent over the rugosa bushes first, thinking what a sweet combination the yellow and white would be, but they were alive in the wind and her fingers were pricked. She turned to start along the path to where the lilies were.

Kevin said, "Well, it was nice seeing you, Mrs. Kitteridge." He glanced at her with a nod meant to signal a goodbye. It was bad luck that she'd encountered him, but he could not be responsible for that. He had felt responsibility about Dr. Goldstein, whom Kevin had genuinely come to love, but even that had receded as he had driven up the turnpike.

Olive Kitteridge was taking a Kleenex from her big black bag. She touched it to her forehead, her hairline, didn't look at Kevin. She said, "I wish I hadn't passed those genes on to him."

Kevin gave the slightest roll of his eyes. The question of genes, DNA, RNA, chromosome 6, the dopamine, serotonin crap; he had lost interest in all that. In fact, it angered him the way a betrayal might. "We are on the edge of understanding the essence of how the mind works in a molecular, real way," a noted academic had said at a lecture last year. The dawning of a new age.

There was always a new age dawning.

"Not that the kid didn't get a few wicky-wacky genes from Henry's side, God knows. His mother was a complete nut, you know. Horrid."

"Whose mother?"

"Henry's. My husband's." Mrs. Kitteridge pulled out her sunglasses and put them on. "I guess you're not supposed to say 'nut' these days, are you?" She looked over at him. He'd been about to start with his wrist again, but he put his hands back into his lap.

Please go, he thought.

"But she had three breakdowns and shock treatments. Doesn't that qualify?"

He shrugged.

"Well, she was wired funny. I guess I can at least say that."

Nuts was when you took a razor blade and cut long strips into your torso. Your thighs, your arms. COMPLETELY CRAZY CLARA. That was nuts. The first night together in the dark he had felt the lines. "I fell," she had whispered. He had pictured living with her. Art on the wall, light shining through a bedroom window. Friends at Thanksgiving, a Christmas tree because Clara would want one.

"The girl is nothing but trouble," Dr. Goldstein had said.

It was not Dr. Goldstein's place to say such a thing. But she had been nothing but trouble: loving and tender one minute, furious the next. The business of cutting herself—it had made him crazy. Crazy breeds crazy. And then she had left, because that's what Clara did—left people and everything else. Off to somewhere new with her obsessions. She was crazy about the lunatic Carrie A. Nation, the first woman prohibitionist who had gone around chopping up saloons with hatchets, and then selling the hatchets. "Is that the coolest thing you ever heard?" Clara had asked, sipping her soy milk. It was like that. Cartwheeling from one thing to the next.

"Everyone suffers through a bad love affair," Dr. Goldstein had said.

That—actually—was just not true. Kevin knew people who had not suffered through a bad love affair. Not many, perhaps, but a few. Olive Kitteridge blew her nose.

"Your son," Kevin said suddenly. "He's still able to practice?"

"What do you mean?"

"With his depression? He still goes to work every day?"

"Oh, sure." Mrs. Kitteridge took off her sunglasses, gave him a quick, penetrating look.

"And Mr. Kitteridge. Is he well?"

"Yes, he is. He's thinking about retiring early. They sold the pharmacy, you know, and he'd have to work for the new chain, and they require all sorts of goofy regulations. Sad, the way the world is going."

It was always sad, the way the world was going. And always a new age dawning.

"What's your brother up to?" Mrs. Kitteridge asked.

Kevin felt weary now. Maybe that was good. "The last I knew he was living on the streets of Berkeley. He's a drug addict." Most of the time Kevin didn't think of himself as having a brother.

"Where'd you go after here? Texas? Is that what I remember? Your father took a job there?"

Kevin nodded.

"I suppose he wanted to get as far away from here as possible. Time and distance, they always say. I don't know as that's true."

To get the conversation over with, Kevin said, dully, "My father died last year of liver cancer. He never remarried. And I never saw much of him once I left."

All the degrees Kevin had acquired, the colleges and universities he had gone to with the fellowships and scholarships he had received, his father had never showed up. But every town had been promising. Every place at first had said, Here you go—You can live here. You can *rest* here. You can fit. The enormous skies of the Southwest, the shadows that fell over the desert mountains, the innumerable cacti—red-tipped, or yellow-blossomed, or flat-headed—all this had lightened him when he'd first moved to Tucson, taking hikes by himself, then with others from the university. Perhaps Tucson had been his favorite, had he been forced to choose—the stark difference between the open dustiness there and the ragged coastline here.

But as with them all, the same hopeful differences—the tall, hot white glassed buildings of Dallas; the tree-lined streets of Hyde Park in Chicago, with the wooden stairs behind each apartment (he had loved those, especially); the neighborhoods of West Hartford, where it looked like a storybook, the houses, the perfect lawns—they all became places that sooner or later, one way or another, assured him that he didn't, in fact, fit.

When he got his medical degree from Chicago, attending the ceremony only because of one of his teachers—a kind woman, who had said it would sadden her to have him not there—he sat beneath the full sun, listening to the president of the university say, in his final words to them, "To love and be loved is the most important thing in life," causing Kevin to feel an inward fear that grew and spread through him, as though his very soul were tightening. But what a thing to say— the man in his venerable robe, white hair, grandfatherly face—he must've had no idea those words could cause such an exacerbation of the silent dread in Kevin. Even Freud had said, "We must love or we grow ill." They were spelling it out for him. Every billboard, movie, magazine cover, television ad—it all spelled it out for him: We belong to the world of family and love. And you don't.

New York, the most recent, had held the largest hopes. The subways filled with such a variety of dull colors and edgy-looking people; it relaxed him, the different clothes, the shopping bags, people sleeping or reading or nodding their heads to some earphoned tune; he had loved the subways, and for a while the activities of the hospitals. But his affair with Clara, and the end of it, had caused him to recoil from the place, so that the streets now seemed crowded and tiresome—all the same. Dr. Goldstein he loved, but that was it—everyone else had become tiresome, and he had thought more and more how provincial New Yorkers were, and how they didn't know it.

What he began to want was to see his childhood house—a house he believed, even as he sat in his car now, that he had never once been happy in. And yet, oddly, the fact of its unhappiness seemed to have a hold on him with the sweetness of a remembered love affair. For Kevin had some memories of sweet, brief love affairs—so different from the long-drawn-out mess with Clara—and none measured up to the inner desire, the *longing* he felt for that place. That house where the sweatshirts and woolen jackets stank like moist salt and musty wood—the smell made him sick, as did the smell of a wood fire, which his father had sometimes made in the fireplace, poking at it in a distracted way. Kevin thought he must be the only person in the country who hated the smell of a wood fire. But the house, the trees tangled with woodbine, the surprise of a lady's slipper in the midst of pine needles, the open leaves of the wild lilies of the valley—he missed it.

He missed his mother.

I've made this awful pilgrimage . . . I've come back for more . . . Kevin wished, as he often did, that he had known the poet John Berryman.

"When I was young," Mrs. Kitteridge said, holding her sunglasses in her hand, "—little, you know—I'd hide in the wood box when my father came home. And he'd sit down on the wood box and say, 'Where's Olive? Where can Olive be?' This would go on, till I'd knock on the side, and he'd act surprised. 'Olive,' he'd say, 'I had no idea where you were!' And I'd laugh, and he'd laugh."

Kevin looked over at her; she put her sunglasses on. She said, "I don't know how long that continued, probably until I was too big to get into the wood box."

He didn't know what to say to this. He squeezed his hands in as tiny a gesture as possible, looking down at the steering wheel. He felt her big presence, and imagined—fleetingly—that an elephant sat next to him, one that wanted to be a member of the human kingdom, and sweet in an innocent way, as though her stubs of forelegs were folded on her lap, her trunk moving just a little as she finished speaking.

"That's a nice story," he said.

He thought of the boy cleaning the fish, how his father had held his hand out to him. He thought again of John Berryman. *Save us from shotguns & fathers' suicides . . . Mercy! . . . do not pull the trigger or all my life I'll suffer from your anger. . . .* He wondered if Mrs. Kitteridge, being a math teacher, knew much poetry.

"Look how the wind's picked up," she said. "Always kind of exciting, long as you don't have a wharf that floats away, like ours used to do. Henry'd be down on those rocks with the waves—Oh, God what a fracas it was."

Again, Kevin found himself liking the sound of her voice. Through the windshield he saw the waves coming in higher now, hitting the ledge in front of the marina hard enough to send a spray far into the air, the spray then falling back languidly, the drops sifting through shards of sunlight that still cracked its way between the dark clouds. The inside of his head began to feel as choppy as the surf before him. Don't go, his mind said to Mrs. Kitteridge. Don't go.

But this turbulence in him was torture. He thought how yesterday morning, in New York, as he'd walked to his car, he had for one moment not seen it. And there was that prick of fear, because he'd had it all planned and wrapped up, and where was the car? But there it was, right there, the old Subaru wagon, and then he knew what he'd felt had been hope. Hope was a cancer inside him. He didn't want it; he did not want it. He could not bear these shoots of tender green hope springing up within him any longer. That awful story of the man who jumped—and survived—walking back and forth for an hour on the Golden Gate Bridge, weeping, saying that had anyone stopped to ask why he was weeping, he wouldn't have jumped.

"Mrs. Kitteridge, you have to—"

But she was leaning forward, squinting through the windshield. "Wait, what in *hell*—" And moving faster than he would have thought possible, she was out of the car, the door left open, and had gone to the front of the marina, her black bag left on the grass. For a moment she disappeared, then reappeared, waving her arms, shouting, though he couldn't hear what she was saying.

He stepped from the car, and was surprised by the force of the wind that whipped through his shirt. Mrs. Kitteridge was shouting, "Hurry up! Hurry!" Waving her arms like a huge seagull. He ran to where she was and looked down into the water, the tide higher than he'd have thought. Mrs. Kitteridge pointed with a repeated thrust of her arm, and he saw the head of Patty Howe rise briefly above the choppy water, like a seal's head, her hair wet and darkened, and then she disappeared again, her skirt swirling with the swirling dark ropes of seaweed.

Kevin turned, so that as he slid down the high sheet of rock, his arms were spread as though to hug it, but there was nothing to hug, just the flat scraping against his chest, ripping his clothes, his skin, his cheek, and then the cold water rose over him. It stunned him, how cold the water was, as though he'd been dropped into a huge test tube containing a pernicious chemical eating at his skin. His foot hit something steady in the massive swooshing of the water; he turned and saw her reaching for him, her eyes open, her skirt swirled around her waist; her fingers reached for him, missed, reached for him again, and he got hold of her. The water receded for a moment, and as a wave came back to cover them, he pulled her hard, and her grip on him was so tight he would not have thought it possible with her thin arms that she could hold anything as tightly as she held him.

Again the water rose, they both took a breath; again they were submerged and his leg hooked over something, an old pipe, unmoving. The next time, they both reached their heads high as the water rushed back, another breath taken. He heard Mrs. Kitteridge yelling from above. He couldn't hear the words, but he understood that help was coming. He had only to keep Patty from falling away, and as they went again beneath the swirling, sucking water, he strengthened his grip on her arm to let her know: He would not let her go. Even though, staring into her open eyes in the swirling salt-filled water, with sun flashing through each wave, he thought he would like this moment to be for-ever: the dark-haired woman on shore calling for their safety, the girl who had once jumped rope like a queen, now holding him with a fierceness that matched the power of the ocean—oh, insane, ludi-crous, unknowable world! Look how she wanted to live, look how she wanted to hold on.

The Piano Player

Four nights a week Angela O'Meara played the piano in the cocktail lounge at the Warehouse Bar and Grill. The cocktail lounge, commodious and comfortable with its sprawl of couches, plump leather chairs, and low tables, was right there as soon as you walked through the heavy doors of the old establishment; the dining room was farther back, with windows overlooking the water. Early in the week the lounge tended to be rather empty, but by Wednesday night and continuing straight through Saturday, the place was filled with people. When you stepped from the sidewalk through the thick oak doors, there was the sound of piano notes, tinkling and constant; and the talk of the people who were slung back on their couches, or sitting forward in their chairs, or leaning over the bar seemed to accommodate itself to this, so the piano was not so much "background" music as it was a character in the room. In other words, the townspeople of Crosby, Maine, had for many years now taken into their lives the cocktail music and presence of Angie O'Meara.

Angie, in her youth, had been a lovely woman to look at, with her wavy red hair and perfect skin, and in many ways this was still the case.

But now she was into her fifties, and her hair, pinned back loosely with combs, was dyed a color you might consider just a little too red, and her figure, while still graceful, had a thickening of its middle, the more noticeable, perhaps, because she was otherwise quite thin. But she was long-waisted, and when she sat at the piano bench, she did so with the ease of a ballet dancer, albeit past her prime. Her jawline had gone soft and uneven, and the wrinkles near her eyes were quite pronounced. But they were kind wrinkles; nothing harsh—it seemed— had happened to this face. If anything, her face revealed itself too clearly in a kind of simple expectancy no longer appropriate for a woman of her age. There was, in the tilt of her head, the slight messiness of the very bright hair, the open gaze of her blue eyes, a quality that could, in other circumstances, make people uncomfortable. Strangers, for example, who passed her in the Cook's Corner shopping mall were tempted to sneak an extra peek or two. As it was, Angie was a familiar figure to those who lived in town. She was just Angie O'Meara, the piano player, and she had been playing at the Warehouse for many years. She had been in love with the town's first selectman, Malcolm Moody, for a number of years as well. Some people knew this, others did not.

On this particular Friday night, Christmas was a week away, and not far from the baby grand piano stood a large fir tree heavily decorated by the restaurant's staff. Its silver tinsel swung slightly every time the door to the outside was opened, and different-colored lights the size of eggs shone amidst the various balls and strings of popcorn and cranberries that adorned the slightly bent-downward branches of the tree.

Angie was wearing a black skirt and a pink nylon top that parted at her collarbone, and there was something about the tiny string of pearls she wore, and the pink top, and the bright red of her hair that seemed to glow along with the Christmas tree, as if she were some extension of its festivities. She had arrived, as she always did, at precisely six o'clock, smiling her vague, childlike smile, chewing on mints, saying hello to the bartender, Joe, and to Betty, the waitress, then tucking her handbag and coat near the end of the bar. Joe, a thickset man who had tended that bar for many years and had the watchful eye of any good bartender, had come to the private conclusion that Angie O'Meara was really very frightened when she showed up at work each night. This would account for the whiff of booze on her minty breath if you happened to be close enough to smell it, and it accounted for the fact that she never took her twenty-minute break—although she was allowed to by the music union, and encouraged to by the Warehouse owner. "I hate to get started again," she said to Joe one night, and that's when he put it together, that Angie must have suffered from stage fright.

If she suffered from anything more, it was considered nobody's business. It was the case with Angie that people knew very little about her, assuming at the same time that other people knew her moderately well. She lived in a rented room on Wood Street and did not own a car. She was within walking distance of a grocery store and also the Warehouse Bar and Grill—a walk that took precisely fifteen minutes in her black very-high-heeled shoes. In the winter she wore very-high-heeled black boots, and a white fake fur coat, and carried a little blue pocketbook. She could be seen picking her way carefully along the snow-covered sidewalks, then crossing through the big parking lot by the post office, and finally going down the little walkway toward the bay, where the squatty white clapboard Warehouse sat.

Joe was right when he imagined that Angie suffered from stage fright, and she had years ago learned to begin swallowing vodka at five fifteen, so that by the time she left her room half an hour later, she had to hold the wall as she went down the hall stairs. But the walk cleared her head, while leaving her with enough confidence to make her way to the piano, open the keyboard, sit down, and play. What frightened her the most was the moment of those first notes, because that was when people really listened: She was changing the atmosphere in the room. It was the responsibility of this that frightened her. And it was why she played straight through for three hours, without taking a break, in order to avoid the quiet that would fall over the room, to avoid again the way people smiled at her when she sat down to play; no, she didn't like the attention at all. What she liked was playing the piano. Two bars into the first song, Angie was always happy. For her, it was as though she had slipped inside the music. *We are one,* Malcolm Moody used to say. *Let's become one, Angie—what do you say?*

Angie had never taken piano lessons, although people tended not to believe this. So she had stopped telling people this long ago. When she was four years old, she sat down at the piano in the church and began to play, and it didn't surprise her then, or now. "My hands are hungry," she would say to her mother when she was young, and it was like that—a hunger. The church had given her mother a key, and these days Angie could still go there anytime and play the piano.

Behind her she heard the door open, felt the momentary chill, saw the tinsel on the tree sway, and heard the loud voice of Olive Kitteridge say, "Too damn bad. I like the cold."

The Kitteridges, when they came alone to the Warehouse, tended to come early and did not sit in the lounge first but went straight through to the dining room. Still, Henry would always call out, "Evening there, Angie," smiling broadly on his way through, and Olive would wave her hand over her head in a kind of hello. Henry's favorite song was "Good Night, Irene," and Angie would try to remember to play this later as the Kitteridges walked back through on their way out. Lots of people had favorite songs, and Angie would sometimes play them, but not always. Henry Kitteridge was different. She always played his song because whenever she saw him, it was like moving into a warm pocket of air.

Tonight Angie was shaky. There were nights, now, when her vodka did not do what it had done for many years, which was to make her happy and make everything feel pleasantly at a distance. Tonight, as sometimes happened now, she felt a little queer in the head—off-kilter. She made sure to keep a smile on her face and didn't look at anyone except Walter Dalton, who sat at the end of the bar. He blew her a kiss. She winked, a tiny gesture; you would have thought it was a blink except she did it with only one eye.

There was a time when Malcolm Moody loved to see her blink like that. "God, but you get me going," he'd say on those afternoons he came to her room on Wood Street. Malcolm did not like Walter Dalton and referred to him as a fairy, which he was. Walter was also an alcoholic, and the college had let him go, and now he lived in a house on Coombs Island. Walter came into the bar every night that Angie played. Sometimes he brought her a gift—a silk scarf once, a pair of leather gloves with tiny buttons on the side. He always handed his car keys to Joe, and then after closing, Joe often drove him home, with one of the busboys driving Joe's car to give Joe a drive back.

"What a pathetic life," Malcolm had said to Angie, about Walter. "Sitting there every night getting stewed."

Angie didn't like to have people called pathetic, but she didn't say anything. Sometimes, not often, Angie would think that people might call her life with Malcolm pathetic. This would occur to her as she walked down a sunny sidewalk, or it might happen when she woke in the night. It made her heart race, and she would go over in her mind the kinds of things he had said to her over the years. At first he had said, "I think about you all the time." He still said, "I love you." Sometimes, "What would I do without you, Angie?" He never bought her gifts and she wouldn't have wanted him to.

She heard the street door open and close, felt the brief chill from the outdoors once again. From the corner of her eye she caught the motion of a man in a dark coat sinking into a chair in the far corner, and there was something in the way he ducked, or moved, that ever so slightly jogged her mind. But she was shaky tonight.

"Dear," she whispered to Betty, who was moving past with a tray of glasses. "Could you tell Joe I need a little Irish coffee?"

"Sure," said Betty, a nice girl, small as a child. "No problem."

She drank it with one hand, still playing the notes of "Have a Holly Jolly Christmas," and gave a wink to Joe, who nodded gravely. At the end of the night, she would have a drink with Joe and Walter, and she would tell them about visiting her mother in the nursing home today; she might or might not mention the bruises on her mother's arm.

"A request, Angie." Betty dropped a cocktail napkin on her way past, while she held the tray of drinks in the flat of her uplifted hand; you could see how heavy it was for her by the way she swayed her back as she moved around the chairs. "From that man," she added, moving her head toward the corner.

"Bridge Over Troubled Water" was written on the napkin and Angie kept playing Christmas carols, smiling her smile. She did not look at the man in the corner. She played every Christmas carol she could think of, but she was not inside the music now. Perhaps another drink would help, but the man in the corner was watching and he would know it was not coffee alone in the cup Betty brought her. His name was Simon. He had once been a piano player, too.

Fall on your knees, O hear the angels' voices. . . . But it was like she had fallen overboard and had to swim through seaweed. The darkness of the man's coat seemed to press against her head, and there was a watery terror that had to do with her mother; get inside, she thought. But she was very shaky. She slowed down, played "The First Noel" quite lightly. She saw a large snowy field now, with a crack of gentle light along the horizon.

When she finished, she did something that really surprised her. Later she had to wonder how long she had been planning this without quite knowing. The way she didn't quite allow herself to know when Malcolm had stopped saying "I think about you all the time."

Angie took a break.

Delicately, she pressed the cocktail napkin to her lips, slipped out from behind the piano, and walked toward the restroom, where there was a pay phone. She did not want to bother Joe for her pocketbook.

"Darling," she said quietly to Walter, "do you have some change?"

He stretched out a leg, reached into his pocket, handed her the coins. "You're the candy shop, Angie," Walter said slurringly.

His hand was moist; even the coins felt moist. "Thank you, sweetheart," she said.

She went to the phone and dialed Malcolm's number. Not once, in twenty-two years, had she called him at home, although she had memorized his number long ago. Twenty-two years, she thought, as she listened to the buzz of the ring, would be considered a very long time by most people, but for Angie time was as big and round as the sky, and to try to make sense of it was like trying to make sense of music and God and why the ocean was deep. Long ago Angie had known not to try to make sense of these things, the way other people tried to do.

Malcolm answered the phone. And here was a curious thing—she didn't like the sound of his voice. "Malcolm," she said softly. "I can't see you anymore. I'm so terribly sorry, but I can't do this anymore."

Silence. His wife was probably right there. "Bye, now," she said.

On her way past Walter, she said, "Thank you, darling," and he said, "Anything for you, Angie." Walter's voice was thick with drunkenness, his face glistening.

She played the song Simon wanted then, "Bridge Over Troubled Water," but it wasn't until she was almost through that she allowed herself to look at him. He did not return her smile, and a flush went through her.

She smiled at the Christmas tree. The colored lights seemed terribly bright, and for a moment she felt baffled that people did this to trees—decorated them with all that glitter; some people looked forward to this all year. And then another flush of heat rose through her, to think how in a few weeks the tree would be stripped, taken down, hauled out onto the sidewalk with tinsel still sticking to it; she could picture how awkward this tree would look, perched sideways on the snow, its chopped little trunk sticking at an angle in the air.

She began to play "We Shall Overcome," but somebody from the bar called out, "Hey, a little serious there, Angie," and so she smiled even more brightly and played ragtime instead. Stupid to play that—to play "We Shall Overcome." Simon would think it was stupid, she realized that now. "You're so schmaltzy," he used to say.

But he had said other things. When he took her to lunch with her mother that first time: "You're like a person in a beautiful fairy tale," he had said, sunlight falling across the table on the deck.

"You're the perfect daughter," he had said, out in the rowboat in the bay, her mother waving from the rocks. "You have the face of an angel," he said the day they stepped from the boat onto Puckerbrush Island. Later he sent her one white rose.

Oh, she had been just a girl. She had come into this very bar with her friends one night that summer, and there he was playing "Fly Me to the Moon." It was like he'd had little lights flickering off him.

A nervous fellow, though, Simon had been, his whole body jerking around like a puppet pulled by strings. A lot of force in his playing. But it lacked—well, deep in her heart she had known even then that his playing lacked—well, *feeling*. "Play 'Feelings,' " people sometimes requested then, but he never did. Too corny, he said. Too schmaltzy.

He had come up from Boston just for the summer but stayed two years. When he broke it off with Angie, he said, "It's like I have to date both you and your mother. It gives me the creeps." Later, he wrote to her. "You're neurotic," he wrote. "You're wounded."

She couldn't use the pedal; her leg was shaking beneath her black skirt. He was the only person she'd ever told that her mother had taken money from men.

A burst of laughter came from the bar and Angie looked over, but it was just some of the fishermen telling stories with Joe. Walter Dalton smiled sweetly at her, rolled his eyes toward the fishermen.

Her mother had knit the three of them matching blue sweaters for Christmas. When her mother left the room, Simon said, "We will never wear these at the same time." Her mother bought him a whole stack of Beethoven records. When Simon left, her mother wrote and asked him for the records back, but he didn't send them. Her mother said they could still wear the blue sweaters, and when her mother wore the blue sweater, she had Angie wear hers as well. Her mother said to her one day, "Simon got rejected from music school, you know. He's a real estate lawyer in Boston. Bob Beane bumped into him down there."

"Okay," Angie had said.

She thought, then, she wouldn't see him again. Because she had seen a shadow of envy flicker darkly over his face the day she'd told him (oh, she had told him everything, child that she was in that shack with her mother!) how once, when she was fifteen, a man from

Chicago had heard her play at a local wedding. He ran a music school and had talked with her mother for two days. Angie should be at the school. There would be a scholarship, room and board. No, Angie's mother had said. She's Mommy's girl. But for years Angie had pictured the place: a white, sprawling place where young people played the piano all day. She would be taught by kind men and women; she would learn to read music. All the rooms would be heated. There would be none of the sounds that came from her mother's room, sounds that made her push her hands to her ears at night, sounds that made her leave the house and go to the church to play the piano. But no, Angie's mother had decided. She was Mommy's girl.

She glanced again at Simon. He was leaning back in his chair watching her. There was no pocket of warmth, the way there was whenever Henry Kitteridge walked through the door, or the way there was right now at the bar where Walter sat.

What was it he had come to see? She pictured him leaving a law office early, driving up the coast in the dark. Perhaps he was divorced; having the kind of crisis men often had in their late fifties, looking back over their lives, wondering why things had worked out the way they had. And so he—after how many years—had thought, or not thought, of her, but for some reason had driven to Crosby, Maine. Had he known she would be working here?

From the corner of her eye she saw him rise, and there he was leaning against the open baby grand, looking straight at her. He had lost most of his hair.

"Hello, Simon," she said. She was playing stuff she'd made up now, her fingers going over the keys.

"Hello, Angie." He wasn't a man you'd look twice at now. Probably back then he wasn't a man you'd have looked twice at, but that didn't matter the way people thought it did. It didn't matter how once he'd had an ugly brown leather jacket and thought it was cool. You couldn't make yourself stop feeling a certain way, no matter what the other person did. You had to just wait. Eventually the feeling went away because others came along. Or sometimes it didn't go away but got squeezed into something tiny, and hung like a piece of tinsel in the back of your mind. She was slipping into the music now.

"How are you, Simon," she said, smiling.

"Very well, thanks." He gave a small nod. "Quite well." And then she felt the ping of danger. His eyes were not warm. They had been warm eyes. "I see you still have your red hair," he said.

"I put a rinse through it these days, I'm afraid."

He just looked at her; his coat hung loosely. His clothes had always hung loosely.

"Are you still a lawyer, Simon? I heard you were a lawyer."

He nodded. "The truth is, Angie, I'm good at it. It's nice to be good at something."

"Yes. Of course it is. What kind of law?"

"Real estate." He looked down. But he raised his chin in a moment. "It's fun. Like a puzzle."

"Oh. Well, that's nice." She crossed her left hand over, did a light run.

"Ever marry, Angie?"

"No. No, I didn't. And you?" She had already seen the wedding ring. A broad band. She would not have thought him the type to wear such a broad band.

"Yes. I have three children. Two boys and a girl, all grown." He shifted his feet, still leaning against the piano.

"Oh, lovely, Simon. That's lovely." She had forgotten "O Come All Ye Faithful." She began playing that, her fingers reaching deeply into it; sometimes when she played, it was like being a sculptress, she thought, pulling at the lovely thick clay.

He looked at his watch. "You're off at nine, then?"

"I am. Yes. But I have to skedaddle right out of here, I'm afraid. Sorry to say." She had stopped blushing; her skin felt chilly now. She had quite a headache.

"Okay, Angie." He stood up straight. "I'll be taking off. Nice to see you after all these years."

"Yes, Simon. Nice to see you."

Betty's arm placed a cup of coffee down on the other side. "From Walter," Betty said, moving past.

Angie turned her head, gave Walter that small blink of a wink; Walter, watching her, bleary in his eyes.

Simon was walking away. And there were the Kitteridges, leaving, Henry waving his hand. "Good Night, Irene," she played.

Simon turned back; in two jerky motions he was at her side, leaning his face next to hers. "You know, your mother came to Boston to see me."

Angie's face got very warm.

"She took the Greyhound bus," said Simon's voice in her ear. "And then took a taxi to my apartment. When I let her in, she asked for a drink and started taking off her clothes. Unbuttoned that button slowly at the top of her neck."

Angie's mouth had gone dry.

"And I've been feeling pretty sorry for you, Angie, all these years."

She smiled straight ahead of her. "Good night, Simon," she said.

She drank, with one hand, all the Irish coffee. And then she played all sorts of songs. She didn't know what she played, couldn't have said, but she was inside the music, and the lights on the Christmas tree were bright and seemed far away. Inside the music like this, she understood many things. She understood that Simon was a disappointed man if he needed, at this age, to tell her he had pitied her for years. She understood that as he drove his car back down the coast toward Boston, toward his wife with whom he had raised three children, that something in him would be satisfied to have witnessed her the way he had tonight, and she understood that this form of comfort was true for many people, as it made Malcolm feel better to call Walter Dalton a pathetic fairy, but it was thin milk, this form of nourishment; it could not change that you had wanted to be a concert pianist and ended up a real estate lawyer, that you had married a woman and stayed married to her for thirty years, when she did not ever find you lovely in bed.

The lounge was mostly empty now. And warmer, since the door

wasn't being opened all the time. She played "We Shall Overcome"; she played it twice, slowly, grandly, and looked over at the bar to where Walter was smiling at her. He raised a fist into the air.

"Want a ride, there, Angie?" Joe asked as she closed the top of the piano, went and gathered her coat and pocketbook.

"No, thank you, dear," she said as Walter helped her into her white fake fur coat. "The walk will do me good."

Clutching her little blue pocketbook, she picked her way over the snowbank by the sidewalk, across the parking lot of the post office. The green numbers by the bank said minus three degrees, but she didn't feel cold. Her mascara was frozen, though. Her mother had taught her not to touch her eyelashes when it was this cold, or they could break off.

Turning onto Wood Street, the streetlamps pale in the dark cold, she said out loud, "Huh!" because she was baffled by many things. That often happened after being inside the music the way she'd been tonight.

She stumbled a little with her high-heeled boots, put her hand against the porch rail.

"Cunt."

She had not seen him standing beside the house, in the dark shadow from the overhang.

"You cunt, Angie." He stepped toward her.

"Malcolm," she said softly. "Now, please."

"Calling my house. Who the fuck do you think you are?"

"Well," she said. She pressed her lips together, put a finger to her mouth. "Well," she said. "Let's see." It was not her style to call his house, but even less so to remind him that she, in twenty-two years, had never done so before.

"You're a fucking nut," he said. "And you're a drunk, too." He walked away. She saw his truck parked on the next block. "You call me at work when you sober up," he said over his shoulder. And then, more quietly, "And don't go pulling this shit again."

Even drunk, she knew she would not call him when she sobered up. She let herself into the apartment house and sat down on the stairwell. Angela O'Meara.

A face like an angel. A drunk. Her mother sold herself to men. Never married, Angela?

But sitting on the stairwell, she told herself that she was no more, no less, pathetic than any of them, including Malcolm's wife. And people were kind: Walter, Joe, and Henry Kitteridge. Oh, definitely, there were kind people in the world. Tomorrow she would get to work early and tell Joe about her mother and the bruises. "Imagine," she would say to Joe. "Imagine someone pinching an old paralyzed woman like that."

Angie, leaning her head now against the hallway wall, fingering her black skirt, felt she had figured something out too late, and that must be the way of life, to get something figured out when it was too late. Tomorrow she would go play the piano in the church, stop thinking about the bruises on her mother's upper arm, that thin arm with its slack soft skin, so loose from the bone that when you squeezed it in your fingers, it was hard to imagine it could feel anything.

A Little Burst

Three hours ago, while the sun was shining full tilt through the trees and across the back lawn, the local podiatrist, a middle-aged man named Christopher Kitteridge, was married to a woman from out of town named Suzanne. This is the first marriage for both of them, and the wedding has been a smallish, pleasant affair, with a flute player and baskets of yellow sweetheart roses placed inside and outside the house. So far, the polite cheerfulness of the guests seems to show no sign of running down, and Olive Kitteridge, standing by the picnic table, is thinking it's really high time everyone left.

All afternoon Olive has been fighting the sensation of moving underwater—a panicky, dismal feeling, since she has somehow never managed to learn to swim. Wedging her paper napkin into the slats of the picnic table, she thinks, All right, I've had enough, and dropping her gaze so as to avoid getting stuck in one more yakkety conversation, she walks around to the side of the house and steps through a door that opens directly into her son's bedroom. Here she crosses the pine floor, gleaming in the sunshine, and lies down on Christopher's (and Suzanne's) queen-size bed.

Olive's dress—which is important to the day, of course, since she is the mother of the groom—is made from a gauzy green muslin with big reddish-pink geraniums printed all over it, and she has to arrange herself carefully on the bed so it won't wind up all wrinkly, and also, in case someone walks in, so she will look decent. Olive is a big person. She knows this about herself, but she wasn't always big, and it still seems something to get used to. It's true she has always been tall and frequently felt clumsy, but the business of being *big* showed up with age; her ankles puffed out, her shoulders rolled up behind her neck, and her wrists and hands seemed to become the size of a man's. Olive minds—of course she does; sometimes, privately, she minds very much. But at this stage of the game, she is not about to abandon the comfort of food, and that means right now she probably looks like a fat, dozing seal wrapped in some kind of gauze bandage. But the dress worked out well, she reminds herself, leaning back and closing her eyes. Much better than the dark, grim clothes the Bernstein family is wearing, as though they had been asked to a funeral, instead of a wedding, on this bright June day.

The inside door of her son's bedroom is partly open, and voices and sounds make their way from the front of the house, where the party is also going on: high heels clicking down the hallway, a bathroom door pushed aggressively shut. (Honestly, Olive thinks—why not just close a door nicely?) A chair in the living room gets scraped over the floor, and in there with the muted laughter and talk is the odor of coffee, and the thick, sweet smell of baked goods, which is the way the streets near the Nissen bread factory used to smell before it closed down. There are different perfumes as well, including one that all day has smelled to Olive like that bug spray Off! All these smells have managed to move down the hall and drift into the bedroom.

Cigarette smoke, too. Olive opens her eyes: Someone is smoking a cigarette in the back garden. Through the open window she hears a cough, the click of a lighter. Really, the place has been overrun. She pictures heavy shoes stepping through the gladiola bed, and then, hearing a toilet flush down the hall, she has a momentary image of the house collapsing; pipes breaking, floorboards snapping, walls folding over. She sits up slightly, rearranges herself, and puts another pillow against the headboard.

She built the house herself—well, almost. She and Henry, years ago, did all the design and then worked closely with the builder, so that Chris would have a decent place to live when he came back from podiatry school. When you build a house yourself, you're going to have a different feeling about it than other people do. Olive is used to this because she has always liked to make things: dresses, gardens, houses. (The yellow roses were arranged in their baskets by her this morning, before the sun was up.) Her own house, a few miles down the road, she and Henry also built, years ago, and just recently she fired the cleaning woman because of the way the foolish girl dragged the vacuum cleaner across the floor, banging it into walls and bumping it down the stairs.

At least Christopher appreciates this place. Over the last few years, the three of them, Olive and Henry and Christopher, have taken care of it together, clearing more woods, planting lilacs and rhododendrons, digging postholes for the fence. Now Suzanne (Dr. Sue is what Olive calls her in her head) will take over, and coming from money the way she does, she will probably hire a housekeeper, as well as a gardener. ("Love your pretty nasturtiums," Dr. Sue said to Olive a few weeks ago, pointing to the petunia rows.) But never mind, Olive thinks now. You move aside and make way for the new.

Through her closed eyelids Olive sees a red light slanting through the windows; she can feel sunlight warming her calves and ankles on the bed, can feel beneath her hand how it warms the soft fabric of her dress, which really did come out nicely. It pleases her to think of the piece of blueberry cake she managed to slip into her big leather handbag—how she can go home soon and eat it in peace, take off this panty girdle, get things back to normal.

Olive senses someone in the room, and opens her eyes. A small child stands staring from the doorway; one of the bride's little nieces from Chicago. It's the one who was supposed to sprinkle rose petals on the ground right before the ceremony but at the last minute decided she didn't want to, and hung back, sulking. Dr. Sue was nice about it, though, speaking reassuringly to the little girl, cupping her hand gently around the child's head. Finally Suzanne called out good-naturedly "Oh, go ahead" to a woman standing near a tree, who started playing a flute. Then Suzanne walked over to Christopher—who was not smiling, looking as stiff as driftwood—and the two stood there, getting married, on the lawn.

But the gesture, the smooth cupping of the little girl's head, the way Suzanne's hand in one quick motion caressed the fine hair and thin neck, has stayed with Olive. It was like watching some woman dive from a boat and swim easily up to the dock. A reminder how some people could do things others could not.

"Hello," Olive says to the little girl, but the child does not reply. After a moment, Olive says, "How old are you?" She is no longer familiar with young children, but she guesses this one is around four, maybe five; nobody in the Bernstein family seems tall.

Still the child says nothing. "Run along now," Olive tells her, but the girl leans against the doorjamb and sways slightly, her eyes fixed on Olive. "Not polite to stare," Olive says. "Didn't anyone teach you that?"

The little girl, still swaying, says calmly, "You look dead."

Olive lifts her head up. "Is that what they teach you to say these days?" But she feels a physical reaction as she leans back down, a soft ache beating on her breastbone for a moment, like a wing inside her. The child ought to have her mouth washed out with soap.

Anyway, the day is almost over. Olive stares up at the skylight over the bed and reassures herself that she has, apparently, lived through it. She pictured herself having another heart attack on the day of her son's wedding: She would be sitting on her folding chair on the lawn, exposed to everyone, and after her son said, "I do," she would silently, awkwardly fall over dead, with her face pressed into the grass, and her big hind end with the gauzy geranium print stuck up in the air. People would talk about it for days to come.

"What are those things on your face?"

Olive turns her head toward the door. "Are you still there? I thought you'd gone away."

"There's a hair coming out of one of those things on your face," the child says, bolder now, taking a step into the room. "The one on your chin."

Olive turns her gaze back to the ceiling and receives these words without an accompanying wing beat in her chest. Amazing how nasty kids are these days. And it was very smart to put that skylight over the bed. Chris has told her how in the winter sometimes he can lie in bed and watch it snow. He has always been like that—a different kind of person, very sensitive. It was what made him an excellent oil painter, though such a thing was not usually expected of a podiatrist. He was a complicated, interesting man, her son, so sensitive as a child that once, when he was reading *Heidi* he painted a picture to illustrate it—some wildflowers on an Alpine hillside.

"What is that on your chin?"

Olive sees that the little girl has been chewing on a ribbon from her dress. "Crumbs," Olive says. "From little girls I've eaten up. Now go away before I eat you, too." She makes her eyes big.

The girl steps back slightly, holding the doorjamb. "You're making that up," she finally says, but she turns and disappears.

" 'Bout time," Olive murmurs.

Now she hears the sound of high heels clattering unevenly down the hallway. "Looking for the little girls' room," a woman's voice says, and Olive recognizes the voice of Janice Bernstein, Suzanne's mother. Henry's voice answers, "Oh, right there, right there."

Olive waits for Henry to look into the bedroom, and in a moment he does. His big face is shiny with the affability that comes over him in large groups of people. "You all right, Ollie?"

"Shhh. Shut *up*. I don't need everyone knowing I'm in here."

He steps farther into the room. "You all right?" he whispers.

"I'm ready to go home. Though I expect you'll want to stay until the last dog dies. Don't I hate a grown woman who says 'the little girls' room.' Is she drunk?"

"Oh, I don't think so, Ollie."

"They're smoking outside there." Olive nods toward the window. "I hope they don't set the place on fire."

"They won't." Then, after a moment, Henry says, "Everything went well, I think."

"Oh, sure. You go say your goodbyes now, so we can get going."

"He's married a nice woman," Henry says, hesitating by the foot of the bed.

"Yes, I think he has." They are silent for a moment; it is a shock, after all. Their son, their only child, married now. He is thirty-eight years old; they'd gotten pretty used to him.

They expected at one point that he would marry his office assistant, but that didn't last very long. Then it seemed that he would marry the teacher who lived out on Turtleback Island, but that didn't last long either. Then it happened, right out of the blue: Suzanne Bernstein, M.D., Ph.D., showed up in town for a conference and trotted around all week in a new pair of shoes. The shoes inflamed an ingrown toenail and caused a blister the size of a big marble to appear on her sole; Suzanne was telling the story all day. "I looked in the yellow pages, and by the time I got to his office, I had *ruined* my feet. He had to drill through a toenail. What a way to meet!"

Olive found the story stupid. Why hadn't the girl, with all her money, simply bought a pair of shoes that fit?

However, that was how the couple met. And the rest, as Suzanne was saying all day, was history. If you call six weeks history. Because that part was surprising as well—to get married quick as a thunderclap. "Why wait?" Suzanne said to Olive the day she and Christopher stopped by to show off the ring. Olive said agreeably, "No reason at all."

"Still, Henry," Olive says now. "How come a gastroenterologist? Plenty of other kinds of doctors to be, without all that poking around. You don't like thinking about it."

Henry looks at her in his absent way. "I know it," he says.

Sunlight flickers on the wall and the white curtains move slightly. The smell of cigarette smoke returns. Henry and Olive are silent, gazing at the foot of the bed, until Olive says, "She's a very positive person."

"She's good for Christopher," Henry says.

They have been almost whispering, but at the sound of footsteps in the hallway, both of them turn toward the half-open door with perky, pleasant expressions on their faces. Except that Suzanne's mother doesn't stop; she goes right on past in her navy-blue suit, holding a pocketbook that looks like a miniature suitcase.

"You better get back out there," Olive says. "I'll come say my good-byes in a minute. Just give me a second to rest."

"Yes, you rest, Ollie."

"How about we stop at Dunkin' Donuts," she says. They like to sit in the booth by the window, and there's a waitress who knows them; she'll say hi nicely, then leave them alone.

"We can do that," Henry says, at the door.

Lying back against the pillows, she thinks how pale her son was standing there getting married. In his guarded Christopher way he looked gratefully at his bride, who stood, thin and small-breasted, gazing up at him. Her mother cried. It was really something—Janice Bernstein's eyes positively streaming. Afterward she said to Olive, "Don't you cry at weddings?"

"I don't see any reason to cry," Olive said.

Weeping would not have come close to what she felt. She felt fear, sitting out there on her folding chair. Fear that her heart would squeeze shut again, would stop, the way it did once before, a fist punched through her back. And she felt it, too, at the way the bride was smiling up at Christopher, as though she actually *knew* him. Because did she know what he looked like in first grade when he had a nosebleed in Miss Lampley's class? Did she see him when he was a pale, slightly pudgy child, his skin broken out in hives because he was afraid to take a spelling test? No, what Suzanne was mistaking for knowing someone was knowing sex with that person for a couple of weeks. You never could have told her that, though. If Olive had told her that the nasturtiums were actually petunias (which she did not do), Dr. Sue might have said, "Well, I've seen nasturtiums that look just like that." But, still, it was disconcerting how Suzanne looked at Christopher while they were getting married, as though saying, "I know you—yes, I do. *I do.*"

A screen door bangs. A man's voice asking for a cigarette. Another click of a lighter, the deep murmur of men's voices. "Stuffed myself. . . ."

Olive can understand why Chris has never bothered having many friends. He is like her that way, can't stand the blah-blah-blah. And they'd just as soon blah-blah-blah about you when your back is turned. "Never trust folks," Olive's mother told her years ago, after someone left a basket of cow flaps by their front door. Henry got irritated by that way of thinking. But Henry was pretty irritating himself, with his steadfast way of remaining naïve, as though life were just what a Sears catalogue told you it was: everyone standing around smiling.

Still, Olive herself has been worried about Christopher's being lonely. She was especially haunted this past winter by the thought of her son's becoming an old man, returning home from work in the darkness, after she and Henry were gone. So she is glad, really, about Suzanne. It was sudden, and will take getting used to, but all things considered, Dr. Sue will do fine. And the girl has been perfectly friendly to her. ("I can't believe you did the blueprints *yourself*!" Blond eyebrows raised sky-high.) Besides, Christopher, let's face it, is gaga over her. Of course, right now their sex life is probably very exciting, and they undoubtedly think that will last, the way new couples do. They think they're finished with loneliness, too.

This thought causes Olive to nod her head slowly as she lies on the bed. She knows that loneliness can kill people—in different ways can actually make you die. Olive's private view is that life depends on what she thinks of as "big bursts" and "little bursts." Big bursts are things like marriage or children, intimacies that keep you afloat, but these big bursts hold dangerous, unseen currents. Which is why you need the little bursts as well: a friendly clerk at Bradlee's, let's say, or the waitress at Dunkin' Donuts who knows how you like your coffee. Tricky business, really.

"Nice spot Suzanne's getting here," says one of the deep voices outside the window. Heard very clearly; they must have shifted their feet around now, facing the house.

"Great spot," says the other voice. "We came up here when I was a kid and stayed at Speckled Egg Harbor, I think. Something like that."

Polite men having their cigarettes. Just keep your feet off the glads, Olive thinks, and don't burn down that fence. She is sleepy, and the feeling is not unpleasant. She could take a nap right here if they'd give her twenty minutes, then go make her rounds and say goodbye, clear-headed and calm from a little sleep. She will take Janice Bernstein's hand and hold it a moment; she will be a gracious gray-haired, pleasantly large woman in her soft, red-flowered dress.

A screen door slams. "The emphysema brigade," comes Suzanne's bright voice, and the clapping of her hands.

Olive's eyes flip open. She feels a jolt of panic, as if she herself has just been caught smoking in the woods.

"Do you know those things will kill you?"

"Oh, I've never heard that," the man says jovially. "Suzanne, I don't think I've ever heard that before."

The screen door opens and closes again; someone has gone in. Olive sits up, her nap spoiled.

Now a softer voice comes through the window. That skinny little friend of Suzanne's, Olive thinks, whose dress looks like a piece of wrapped seaweed. "You holding up okay?"

"Yeah." Suzanne draws the word out, somehow—enjoying the attention, Olive thinks.

"So, Suzie, how do you like your new in-laws?"

Olive's heart goes beat-beat as she sits on the edge of the bed.

"It's interesting," Suzanne says, her voice lowered and serious: Dr. Sue, the professional, about to give a paper on intestinal parasites. Her voice drops and Olive can't hear.

"I can see that." Murmur, murmur. "The father—"

"Oh, Henry's a *doll*."

Olive stands up and very slowly moves along the wall closer to the open window. A shaft of the late-afternoon sun falls over the side of her face as she strains her head forward to make out words in the sounds of the women's murmuring.

"Oh, God, yes," says Suzanne, her quiet words suddenly distinct. "I couldn't believe it. I mean that she would really *wear* it."

The dress, Olive thinks. She pulls herself back against the wall.

"Well, people dress differently up here."

By God, we do, Olive thinks. But she is stunned in her underwater way.

Seaweed Friend murmurs again. Her voice is difficult to make out, but Olive hears her say, "Chris."

"Very special," Suzanne answers seriously, and for Olive it is as if these women are sitting in a rowboat above her while she sinks into the murky water. "He's had a hard time, you know. And being an only child—that really sucked for him."

Seaweed murmurs, and Suzanne's oar slices through the water again. "The expectations, you know."

Olive turns and gazes slowly around the room. Her son's bedroom. She built it, and there are familiar things in here, too, like the bureau, and the rug she braided a long time ago. But something stunned and fat and black moves through her.

He's had a hard time, you know.

Almost crouching, Olive creeps slowly back to the bed, where she sits down cautiously. What did he tell Suzanne? *A hard time.* Underneath her tongue, back up by her molars, Olive's mouth begins to secrete. She pictures fleetingly, again, how Suzanne's hand so easily, gently cupped that little girl's head. What had Christopher said? What had he remembered? A person can only move forward, she thinks. A person *should* only move forward.

And there is the sting of deep embarrassment, because she loves this dress. Her heart really opened when she came across the gauzy muslin in So-Fro's; sunlight let into the anxious gloom of the upcoming wedding; those flowers skimming over the table in her sewing room. Becoming this dress that she took comfort in all day.

She hears Suzanne say something about her guests, and then the screen door slams and it is quiet in the garden. Olive touches her open palm to her cheeks, her mouth. She is going to have to go back into the living room before somebody finds her in here. She will have to bend down and kiss the cheek of that bride, who will be smiling and looking around, with her know-it-all face.

Oh, it hurts—actually makes Olive groan as she sits on the bed. What does Suzanne know about a heart that aches so badly at times that a few months ago it almost gave out, gave up altogether? It is true she doesn't exercise, her cholesterol is sky-high. But all that is only a good excuse, hiding how it's her soul, really, that is wearing out.

Her son came to her last Christmastime, before any Dr. Sue was on the scene, and told her what he sometimes thought about. *Sometimes I think about just ending it all—*

An uncanny echo of Olive's father, thirty-nine years before. Only, that time, newly married (with disappointments of her own, and pregnant, too, but she hadn't known that part then), she said lightly, "Oh, Father, we all have times when we feel blue." The wrong response, as it turned out.

Olive, on the edge of the bed, leans her face into her hands. She can almost not remember the first decade of Christopher's life, although some things she does remember and doesn't want to. She tried teaching him to play the piano and he wouldn't play the notes right. It was how scared he was of her that made her go all wacky. But she loved him! She would like to say this to Suzanne. She would like to say, Listen, Dr. Sue, deep down there is a thing inside me, and sometimes it swells up like the head of a squid and shoots blackness through me. I haven't wanted to be this way, but so help me, I have loved my son.

It is true. She has. That is why she took him to the doctor this past Christmas, leaving Henry at home, and sat in the waiting room while her heart pumped, until he emerged—this grown man, her son—with a lightened countenance and a prescription for pills. All the way home he talked to her about serotonin levels and genetic tendencies; it might have been the most she had ever heard him say at one time. Like her father, he is not given to talk.

Down the hall now comes the sudden sound of clinking crystal. "A toast to Fidelity Select," a man's voice calls out.

Olive straightens up and runs her hand across the sun-warmed bureau top. It is the bureau that Christopher grew up with, and that stain from a jar of Vicks VapoRub is still there. Next to it now is a stack of folders with Dr. Sue's handwriting on them, and three black Magic Markers, too. Slowly, Olive slides open the top drawer of the bureau. Once a place for a boy's socks and T-shirts, the drawer is now filled with her daughter-in-law's underwear—tumbled together, slippery, lacy, colorful things. Olive tugs on a strap and out comes a shiny pale blue bra, small-cupped and delicate. She turns it slowly in her thick hand, then balls it up and pokes it down into her roomy handbag. Her legs feel swollen, not good.

She looks at the Magic Markers lying on the bureau, next to Suzanne's folders. Miss Smarty, Olive thinks, reaching for a marker and uncapping it, smelling the schoolroom smell of it. Olive wants to smear the marker across the pale bedspread that this bride has brought with her. Looking around the invaded bedroom, she wants to mark every item brought in here over the last month.

Olive walks to the closet, pulls open the door. The dresses there do make her feel violent, though. She wants to snatch them down, twist the expensive dark fabric of these small dresses hanging pompously on wooden hangers. And there are sweaters, different shades of brown and green, folded neatly on a plastic quilted hanging shelf. One of them near the bottom is actually beige. For God's sake, what's wrong with a little *color*? Olive's fingers shake because she is angry, and because anyone of course could walk down the hall right now and stick his head through the open door.

The beige sweater is thick, and this is good, because it means the girl won't wear it until fall. Olive unfolds it quickly and smears a black line of Magic Marker down one arm. Then she holds the marker in her mouth and refolds the sweater hurriedly, folding it again, and even again, to get it as neat as it was at first. But she manages. You would never, opening this closet door, know that someone had pawed through it, everything so neat.

Except for the shoes. All over the floor of the closet shoes are tossed and scattered. Olive chooses a dark, scuffed loafer that looks as though it is worn frequently; in fact, Olive has often seen Suzanne wearing these loafers—having bagged a husband, Olive supposes, she can now flop around in beaten-up shoes. Bending over, scared for a moment that she won't get up, Olive pushes the loafer down inside her handbag, and then, hoisting herself, she does get up, panting slightly, and arranges the tinfoil-wrapped package of blueberry cake so that it covers the shoe.

"You all set?"

Henry is standing in the doorway, his face shiny and happy now that he's made the rounds, now that he's been the sort of man who is well liked, a *doll*. Much as she wants to tell him what she has just heard, much as she wants relief from the solitary burden of what she's done, she will not tell.

"You want to stop at Dunkin' Donuts on the way?" Henry asks, his big ocean-colored eyes looking at her. He is an innocent. It's how he has learned to get through life.

"Oh," says Olive, "I don't know if I need a doughnut, Henry."

"That's all right. I just thought you said—"

"Okay. Sure, let's stop."

Olive tucks her handbag under her large arm, pressing it to her as she walks toward the door. It does not help much, but it does help some, to know that at least there will be moments now when Suzanne will doubt herself. Calling out, "Christopher, are you *sure* you haven't seen my shoe?" Looking through the laundry, her underwear drawer, some anxiety will flutter through her. "I must be losing my mind, I can't keep track of anything. . . . And, my God, what happened to my sweater?" And she would never know, would she? Because who would mark a sweater, steal a bra, take one shoe?

The sweater will be ruined, and the shoe will be gone, along with the bra, covered by used Kleenex and old sanitary napkins in the bathroom trash of Dunkin' Donuts, and then squashed into a dumpster the next day. As a matter of fact, there is no reason, if Dr. Sue is going to live near Olive, that Olive can't occasionally take a little of this, a little of that— just to keep the self-doubt alive. Give herself a little burst. Because Christopher doesn't need to be living with a woman who thinks she knows everything. Nobody knows everything—they shouldn't think they do.

"Let's go," Olive says finally, and she clutches her bag beneath her arm, preparing for a journey through the living room. Picturing her heart, a big red muscle, banging away beneath her flowered dress.

Starving

At the marina on Sunday morning, Harmon had to work not to stare at the young couple. He had seen them before in town, walking along Main Street; the girl's thin hand—cuffed at the wrist by fake fur on the end of her denim jacket sleeve—had been holding the boy's hand loosely as the two had looked in store windows with the same laconic, unqualified comfortableness they had now leaning against the railing by the stairs. The boy was said to be a cousin of Kathleen Burnham and was up from New Hampshire, working at the sawmill, though he was no bigger, and looked no older, than an adolescent sugar maple. But his eyes behind the black-framed glasses were easy, his body was easy. They wore no wedding bands, Harmon noticed, and he turned his gaze out to the bay, which was sparkling in the morning sunlight and was as flat as a coin on the windless day.

"I'm mad at Victoria," Harmon heard the girl say. Her voice was high, and in that way sounded too loud. She seemed not to care that everyone could hear, though there were just a few of them—Harmon, two fishermen—waiting to get inside. Recently the marina had become a popular breakfast spot on Sunday mornings; a wait for a table was not unusual. Harmon's wife, Bonnie, wouldn't do it. "People waiting gets me anxious," she said.

"Why?" the boy asked. His voice was softer, but Harmon, not far away, could hear it. He turned, gave them a long glance through his squinted eyes.

"Well." The girl seemed to consider this, her mouth moving back and forth. Her skin was flawless, and had the faintest blush of cinnamon color. Her hair had been dyed to match this coloring—or so Harmon thought. Girls did brilliant things with their hair these days. His niece worked in a salon in Portland and had told Bonnie hair coloring had been a whole different ball game for years. You could make it any number of colors, and it was good for your hair. Bonnie said she didn't care, she'd take the hair God gave her. Harmon had been sorry.

"She's been kind of a bitch lately," the girl said. Her voice was energetic, but ruminative. The boy nodded.

The marina door opened, two fishermen came out, the two waiting went in. The boy took a seat on the wooden bench and the girl, instead of sitting next to him, sat on his lap as though he were a chair. "Here," she said to Harmon, nodding to the space left.

He started to raise a hand to indicate no, that was all right, but she looked at him with such open-faced matter-of-factness that he sat down next to them.

"Stop smelling me," the girl said. She was gazing out at the water; her denim jacket with its fake fur lining in the hood caused her head to be thrust forward. "You're smelling me, I know you are." She made a small motion, perhaps to hit the boy lightly. Harmon, who had been looking from the corner of his eye, now stared straight ahead. In just those few moments a breeze seemed to have picked up—the bay was one long ripple. He heard the sound of an oar being tossed into a dinghy and watched as the young Coombs boy slipped the rope off the post on the wharf. He'd heard it said the kid didn't want to take over his father's store, that he wanted to go into the coast guard instead.

A car driving into the parking lot allowed Harmon to turn his head, and he saw the girl was sniffing herself, the shoulder of her denim jacket. "I know," she said. "I smell like pot."

"Potheads," Bonnie would say, and dismiss them. Also the way the girl was sitting on the boy's lap, she wouldn't like that. But Harmon had the impression that everyone young smoked pot these days, as much as they had in the sixties. His own sons probably had, and maybe Kevin still did, but not when his wife was around. Kevin's wife drank soy milk, made up baggies of granola, talked about her yoga class— Harmon and Bonnie would roll their eyes. Still, Harmon admired the vigor behind it, just as he admired the couple next to him. The world was their oyster. It was in their easiness, in the clarity of the girl's skin, her high and strong voice. Harmon felt the way he had as a child when he'd been walking along a dirt road after a rainstorm and had found a quarter in a puddle. The coin had seemed huge and magical. This couple had the same pull on his excitement—such abundance sitting next to him.

"We could take a nap," the girl was saying. "This afternoon. Then we'll be able to stay up. We'll want to, everyone's going to be there."

"We can do that," the boy answered.

At the counter there was no room to read the paper, and Harmon ate his eggs and corn muffin watching the young couple, seated at a table by the window. The girl was thinner than he'd have thought; her torso—even with its little denim jacket—was no bigger than a washboard as she leaned forward over the table. At one point, she folded her arms and put her head down. The boy spoke, his relaxed face never changing. When she sat up, he touched her hair, rubbing the ends between his fingers.

Harmon got two doughnuts in two separate bags, and left. It was early September and the maples were red at their tops; a few bright red leaves had fallen onto the dirt road, perfect things, star-shaped. Years earlier when his sons were small, Harmon might have pointed to them, and they'd have picked them up with eagerness—Derrick, especially, had loved leaves, and twigs, and acorns. Bonnie would find half the woods under his bed. "You'll get a squirrel living in here," she'd say, directing him to clean it out, while the boy cried. Derrick had been a pack rat with a sentimental streak. Harmon walked along, leaving his car at the marina, the air like a cold washcloth on his face. Each of his sons had been his favorite child.

Daisy Foster lived in a small winterized cottage at the very top of the dirt road that wound its way down past the marina to the water. From her little living room you could see a small strip of the water far out. From her dining room you could see the dirt road just a few feet away, although in the summer there were the brambly bridal wreaths that flowered up against her window. Today the shrubs were twiggy and bare, and it was cold; she had started a fire in the stove in the kitchen. Earlier, she had changed out of her church clothes, putting on a pale blue sweater that matched her eyes, and now she sat smoking a cigarette at the dining room table, watching the tips of the branches of the Norwegian pine across the road move up and down just slightly.

Daisy's husband, old enough to be her father, had died three years ago. Her lips moved, thinking of him coming to her last night in that dream, if you wanted to call it a dream. She tapped her cigarette ash into the big glass ashtray. A natural lover, he'd always said. Through the window she saw the young couple drive by—Kathleen Burnham's cousin and his girlfriend. They drove a dented Volvo with bumper stickers all over it, reminding Daisy of the way old suitcases used to look, covered with stamped visas, back in the day. She saw the girl was talking, while the boy, driving, nodded. Peering through the twiggy bridal wreath that touched the window, Daisy thought she saw a bumper sticker that said VISUALIZE SWIRLED PEAS, over a picture of the earth.

She squashed her cigarette in the big glass ashtray just as Harmon came into sight. Harmon's slow walk, his slumped shoulders, made him look older than he was, and just in this quick glimpse she could see how he carried within him a sadness. But his eyes, when she opened the door, looked at her with that flash of liveliness and inno- cence. "Thank you, Harmon," she said, when he handed her the bag containing the doughnut he always brought. She left it on the kitchen table's red-checked cloth, next to the other one Harmon put there. She would eat the doughnut later, with a glass of red wine.

In the living room Daisy sat on the couch, crossing her plump an- kles. She lit another cigarette. "How are you, Harmon?" she said. "How are the boys?" For she knew this was his sadness: His four sons had grown and scattered. They visited, appearing in town as great grown men, and she remembered when, in years past, you never saw Harmon alone. Always one or more of these small, then teenage, boys were with him, running around the hardware store on Saturdays, yelling across the parking lot, throwing a ball, calling out to their father to hurry.

"They're good. They seem good." Harmon sat next to her; he never sat in Copper's old easy chair. "And you, Daisy?"

"Copper came to me in a dream last night. It didn't seem like a dream. I could swear he came—well, from wherever he is, to visit me." She tilted her head at him, peering through the smoke. "Does that sound crazy?"

Harmon raised a shoulder. "I don't know as anyone's got a corner on the market of that stuff, no matter what people say they believe, or don't."

Daisy nodded. "Well, he said everything was fine."

"Everything?"

She laughed softly, her eyes squinting again as she put the cigarette to her mouth. "Everything." Together they looked about the small, low- ceilinged room, the smoke leveling above them. Once, during a sum- mer thunderstorm, they had sat in this room while a small ball of electricity had come through the partly opened window, buzzed ludi- crously around the walls, and then gone out the window again.

Daisy sat back, tugging the blue sweater over her large, soft stom- ach. "No need to tell anyone I saw him like that."

"No."

"You're a good friend to me, Harmon."

He said nothing, ran his hand over the couch cushion.

"Say, Kathleen Burnham's cousin is in town with his girlfriend. I saw them drive by."

"They were just at the marina." He told how the girl had put her head down on the table. How she had said to the fellow, Stop smelling me.

"Oh, sweet." Daisy laughed softly again.

"God, I love young people," Harmon said. "They get griped about enough. People like to think the younger generation's job is to steer the world to hell. But it's never true, is it? They're hopeful and good—and that's how it should be."

Daisy kept smiling. "Everything you say is true." She took a final drag on her cigarette, leaned forward to squish it out. She had told him once how she'd thought with Copper she was pregnant, how happy they'd been—but it wasn't to be. She wasn't going to mention this again. Instead she put her hand over his, feeling the thickness of his knuckles.

In a moment they both stood, and climbed the narrow staircase to the little room where sunlight shone through the window, making a red glass vase on the bureau glow.

"I take it you had to wait." Bonnie was ripping long strips of dark green wool. A soft pile of these strips lay at her feet, the late morning sun making a pattern across the pine floor from the small-paned window she sat near.

"I wish you'd come. The water's beautiful. Calm, flat. But it's picking up now."

"I guess I can see the bay from here." She had not looked up. Her fingers were long. Her plain gold band, loose behind the knuckle, caught the sun with each rip. "I suppose it's mostly out-of-staters making you wait."

"No." Harmon sat down in the La-Z-Boy that looked out over the water. He thought of the young couple. "Maybe. Mostly, it was the usual."

"Did you bring me back a doughnut?"

He sat forward. "Oh, gosh. Gosh, no. I left it there. I'll go back, Bonnie."

"Oh, stop it."

"I will."

"Sit down."

He had not stood up, but had been ready, with his hands on the chair's arms, his knees bent. He hesitated, sat back. He picked up a *Newsweek* magazine on the small table beside the chair.

"Would've been nice if you'd remembered."

"Bonnie, I said—"

"And I said stop it."

He turned the pages of the magazine, not reading. There was only the sound of her ripping the strips of wool. Then she said, "I want this rug to look like the forest floor." She nodded toward a piece of mustard-colored wool.

"That'll be nice," he said. She had braided rugs for years. She made wreaths from dried roses and bayberry, and made quilted jackets and vests. It used to be she'd stay up late doing these things. Now she fell asleep by eight o'clock most nights, and was awake before it was light; he often woke to hear her sewing machine.

He closed the magazine, and watched as she stood, flicking off tiny bits of green wool. She bent gracefully and put the strips into a large basket. She looked very different from the woman he had married, though he didn't mind that especially, it only bewildered him to think how a person could change. Her waist had thickened considerably, and so had his. Her hair, gray now, was clipped almost as short as a man's, and she had stopped wearing jewelry, except for her wedding band. She seemed not to have gained weight anywhere except around the middle. He had gained weight everywhere, and had lost a good deal of hair. Perhaps she minded this about him. He thought again of the young couple, the girl's clear voice, her cinnamon hair.

"Let's go for a drive," he said.

"You just got back from a drive. I want to make some applesauce and get started on this rug."

"Any of the boys call?"

"Not yet. I expect Kevin will call soon."

"I wish he'd call to say they were pregnant."

"Oh, give it time, Harmon. Goodness."

But he wanted a whole bushel of them—grandchildren spilling everywhere. After all the years of broken collarbones, pimples, hockey sticks, and baseball bats, and ice skates getting lost, the bickering, schoolbooks everywhere, worrying about beer on their breath, waiting to hear the car pulling up in the middle of the night, the girlfriends, the two who'd had no girlfriends. All that had kept Bonnie and him in a state of continual confusion, as though there was always, always, some leak in the house that needed fixing, and there were plenty of times when he'd thought, God, let them just be grown.

And then they were.

He had thought Bonnie might have a bad empty-nest time of it, that he'd have to watch out for her. He knew, everyone knew, of at least one family these days where the kids grew up and the wife just *took off,* lickety-split. But Bonnie seemed calmer, full of a new energy. She had joined a book club, and she and another woman were writing a cookbook of recipes from the early settlers that some small press in Camden had said they might publish. She'd started braiding more rugs to sell in a shop in Portland. She brought home the first check with her face flushed with pleasure. He just never would have thought, that's all.

Something else happened the year Derrick went off to college. While their bedroom life had slowed considerably, Harmon had accepted this, had sensed for some time that Bonnie was "accommodating" him. But one night he turned to her in bed, and she pulled away. After a long moment she said quietly, "Harmon, I think I'm just done with that stuff."

They lay there in the dark; what gripped him from his bowels on up was the horrible, blank knowledge that she meant this. Still, nobody can accept losses right away.

"Done?" he asked. She could have piled twenty bricks onto his stomach, that was the pain he felt.

"I'm sorry. But I'm just done. There's no point in my pretending. That isn't pretty for either of us."

He asked if it was because he'd gotten fat. She said he hadn't really gotten *fat,* please not to think that way. She was just done.

But maybe I've been selfish, he said. What can I do to please you? (They had never really talked about things in this way—in the dark he blushed.)

She said, couldn't he understand—it wasn't *him,* it was her. She was just done.

He opened the *Newsweek* again now, thinking how in a few years the house would be full again; if not all the time, at least a lot. They'd be good grandparents. He read the magazine's paragraph over again. They were making a film about the towers going down. It seemed to him he should have some opinion about this, but he did not know what to think. When had he stopped having opinions on things? He turned and looked out at the water.

The words *cheating on Bonnie* were as far away as seagulls circling Longway Rock, not even dots to the eye of anyone standing on shore— they had no real meaning to Harmon. Why would they? They implied a passion that would turn him away from his wife, and this was not the case. Bonnie was the central heating of his life. His brief Sunday moments with Daisy were not untender, but it was more a shared interest, like bird-watching. He turned back to the magazine, an inner shudder to think if one of his sons had gone down in one of those planes.

On Thursday it was just getting dark when the couple came into the hardware store. Harmon heard the high voice of the girl before he actually saw her. Stepping around from behind the rack of drill bits, he was surprised at her forthright "Hi." She said it in almost two syllables, and while she didn't smile, her face had that same matter-of-factness that he had seen outside the marina.

"Hi there," Harmon said. "How're you folks today?"

"Good. We're just looking." The girl put her hand into the boy's pocket. Harmon gave a little bow, and they wandered down toward the lightbulbs. He heard her say, "He reminds me of Luke in the hospital. I wonder what happened to him. Remember Muffin Luke who ran the fucking place?"

The boy answered in a murmur.

"Luke was fucking weird. Remember I told you he said he was going in for heart surgery? I bet he made a terrible patient—he was so used to being in charge. He got scared about his stupid heart, though. Remember I told you he said he didn't know if he'd wake up dead or alive?"

Again, a murmur, and Harmon got the broom from the back of the store. Sweeping, he glanced at the back of them, the girl standing close to the boy, who had a coat with baggy pockets. "But you don't wake up dead, do you?"

"Let me know if you need my help," Harmon said, and they both turned, the girl looking startled.

"Okay," she said.

He took the broom up front. Cliff Mott came in to ask if there were snow shovels yet, and Harmon told him the new ones would be in next week. He showed Cliff one from last year and Cliff looked at it a long time, said he'd be back.

"We should get this for Victoria," Harmon heard the girl say. With the broom, he moved up to the front of the gardening aisle, and saw she had picked up a watering can. "Victoria says her plants listen when she talks, and I believe her." The girl put the can back on the shelf, and the boy, slouchy, easygoing, nodded. He was looking at the coiled hoses hanging on the wall. Harmon wondered why they would want a hose this time of year.

"You know how she's been such a bitch?" The girl was wearing the same denim jacket with the fake fur at the cuffs. "It's because the guy she likes has a fuck buddy and he didn't tell her. She found out from someone else."

Harmon stopped sweeping.

"But a fuck buddy—I mean, who cares. That's the point of a fuck buddy." The girl put her head against her boyfriend's shoulder.

The boy nudged her toward the door. "Night, now," Harmon said. The girl pulled the handle with her small hand. On her feet were big suede shapeless boots, her legs as skinny as spider legs rising from them. It was not until they were out of sight down the sidewalk that Harmon recognized the uneasy feeling he had. He didn't know, but years of experience in the store made him think the boy had shoplifted something.

The next morning, he called his son Kevin at work.

"Everything all right, Dad?" the kid asked.

"Oh, sure, sure." Harmon was suddenly overcome with a bashfulness. "Everything okay with you?" he asked.

"The same. Work's okay. Martha's talking about wanting a kid, but I say we wait."

"You're both young," Harmon said. "You can wait. *I* can't wait. But don't rush. You just got married."

"It makes you feel old, though, doesn't it? Once that ring is on the finger."

"It does, I guess." It was hard for Harmon to remember the emotions of his first years of marriage. "Say, listen, Kev. Are you smoking pot?"

Kevin laughed through the phone. It was, to Harmon's ear, a healthy sound, straightforward, relaxed. "Jesus, Dad. What's gotten into you?"

"I wondered, is all. Couple of kids have moved into the Washburn place. People are afraid they're potheads."

"Weed makes me antisocial," Kevin said. "Makes me turn my face to the wall. So no, I don't smoke it anymore."

"Let me ask you something," Harmon said. "And don't tell your mother, for Christ's sake. But these kids came in the store yesterday, they were talking, casual, you know, and they mentioned 'fuck buddies.' You heard of that?"

"You're kind of surprising me here, Dad. What's going on?"

"I know, I know." Harmon waved a hand. "I just hate getting old, one of those old people that don't know anything about young people. So I thought I'd ask."

"Fuck buddies. Yeah. That's a thing these days. Just what it says. People who get together to get laid. No strings attached."

"I see." Now Harmon didn't know what more to say.

"I gotta go, Dad. But listen, stay cool. You're cool, Dad. You're not an old fart, don't worry about that."

"All right," Harmon said, and after he hung up, he stared out the window for a long time.

"That's fine, honestly," Daisy said when he called her the next morning. "I mean it, Harmon." He could hear her smoking as they spoke. "You're not to worry," she said.

Within fifteen minutes, she called back. He had a customer in the store, but Daisy said, "Say, listen. Why don't you stop by anyway and we'll just talk. Talk."

"All right," he said. Cliff Mott brought the snow shovel up to the register. Cliff Mott, who had heart disease, and could go any minute. "All set, then," Harmon said, handing the man his change.

Harmon still did not sit in Copper's chair; he sat on the couch beside Daisy, and once or twice they might briefly touch hands. Otherwise, they did what she had suggested—talked. He told her of trips to his grandmother's house, the way her pantry smelled of ammonia, the homesickness he had felt. "I was small, see," he said to the responsive face of Daisy. "And I understood it was meant to be *fun*. That was the idea, you see. But I couldn't tell anyone it wasn't fun."

"Oh, Harmon," said Daisy, her eyes moistening. "Yes. I know what you mean."

She told him about the morning she took a pear from the front yard of Mrs. Kettleworth, and her mother made her take it back, how embarrassed she'd been. He told about finding the quarter in the mud puddle. She told of going to her first high school dance, wearing a dress of her mother's, and the only person who asked her to dance was the principal.

"I'd have asked you," Harmon said.

She told him her favorite song was "Whenever I Feel Afraid," and she sang it to him softly, her blue eyes sparkling with warmth. He said the first time he heard Elvis on the radio singing "Fools Rush In," it made him feel like he and Elvis were friends.

Walking back to his car at the marina on those mornings, he was sometimes surprised to feel that the earth was altered, the crisp air a nice thing to move through, the rustle of the oak leaves like a murmuring friend. For the first time in years he thought about God, who seemed a piggy bank Harmon had stuck up on a shelf and had now brought down to look at with a new considering eye. He wondered if this was what kids felt like when they smoked pot, or took that drug ecstasy.

One Monday in October, there was an article in the local paper saying arrests had been made at the Washburn residence. Police broke up a party where marijuana was found growing in pots along a windowsill. Harmon perused the paper carefully, finding the name Timothy Burnham, and his "girlfriend, Nina White," who had the extra charge of assaulting a police officer.

Harmon couldn't imagine the girl with the cinnamon hair and skinny legs assaulting a police officer. He pondered this as he moved around the hardware store, finding some ball bearings for Greg Marston, a toilet plunger for Marlene Bonney. He made a sign that said 10% OFF, and put it on the one remaining barbecue up front. He hoped Kathleen Burnham would come in, or someone from the sawmill so he could ask, but they didn't, and none of his customers mentioned it. He telephoned Daisy, who said she'd seen the article, and hoped the girl was all right. "Poor little thing," Daisy said, "must've been scared."

Bonnie came home from her book club that night and reported how Kathleen said her nephew Tim just had the bad luck of inviting a bunch of friends over who turned up the music too loud, and some were smoking pot, including Tim's girlfriend. When the police came, the girl, Nina, started to kick like a wildcat and they had to cuff her, though probably the charges would be dropped, and they'd just all have to pay a fine, and be on probation a year.

"Idiots," Bonnie said, shaking her head.

Harmon said nothing.

"She's sick, you know," Bonnie added, dropping the book onto the couch. It was a book by Anne Lindbergh; she'd told him about it. Anne Lindbergh liked to get away from it all.

"Who's sick?"

"That girl. The girlfriend of Tim Burnham."

"What do you mean *sick*?"

"She's got that disease where you don't eat anything. Apparently she's had it long enough there's some damage to her heart, so she really *is* an idiot."

Harmon felt a sprinkle of perspiration arrive on his forehead. "Are you sure?"

"That she's an idiot? Think about it, Harmon. If you're young and you've got heart damage, then you're not supposed to be partying. And you're *certainly* not supposed to go on starving yourself."

"She's not starving herself. I saw her in the marina with the fellow. They were sitting in a booth, ordering breakfast."

"And how much of the breakfast did she eat?"

"I don't know," he admitted, remembering her small back as she'd leaned over the table. "But she doesn't look sick. She's a pretty girl."

"That's what Kathleen says. Tim met her when he was driving around the country following some band. I guess people just follow this band around, Fish or Pish. Something. Remember Kevin talking about Dead Heads, people who followed around that mess—what were they called? The Grateful Dead? I always found that offensive."

"He died," said Harmon. "That fat fellow Jerry of that band."

"Well, I hope he died gratefully," Bonnie said.

The leaves were half-gone now. The Norway maples still hung on to their yellow, but most of the orangey-red of the sugar maples had found their way to the ground, leaving behind the stark branches that seemed to hang like stuck-out arms and tiny fingers, skeletal and bleak. Harmon sat on the couch next to Daisy. He had just mentioned to her that he never saw the young couple anymore, and she told him that Les Washburn had kicked them out after the party that had led to the arrests, but she didn't know where they were living, only that Tim still worked at the sawmill.

"Bonnie said the girl had that disease where you starve yourself," Harmon said. "But I don't know if that's true."

Daisy shook her head. "Pretty young girls starving themselves. I've read articles about it. They do it so they can feel in control, and then *it* goes out of control and they can't stop. It's just the saddest thing."

Harmon himself had been losing weight. It wasn't that hard to do; he just stopped taking the extra portion at night, had a smaller slice of cake. He felt better. He told this to Daisy, and she nodded.

"Same with my smoking. I've been putting off the first cigarette of the day, and I've got it pushed back now—three in the afternoon."

"That's great, Daisy." He had seen that she'd not been smoking on Sunday mornings, but wasn't going to mention it. The appetites of the body were private battles.

"Tell me, Harmon," Daisy said, brushing something from her pant leg, glancing over with a mischievous smile. "Who was your first girlfriend?"

In fourth grade he'd had a crush on Candy Connelly. He'd stand behind her to watch her take the steps up the big metal slide on the playground, and one time she had fallen. When she'd cried, he had felt helpless with love. All that at nine years old. Daisy said when she was nine, her mother sewed her a yellow dress to wear to the spring concert the school had every year. "She pinned a white lilac to it just as we left that evening," Daisy said, with her soft laugh. "Walking to the school—oh, I felt so pretty."

Harmon's mother didn't sew, but she used to make popcorn balls at Christmas. Speaking of this, he felt something had been returned to him, as though the inestimable losses of life had been lifted like a boulder, and beneath he saw—under the attentive gaze of Daisy's blue eyes—the comforts and sweetness of what had once been.

When he got home, Bonnie said, "What took you so long? I need you to climb up and fix those gutters like you've been promising to do."

He handed her the bag with her doughnut.

"And the pipe under the sink has been dripping into that bucket for weeks. Ironic you should own a hardware store."

Unexpectedly, a ripple of terror went through him. He sat down in his La-Z-Boy. In a moment he said, "Hey, Bonnie, would you ever want to move?"

"Move?"

"Say to Florida or somewhere."

"Are you crazy? Or are you kidding."

"Where there's sun all year long. Where the house isn't so big and empty."

"I'm not even going to answer such a ludicrous thing." She peered into the bag with the doughnut. "Cinnamon? You know I hate cinnamon."

"It's all they had." He picked up a magazine, so as not to look at her. But in a moment, he said, "Has it ever bothered you, Bonnie, that none of the boys want to take over the store?"

Bonnie frowned. "We've talked about that, Harmon. Why in the world should it bother us? They're free to do what they like."

"Of course they are. But it would've been nice. Have at least one of them around."

"This negativity of yours. It's driving me nuts."

"Negativity?"

"I just wish you'd perk up." She crumpled the doughnut bag closed. "And clean out those gutters. It isn't pleasant, Harmon, having to feel like a nag."

By November, the leaves were gone, the trees along Main Street were bare, and the sky was often overcast. The shortening days made Harmon recall a soberness of heart that he had felt off and on for a long time; no wonder Bonnie had told him to perk up. In a small, private way, he was perking up. Because now, as he went around closing up the store, selling nails to a last-minute customer, he found himself looking forward to his Sunday mornings with Daisy with a sense of gladness, not the furtive urgency of those few months they'd been . . . "buddies." It was as though a lightbulb glowed in a town where nighttime came swiftly, and sometimes driving home he would go the long way to pass by her house. Once he saw a dented Volvo parked in her driveway; it was covered with bumper stickers, and he wondered if some of Copper's family had come from Boston to visit.

The next Sunday, Daisy said, in a hushed tone at the door, "Come in, Harmon. Have I got a story to tell you." She put a finger to her lips, then said, "Nina's asleep upstairs in the little room." They sat at the dining room table as Daisy told him in a whisper that the girl, a few days earlier, had had a fight with Tim—they'd been staying at some motel on Route 1 since getting kicked out of the Washburn place—and he'd gone off with their cell phone. Nina knocked on Daisy's door, so distraught Daisy thought she might have to get her to a doctor. Nina got hold of the boy, though, and he'd come by to get her. Daisy thought they'd made up. But last night the girl knocked again, another fight, and she didn't have a place to stay. So now she was upstairs. Daisy clasped her hands together on the table. "Boy, do I want a cigarette."

Harmon sat back. "Well, hold off if you can. We'll get this figured out."

Above them the floor creaked, there was a motion on the stairs, and here was the girl, wearing flannel pants and a T-shirt. "Hello," said Harmon, so as not to frighten her, being startled himself. He had not seen her for weeks, since she'd been in the store; she was hardly recognizable. The girl's head seemed much too large for her body; veins were visible on the sides of her forehead, and her bare arms were as skinny as the slats of the chair back she took hold of. He almost couldn't look.

"Sit, dear," said Daisy. The girl sat, her long, long arms placed on the table. Truly, it was as though a skeleton had sat down with them.

"Did he call?" the girl asked Daisy. Her skin was not cinnamon-looking now, but pallid, and her hair, uncombed, looked like the hair of a stuffed animal, not real.

"No, dear. He didn't." Daisy handed her a tissue, and Harmon saw the girl was weeping.

"What'm I going to do?" she asked. She looked past Harmon, out the window at the road. "I mean, *Victoria,* of all people. Jesus, she was my *friend.*"

"You can stay another day while you get it figured out," said Daisy. The girl turned her big light-brown eyes toward Daisy, as though studying her from somewhere far off.

"You should eat something, dear," Daisy said. "I know you don't want to, but you should."

"She's right," Harmon said. It worried him to think of this girl falling faint or dead in Daisy's little cottage. He thought of Bonnie saying how she had already damaged her heart. "Look." He pushed forward the two bags from the marina. "Doughnuts."

The girl eyed the bags. "Doughnuts?"

"How about just half a glass of milk, and a bit of doughnut?" Daisy asked. The girl began to weep again. While Daisy went to get the milk, Harmon reached into his pocket and handed her his white folded handkerchief. The girl stopped crying, started to laugh.

"Hey, cool," she said. "I didn't know anyone used these anymore."

"Go ahead and use it," Harmon said. "But for the love of God, drink that milk."

Daisy brought in the milk, took the doughnut from its bag, broke it in two.

"Fucking Luke," the girl said, with sudden energy. "He put me on fucking probation for being a muffin cutter."

"A what?" asked Daisy, sitting down.

"In the hospital. One time I cut my muffin in half. The rules are, you're not supposed to engage—that's the word they use, *engage*—with the food except to eat it. So I have this plastic knife in my pocket and I cut the muffin in half, and I get reported to Luke. 'We heard you've been cutting your muffins, Nina,' he said, with his arms folded across his chest." The girl rolled her eyes extravagantly when she finished telling this. "Muffin Luke. The fucker."

Daisy and Harmon looked at each other.

"How did you get out of the hospital?" asked Harmon.

"I ran away. But next time, my parents said they'd commit me, and then I'm fucked."

"Better eat the doughnut," Harmon said.

The girl giggled. "You're kind of goofy."

"He's not goofy. He's concerned about you. Now eat the doughnut," Daisy said, in a melodious voice.

"So, like, what's the story with you two?" The girl looked from one to the other.

"We're friends," said Daisy, but Harmon saw that her cheeks colored.

"Okay." Nina looked again from one to the other. Tears swelled in her eyes and spilled over. "I don't know what to do without Tim," she said. "And I don't want to go back to the hospital." She had begun to shiver. Harmon took off his big woolen cardigan and put it over her shoulders.

"Of course you don't," said Daisy. "But you need to eat. You're going to have other boyfriends, you know."

94 | *Olive Kitteridge*

Harmon realized by a shift in the girl's expression that this was what she feared—being without love. Who didn't fear that? But he knew her problems had roots that were long and tangled, and the safety of Daisy's cottage could not provide any lasting relief. She was very sick. "How old are you?" he asked.

"Twenty-three. So you can't make me go to the hospital. I know this shit," she added. "So don't try anything."

He held both palms toward her. "I am trying nothing." He put his hands down. "Didn't you get arrested?"

Nina nodded. "I had to show up in court. We both got ACD's, but I got an extra lecture because I'd been, you know, an asshole to that fucker police."

"What's an ACD?"

But Nina was exhausted; she folded her arms, putting her head down, like he had seen her do in the marina that day. He and Daisy glanced at each other. "Nina," he said softly, and she rolled her eyes toward him. He picked up the doughnut. He said, "To my memory, I have never begged for anything." Just slightly the girl smiled at him. "And I am begging you to eat."

The girl sat up slowly. "Only because you've been nice," she said. She ate the doughnut so ravenously, Daisy had to tell her to slow down.

"He stole from you," Nina said to Harmon, with her mouth full. "He stole some tubing that day to make a bong." She lifted the glass of milk.

"You're better off without him," Daisy said.

A loud knocking on the kitchen door caused them all to turn; the door opened, banged shut. "Hello!"

The girl gave a whimper, spit the doughnut into Harmon's handkerchief, started to rise from her chair. Harmon's sweater fell from her shoulders to the floor.

"No, dear." Daisy put her hand on the girl's arm. "It's only a woman come to collect money for the Red Cross."

Olive Kitteridge stood in the doorway to the dining room, almost filling the space up. "Well, look at the tea party. Hello, Harmon." To the girl: "Who are you?"

The girl looked at Daisy, then at the table, her hand clenching the handkerchief. Looking back at Olive, she said sarcastically, "Who are *you*?"

"I'm Olive," said Olive. "And if you don't mind, I'd like to sit down. Begging for money seems to knock me out. I think this is the last year I'll canvass."

"Can I get you some coffee, Olive?"

"Nope. Thank you." Olive had gone round to the other side of the table, seated herself in a chair. "But that doughnut looks good. You have any more?"

"In fact, we do." Daisy opened the other bag, glancing at Harmon—it was the doughnut meant for Bonnie—and pushed the paper bag toward Olive, the doughnut on it. "I could get you a plate."

"Oh, hell no." Olive ate the doughnut, leaning forward over the table. A silence fell.

"Let me get you the check." Daisy stood and went into the next room.

"Henry okay?" Harmon asked. "Christopher?"

Olive nodded, her mouth moving with the doughnut. Harmon knew—as most people in town did—that she didn't like her son's new wife, but, then, Harmon didn't think Olive would like any wife of her son. The new wife was a doctor, smart, and from some city, he didn't remember where. Maybe she made baggies of granola, did yoga—he had no idea. Olive was watching Nina, and Harmon followed her gaze. Nina sat motionless, slumped forward, the back of each rib bone defined against her thin T-shirt; she clutched his handkerchief with a hand that looked like the claw of a seagull. Her head looked too big to be supported by the ridged stick of her backbone. The vein running from her hairline across to her brow was a greenish-blue color.

Olive finished the doughnut, wiped the sugar from her fingers, sat back, and said, "You're starving."

The girl didn't move, only said, "Uh—*duh*."

"I'm starving, too," Olive said. The girl looked over at her. "I am," Olive said. "Why do you think I eat every doughnut in sight?"

"You're not starving," Nina said with disgust.

"Sure I am. We all are."

"Wow," Nina said, quietly. "Heavy."

Olive looked through her big black handbag, took a tissue, wiped at her mouth, her forehead. It took a moment for Harmon to realize she was agitated. When Daisy returned and said, "Here you go, Olive," slipping her an envelope, Olive only nodded, put it into her bag.

"Jesus," said Nina. "Okay, I'm sorry." Olive Kitteridge was crying. If there was anyone in town Harmon believed he would never see cry, Olive was that person. But there she sat, large and big-wristed, her mouth quivering, tears coming from her eyes. She shook her head slightly, as though to indicate the girl needn't apologize.

"Excuse me," she finally said, but she stayed where she was.

"Olive, is there anything—" Daisy leaned forward.

Olive shook her head again, blew her nose. She looked at Nina, and said quietly, "I don't know who you are, but young lady, you're breaking my heart."

"I'm not trying to," Nina said, defensively. "It's not like I can help it."

"Oh, I know that. I know." Olive nodded. "I taught school for thirty-two years. I never saw a girl sick like you, it wasn't around then—not up here, anyway. But I know from all those years with kids, and—and just *living*—" Olive stood up, wiped crumbs from her front. "Anyway, I'm sorry." She started to move away, stopped when she was near the girl. Hesitantly, she raised her hand, started to put it down, then raised it again, and touched the girl's head. She must have felt, beneath her large hand, something Harmon didn't see, because she slid her hand down to the girl's bone of a shoulder, and the girl—tears creeping from her closed eyes—leaned her cheek on Olive's hand.

"I don't want to be like this," the girl whispered.

"Of course you don't," said Olive. "And we're going to get you help."

The girl shook her head. "They've tried. I just keep getting sick again. It's hopeless."

Olive reached and pulled over a chair, so that she could sit with the girl's head on her big lap. She stroked the girl's hair, and held a few pieces in her fingers, giving Daisy and Harmon a meaningful nod before flicking the hair to the floor. You lost your hair when you starved. Olive had stopped her own weeping, and said, "Are you too young to know who Winston Churchill was?"

"I know who he was," the girl said, tiredly.

"Well, he said, never, never, never, never give up."

"He was fat," said Nina, "so what did he know?" She added, "It's not that I want to give up."

"Of course not," said Olive. "But your body's going to give up without some fuel. I know you've heard this all before, so you just lie there and don't answer. Well, answer this: Do you hate your mother?"

"No," Nina said. "I mean, she's kind of pathetic, but I don't hate her."

"All right, then," Olive said, her big body giving a shudder. "All right, then. That's a start."

For Harmon, the scene would always remind him of the day the ball of lightning came through the window and buzzed around. For there was a kind of warm electricity, something astonishing and unworldly in the feeling of the room, as the girl began to cry, and Daisy eventually got the mother on the telephone, arrangements made for her to be picked up that afternoon, promises that she would not go to the hospital. Harmon left with Olive, the girl wrapped in a blanket on the couch. He helped Olive Kitteridge get into her car, then he walked back to the marina and went home, knowing that something in his life had changed. He did not speak of it to Bonnie.

"Did you bring me my doughnut?" she asked.

"There was only cinnamon," he said. "The boys call?"

Bonnie shook her head.

You started to expect things at a certain age. Harmon knew that. You worried about heart attacks, cancer, the cough that turned into a ferocious pneumonia. You could even expect to have a kind of midlife crisis—but there was nothing to explain what he felt was happening to him, that he'd been put into a transparent plastic capsule that rose off the ground and was tossed and blown and shaken so fiercely that he could not possibly find his way back to the quotidian pleasures of his past life. Desperately, he did not want this. And yet, after that morning at Daisy's, when Nina had cried, and Daisy had gotten on the phone, making arrangements for the parents to come and get her—after that morning, the sight of Bonnie made him feel cold.

The house felt like a damp, unlit cave. He noticed how Bonnie never asked him how things were at the store—perhaps after all these years, she didn't need to ask. Without wanting to, he began to keep score. A whole week might go by when she asked him nothing more personal than if he "had any thoughts about dinner."

One night he said, "Bonnie, do you know my favorite song?"

She was reading and didn't look up. "What?"

"I said—Do you know my favorite song?"

Now she looked at him over the tops of her glasses. "And I said, what? What is it?"

"So you don't know?"

She put her glasses onto her lap. "Am I supposed to know? Is this twenty questions?"

"I know yours—'Some Enchanted Evening.'"

"Is that my favorite song? I didn't know."

"Isn't it?"

Bonnie shrugged, put her glasses back on, looked at her book. "'I'm Always Chasing Rainbows.' Last time I checked, that was yours."

When would be the last time she checked? He barely remembered that song. He was going to say, "No—it's 'Fools Rush In.'" But she turned the page, and he didn't say anything.

On Sundays he visited Daisy, sitting on the couch. They spoke frequently of Nina. She was in a program for eating disorders, and having private psychotherapy, and family therapy, too. Daisy was in touch with the girl by phone, and frequently spoke to her mother. Talking all this over, Harmon sometimes felt that Nina was their child, his and Daisy's—that every aspect of her well-being was their great concern.

When she gained weight, they broke a doughnut in half, and touched it together as a toast. "To doughnut breakers," Harmon said. "To Muffin Luke."

When he was in town, it seemed he saw couples everywhere; arms tucked against the other in sweet intimacy; he felt he saw light flash from their faces, and it was the light of life, people were *living*. How much longer would he live? In theory, he could live twenty more years, even thirty, but he doubted that he would. And why would he want to, unless he was altogether healthy? Look at Wayne Roote, only a couple years older than Harmon, and his wife had to tape a note to the television saying what day it was. Cliff Mott, just a ticking bomb waiting to go off, all those arteries plugged. Harry Coombs'd had a stiff neck, and was dead from lymphoma by the end of last year.

"What will you do for Thanksgiving?" Harmon asked Daisy.

"I'll go to my sister's. It'll be fine. And what about you? Will all the boys be home?"

He shook his head. "We have to drive three hours to have it with Kevin's in-laws." As it turned out, Derrick didn't come, choosing to go to his girlfriend's instead. The other boys were there, but it wasn't their house, and seeing them was almost like visiting relatives, not *sons*.

"Christmas will be better," Daisy promised. She showed him a gift she was sending Nina—a pillow cross-stitched with the words *I AM LOVED*. "Don't you think that might help her, to glance at that sometimes?"

"That's nice," Harmon said.

"I spoke to Olive, and I'm signing the card from the three of us."

"That's very nice, Daisy."

He asked Bonnie if she wanted to make popcorn balls for Christmas. "God in heaven, no," Bonnie said. "Whenever your mother made those, I thought my teeth would come out." For some reason, this made Harmon laugh, the long familiarity of his wife's voice—and when she laughed with him, he felt a splintering of love and comfort and pain spread through him. Derrick came home for two days; he helped his father chop down a Christmas tree, helped him put it up, and then the day after Christmas, he left to go skiing with some friends. Kevin was not as jovial as Harmon remembered him; he seemed grown-up and serious, and maybe a little bit afraid of Martha, who wouldn't eat the carrot soup when she found it had been made with a chicken stock base. The other boys watched sports on television, and went off to visit their girlfriends in towns far away. It occurred to Harmon it would be years before they had a house full of grandchildren.

On New Year's, he and Bonnie were in bed by ten. He said, "I don't know, Bonnie. The holidays made me kind of blue this year."

She said, "Well, the boys have grown up, Harmon. They have their own lives."

One afternoon at work, when the store was especially slow, he called Les Washburn and asked if the place he had rented to the Burnham boy was still empty. Les said it was, he wasn't renting to kids again. Tim Burnham had left town, which Harmon hadn't known. "Went off with a different girl, not that pretty hellion who was sick."

"Before you rent it to anyone," Harmon said, "just let me know, would you? I might be looking for a work space."

Then one day in January, when there had been one of those days of midwinter thaw, the snow melting for just a few moments, making the sidewalks wet and the fenders of cars sparkle, Daisy called him at the store. "Can you stop by?" she asked.

Olive Kitteridge's car was in Daisy's little driveway, and when he saw it, he knew. Inside, Daisy was crying and making tea, and Olive Kitteridge was sitting at the table not crying, tapping a spoon against the table relentlessly. "That goddamn know-it-all daughter-in-law of mine," she said. "To hear her talk, you'd think she was an expert on every goddamn thing. She said, 'Olive, you couldn't *really* have expected her to get well. People with that disease never actually get over it.' And I said to her, 'Well, they don't all *die*, Suzanne,' and she said, 'Well, Olive, many of them actually do.' "

"The funeral's private," Daisy told Harmon. "Just the family."

He nodded.

"She was taking laxatives," Daisy said, putting a cup of tea in front of him, wiping at her nose with a tissue. "Her mother found them in a drawer in her room, and it made sense, I guess, because she'd stopped gaining the few ounces she'd been gaining. And so she went into the hospital on Thursday—" Here Daisy had to sit down and put her face into her hands.

"It was an awful scene," Olive told him. "From what the mother described. Nina didn't want to go, of course. They had to call people, get officials involved, and off she went kicking and biting."

"Poor little thing," said Daisy.

"She had the heart attack last night," Olive said to Harmon. Olive shook her head, slapped lightly at the table with her hand. "For the love of Jesus," she said.

It had been dark a long while by the time he left.

"Where in the world have you been?" Bonnie said. "Your supper's all cold."

He didn't answer, just sat down. "I'm not that hungry, Bonnie. I'm sorry."

"You better tell me where you've been."

"Driving around," he said. "I told you I've been kind of blue."

Bonnie sat down across from him. "Your being so blue makes me feel awful. And I don't *feel* like feeling awful."

"I don't blame you," he said. "I'm sorry."

Kevin called him at the store a few mornings later. "You busy, Dad? Got a minute?"

"What's up?"

"I just wanted to know if you're okay, if everything's okay."

Harmon watched Bessie Davis looking through the lightbulbs. "Sure, son. Why?"

"I was thinking you seemed a little depressed these days. Not yourself."

"No, no. Swimmingly, Kevin." A phrase they'd used since Kevin had learned to swim late, when he was almost a teenager.

"Martha thinks you might be mad because of Christmas and the carrot soup."

"Oh, Jesus, no." He saw Bessie turn, walk down toward the brooms. "Is that what your mother said?"

"No one said anything. I was just wondering."

"Has your mother been complaining to you?"

"No, Dad. I just told you. It's me. Wondering, that's all."

"Don't you worry," Harmon said. "I'm just fine. And you?"

"Swimmingly. Okay. Stay cool."

Bessie Davis, the town's old maid, stood and talked for a long time while she bought a new dustpan. She spoke of her hip problems, her bursitis. She spoke of her sister's thyroid condition. "Hate this time of year," she said, shaking her head. Harmon felt a rush of anxiety as she left. Some skin that had stood between himself and the world seemed to have been ripped away, and everything was close, and frightening. Bessie Davis had always talked on, but now he saw her loneliness as a lesion on her face. The words *Not me, not me* crossed over his mind. And he pictured the sweet Nina White sitting on Tim Burnham's lap outside the marina, and he thought, *Not you, not you, not you.*

On Sunday morning, the sky had a low overcast, and the lights in Daisy's living room glowed from beneath the little lamp shades. "Daisy, I'm just going to say this. I don't want you to answer, or in any way feel responsible. This is not because of anything you've done. Except be you." He waited, looked around the room, looked into her blue eyes, and said, "I've fallen in love with you."

He felt so certain of what was coming, her kindness, her tender refusal, that he was amazed when he felt her soft arms around him, saw the tears in her eyes, felt her mouth on his.

He paid the rent to Les Washburn from their savings account. How soon before Bonnie would notice, he couldn't say. But he thought he had a few months. What was he waiting for? The labor pains to squeeze so hard his new life would shoot forth? By February, as the slow opening of the world began once more—the air having a lightness of smell at times, the extra minutes of daylight as the sun lingered across a snow-covered field and made it violet in color—Harmon was afraid. What had begun—not when they were "fuck buddies," but as a sweet interest in the other—questions probing the old memories, a shaft of love moving toward his heart, sharing the love and grief of Nina's brief life, all this was now, undeniably, a ferocious and full-blown love, and his heart itself seemed to know this. He thought it beat irregularly. Sitting in his La-Z-Boy, he could hear it, feel it pulsing right behind his ribs. It seemed to be warning him in its heavy pounding, that it would not be able to continue like this. Only the young, he thought, could withstand the rigors of love. Except for little cinnamon-colored Nina; and it seemed all inside out, backward to forward, that he had been handed the baton by her. Never, never, never give up.

He went to the doctor he'd known for years. The doctor stuck metal disks onto his bare chest, wires attached to each one. Harmon's heart showed no signs of trouble. As he sat in front of the doctor's big wooden desk, he told the man he perhaps was going to leave his marriage. The doctor said quietly, "No, no, this is no good," but it was the doctor's body, the sudden way he moved the folders on his desk, the way he moved back from Harmon, that Harmon would always remember. As though he had known what Harmon didn't know, that lives get knit together like bones, and fractures might not heal.

But there was no telling Harmon anything. There is no telling anyone anything when they have been infected this way. He was waiting now—living in the hallucinatory world of Daisy Foster's generous body—waiting for the day, and he knew it would come, when he left Bonnie or when she kicked him out; he didn't know which of the two would happen, but it would—waiting like Muffin Luke for open-heart surgery, not knowing if he would die on the table, or live.

A Different Road

An awful thing happened to the Kitteridges on a chilly night in June. At the time, Henry was sixty-eight, Olive sixty-nine, and while they were not an especially youthful couple, there was nothing about them that gave the appearance of being old, or ill. Still, after a year had gone by, people in this small New England coastal town of Crosby agreed: Both Kitteridges were changed by the event. Henry, if you met him at the post office now, only lifted his mail as a hello. When you looked into his eyes, it was like seeing him through a screened-in porch. Sad, because he had always been an open-faced and cheerful man, even when his only son had—out of the blue—moved to California with his new wife, something people in town understood had been a great disappointment for the Kitteridges. And while Olive Kitteridge had *never* in anyone's memory felt inclined to be affable, or even polite, she seemed less so now as this particular June rolled around. Not a chilly June this year, but one that showed up with the suddenness of summer, days of dappled sunlight falling through the birch trees, making the people of Crosby uncharacteristically chatty at times.

Why else would Cynthia Bibber have approached Olive in the

shopping mall out at Cook's Corner to explain how Cynthia's daughter, Andrea, who after years of evening classes had earned a social work degree, thought maybe Henry and Olive hadn't been able to absorb the experience they'd had last year? Panic, when it wasn't expressed, became internalized—and *that,* Cynthia Bibber was saying, in an earnest half whisper, as she stood next to a plastic ficus tree, could lead to a depressive situation.

"I see," said Olive loudly. "Well, you tell Andrea that's pretty impressive." Olive, years ago, had taught math at the Crosby Junior High School, and while her emotions at times had attached themselves fiercely to particular students, Andrea Bibber had never seemed to her to be anything more than a small, dull, asseverating mouse. Like her mother, Olive thought, glancing past her at the silk daffodils that were stuck in rows of fake straw by the benches near the frozen yogurt place.

"It's a specialty now," Cynthia Bibber was saying.

"What is?" asked Olive, considering the possibility of some frozen chocolate yogurt if this woman would move on.

"Crisis counseling," said Cynthia. "Even before nine-eleven"—she shifted a package under her arm—"but when there's a crash, or a school shooting, or anything nowadays, they bring in psychologists right off the bat. People can't process this stuff on their own."

"Huh." Olive glanced down at the woman, who was short and small-boned. Olive, big, solidly built, towered over her.

"People have noticed a change in Henry," Cynthia said. "And you, too. And it's just a thought that crisis counseling might have helped. Could still help. Andrea has her own practice, you know—gone in with another woman part-time."

"I see," said Olive again, quite loudly this time. "Aren't they ugly words, Cynthia, that those people think up—process, internalize, depressive whatever. It'd make me *depressive* to go around saying those words all day." She held up the plastic bag she carried. "D'you see the sale they're having at So-Fro?"

In the parking lot she couldn't find her keys and had to dump the contents of her pocketbook out onto the sun-baked hood of the car. At the stop sign she said, "Oh, hells bells to you," into the rearview mirror when a man in a red truck honked his horn, then she pulled into traffic, and the bag from the fabric store slid onto the floor, a corner of denim material poking out onto the gravelly mat. "Andrea Bibber wants us to make an appointment for crisis counseling," she'd have said in the old days, and it was easy to picture Henry's big eyebrows drawing together as he stood up from weeding the peas. "Godfrey, Ollie," he'd have answered, the bay spread out behind him and seagulls flapping their wings above a lobster boat. "Imagine." He might even have put his head back to laugh the way he did sometimes, it would have been that funny.

Olive merged onto the highway, which was how she'd gotten home from the mall ever since Christopher had moved to California. She didn't care to drive by the house with its lovely lines, and the big bowed window where the Boston fern had done so well. Out here by Cook's Corner the highway went along the river, and today the water was shimmery and the leaves of poplars fluttered, showing the paler green of their undersides. Maybe, even in the old days, Henry wouldn't have laughed about Andrea Bibber. You could be wrong thinking you knew what people would do. "Bet you anything," Olive said out loud, as she looked over at the shining river, the sweet ribbon of it there beyond the guardrails. What she meant was: Bet you anything Andrea Bibber has a different idea of crisis than I do. "Yup, yup," she said. Weeping willows were down there on the bank, their swooping, airy boughs a light, bright green.

She had needed to go to the bathroom. "I need to go to the bathroom," she had said to Henry that night as they were pulling into the town of Maisy Mills. Henry had told her, pleasantly, she'd have to wait.

"Ay-yuh," she had said, pronouncing the word with exaggeration in order to make fun of her mother-in-law, Pauline, dead for some years, who used to say that in response to anything she didn't want to hear.

"Ay-yuh," Olive had repeated. "Tell my insides," she added, shifting slightly in the darkened car. "Good Lord, Henry. I'm about ready to explode."

But the truth was, they had had a pleasant evening. Earlier, farther up the river, they had met their friends Bill and Bunny Newton, and had gone to a restaurant recently opened, enjoying themselves a good deal. The mushrooms stuffed with crabmeat were marvelous, and all evening the waiters bowed politely, filling water glasses before the water had gone halfway down.

More gratifying, however, was the fact that for Olive and Henry the story of Bill and Bunny's offspring was worse than their own. Both couples had only the one child, and Karen Newton—the Kitteridges privately agreed—had created a different level of sadness for her parents. Even if Karen did live next door to Bill and Bunny and they got to see her, and her family, all the time. Last year Karen had carried on a brief affair with a man who worked for Midcoast Power, but decided in the end to stay in her marriage. All this, of course, worried the Newtons profoundly, even though they had never cared a great deal for their son-in-law, Eddie.

And while it had been a really ghastly blow for the Kitteridges to have Christopher so suddenly uprooted by his pushy new wife, after they had planned on him living nearby and raising a family (Olive had pictured teaching his future children how to plant bulbs)—while it had certainly been a blow to have this dream disintegrate, the fact that Bill and Bunny had their grandchildren right next door and the grandchildren were *spiteful* was a source of unspoken comfort to the Kitteridges. In fact, the Newtons told a story that night about how their grandson had said to Bunny just last week, "You may be my grandmother, but that doesn't mean I have to love you, you know." It was a frightful thing—who would expect such a thing? Bunny's eyes had glistened in the telling of this. Olive and Henry did what they could, shaking their heads, saying what a shame it was that Eddie essentially trained the children to say these things under the guise of "expressing themselves."

"Well, Karen's responsible, too," Bill said gravely, and Olive and Henry murmured, Well, sure, that was true.

"Oh, boy," said Bunny, blowing her nose. "Sometimes it seems like you can't win."

"You can't win," Henry said. "You do your best."

How was the California contingent, Bill wanted to know.

"Grumpy," Olive said. "Grumpy as hell when we called last week. I told Henry we're going to stop calling. When they feel like speaking to us, we'll speak to them."

"You can't win," said Bunny. "Even when you do your best." But they had been able to laugh, as if something about it were ruefully funny.

"Always nice to hear other people's problems," Olive and Bunny had agreed in the parking lot, pulling on their sweaters.

It was chilly in the car. Henry said they could turn the heat on if she wanted, but she said no. They drove along through the dark, an occasional car coming toward them with headlights shining, then the road dark again. "Awful what that boy said to Bunny," Olive remarked, and Henry said it was awful. After a while Henry said, "That Karen's not much." "No," Olive said, "she's not." But her stomach, grumbling and shifting in familiar ways, began some acceleration of its own and Olive became alert, then alarmed. "God," she said, as they stopped for a red light by the bridge that crossed into the town of Maisy Mills. "I really am ready to explode."

"I'm not sure what to do," Henry said, leaning forward to peer through the windshield. "The gas stations are across town, and who knows if they're open at this hour. Can't you sit tight? We'll be home in fifteen minutes."

"No," said Olive. "Believe me, I'm sitting as tight as I can."

"Well—"

"Green, *go*. Pull into the hospital, Henry. They ought to have a bathroom."

"The hospital? Ollie, I don't know."

"Turn into the hospital, for crying out loud." She added, "I was born there. I guess they'll let me use a bathroom."

There was the hospital at the top of the hill, bigger now with the new wing that had been built. Henry turned the car in, and then drove right past the blue sign that spelled out EMERGENCY.

"What are you *doing*?" asked Olive. "For God's sake."

"I'm taking you around to the front door."

"Stop the goddamn car."

"Oh, Olive." His voice was filled with disappointment, she supposed because of how he hated to have her swear. He backed the car up and stopped in front of the big, well-lighted blue door that said EMERGENCY.

"Thank you," said Olive. "Now, was that so hard to do?"

The nurse had looked up from her desk in a lobby cleanly bright, and empty. "I need a bathroom," Olive said, and the nurse raised her white-sweatered arm and pointed. Olive waved her hand over her head and stepped through the door.

"Whew," she said to herself out loud. "Whewie." *Pleasure is the absence of pain,* according to Aristotle. Or Plato. One of them. Olive had graduated magna cum laude from college. And Henry's mother had actually not liked that. Imagine. Pauline had actually said something about magna cum laude girls being plain and not having much fun. . . . Well, Olive was not going to spoil this moment thinking of Pauline. She finished up, washed her hands, and looked around as she stuck them under the dryer, thinking how the bathroom was huge, big enough to do surgery in. It was because of people in wheelchairs. Nowadays you got sued if you didn't build something big enough for a wheelchair, but she'd rather somebody just shoot her if it came to that.

"You all right?" The nurse was standing in the hallway, her sweater and pants droopy. "What'd you have? Diarrhea?"

"Explosive," said Olive. "My goodness. I'm fine now, thank you very much."

"Vomiting?"

"Oh, no."

"Do you have any allergies?"

"Nope." Olive looked around. "You seem pretty short on business tonight."

"Well. Weekends it picks up."

Olive nodded. "People party, I suppose. Drive into a tree."

"More often than not," the nurse said, "it's families. Last Friday we had a brother push his sister out the window. They were afraid she broke her neck."

"My word," said Olive. "All this in little Maisy Mills."

"She was okay. I think the doctor's ready to see you now."

"Oh, I don't need a doctor. I needed a bathroom. We had dinner with friends and I ate everything came my way. My husband's waiting for me in the parking lot."

The nurse reached for Olive's hand and looked at it. "Let's just be careful for a minute here. Have your palms been itching? Soles of your feet?" She peered up at Olive. "Are your ears always this red?"

Olive touched her ears. "Why?" she said. "Am I getting ready to die?"

"Lost a woman in here just last night," the nurse said. "About your age. Like you, she'd been out to eat with her husband and came in here later with diarrhea."

"Oh, for God's sake," Olive said, but her heart banged fast, and her face heated up. "What in hell ailed her?"

"She was allergic to crabmeat and went into anaphylactic shock."

"Well, there you are. I'm not allergic to crabmeat."

The nurse nodded calmly. "This woman'd been eating it for years with no problem. Let's just have the doctor give you a look. You did come in here flushed, showing signs of agitation."

Olive felt a great deal more agitated now, but she wasn't going to let the nurse know that, nor was she going to mention to her the mushrooms stuffed with crabmeat. If the doctor was nice, she'd tell him.

Henry was parked straight in front of the emergency room with the engine still running. She gestured for him to put the window down. "They want to check me," she said, bending her head down.

"Check you in?"

"*Check* me. Make sure I haven't gone into shock. Turn that damn thing down." Although he had already reached over to turn off the Red Sox game.

"Ollie, good Lord. Are you all right?"

"Some woman choked on crabmeat last night and now they're afraid they'll be sued. They're going to check my pulse and I'll be right out. But you ought to move the car."

The nurse was holding back a huge green curtain farther down the hall.

"He's listening to the ball game," Olive said, walking toward her. "When he thinks I've died, I expect he'll come in."

"I'll keep an eye out for him."

"He's got on a red jacket." Olive put her pocketbook on a nearby chair and then sat on the examining table while the nurse took her blood pressure.

"Better safe than sorry," the nurse said. "But I expect you're all right."

"I expect I am," said Olive.

The nurse left her with a form on a clipboard, and Olive sat on the examining table filling it out. She looked closely at her palms, and set the clipboard aside. Well, if you came stumbling into an emergency room it was their job to examine you. She'd stick her tongue out, have her temperature taken, go home.

"Mrs. Kitteridge?" The doctor was a plain-faced man who did not appear old enough to have gone through medical school. He held her large wrist gently, taking her pulse, while she told him about going to the new restaurant and that she'd only come in here to use the bathroom on the drive home, and yes, she'd had some terrific diarrhea, which had surprised her, but no itchy hands or feet.

"What did you have to eat?" the doctor asked as though he were interested.

"I started off with mushrooms stuffed with crabmeat, and I know some old lady died from that last night."

The doctor touched Olive's ear lobe, squinting. "I don't see any signs of a rash," he said. "Tell me what else you had to eat."

She appreciated how this young man did not seem bored. So many doctors made you feel like hell, like you were just a fat lump moving down the conveyor belt.

"Steak. And a potato. Baked. Big as your hat. And creamed spinach. Let's see." Olive closed her eyes. "Puny little salad, but a nice dressing on it."

"Soup? A lot of additives in soup that can cause allergic reactions."

"No soup," Olive said, opening her eyes. "But a lovely slab of cheesecake for dessert. With strawberries."

The doctor said, as he wrote things down, "This is probably just a case of active gastro-reflux."

"Oh, I see," said Olive. She considered for a moment before adding quickly, "Statistically speaking, it doesn't seem you'd have two women die of the same thing two nights in a row."

"I think you're okay," the doctor said. "But I'd like to examine you just the same, palpate your abdomen, listen to your heart." He handed her a blue papery-plastic square. "Put this on, open in front. Everything off, please."

"Oh, for heaven's sake," said Olive, but he had already stepped past the curtain. "Oh, for heaven's sake," she said again, rolling her eyes, but she did as she was told because he had been pleasant, and because the crabmeat woman had died. Olive folded her slacks and put them on the chair, careful to tuck her underpants beneath them where they couldn't be seen when the doctor walked back in.

Silly little plastic belt, made for a skinny pinny; it could barely tie around her. She managed, though—a tiny white bow. Waiting, she folded her hands and realized how every single time she went by this hospital, the same two thoughts occurred to her: that she'd been born here and that her father's body had been brought here after his suicide. She'd been through some things, but never mind. She straightened her back. Other people had been through things, too.

She gave a small shake of her head as she thought of the nurse saying someone had tossed his sister out the window like that. If Christopher had had a sister, he never would have thrown her out a window. If Christopher had married his receptionist, he'd still be here in town. Although the girl had been stupid. Olive could see why he'd passed on her. His wife was not stupid. She was pushy and determined, and mean as a bat from hell.

Olive straightened her back and looked at the little glass bottles of different things lined up on the counter, and the box of latex gloves. In the drawers of that metal cabinet, she bet there were all sorts of syringes ready for all sorts of problems. She flexed her ankle one way, then the other. In a minute she was going to poke her nose out to see if Henry was all set; she knew he wouldn't stay out there in the car, even with the ball game on. She'd call Bunny tomorrow, tell her about this little fiasco.

After that, it was like painting with a sponge, like someone had pressed a paint-wet sponge to the inside of her mind, and only what it painted, those splotches there, held what she remembered of the rest of that night. There was a quick, rushing sound—the curtain flung back with the tinny whoosh of its rings against the rod. There was a person in a blue ski mask waving an arm at Olive, shouting, "Get down!" There was the weird confusion, for a second the schoolteacher in her saying, "Hey, hey, hey," while he said, "Get *down,* lady. Jesus." "Get down where?" she might have said, because they were both confused—she was sure of that; she, clutching her papery robe, and this slender person in a blue ski mask waving his arm. "Look," she did say, her tongue as sticky as flypaper. "My handbag is right on that chair."

But there was a shout from down the hall. A man shouting, coming closer, and it was the quick thrust of a booted foot kicking over the chair that swept her into the black of terror. A tall man holding a rifle, wearing a big khaki vest with pocket flaps. *But it was the mask he wore,* a Halloween mask of a pink-cheeked smiling pig, which seemed to pitch her forward into the depths of ice-cold water—that ghoulish plastic face of a pink smiling pig. Underwater she saw the seaweed of his camouflage pants and knew he was shouting at her but couldn't hear his words.

They made her walk down the hall in her bare feet and papery blue robe while they walked behind her; her legs ached and felt enormous, like big sacks of water. A shove behind smacked into her, and she stumbled, clutching her papery robe as she was pushed through the door of the bathroom she had been in. On the floor with their backs against the separate walls sat the nurse and the doctor and Henry. Henry's red jacket was unzipped and askew, one of his pant legs caught halfway up.

"Olive, have they hurt you?"

"Shut the *fuck up*," said the man with the smiling pink pig face, and he kicked Henry's foot. "Say another word and I'll blow your mother-fucking head off *right now.*"

A paint splotch of memory that quivered every time: the sound of the duct tape behind her that night, the quick stripping of duct tape from its roll, and the grabbing of her hands behind her back, the wrapping of the tape around them, because then she knew she was going to die—that they would, all of them, be shot execution style; they would have to kneel. She was told to sit, but it was hard to sit down when your hands were taped behind you and your head inside was tilting. She had thought: *Just hurry.* Her legs were shaking so hard, they actually made a little slapping sound against the floor.

"Move, you get shot in the head," Pig-Face said. He was holding the rifle, and he kept turning quickly, while the flaps of his vest bulged, swinging when he turned. "You even look at each other, and this guy shoots you in the head."

But when did the things get said? Different things got said.

Along the exit ramp now were lilac trees and a red berry bush. Olive pulled up at the stop sign, and then almost pulled out in front of a car passing by; even as she looked at the car, she almost pulled out in front of it. The driver shook his head at her as though she were crazy. "Hells bells to you," she said, but she waited so she wouldn't end up right behind someone who had just looked at her as though she were crazy. And then she decided to go in the other direction, heading the back way to Maisy Mills.

Pig-Face had left them in the bathroom. ("It just doesn't make sense," different people said to the Kitteridges soon after this happened, after they read about it in the paper, saw it on TV. "It doesn't make sense, two fellows barging into a hospital hoping to get drugs." Before people realized the Kitteridges were not going to say three words about the ordeal. What does "making sense" have to do with the price of eggs, Olive could have said.) Pig-Face had left them, and Blue-Mask reached for the doorknob, locking it with the same *click* sound it had made for Olive not so long before. He sat down on the toilet seat cover, leaning forward, his legs apart, a small, squarish gun in his hand. Made of pewter, it looked like. Olive had thought she would vomit and choke on the vomit. It seemed a certainty; being unable to move her bulky, handless self, she would aspirate the vomit that was on its way up, and she would do it sitting right next to a doctor who wouldn't be able to help her because his hands were taped, too. Sitting next to a doctor, and across from a nurse, she would die on her vomit the way drunks did. And Henry would watch it and never be the same. *People have noticed the change in Henry.* She didn't vomit. The nurse had been crying when Olive was first pushed into the bathroom, and she was still crying. A lot of things were the nurse's fault.

At some point the doctor, whose white lab coat had been partly bunched beneath his leg that was closest to Olive, had said, "What's your name?" using the same pleasant voice he'd used earlier with Olive.

"Listen," said Blue-Mask. "Fuck you. Okay?"

At different times Olive thought: I remember this clearly, but then later couldn't remember when she'd thought that. Paint streaks, though, of this: They were quiet. They were waiting. Her legs had stopped shaking. Outside the door a telephone rang. It rang and rang, then stopped. Almost immediately it rang again. Olive's kneecaps bumped up, like big, uneven saucers beyond the edge of the papery blue robe. She didn't think she would have picked them out as her own, if someone had passed before her a series of photographs of old ladies' fat knees. Her ankles and bunioned toes seemed more familiar, stuck out in the middle of the room. The doctor's legs were not as long as hers, and his shoes didn't seem very big. Plain as a child's, his shoes. Brown leather and rubber-soled.

Where Henry's pant leg was caught up, the liver spots showed on his white hairless shin. He said, "Oh, gosh," quietly. And then: "Do you think you could find a blanket for my wife? Her teeth are chattering."

"You think this is a fucking hotel?" said Blue-Mask. "Just shut the fuck *up*."

"But she's—"

"Henry," Olive said sharply. "Be quiet."

The nurse kept crying silently.

No, Olive could not get the splotches arranged in order, but Blue-Mask was very nervous; she understood early on he was frightened to death. He kept bouncing his knees up and down. Young—she had understood that right away, too. When he pushed up the sleeves of his nylon jacket, his wrists were moist with perspiration. And then she saw how he had almost no fingernails. She had never, in all her years of school teaching, come across nails that had been bitten so extremely to the quick. He kept bringing his fingertips to his mouth, pressing them into the slots of the mask with a ferociousness; even the hand that held the gun would move to his mouth and he would chew the thumb tip quickly; a big bump of bright red.

"Get your fucking head down," he said to Henry. "Stop fucking *watching* me."

"You don't need to speak so filthy," Henry said, looking at the floor, his wavy hair headed in the wrong direction across his head.

"What'd you say?" The boy's voice rose like it was going to break. "What the *fuck* did you say, old man?"

"Henry, please," Olive said. "Keep quiet before you get us all killed."

This: Blue-Mask leaning forward, interested in Henry. "Old man. What the fucking-fuck did you say to me?" Henry turning his face to the side, his big eyebrows frowning. Blue-Mask getting up and pushing the gun into Henry's shoulder. "Answer me! What the fuck did you say to me?" (And Olive, turning down past the mill now, approaching the town, remembered the familiarity of that kind of frenzied frustration, saying to Christopher when he was a child, *Answer me!* Christopher always a quiet child, quiet the way her father had been.)

Henry blurted: "I said you don't need to talk so filthy." Blurted out further: "You should be ashamed of your mouth." And then the guy had pushed the gun against Henry's face, right into his cheek, his hand on the trigger.

"Please!" Olive cried out. "Please. He got that from his mother. His mother was impossible. Just ignore him."

Her heart thumped so hard she thought it made her papery blue gown move on her chest. The boy stood there watching Henry, then finally stepped back, tripping over the nurse's white shoes. He kept the gun pointed at Henry but turned to look at Olive. "This guy's your husband?"

Olive nodded.

"Well, he's a fuckin' nut."

"He can't help it," Olive said. "You'd have to know his mother. His mother was *full* of pious crap."

"That's not true," said Henry. "My mother was a good, decent woman."

"Shut up," the boy said tiredly. "Everyone *please* just shut the fuck up." He sat back down on the toilet seat cover, his legs spread, holding the gun over a knee. Olive's mouth was so dry, she thought of the word *tongue* and pictured a slab of cow's tongue packaged for sale.

The boy suddenly pulled off his ski mask. And how startling—it was as though she knew him then, as if seeing him *made sense.* Quietly, he said, "Motherfucker." His skin had become tender beneath the heat of the ski mask; his neck had streaks, patches of red. Crowded together high on his cheeks were inflamed pimples. His head was shaved, but she saw he was a redhead; there was the orangey effervescence of his scalp; the tiny flickers of bright stubble, the almost parboiled look of his tender, pale skin. The boy wiped his face in the crook of his nylon-sleeved elbow.

"I bought my son a ski mask like that," Olive told him. "He lives in California and skis in the Sierra Nevada Mountains."

The boy looked at her. His eyes were pale blue, and his eyelashes were almost colorless. The whites of his eyes had spidery red veins. He kept staring at Olive without changing his hangdog expression. "Just please shut up," he finally said.

Olive sat in her car in the far back of the hospital's parking lot, where she could see the blue door of the emergency room, but there was no shade and the sun baked through the windshield; even with the windows open, she was too warm. The lack of shade had not been a problem all year, of course. In the winter, she would come and sit with the car running. Never did she stay long. Only enough to gaze at the door and to remember the clean, bright lobby, the huge bathroom with its shiny chrome rail that ran along part of one wall; a rail that right now, perhaps, some old doddering lady was holding on to, in order to hoist herself off the toilet—the rail Olive had stared at as they all sat, legs splayed out, hands behind their backs. In hospitals, lives were changed all the time. A newspaper said the nurse had not returned to work, but maybe by now she had. About the doctor, Olive didn't know.

The kid kept getting up and sitting back down on the toilet seat. When he sat, he'd be hunched forward, the gun in one hand, the other hand folded in front of his mouth, him chewing the hell out of those fingertips. The sirens did not sound for very long. She had thought that, but maybe they had sounded for a long time. It was the pharmacist who'd been able to signal a janitor to call the police, a special unit brought to negotiate with Pig-Face, but none of them had known that then. A telephone kept ringing and stopping. They waited, the nurse rolling her head back, closing her eyes.

Olive's little plastic strip of a belt had come untied. The memory of this was a splotch of thick, dense paint. The belt, somewhere along the line, had come untied, and the papery gown was open. She tried crossing one leg over the other, but that made the gown open more, and she could see her big stomach with its folds, and her thighs, white as two massive fish bellies.

"Honestly," Henry said. "Can't you find something to cover my wife? She's all exposed."

"Shut up, Henry," Olive said. The nurse opened her eyes and gazed over at Olive, and the doctor of course turned his head to look at her. They were all looking at her now. "God, Henry."

The boy leaned forward, and said softly to Henry, "See—you gotta be quiet, or someone's gonna blow your head off. Your motherfucking head," he added.

He sat back. His glance, as he looked around, fell on Olive, and he said, "Oh, Jesus, lady," a look of real discomfort passing over his face.

"Well, what am I supposed to do?" she said, furious—oh, she was furious; and if her teeth had been chattering before, she now felt sweat rolling down her face; she seemed to be one moist, furious sack of horror. She tasted salt and did not know if these were tears or rivulets of sweat.

"Okay, listen." The kid took a deep, quick breath. He got up and came over to her, squatting down, putting the gun on the tile floor. "Any of you move, I'll kill you." He looked around. "Just give me a fucking second here." And then he tugged quickly on both sides of her papery blue robe, tied the white plastic strip in a knot right there on her stomach. His shaved head with the tiny glints of orange stubble was close to her. The top of his forehead was still red from where the ski mask had excited the skin. "Okay," he said. He took his gun and went back and sat on the toilet.

That moment, right there, when he sat back down and she wanted him to look at her—that was a vivid paint spot on her mind. How much she wanted him to look at her right then, and he didn't.

In the car, Olive started the engine and pulled out of the parking lot. She drove past a drugstore, the doughnut shop, a dress shop that had been there forever, then she drove over the bridge. Farther ahead, if she continued that way, was the cemetery where her father was buried. Last week she had taken lilacs to put on his grave, though she wasn't one who went in, especially, for decorating graves. Pauline was down there in Portland, and this was the first year that Olive had not accompanied Henry on Memorial Day to plant geraniums at the head of Pauline's grave.

There had been a pounding on the bathroom door (locked from the inside by the kid, the way Olive herself had locked it) and the hurried, "Come on, come on, open up, it's *me*!" And then she had seen—Henry couldn't because of where he was sitting, but she had seen, when the kid opened the bathroom door that was being pounded upon—the horrible Pig-Face guy with the rifle hit the boy hard, crack him right across the face, shouting, "You took off your *mask*! You dumb-shit motherfucker!" Screaming, "You dumb *shit*!" There was an immediate resurgence of the thickening of her limbs, her eye muscles seemed to thicken, the air got thick; the whole thick, slow feeling of things not being real. Because now they would die. They had been thinking they wouldn't, but they saw again that they would: This was clear in Pig-Face's panicky voice.

The nurse started saying Hail Mary's quickly and loudly, and as far as Olive could remember, it was after the nurse had repeated for the umpteenth time "Blessed is the fruit of thy womb" that Olive said to her, "God, will you shut up with that crap?" And Henry said, "Olive, stop." Siding with the nurse like that.

Olive, stopping at a red light, reaching down to put the bag from the fabric store back up onto the seat next to her, still didn't get it. She didn't get it. No matter how many times she went over it in her mind, she didn't understand why Henry had sided with the nurse like that. Unless it was because the nurse didn't swear (Olive bet that nurse could swear) and Henry, trussed up like a chicken and about to be shot, had been mad at Olive for swearing. Or for putting down Pauline earlier, when Olive had been trying to save his life.

Well, she had said some things about his mother then. After Pig-Face had screamed at the kid, and then disappeared again, and they all knew he'd be back to shoot them—in that blurry, thick, awful part when Henry said, "Olive, stop," she, Olive, said some things about his mother then.

She said: "*You're* the one who can't stand these Hail-Mary Catholics! Your mother taught you that! Pauline was the only real Christian in the world, as far as Pauline was concerned. And her good boy, Henry. You two were the only good Christians in the whole goddamn world!"

She said things like that. She said: "Do you know what your mother told people when my father died? That it was a *sin*! How's that for Christian charity, I ask you?" The doctor said, "Stop now. Let's stop this," but it was like an engine inside Olive had the switch flipped on, and the motor was accelerating; how did you stop such a thing?

She said the word *Jew.* She was crying, everything was all mixed up, and she said, "Did it ever occur to you that's why Christopher left? Because he married a Jew and knew his father would be judgmental—did you ever think of that, Henry?"

In the sudden silence in the room, the kid sitting on the toilet seat hiding his hit face in his arm, Henry said quietly, "That's a despicable thing to accuse me of, Olive, and you know it isn't true. He left because from the day your father died, you took over that boy's life. You didn't leave him any room. He couldn't stay married and stay in town, too."

"Shut up!" Olive said. "Shut up, shut up."

The boy stood up, holding that gun, saying, "Jesus fucking Christ. Oh *fuck*, man."

Henry said, "Oh, no," and Olive saw that Henry had wet himself; a dark stain grew in his lap, and down his trouser leg. The doctor said, "Let's try and be calm. Let's try and be quiet."

And they could hear the crackling of walkie-talkies out in the hall, the sound of the strong, unexcited speech of people in charge, and the boy started to cry. He cried without trying to hide it, and he held the small gun, still standing up. There was a gesture with his arm, a tentative move, and Olive whispered, "Oh, *don't*." For the rest of Olive's life she would be certain the boy had thought of turning the gun on himself, but the policemen then were everywhere, covered with dark vests and helmets. When they cut the duct tape from her wrists, her arms and shoulders ached so that she couldn't put her arms down by her sides.

Henry was standing on the front deck, looking over the bay. She had thought he would be working in the garden, but there he was, just standing, looking out over the water.

"Henry." Her heart was thumping ferociously.

He turned. "Hello, Olive. You're back. You were gone longer than I thought you'd be."

"I bumped into Cynthia Bibber and she wouldn't shut up."

"What's new with Cynthia?"

"Nothing. Not one thing."

She sat down in the canvas deck chair. "Listen," she said. "I don't remember. But you defended that woman, and I was just trying to help you. I didn't think you'd want to hear that Catholic mumbo jumbo crap."

He shook his head once, as though he had water in his ear that he was trying to shake out. After a moment he opened his mouth, then closed it. He turned back to look at the water, and for a long time neither said anything. Earlier in their marriage, they'd had fights that had made Olive feel sick the way she felt now. But after a certain point in a marriage, you stopped having a certain kind of fight, Olive thought, because when the years behind you were more than the years in front of you, things were different. She felt the sun's warmth on her arms, although down here under the hill by the water, the air held the hint of nippiness.

The bay was sparkling brilliantly in the afternoon sun. A small outboard cut across toward Diamond Cove, its bow riding high, and farther out was a sailboat with a red sail, and a white one. There was the sound of the water touching against the rocks; it was almost high tide. A cardinal called from the Norwegian pine, and there was the fragrance of bayberry leaves from the bushes that were soaking up the sun.

Slowly, Henry turned and lowered himself onto the wooden bench there, leaning forward, resting his head in his hands. "Do you know, Ollie," he said, looking up, his eyes tired, the skin around them red. "In all the years we've been married, all the years, I don't believe you've ever once apologized. For anything."

She flushed immediately and deeply. She could feel her face burn beneath the sunshine that fell upon it. "Well, sorry, sorry, sorry," she said, taking her sunglasses from where they'd been resting on top of her head, and putting them back on. "What exactly are you saying?" she asked. "What in hell ails you? What in hell is this all about? Apologies? Well, I'm sorry then. I *am* sorry I'm such a hell of a rotten wife."

He shook his head and leaned forward, placing his hand on her knee. You rode along in life a certain way, Olive thought. Just like she'd ridden home from Cook's Corner for years, past Taylor's field, before Christopher's house had even been there; then his house was there, Christopher was there; and then after a while he wasn't. Different road, and you had to get used to that. But the mind, or the heart, she didn't know which one it was, but it was slower these days, not catching up, and she felt like a big, fat field mouse scrambling to get up on a ball that was right in front of her turning faster and faster, and she couldn't get her scratchy frantic limbs up onto it.

"Olive, we were scared that night." He gave her knee a faint squeeze. "We were both scared. In a situation most people in a whole lifetime are never in. We said things, and we'll get over them in time."

But he stood up, and turned and looked out over the water, and Olive thought he had to turn away because he knew what he said wasn't true.

They would never get over that night. And it wasn't because they'd been held hostage in a bathroom—which Andrea Bibber would think was the crisis. No, they would never get over that night because they had said things that altered how they saw each other. And because she had, ever since then, been weeping from a private faucet inside her, unable to keep her thoughts from the red-haired boy with his blemished, frightened face, as in love with him as any schoolgirl, picturing him at his sedulous afternoon work in the prison garden; ready to make him a gardening smock as the prison liaison had told her she could do, with the fabric she bought at So-Fro today, unable to help herself, as Karen Newton must have been with her man from Midcoast Power—poor, pining Karen, who had produced a child who'd said, Just because you're my grandmother doesn't mean I have to love you, you know.

Winter Concert

In the dark of the car, his wife, Jane, sat with her nice black coat buttoned up all the way—the coat they'd bought together last year, going through all those stores. Hard work; they'd get thirsty and end up having a sundae at the place on Water Street, the sullen young waitress always giving their senior discount even though they never asked; they had joked about that—how the girl had no idea, as she plunked down their mugs of coffee, that her own arm would someday be sprinkled with age spots, or that cups of coffee had to be planned since blood pressure medicine made you widdle so much, that life picked up speed, and then most of it was gone—made you breathless, really.

"Oh, this is fun," his wife said now, gazing through the night at all the houses they passed, lit up with different Christmas lights, and it made Bob Houlton smile as he drove; his wife contented, her hands folded on her lap. "All these lives," she said. "All the stories we never know." And he smiled further, reaching to touch her mittened hand because he had known she might be thinking that.

Her small gold earring caught the light from a streetlamp as she turned her head. "Remember on our honeymoon," she asked, "when you wanted me to care about those old Mayan ruins the way you did, and all I wanted to know was which people on the bus had pom-poms on their shower curtains back home? And we had that fight, because deep down you were scared you'd married a dull thing? Pleasant, but dull."

He said no, he didn't remember that at all, and she sighed deeply to let him know she thought he did, pointing, then, to a house on the corner done all in blue lights, strings of blue lights up and down the whole front of it, turning her head to keep looking as the car moved past.

He said, "I'm mental, Janie."

"Very mental," she agreed. "You have the tickets?"

He nodded.

"Funny to have tickets in order to get into a church."

In fact, it made sense to move the concert into St. Catherine's after this latest storm had caused the roof of Macklin Music Hall to cave in. No one had been hurt, but it made Bob Houlton shudder; he had an image of sitting in the plush red seats, he and Jane, and the roof falling in, the two of them suffocating, their life together ending in that horrible way. He was prone to that sort of thinking these days. He had even had a sense of foreboding coming out tonight, but it wasn't something he'd say; and she loved seeing all these lights.

And she was happy right now, it was true. Jane Houlton, shifting slightly inside her nice black coat, was thinking that, after all, life was a gift—that one of those things about getting older was knowing that so many moments weren't just moments, they were gifts. And how nice, really, that people should celebrate with such earnestness this time of year. No matter what people's lives might hold (some of these houses they were passing would have to hold some woeful tribulations, Janie knew), still and all, people were compelled to celebrate because they knew somehow, in their different ways, that life was a thing to celebrate.

He put the blinker on, pulled out onto the avenue. "Well, that was nice," she said, sitting back. They had fun together these days, they really did. It was as if marriage had been a long, complicated meal, and now there was this lovely dessert.

Downtown the cars moved slowly on Main Street, passing by streetlamps that had large wreaths hung on their poles, and shop windows and restaurants that were lit up. Just past the movie theater, Bob saw a parking spot next to the curb and pulled the car over; it took some time, he had to work hard to ease in between the others. Someone from behind them honked with annoyance.

"Oh, phooey to you." Jane made a face through the dark.

He straightened the wheels, turned the engine off. "Wait there, Janie, till I come around."

They weren't young anymore, this was the thing. They kept telling each other as though they couldn't believe it. But they had each of them in this last year suffered a mild heart attack; hers first—feeling, she said, as though she had eaten too many of the grilled onions at dinner that night. And then his, months later, not feeling like that at all, more like someone had sat hard on his chest, but with his jaw aching the same way Jane's had.

They felt okay now. But she was seventy-two and he was seventy-five and unless a roof fell down on them both together, one would, presumably, be living without the other at some point in time.

Shop windows twinkled with Christmas lights, and the air smelled like snow. He took Jane's arm and they walked down the street, where restaurant windows displayed different arrangements of holly or wreaths, and some windowpanes had their corners spray-painted white. "The Lydias," Jane said. "Wave, honey."

"Where?"

"Just wave, honey. Over there."

"There's no point in my waving if I don't see who I'm waving to."

"The Lydias, right there in the steak house. Ages since we've seen them." Jane was waving cheerfully, excessively. He saw the couple through the window now, on either side of a white tablecloth, and he waved, too. Mrs. Lydia was motioning for them to come in.

Bob Houlton put his arm through Jane's. "I don't want to," he said, waving his other hand at the Lydias.

Jane waved more, shook her head, gestured, mouthing each word with exaggeration: "We'll see you lay-ter. At the concert?" Nodding. More waving, they were on their way. "She looks good," Jane said. "I'm kind of surprised how good she looks. She must have colored her hair."

"Did you want to go in?"

"No," said Jane. "I want to look in store windows. It's nice out here, not too cold."

"Now fill me in," he said, as they continued walking, thinking of the Lydias, whose name was not actually Lydia, but Granger—Alan and Donna Granger. The daughter, Lydia Granger, had been friends with the middle Houlton girl, and Patty Granger had been friends with the youngest Houlton girl. Bob and Jane referred to the parents of their daughters' friends, even now, by the children's names.

"Lydia's been divorced a few years now. The guy bit her. That part's supposed to be a secret, I think."

"Bit her? Or beat her?"

"Bit." Jane snapped her teeth together twice. "You know, chomp, chomp. He was a veterinarian, I think."

"Did he bite the kids, too?"

"I don't believe he bit the children. Two children. One of them is hyperactive, can't concentrate, whatever it is these days when a kid can't sit still. The Lydias won't mention it, so don't bring it up. The woman with the pink hair in the library told me all this. Let's go. I want to be able to sit on an aisle."

Ever since her heart attack, Jane had been worried about dying in public. She had had her attack in the kitchen of her home, but the idea that she might fall over in front of people made her very anxious. Years ago, she had witnessed such a thing, a man dead on the sidewalk. The medics had ripped his shirt open, and it could still make her cry if she thought about it hard enough—the tender unknowingness, the *gone-ness* of his flung-wide arms, his belly showing. Poor darling thing, she had thought, to be lying there dead.

"And I want to sit toward the back," her husband said. She nodded. His bowels weren't what they used to be; sometimes he had to leave a place in a hurry.

The church was dark and cold, almost empty. They handed over their tickets and were given programs, which they held with a tentativeness while they walked into one of the back pews, settling in, unbuttoning their coats, but leaving them on.

"Keep an eye out for the Lydias," Jane said, turning her head.

He held her hand, picked nervously at her fingertips.

"Was it Lydia who slept over every weekend for a while there, or was that her sister?" Bob asked, while Jane craned her neck back, looking up at the ceiling of the church, the large, dark rafters.

"That was Patty, her sister. Not as nice a girl as Lydia." Jane leaned in closer toward her husband and whispered, "Lydia had an abortion in high school, you know."

"I know, I remember."

"You do?" Jane looked at her husband, surprised.

"Sure," Bob said. "You told me she used to come to your office with cramps. She came in once and cried for two days."

"That's right," said Jane, warmer now inside her coat. "Poor thing. I suspected it right then, frankly, and pretty soon after that Becky told me it was true. I'm really surprised you remember that." She chewed her lip pensively, rocked her foot up and down a few times.

"What?" Bob said. "You thought I never listened? I listened, Janie."

But she waved a hand and sighed, and settled herself against the back of the pew before she said, musingly, "I liked working there." And she had. She had liked, especially, the adolescent girls, the young, bumbling, oily-skinned, scared girls that talked too loud, or snapped their gum ferociously, or slunk through the corridor with their heads down—she'd loved them, really. And they knew it. They would come to her office with their terrible cramps, lying on the couch gray-faced and dry-lipped with pain. "My father says it's all in my head," more than one girl had said, and oh, it broke her heart. What a lonely thing to be a young girl! She would let them stay sometimes all afternoon.

The church was slowly beginning to fill up. Olive Kitteridge walked in, tall and broad-shouldered in a navy-blue coat, her husband behind her. Henry Kitteridge touched his wife's arm, indicating they take a seat in a pew nearby, but Olive shook her head and they sat instead two pews closer to the front of the church. "I don't know how he can stand her," Bob murmured to Jane.

They watched the Kitteridges settle into their pew, Olive shaking off her coat, then placing it back on her shoulders, Henry helping her. Olive Kitteridge had taught math at the school Jane had worked at; very seldom had the two women spoken at length. Olive had a way about her that was absolutely without apology, and Jane had kept her distance. In response to Bob's remark now, Jane merely shrugged.

Turning her head, she saw the Lydias going up the back steps to the balcony. "Oh, there they are," she said to Bob. "Such a long time since we've seen them. She looks pretty good."

He squeezed her hand and whispered, "So do you."

The members of the orchestra came out in their black clothes and took their seats up front by the pulpit. Music stands were adjusted, legs set at an angle, chins tilted, bows picked up—and then the disharmonious sound of an orchestra warming up.

It bothered Jane that she knew something about Lydia Granger that Mrs. Lydia might not, even now, know. It felt indecent, invasive. But people ended up knowing things. When you were a school nurse, or a pink-haired librarian, you ended up knowing who married alcoholics, whose kids had attention deficit disorder (that's what it was), who threw dishes, who slept on the couch. She didn't want to think there were people in this church right now who knew things about her children that she didn't know herself. She ducked her head toward Bob and said, "I hope there aren't people in this church right now who know things about my kids that I don't know."

The music started, and he winked one eye at her slowly, reassuringly.

During Debussy he fell asleep, his arms folded across his chest. Glancing at her husband, Jane felt her heart swell with the music, and with love for him, this man next to her, this old (!) man, who had been followed through life by his own childhood troubles—a mother always, always mad at him. In his face right now she felt she could see the little boy, furtive, forever scared; even as he slept here at this very moment there was a tautness of anxiety on his face. A gift, she thought again, placing her mittened hand lightly on his leg, a gift to be able to know someone for so many years.

Mrs. Lydia had had her eyes done; they stared out of her head like a sixteen-year-old's.

"You look wonderful," Jane told her, although close-up the effect was frightening. "Just wonderful," she repeated, because it must have been scary, having someone take a scalpel so close to your eyes. "How's Lydia?" Jane asked. "And the others?"

"Lydia's getting married again," Mrs. Lydia said, moving aside to let someone get by. "We're happy about it."

Her husband, squatty, round-shouldered, rolled his eyes and jiggled change in his pocket. "Gets expensive," he said, and his wife, a red felt hat tucked over her gold hair, gave him a fleeting look, which he seemed to ignore. "All those damn psychiatrist bills," he added, saying this to Bob with a kind of man-to-man laugh.

"Sure," said Bob, affably.

"But tell us, what are your bunny rabbits up to?" Mrs. Lydia's lipstick was dark, perfectly lined on her lips.

And so Jane recited the ages of their grandchildren, described the jobs held by her sons-in-law, the girl they were hoping Tim would marry soon. And because the Lydias only nodded at all this, without even saying "How nice," Jane felt compelled to go on, to fill the space between their close, almost hovering, faces. "Tim went skydiving this year," she said, and told them how this had scared her to death. It seemed he'd gotten over it after a few times; he hadn't mentioned it again. "But honestly," Jane said, shivering, hugging her black coat close. "Jumping out of a plane, can you imagine?" She herself could imagine it only too well, and it made her heart race.

"Not really a risk taker, are you, Jane?" Mrs. Lydia was looking at her with those new eyes; unnerving to have a sixteen-year old's eyes looking at you from an old woman's head.

"No," said Jane, but she felt indistinctly that she had been insulted, and when Bob's arm came up to touch her elbow, she felt he had received this, for her, in that way, too.

"You've always been a favorite of mine, Janie Houlton," said the squat, red-faced Mr. Lydia then, abruptly reaching over and rubbing her shoulder through her nice black coat.

She felt exhausted, suddenly, by this silliness. What were you supposed to say when a squat, homely little man whose path you had crossed briefly for a number of years said you had always been a favorite of his? "Do you have any plans to retire soon, Alan?" is what she pleasantly said.

"Never," the man answered. "I'll retire the day I die." He laughed, and they laughed with him, and in the quick glance he gave to Mrs. Lydia, the way she briefly rolled her brand-new eyes, Jane Houlton realized that he did not want to be home all day with his wife, that his wife did not want him there either. Mrs. Lydia said to Bob, "You've retired now, since we last saw you? Wasn't it funny, meeting you in the Miami airport the way we did?

"It's a small world," Mrs. Lydia added, tugging on her ear with a gloved hand, glancing at Jane, and then turning her head, looking up the balcony stairs.

Bob stepped to the side, ready to go back into the church.

"When was this?" Jane said. "Miami?"

"Couple years ago. We visited those friends we told you about"— Mr. Lydia nodded at Bob—"in their little gated community. That's not my dish of ice cream, I can tell you." He shook his head, then squinted up at Bob. "Doesn't it make you crazy to be home all day?"

"Love it," Bob said firmly. "I love it."

"We do things," Jane added, as though she needed to explain something.

"What things?"

And then Jane hated her, this tall woman with her painted face, the hard eyes staring out from under the red felt hat; she didn't want to tell Mrs. Lydia how every morning she and Bobby, early, first thing, took a walk, how they came back and made coffee and ate their bran cereal and read the paper to each other. How they planned their day, went shopping—for her coat, for a special pair of shoes since he had such trouble now with his feet.

"We bumped into someone else that trip," Mr. Lydia said. "The Shepherds. They were at a golf resort north of the city."

"Small world," Mrs. Lydia said again, tugging at her ear with her gloved hand again, not looking at Jane this time, just looking up the stairs at the balcony.

Olive Kitteridge was moving through the crowd of people. Taller than most, her head was visible as she seemed to say something to her husband, Henry, who nodded, an expression of suppressed mirth on his face.

"Better get back in there," said Bob, nodding toward the inside of the church, touching Jane's elbow.

"Come on," said Mrs. Lydia, tapping her husband's sleeve with a program. "Let's go. Lovely to see you." She wiggled her fingers at Jane, then moved up the stairs.

Jane squeezed past a group of people standing right in the doorway, and she and Bob went back to their pew, her tugging her coat around her, crossing her legs, cold inside their black wool slacks. "He loves her," said Jane, with a tone of admonishment. "That's how he can stand her."

"Mr. Lydia?"

"No. Henry Kitteridge."

Bob didn't answer, and they watched as others came in, took their seats again, the Kitteridges among them. "Miami?" Jane said to her husband. "What was he talking about?" She looked at him.

Bob thrust out his lower lip and shrugged, to indicate he didn't know.

"When were you in *Miami*?"

"He must have meant Orlando. Remember when I had that account I was closing down there?"

"You bumped into the Lydias at the airport in Florida? You never told me that."

"I'm sure I did. It was ages ago."

The music took over the church. It took up all the space that wasn't filled with people or coats or pews, it took up all the space in Jane Houlton's head. She actually moved her neck back and forth as though to shake off the cumbersome weight of the sound, and realized that she had never liked music. It seemed to bring back all the shadows and aches of a lifetime. Let others enjoy it, these people listening so seriously in their fur coats, their red felt hats, their tiresome lives—a pressure on her knee, her husband's hand.

She gazed at his hand, spread over her black coat that they had bought together. It was the large hand of an old man; a beautiful hand with the long fingers and the veins rising across; as familiar, almost, as her own hand was to her.

"Are you all right?" He had put his mouth against her ear, but she thought he had whispered too loudly. She made a circular motion with two fingers, their own sign language from years back, *Let's go,* and he nodded.

"You all right, Janie?" he asked on the sidewalk, his hand under her elbow.

"Oh, I get tired of that heavy music somehow. Do you mind?"

"No. I'd had enough."

In the car, in the darkness and the silence of the car, she felt some knowledge pass between them. And it had been sitting there in church with them, too, like a child pressed between them in the pew, this thing, this presence that had made its way into their evening.

She said quietly, "Oh, God."

"What, Janie?"

She shook her head, and he did not ask again.

A traffic light up ahead turned yellow. He slowed down, drove slowly; he stopped.

Jane blurted out: "I hate her."

"Who?" His tone was surprised. "Olive Kitteridge?"

"Of course not Olive Kitteridge. Why would I hate her? Donna Granger. I hate her. There's something creepy about her. Smug. Your *bunny rabbits.* I hate her." Jane actually stamped a foot against the floor of the car.

"I can't think it's worth all that emotion, Janie. I mean, really, do you?" asked Bob, and from the corner of her eye, she saw that he didn't turn his head to look at her as he asked this.

In the silence that followed, Jane's anger grew; it became immense, swelling like water around them, as if they had suddenly driven over a bridge and into a pond below—stagnant, cold stuff filled up around them.

"She was so busy getting her hair done that she didn't even know her kid was pregnant. Didn't even know it! Still doesn't know it, probably. She still doesn't *know* that I was the one to comfort the girl years ago, *I* was the one to worry myself sick!"

"You were nice to those girls."

"That younger sister, though—Patty. She was a nasty thing. I never trusted her, and Tracy shouldn't have either."

"What in the world are you talking about?"

"Tracy was too innocent, you know. Don't you remember that night she had a slumber party and ended up so crushed?"

"There must have been a hundred slumber parties over the years, Jane. No, I don't remember that one."

"Patty Granger told Tracy how some other girl didn't like her, some girl. *She really doesn't like you, you know.*" Jane was almost ready to cry, recalling this. Her chin tingled.

"What are you talking about? You loved Patty."

"I fed Patty," Jane answered fiercely. "I fed the goddamn girl for years. Those parents were never home, going this place and that, some party here, some evening there, leaving *other people* to take care of their kids."

"Janie, calm down."

"Please don't tell me to calm down," she said. "Please don't do that, Bob."

She heard him sigh quietly, could picture in the dark how he rolled his eyes.

They drove the rest of the way in silence, passing Christmas lights, twinkling reindeer; Jane looked out the window, her hands jammed into the pockets of her coat. It wasn't until they were through town, out on the final long stretch of Basing Hill Road, that Jane spoke again, quietly, with genuine confusion in her voice. "Bobby, I didn't know you'd ever run into the Lydias at the Orlando airport. I don't think you ever told me that."

"You probably forgot. It was a long time ago."

Ahead of them through the trees the moon gleamed like a shiny little curved particle in the black sky of the night, and something moved in Jane's water-filled mind. It was the way the Lydia woman had looked at her, and then looked away, right before going up the balcony stairs. Purposefully now, Jane made her voice calm, almost conversational. "Bobby," she said, "please tell me the truth. You did see them at the Miami airport, didn't you?"

And when he didn't answer, she felt her bowels ache, and an age-old sliver of anguish shuddered deep within her—how tired it made her, that particular, familiar pain; a weight that seemed to her to be like a thick, tarnished silver spreading through her, and then it rolled over everything, extinguishing Christmas lights, streetlamps, fresh snow; the loveliness of all things—all gone.

"Oh, God," she said. "I can't believe it." She added, "I really can't believe it."

Bob pulled the car into the driveway and turned off the engine. They sat. "Janie," he said.

"Tell me." So calm. She even sighed. "Tell me, please," she said.

She could hear in the darkness of the car how his breathing was quicker now; and her own was, too. She wanted to say their hearts were too old for this now; you can't keep doing this to a heart, can't keep on expecting your heart to pull through.

In the dim light that shone from their front porch, his face looked ghastly and ghostly. He must not die right now. "Just tell me," she said again, kindly.

"She got breast cancer, Janie. She called me at the office that spring before I retired, and I hadn't heard from her in years. Really years, Janie."

"Okay," Jane said.

"She was very unhappy. I felt bad." He still did not look at her; he stared over the steering wheel. "I felt . . . I don't know. I can tell you I wish she hadn't called." Now he sat back, taking a deep breath. "I had to go to Orlando to close down that account, so I told her I'd come see her, and I did. I went down to Miami and I saw her, and it was awful, it was pathetic, and the next day I flew back from Miami, where I saw the Grangers."

"You spent the night with her in Miami?" Jane was shivering now, her teeth would chatter if she let them.

Bob was slumped in his seat. He put his head back on the headrest and closed his eyes. "I wanted to drive back to Orlando that night. That's what I'd planned. But it was too late. I didn't feel like I could leave, and then, frankly, it was too late for me to feel I could safely drive back. It was awful, Janie. If you could know how stupid and awful and miserable it was."

"So how much have you spoken with her since then?"

"I called her once, a few days after I got back, and that was it. I'm telling you the truth."

"Is she dead?"

He shook his head. "I have no idea. I probably would have heard from Scott or Mary maybe, if she'd died, so I assume she hasn't. But I have no idea."

"Do you think about her?"

He looked at her pleadingly in the semidarkness. "Jane, I think of you. I care about you. Only you. Janie, it was four years ago. That's a long time."

"No, it isn't. At our age, it's like turning a couple of quick pages. Blip-blip." She made a hand gesture in the dark, a quick back and forth.

He didn't answer this but only looked at her with his head still back against the headrest, as though he had fallen out of some tree and lay now, unable to sit up, his eyes rolling sideways to look at her with exhaustion and terrible sadness. "All that matters is you, Janie. She doesn't matter to me. Seeing her—it didn't matter to me. I just did it because she wanted me to."

Jane said, "But I just don't understand. I mean, at this point in our lives, I just don't understand. Because she *wanted* you to?"

"I don't blame you, Janie. It's ridiculous. It was so—nothing." He put a large gloved hand over his face.

"I have to go in. I'm freezing." She got out of the car and went up the front steps of their home as though she were stumbling, but she didn't stumble. She waited for him to unlock the door and then moved past him into the kitchen, then through the dining room into the living room, where she sat down on the couch.

He followed her, and turned on the lamp, then sat on the coffee table, facing her. For a long time they just sat. And she felt that her heart was broken again. Only now she was old, so it was different. He slipped off his coat.

"Can I get you anything?" he asked. "You want some hot chocolate? Tea?"

She shook her head.

"Take your coat off, though, Janie."

"No," she said. "I'm cold."

"Oh, please, Janie." He went upstairs and came back down with her favorite sweater, a yellow angora cardigan.

She put the sweater on her lap.

He sat down next to her on the couch. "Oh, Janie," he said. "I've made you so sad."

She let him help her, in a moment, put the sweater on. "We're getting old," she said then. "One day we're going to die."

"Janie."

"I'm scared of it, Bobby."

"Come to bed now," he said. But she shook her head. She asked, pulling back from his arm, which had gone around her, "Didn't she ever marry?"

"Oh, no," he said. "No, she never married. She's mental, Janie."

After a moment, Jane said, "I don't want to talk about her."

"I don't either."

"Never again."

"Never again."

She said, "It's that we're running out of time."

"No, we're not, Janie. We still have time together. We could still have twenty years together."

When he said that, she felt a deep and sudden pity for him. "I need to sit here for just a few more minutes," she said. "You go on up to bed."

"I'll stay with you." And so they sat. The lamp from the side table threw a dim and serious light throughout the silent room.

She took a deep, quiet breath and thought how she did not envy those young girls in the ice cream shop. Behind the bored eyes of the waitresses handing out sundaes there loomed, she knew, great earnestness, great desires, and great disappointments; such confusion lay ahead for them, and (more wearisome) anger; oh, before they were through, they would blame and blame and blame, and then get tired, too.

Next to her she heard her husband's breathing change; he had drifted into a sudden sleep, his head thrown back against the cushions of the couch. And then she saw him give a start.

"What is it?" She touched his shoulder. "Bobby, what were you just dreaming?"

"Whew," he said, raising his head. In the dim light of the living room he looked like a half-plucked bird, his thin, dry hair sticking out in different angled patches from his head.

"The concert hall roof fell in," he said.

She leaned toward him. "I'm right here," she said, putting her palm to the side of his face. Because what did they have now, except for each other, and what could you do if it was not even quite that?

Tulips

People thought the Larkin couple would move after what happened. But they didn't move—perhaps they had nowhere to go. Their blinds remained drawn, however, day and night. Although sometimes in the dusk of winter, Roger Larkin would be found shoveling his driveway. Or in the summer, after the grass got high and sad-looking, you might find him out mowing the lawn. In both cases he wore a hat far down over his face and never looked up when someone drove by. Louise, there was never any sight of at all. Apparently she'd been in a hospital down in Boston for a while—the daughter lived near Boston, so that would make sense—but Mary Blackwell, who was an X-ray technician in Portland, said Louise had spent time in the hospital there. What was interesting was that Mary was criticized for reporting this, even though at the time there wasn't a soul in town who wouldn't have chopped off a baby finger for news of any kind. But there was that small outpouring against Mary. With the HIPAA privacy laws these days, she could have lost her job, people said. Remind *me* never to have shock treatments in Portland, people said. And Cecil Green, who brought hot coffee and doughnuts to the reporters who hung around the house those days, took a scolding from Olive Kitteridge.

"What in hell ails you?" Olive demanded over the phone. "Feeding the vultures like that—good God." But Cecil was known to be a little "slow," and Henry Kitteridge asked his wife to leave the fellow alone.

How the Larkins got groceries, nobody knew. It was assumed the daughter from Boston must have some hand in getting her parents food, because once a month or so there would be a car parked in the driveway with a Massachusetts license plate, and while she was never seen in the local grocery store, perhaps she brought with her her husband, whom nobody in the town of Crosby would recognize anymore, and maybe he did some shopping in Mardenville.

Had the Larkins stopped going to visit their son? Nobody knew, and after a while people did not talk too much about it; sometimes people driving past the house—large and square, painted pale yellow—even turned their heads away, not wanting to be reminded of what could happen to a family that had seemed as pretty and fresh as blueberry pie.

It was Henry Kitteridge, responding in the middle of the night to a police call that the alarm in his pharmacy had gone off (a raccoon had made his way inside), who saw the Larkins pulling out of their driveway, Roger driving, Louise—presumably Louise, for the woman had a scarf around her head and was wearing dark glasses—sitting motionless beside him. It was two o'clock in the morning, and that's when Henry understood that this couple came and went under cover of night; that most likely, most certainly, they would drive to Connecticut to visit the son—but they did it with a furtiveness, and he thought perhaps they would always live this way. He told Olive this, and she said "Yikes" softly.

In any event, the Larkins and their home and whatever their story was inside it eventually receded so that their house with its drawn shades took on, over time, the nature of one more hillock in the dramatic rise and fall of the coastal landscape. The natural rubber band around people's lives that curiosity stretched for a while had long ago returned to encompass their own particularities. Two, five, then seven years passed by—and in the case of Olive Kitteridge, she found herself positively squeezed to death by an unendurable sense of loneliness.

Her son, Christopher, had married. Olive and Henry had been appalled by the bossiness of their new daughter-in-law, who had grown up in Philadelphia, and who expected things like a diamond tennis bracelet for Christmas (what was a *tennis* bracelet? but Christopher bought her one), and who would send back meals in a restaurant, one time demanding the chef be brought to speak to her. Olive, suffering a seemingly endless menopause, would be washed over with extraordinary waves of heat in the girl's presence, and one time Suzanne said, "There's a soy supplement you could take, Olive. If you don't believe in estrogen replacement."

Olive thought: *I believe in minding my own business, that's what I believe in.* She said, "I've got to get the tulips in before the ground freezes."

"Oh?" asked Suzanne, who had proven to be consistently stupid about flowers. "Do you plant those tulips every year?"

"Certainly," said Olive.

"I'm sure my mother didn't plant them every year. And we always had some in the back of the house."

"I think if you ask your mother," Olive said, "you'll find you're mistaken. The bloom of a tulip is already in its bulb. Right there. One shot. That's it."

The girl smiled in a way that made Olive want to slap her.

At home Henry said, "Don't go telling Suzanne she's mistaken."

"Oh, hell," said Olive. "I'll tell her anything I want." But she made some applesauce and took it over to their house.

The couple hadn't been married four months when Christopher called from work one day. "Now, listen," he said. "Suzanne and I are moving to California."

For Olive, everything turned upside down. It was as though she'd been thinking, This is a tree, and here is a kitchen stove—and it wasn't a tree at all, or a kitchen stove either. When she saw the FOR SALE sign in front of the house she and Henry had built for Christopher, it was as though splinters of wood were shoved into her heart. She wept at times with such noise the dog whimpered and trembled and pushed his cold nose into her arm. She screamed at the dog. She screamed at Henry. "I wish she'd drop dead," Olive said. "Just drop dead today." And Henry didn't admonish her.

California? Why all the way across this vast country?

"I like sunshine," Suzanne said. "New England autumns are fine for about two weeks, and then the darkness settles in, and—" She smiled, lifting a shoulder. "I just don't like it, that's all. You'll come visit us soon."

It was hard stuff to swallow. Henry, by then, had retired from the pharmacy—earlier than planned; the rent had skyrocketed, and the building was sold for a big chain drugstore to move in—and he often seemed at a loss for how to fill his days. Olive, who had retired from teaching five years earlier, kept telling him, "Get yourself a schedule, and *stick* to it."

So Henry took a woodworking class at the extension school in Portland and set up a lathe in the basement, eventually producing four uneven, but quite lovely, maple salad bowls. Olive pored over catalogues and ordered one hundred tulip bulbs. They joined the American Civil War Society—Henry's great-grandfather had been at Gettysburg, and they had the old pistol in the hutch to prove it—driving up to Belfast once a month to sit in a circle and hear lectures about battles and heroes and so forth. They found it interesting. It helped. They chatted with other Civil War people, then drove home in the dark, passing the Larkin house, where no lights were on. Olive shook her head. "I always thought Louise was a little off," she said. Louise had been a guidance counselor at the school Olive taught in, and there was something about Louise—she would talk too much and too gaily, and wore all that makeup and put such a fuss into her clothes. "She got absolutely tipsy at the Christmas parties," Olive said. "One year downright drunk. I found her singing 'Onward, Christian Soldiers' sitting on the bleachers in the gym. Honestly, it was disgusting."

"Well," said Henry.

"Yes," agreed Olive. "Well, indeed."

And so they were getting on their feet, Olive and Henry, finding their way in this retirement-land, when Christopher telephoned one night to say calmly that he was getting divorced. Henry was on the phone in the bedroom, Olive on the phone in the kitchen. "But *why*?" they asked in unison.

"She wants to," Christopher said.

"But what happened, Christopher? For God's sake, you've only been married a year."

"Mom, it's happened. That's all."

"Well, then come on home, son," Henry said.

"No," Christopher answered. "I like it out here. And the practice is going well. I have no intention of coming back home."

Henry spent the evening sitting in the living room with his head in his hands.

"Come on. Snap out of it," Olive said. "At least you're not Roger Larkin, for God's sake." But her hands were trembling, and she went and took everything out of the refrigerator and cleaned the inside and the racks with a sponge that she dipped into a bowl of cool water and baking soda. Then she put everything back into the refrigerator. Henry was still sitting with his head in his hands.

More and more often, Henry sat in the living room with his head in his hands. One day he said, with sudden cheerfulness, "He'll come back. You'll see."

"And what makes you so sure?"

"It's his home, Olive. This coastline is his home."

As though to prove the strength of this geographical pull on their only offspring, they traced their genealogy, driving to Augusta to work in the library there, going to old graveyards miles away. Henry's ancestors went back eight generations; Olive's went back ten. Her first ancestor had come from Scotland, was indentured for seven years of labor, and then started out on his own. The Scottish were scrappy and tough, surviving things you'd never dream of—scalpings, freezing winters with no food, barns burning from a lightning flash, children dying left and right. But they persevered, and Olive would be temporarily lightened in spirit as she read about this.

Still, Christopher remained gone. "Fine," he would say when they called him. "Fine."

But who was he? This stranger living in California. "No, not right now," he said when they wanted to fly out to visit. "Now isn't a good time."

Olive had trouble sitting still. Instead of a lump in her throat, she felt a lump in her whole body, a persistent ache that seemed to be holding back enough tears to fill the bay seen through the front window. She was flooded with images of Christopher: As a toddler, he had reached to touch a geranium on the windowsill, and she had slapped his hand. But she had loved him! By God, she had loved him. In second grade, he had almost set himself on fire, trying to burn his spelling test out back in the woods. But he knew she loved him. People know exactly who loves them, and how much—Olive believed this. Why would he not allow his parents to even visit him? What had they done?

She could make the bed, do the laundry, feed the dog. But she could not be bothered with any more meals.

"What'll we have for supper?" Henry would ask, coming upstairs from the basement.

"Strawberries."

Henry would chide her. "You wouldn't last a day without me, Olive. If I died tomorrow, whatever would become of you?"

"Oh, stop it." It irritated her, that kind of thing, and it seemed to her that Henry enjoyed irritating her. Sometimes she'd get into the car by herself and go for a drive.

It was Henry who bought the groceries now. One day he brought back with him a bunch of flowers. "For my wife," he said, handing them to her. They were the saddest damn things. Daisies dyed blue among the white and ludicrously pink ones, some of them half-dead.

"Put them in that pot," Olive said, pointing to an old blue vase. The flowers sat there on the wooden table in the kitchen. Henry came and put his arms around her; it was early autumn and chilly, and his woolen shirt smelled faintly of wood chips and mustiness. She stood, waiting for the hug to end. Then she went outside and planted her tulip bulbs.

A week later—just a morning with errands to do—they drove into town, into the parking lot of the big Shop 'n Save. Olive was going to stay in the car and read the paper while he went in to get the milk and orange juice and a jar of jam. "Anything else?" He said those words. Olive shook her head. Henry opened the door, swinging his long legs out. The creak of the opening car door, the back of his plaid jacket, then the bizarre, unnatural motion of him falling right from that position to the ground.

"Henry!" she shouted.

She shouted at him, waiting for the ambulance to come. His mouth moved, and his eyes were open, and one hand kept jerking through the air, as though reaching for something beyond her.

The tulips bloomed in ridiculous splendor. The midafternoon sun hit them in a wide wash of light where they grew on the hill, almost down to the water. From the kitchen window, Olive could see them: yellow, white, pink, bright red. She had planted them at different depths and they had a lovely unevenness to them. When a breeze bent them slightly, it seemed like an underwater field of something magical, all those colors floating out there. Even lying in the "bump-out room"—the room Henry had added a few years before, with a bay window big enough to have a small bed tucked right under it—she could see the tops of the tulips, the sun hitting the blooms, and sometimes she dozed briefly, listening to the transistor radio she held to her ear whenever she lay down. She got tired this time of day because she was up so early, before the sun. The sky would just be lightening as she got into her car with the dog and drove to the river, where she walked the three miles one way and the three miles back as the sun rose over the wide ribbon of water where her ancestors had paddled their canoes from one inlet to another.

The walkway had been newly paved, and by the time Olive made her way back, Rollerbladers would be passing by, young and ferociously healthy, their spandexed thighs pumping past her. She'd drive to Dunkin' Donuts and read the paper and give the dog some doughnut holes. And then she would drive to the nursing home. Mary Blackwell was working there now. Olive might have said, "Hope you've learned to keep your mouth shut," because Mary looked at her oddly, but Mary Blackwell could go to hell—they all could go to hell. Propped up in his wheelchair, blind, always smiling, Henry was wheeled by Olive to the recreation room, over by the piano. She said, "Squeeze my hand if you understand me," but his hand did not squeeze her hand. "Blink," she said, "if you hear me." He smiled straight ahead. In the evenings, she went back to spoon the food into his mouth. They let her wheel him into the parking lot one day so the dog could lick his hand. Henry smiled. "Christopher is coming," she told him.

When Christopher arrived, Henry still smiled. Christopher had gained weight, and he wore a collared shirt to the nursing home. When he saw his father, he looked at Olive with a face stricken. "Talk to him," Olive directed. "Tell him you're here." She walked away so they could have some privacy, but it wasn't long before Christopher came to find her.

"Where have you been?" he asked, peevishly. But his eyes were red, and Olive's heart unfolded.

"Are you eating all right out there in California?" she asked.

"My God, how can you stand this place?" her son asked.

"I can't," she said. "The smell stays all over you." She was like some helpless schoolgirl, careful not to let it show: how glad she was to have him there, to not have to go there alone, to have him in the car beside her. But he did not stay the whole week. He said something had come up at work and he had to get back.

"All right, then." She drove him to the airport with the dog in the backseat. The house was emptier than ever; even the nursing home seemed changed with Christopher not being there.

The next morning she wheeled Henry over by the piano. "Christopher will be back soon," she said. "He had some work to finish up, but he's coming back soon. He's crazy about you, Henry. Kept saying what a wonderful father you were." But her voice started to wobble, and she had to move away, looking out the window at the parking lot. She didn't have a Kleenex, and turned to find one. Mary Blackwell stood there. "What's the matter?" Olive said to her. "Haven't you ever seen an old lady cry before?"

She didn't like to be alone. Even more, she didn't like being with people.

It made her skin crawl to sit in Daisy Foster's tiny dining room, sipping tea. "I went to that damn dopey grief group," she told Daisy. "And they said it was normal to feel angry. God, people are stupid. Why in hell should I feel angry? We all know this stuff is coming. Not many are lucky enough to just drop dead in their sleep."

"People react in their own way, I guess," Daisy said, in her nice voice. She didn't have anything except a nice voice, Olive thought, because that's what Daisy was—nice. To hell with all of it. She said the dog was waiting, and left her teacup still full.

It was like that—she couldn't stand anyone. She went to the post office every few days, and she couldn't stand that either. "How are you doing?" Emily Buck asked her every time, and it annoyed Olive. "I'm managing," Olive said, but she hated getting the envelopes, almost all with Henry's name. And the bills! She didn't know what to do with them, didn't even understand some of them—and so much junk mail! She'd stand by the big gray waste bin, throwing it all away, and sometimes a bill would get tossed in and she'd have to lean in and fiddle around to find it, all the while aware of Emily watching her from behind the counter.

A few cards dribbled in. "I'm sorry . . . so sad." "I'm sorry to hear . . ." She answered each one. "Don't be sorry," she wrote. "We all know this stuff is bound to happen. There's not a damn thing to be sorry about." Only once or twice, fleetingly, did it occur to Olive that she might be out of her head.

Christopher called once a week. "What can I do for you, Christopher?" she'd ask, meaning *Do something for me!* "Shall I fly out and visit you?"

"No," he always said. "I'm doing all right."

The tulips died, the trees turned red, the leaves fell off, the trees were bare, snow came. All these changes she watched from the bump-out room, where she lay on her side, clutching her transistor radio, her knees tucked to her chest. The sky was black against the long panes. She could see three tiny stars. On the radio a man's calm voice interviewed people or reported news. When the words seemed to shift in meaning, she knew she had slept for a bit. "Yikes," she said softly, at times. She thought about Christopher, why he would not let her come visit, why he did not come back east. Her mind briefly passed over the Larkins, wondering if they still visited their son. Perhaps Christopher stayed in California hoping to reconcile with his wife—what a fierce know-it-all Suzanne had been. And yet she hadn't known a damn thing about any flower that grew up out of the earth.

One freezing cold morning, Olive took her walk, went to Dunkin' Donuts, read the paper in the car while the dog, in the backseat, kept whining. "Hush," she said. "Stop it." The dog's whimpering became louder. "Stop it!" she shouted. She drove. She drove to the library, and didn't go in. Then she drove to the post office, tossed some junk mail into the waste bin, and then had to bend over and fish out a pale yellow envelope with no return address, the handwriting not one she recognized. In the car she ripped it open, just a plain yellow square. "He was always a nice man, and I'm sure he still is." Signed, Louise Larkin.

The next morning while it was still dark, Olive drove by the Larkin home slowly. There, beneath the blind, was the faintest strip of light.

"Christopher," she said, into the kitchen phone the next Saturday. "Louise Larkin sent me a note about your father."

She heard nothing.

"Are you still there?" she asked.

"Still here," Christopher said.

"Did you hear what I said about Louise?"

"Yup."

"Don't you think that's interesting?"

"Not really."

Pain, like a pinecone unfolding, seemed to blossom beneath her breastbone.

"I don't even know how she found out. Shut up in that house all day."

"Dunno," Christopher said.

"All right, then," Olive said. "Well, I'm off to the library. Goodbye."

She sat at the kitchen table, leaning forward, her hand on her big stomach. The thought that she could, anytime she needed to, kill herself went through her head. It was not the first time in her life that she'd thought this, but before, she would think about the note to leave. Now she thought she would leave no note. Not even: "Christopher, what did I do that you should treat me this way?"

She looked with some caution around the kitchen. There were women, widows, who hated to give up their home, died soon after someone hauled them off to assisted living. But she didn't know how long she could go on living here. She had been waiting to see if there was some way Henry could finally come home. She had been waiting for Christopher to come back east. As she stood up, looking for her car keys—because she had to get out of here—she remembered, in a distant way, how as a much younger woman she had felt the dreariness of domestic life, yelling, while Christopher ducked his head, "I hate being a goddamn slave!" Maybe she hadn't yelled that. She called to the dog and left.

Absolutely stick-thin, and appearing ancient in the way she moved, Louise led Olive into the darkened living room. Louise turned on a lamp, and Olive was surprised by the beauty in the woman's face. "Don't mean to stare," Olive said—she had to say this because she knew she was not going to be able to stop staring—"but you look lovely."

"Do I?" Louise made a sound of soft laughter.

"Your face."

"Ah."

It was as though all of Louise's earlier attempts to be pretty, her dyed blond hair, her heavy pink lipstick, her eagerness of speech and careful clothing, the beads and bracelets and nice shoes (Olive remembered)—all of this had, in fact, been *covering up* the essence of Louise, who, stripped by grief and isolation, and probably drugged to the gills, emerged in her frailty with a face of astonishing beauty. You seldom saw really beautiful old women, Olive thought. You saw the remnants of it, if they'd once been that way, but you seldom saw what she saw now: the brown eyes that shone with an otherworldliness, sunken behind a bone structure as fine as any sculpture, the skin drawn tight across the cheekbones, the lips still full, her hair white and tied off to the side in a little brown ribbon.

"I've made tea," Louise said.

"No, but thank you."

"All right, then." Louise sat down gracefully, in a chair nearby. She was wearing a long, dark green sweater-type robe. Cashmere, Olive realized. The Larkins were the only people in town with money they spent. The kids had gone to private school in Portland. They'd had tennis lessons, and music lessons, and skating lessons, and each summer had gone away to summer camp. People used to laugh about that, because no other kid in Crosby, Maine, went to summer camp. There were summer camps nearby, filled with kids from New York, and why would the Larkins have their children spend the summer with them? It's how they were, is all. Roger's suits (Olive remembered) had been made by a tailor, or so Louise used to say. Later, of course, people assumed they must have gone broke. But maybe there weren't that many expenses, once all the experts got paid.

Olive looked around discreetly. The wallpaper had water stains in one spot, and the wainscoting was faded. It was clean, the room, but not one speck of effort had been given to maintaining it. Olive had not been here for ages—perhaps a Christmas tea, it had been. A Christmas tree in that corner, lit candles and food all over the place, Louise greeting people. Louise had always liked to present a good show.

"It doesn't bother you, staying in this house?" Olive asked.

"Staying anywhere bothers me," Louise answered. "To actually pack up and move—well, that's always seemed too much."

"I guess I can see that."

"Roger lives upstairs," Louise said. "And I live downstairs."

"Huh." Olive was having trouble taking things in.

"Arrangements get made in life. Accommodations get made."

Olive nodded. What she minded was how Henry had bought her those flowers. How she'd just stood there. She'd kept the flowers, dried them out, all the blue daisies brown now, bent over.

"Has Christopher been a help to you?" Louise asked. "He was always such a sensitive boy, wasn't he?" Louise smoothed her bony hand over her cashmere-covered knee. "But then, Henry was a nice man, so that was lucky for you."

Olive didn't answer. Through the bottom of the drawn blind a thin strip of white light shone; it was morning now. She'd be on her walk by the river if she hadn't come here.

"Roger is not a nice man, you see, and that made all the difference."

Olive looked back at Louise. "He always seemed nice enough to me." In truth, Olive didn't remember much about Roger; he had looked like a banker, which he was, and his suits had fit well—if you cared about that kind of thing, and Olive did not.

"He seemed nice to everyone," Louise said. "That's his modus operandi." She laughed lightly. "But in ree-al-it-y"—she spoke with exaggerated enunciation—"his heart beats twice an hour."

Olive sat completely still, her big handbag on her lap.

"Cold, cold man. Brrr . . . But no one cares, because they blame the mother, you know. Always, always, always, they blame the mother for everything."

"I suppose that's true."

"You *know* that's true. Please, Olive. Make yourself comfortable." Louise waved a thin white hand, a strip of poured milk in the dim light. Olive tentatively moved her handbag to the floor, sat back.

Louise folded her hands, and smiled. "Christopher was a sensitive boy just like Doyle. Nobody believes this now of course, but Doyle is the sweetest man alive."

Olive nodded, turned around, and looked behind her. Twenty-nine times, the newspapers had kept reporting. And on the TV, too. Twenty-nine times. That was a lot.

"Maybe you don't like my comparing Doyle to Christopher." Louise laughed lightly again, her tone almost flirtatious.

"How's your daughter?" asked Olive, turning back to face Louise. "What's she up to these days?"

"She lives in Boston, married to a lawyer. Which has been helpful, naturally. She's a wonderful woman."

Olive nodded.

Louise leaned forward, both hands on her lap. She tilted her head back and forth and chanted softly, "Boys go to Jupiter to get more stupider, girls go to college to get more knowledge." She laughed her soft laugh, and sat back. "Roger ran right off to his lady friend in Bangor." Again, the soft laugh. "But she rejected him, poor thing."

For Olive there was more than an inner silent groan of disappointment. There was an almost desperate urge to leave, and yet she could not, of course, having trespassed, having written Louise back, having asked to visit.

"You've probably thought of killing yourself." Louise said this serenely, as though discussing a recipe for lemon pie.

Olive felt a sudden disorientation, as though a soccer ball had just been bounced off her head. "I hardly see that would solve anything," she said.

"Of course it would," Louise said, pleasantly. "It would solve everything. But there's the question of how to do it."

Olive shifted her weight, touched her handbag that was next to her.

"Myself, of course, it would be pills and drink. You—I don't see you as a pill person. Something more aggressive. The wrists, but that would take so long."

"I guess that's enough of that," said Olive. But she couldn't help adding, "There are people who depend on me. For heaven's sake."

"Exactly." Louise held up a bony finger, tilted her head. "Doyle lives for me. So I live for him. I write him every day. I visit every chance it's allowed. He knows he's not alone, and so I stay alive."

Olive nodded.

"But surely Christopher doesn't depend on you? He has a wife."

"She divorced him," Olive said. It was odd how easy it was to say this. The truth was that she and Henry had never told anyone, except their friends up the river, Bill and Bunny Newton. With Christopher in California, it didn't seem anyone needed to know.

"I see," said Louise. "Well, I'm sure he'll find a new one. And Henry doesn't depend on you, dear. He doesn't know where he is, or who is with him."

Olive felt a shoot of fury stab through her. "How do you know that? It's not true. He knows damn well I'm there."

"Oh, I don't think so. That's not what Mary says."

"Mary who?"

Louise put her fingers to her mouth in an exaggerated manner. "Whoops."

"Mary Blackwell? You're in touch with Mary Blackwell?"

"Mary and I go way back," Louise explained.

"Yuh. Well, she told everyone things about you, too." Olive's heart had started to beat fast.

"And I imagine every one of them was true." Louise laughed that soft laugh, and made a gesture, as though she were drying nail polish.

"She shouldn't be telling things from the nursing home."

"Oh, come now, Olive. People are people. It always seemed to me that you—especially—understood that."

A silence came into the room, like dark gases coming from the corners. There were no newspapers, or magazines, or any books.

"What do you do all day?" Olive asked. "How do you manage?"

"Ah," said Louise. "Have you come here for lessons?"

"No," said Olive. "I came because you were nice enough to write me a note."

"I was always sorry my kids didn't have you for a teacher. So many people don't have that *spark,* do they, Olive? Are you sure you wouldn't like that tea? I'm going to have some."

"No, I'm fine." Olive watched as Louise stood and moved through the room. Louise bent to straighten a lamp shade, and the sweater fell across her back, showing the thin form of it. Olive didn't know you could be that thin and still be alive. "Are you ill?" she asked, when Louise returned with a teacup on a saucer.

"Ill?" Louise smiled in that way that reminded Olive once again of flirtation. "In what way ill, Olive?"

"Physically. You're very thin. But you certainly do look beautiful."

Louise spoke carefully, but again with that playful tone. "Physically ill, I am not. Though I have little appetite for food, if that's what you're referring to."

Olive nodded. If she had asked for tea, she'd have been able to leave when she'd finished it. But it was too late now. She sat.

"And mentally, I don't believe, really, that I am one bit more out of my head than any other creature here on earth." Louise sipped her tea. The veins on her hand were pronounced; one went right down her skinny finger. The teacup clattered just slightly against the saucer.

"Has Christopher been out here frequently to help you, Olive?"

"Oh, sure. Sure he has."

Louise pursed her lips, tilted her head again, studied Olive, and Olive could now see that the woman was wearing makeup. Around her eyes was a shadowing of color that matched her sweater. "Why did you come here, Olive?"

"I told you. Because you were nice enough to send that note."

"But I've disappointed you, haven't I?"

"Certainly not."

"You're the last person I expected to lie, Olive."

Olive reached down for her handbag. "I'm going to get going. But I do appreciate that you sent the note."

"Oh," said Louise, laughing softly. "You came here for a nice dose of schadenfreude, and it didn't work." She sang, "Saaaaw-ry."

Overhead, Olive heard the floorboards creak. She stood, holding her bag, looking for her coat.

"Roger is up." Louise continued her smile. "Your coat is in the closet, right as you come in. And I happen to know that Christopher has been back only once. Liar, liar, Olive. Pants on fire, Olive."

Olive went as fast as she could. She had the coat over her shoulder, and turned back briefly. Louise was sitting in her chair, her thin back straight, her face so oddly beautiful; she was no longer smiling. She said to Olive, loudly, "She was a bitch, you know. A slut."

"Who?"

Louise just stared at her with stony beauty. A shiver ran right through Olive.

Louise said, "She was—Oh, she was something, let me tell you, Olive Kitteridge. A cock tease! I don't care what the papers said about how she loved animals and small children. She was evil, a living monster brought into this world to make a sweet boy crazy."

"Okay, okay." Olive was putting her coat on hurriedly.

"She deserved it, you know. She did."

Olive turned and saw Roger Larkin on the stairs behind her. He looked old, and wore a loose sweater; he had slippers on. Olive said, "I'm sorry. I've disturbed her."

He only raised a hand tiredly, the gesture indicating that she was not to worry, life had brought them to this point and he was resigned to living in hell. This is what Olive thought she saw, as she hurried to get her coat on. Roger Larkin opened the door, nodding slightly, and as the door was closing behind her, Olive was certain she heard the tiny, quick smashing sound of glass, and the spat-out word, "Cunt."

A bright haze hung over the river, so you could barely make out the water. You couldn't even see too far ahead on the path, and Olive was consistently startled by the people who passed by her. She was here later than usual, and more people were out and about. Next to the asphalt pathway, the patches of pine needles were visible, and the fringe of tall grasses, and the bark of the shrub oaks, the granite bench to sit on. A young man ran toward her, emerging through the light fog. He was pushing before him a triangular-shaped stroller on wheels, the handles like those of a bicycle. Olive caught sight of a sleeping baby tucked inside. What contraptions they had these days, these self-important baby boomer parents. When Christopher was the age of that baby, she'd leave him napping in his crib, and go down the road to visit Betty Simms, who had five kids of her own—they'd be crawling all over the house and all over Betty, like slugs stuck to her. Sometimes when Olive got back, Chris would be awake and whimpering, but the dog, Sparky, knew to watch over him.

Olive walked quickly. It was unseasonably hot, and the haze was warm and sticky. She felt the sweat run from below her eyes, like tears. The visit to the Larkin home sat inside her like a dark, messy injection of sludge spreading throughout her body. Only telling someone about it would get it hosed out. But it was too early to call Bunny, and not having Henry—the walking, talking Henry—to tell this to grieved her so much that it was as though she had just that morning lost him to his stroke again. She could picture clearly what Henry would say. Always that gentle amazement. "My word," he'd say, softly. "My word."

"On your left!" yelled someone, and a bicycle whizzed past her, coming so close she felt the whir of air on her hand. "Jesus, lady," said the helmeted alien, as he sped by, and confusion rolled through Olive.

"You're supposed to stay on the right side of the line," came a voice from behind her, a young woman on Rollerblades. Her voice was not angry, but it was not kind.

Olive turned and walked back to her car.

At the nursing home, Henry was asleep. With one cheek against the pillow, he looked almost the way he used to look, because his eyes were closed, and the blindness was taken away, so the blank, smiling face was gone. Asleep, with the faintest furrowing of his brows, a hint of anxiety seemed caught within him, making him familiar.

Mary Blackwell was nowhere in sight, but an aide told Olive that Henry had had a "bad night."

"What do you mean?" Olive demanded.

"Agitated. We gave him a pill around four this morning. He'll probably sleep awhile longer."

Olive pulled the chair next to the bed, and sat holding his hand beneath the guardrail. It was still a beautiful hand—large, perfectly proportioned. Surely as a pharmacist all those years, while he counted out pills, people watching had trusted those hands.

Now his handsome hand was the hand of a man half-dead. He had dreaded this, as all people did. Why it should have been his fate, and not (for example) Louise Larkin's, was anyone's guess. The doctor's guess was that Henry should have been on Lipitor or some other statin, since his cholesterol had been a little high. Henry had been one of those pharmacists, though, who seldom took a pill. And Olive's feeling about the doctor was simple: He could go to hell. She waited now, until Henry woke up, so he wouldn't wonder where she was. When she tried to wash him, get him dressed with the help of the aide, he was groggy and heavy and kept falling back asleep. The aide said, "Maybe we should let him rest for a bit."

Olive whispered to Henry, "I'll be back this afternoon."

No one answered the telephone when she called Bunny. She called Christopher—with the time difference, he'd be getting ready for work.

"Is he okay?" Christopher asked immediately.

"He had a bad night. I'll go back up in a while. But Chris, I saw Louise Larkin this morning."

He made no response the whole time she talked. She could hear an urgency in her voice, something desperate, or defensive. "The crazy creature suggested I cut my wrists," Olive said. "Can you imagine that? And then said, well, maybe that would take too long."

Christopher remained silent, even when she finished with the smashed teacup, and the name-calling "Bitch." (She could not bring herself to say the word *cunt*.) "Are you there?" she asked, sharply.

"I can't imagine why you went to see her," Chris finally said, as though accusing her of something. "After all these years. You never even liked her."

"She sent that note," Olive said. "She was reaching out."

"So what," said Christopher. "You couldn't drag me in there to save my life."

"It would hardly save your life. She's all ready to stab someone herself. And she said she knows you've only come back here once."

"How would she know that? I think she's cracked."

"She *is* cracked. Haven't you been listening? But I think she knows that from Mary Blackwell; apparently they're in touch."

Christopher yawned. "I have to get into the shower, Mom. Just let me know if Daddy's all right."

As she drove to the nursing home, a light rain dropped onto the car, and onto the road before her. The sky was gray and low. She felt an upset different from the times before. It stemmed from Christopher, yes. But she seemed caught between the pincers of some intractable remorse. A personal, deep embarrassment flushed through her, as though she had been caught in the act of shoplifting, which she had never done. It was shame that swiped across her soul, like these windshield wipers before her: two large black long fingers, relentless and rhythmic in their chastisement.

Pulling into the parking lot of the nursing home, she turned the car too sharply and came close to hitting a car pulling in beside her. She backed up, pulled in again, leaving more space, but she was unsettled by how close she had come to hitting the car. She took her big handbag, made sure to put her keys where she could find them, and stepped out. The woman—she was ahead of Olive—started to turn toward her, and in less than a few seconds a strange thing happened. Olive said, "I'm awfully sorry about that, my gosh," just as the woman said, "Oh, that's all right," with a kindness that Olive felt was providential in its spontaneous generosity. The woman was Mary Blackwell. And the moment occurred so suddenly, that neither woman seemed to know at first who the other was. But there they were, Olive Kitteridge apologizing to Mary Blackwell, and Mary's face kind, gentle, absolutely forgiving.

"I just didn't see you there, with this rain, I guess," Olive said.

"Oh, I know. It can be bad, this kind of day—twilight before it even gets going."

Mary held the door open for her, and Olive passed in front of her. "Thank you," Olive said. Just to make sure, she glanced at Mary, and the woman's face was tired and noncombative, the remains of sympathy still there. It was like a sheet of paper on which marks of something simple and honest had been drawn.

Who did I think she was? thought Olive. (And then: Who do I think *I* was?)

Henry was still in bed. He had not made it into his chair all day. She sat by him, touching his hand, and fed him some mashed potato, which he ate. It was dark as she prepared to leave. Waiting until she knew she would not be interrupted, she leaned over to Henry and whispered right into his ear, "You can die now, Henry. Go ahead. I'm fine. You can go ahead. It's *all right.*" She did not look back as she left the room.

Dozing in the bump-out room, she expected the phone to ring.

In the morning, Henry was in his wheelchair, a polite smile on his face, his eyes unseeing. At four o'clock, she returned and spooned into his mouth his supper. The next week was the same. And the week after that. Autumn was upon them; soon it would be dark as she fed him his supper from the tray that sometimes Mary Blackwell brought.

One evening when she returned home, she looked through a drawer of old photographs. Her mother, plump and smiling, but still foreboding. Her father, tall, stoic; his silence in life seemed right there in the photo—he was, she thought, the biggest mystery of all. A picture of Henry as a small child. Huge-eyed and curly-haired, he was looking at the photographer (his mother?) with a child's fear and wonder. Another photo of him in the navy, tall and thin, just a kid, really, waiting for life to begin. You will marry a beast and love her, Olive thought. You will have a son and love him. You will be endlessly kind to townspeople as they come to you for medicine, tall in your white lab coat. You will end your days blind and mute in a wheelchair. That will be your life.

Olive slipped the picture back into the drawer, her eye catching a photo of Christopher, taken when he was not yet two. She had forgotten how angelic he'd looked, like some creature newly hatched, as though he had not yet grown a skin and was all light and luminescence. You will marry a beast and she will leave you, Olive thought. You will move across the country and break your mother's heart. She closed the drawer. But you will not stab a woman twenty-nine times.

She went into the bump-out room, lay down on her back. No, Christopher wouldn't stab someone. (She hoped not.) It was not in his cards. Not in his bulb—planted in this particular soil, hers and Henry's, and their parents before them. Closing her eyes, she thought of soil, and green things growing, and the soccer field by the school came into her mind. She remembered the days when she was a school-teacher, how Henry would leave the pharmacy sometimes in the autumn to come and watch the soccer games on the field beside the school. Christopher, never physically aggressive, had spent most of the games sitting on the bench in his uniform, but Olive had suspected he didn't mind.

There was beauty to that autumn air, and the sweaty young bodies that had mud on their legs, strong young men who would throw themselves forward to have the ball smack against their foreheads; the cheering when a goal was scored, the goalie sinking to his knees. There were days—she could remember this—when Henry would hold her hand as they walked home, middle-aged people, in their prime. Had they known at these moments to be quietly joyful? Most likely not. People mostly did not know enough when they were living life that they were living it. But she had that memory now, of something healthy and pure. Maybe it was the purest she had, those moments on the soccer field, because she had other memories that were not pure.

Doyle Larkin had not been at the soccer games—he had not gone to that school. Whether Doyle even played soccer, Olive didn't know. She could not recall Louise ever saying, "I must go to Portland this afternoon to see Doyle in a soccer game." But Louise had loved her children, had bragged about them endlessly; when she'd spoken of Doyle being homesick at summer camp, her eyes had moistened, Olive now remembered this.

There was no understanding any of it.

But she had been wrong to visit Louise Larkin, hoping to feel better by knowing the woman suffered. It was ludicrous, as well, to think that Henry would die because she had told him he could. Who in the world, this strange and incomprehensible world, did she think she was? Olive turned onto her side, drew her knees up to her chest, turned on her transistor radio. She would have to decide soon whether or not to plant the tulips, before the ground was frozen.

Basket of Trips

Town is the church, and the grange hall, and the grocery store, and these days the grocery store could use a coat of paint. But no one's about to mention that to the grocer's wife—a plump, short woman who has brown eyes and two little dimples high up on her cheeks. When she was younger, Marlene Bonney was quite shy, and she would push the numbers on the cash register with a tentativeness, patches of pink spreading over her cheeks; you could see it made her nervous, counting out the change. But she was kind and warm-natured, and would listen carefully, her head bent forward, whenever a customer mentioned a problem they had. The fishermen liked her because she was quick to laugh, a sweet eruption of a deep, soft giggle. And when she made a mistake with the change, as she sometimes did, she would laugh even while blushing clear to her roots. "I guess I'm not going to win any prizes," she'd say. "No prizes for me."

Now, on this April day, people stand in the gravelly parking lot next to the church, waiting for Marlene to come out with her kids. Those who speak do so quietly, and there is a great deal of abstracted gazing, not uncommon in these circumstances, and many long glances at the ground. This same gravel parking lot stretches along the road and goes, eventually, up to the big side door of the grocery store, which in the past was often open during the summer months, and where people could see Marlene out back there, playing cards with the kids, or fixing them hot dogs to eat; good kids, always running around the store when they were small, always underfoot.

Molly Collins, standing next to Olive Kitteridge, both of them waiting along with the rest, has just looked around behind her at that side of the grocery store, and with a deep sigh says, "Such a nice woman. It isn't right."

Olive Kitteridge, who is big-boned and taller by a head than Molly, reaches into her handbag for her sunglasses, and once she has them on, she squints hard at Molly Collins, because it seems such a stupid thing to say. Stupid—this assumption people have, that things should somehow be *right*. But she finally answers, "She's a nice woman, it's true," turning and looking across the road at the budded forsythia near the grange hall.

And it is true, Marlene Bonney is sweet—and as thick as molasses, to boot. Years ago it was Olive who taught Marlene math in the seventh grade; Olive thinks she knows better than most how hard it must've been for the poor girl to take on that cash register when the time came. Still, the reason Olive has come here today, volunteered to help out, is that she knows Henry would be here if things weren't as they are; Henry, who went to church every Sunday, believed in this community stuff. But there they are—Marlene has come out of the church, Eddie Junior next to her, and the girls right behind. Marlene has been crying of course, but she is smiling now, the dimples high on her cheeks twinkling as she thanks people, standing on the side porch of the church in a blue coat that spreads over her rounded behind, but is not long enough to cover the rest of the green flowered dress that sticks to her nylons with static cling.

Kerry Monroe, one of Marlene's cousins (who was in trouble with the law a few years ago, and Marlene helped her out, took her in, gave her a job at the store), stands behind Marlene, slick as a whistle with her black hair and black suit and sunglasses, giving a nod to Eddie Junior, who nudges his mother toward a car and helps her get in. Those people going to the cemetery, and this includes the husband of Molly Collins, get into their cars as well, switching on their headlights in the midst of this sunny day, waiting for the hearse to pull away, then for the black car carrying the rest of the Bonneys to follow. All of it costing an arm and a leg, Olive thinks, walking to her own car along with Molly.

"Direct cremation," Olive says, as she waits for Molly to dig out a seat belt from the mess of dog hairs. "No frills. Door to door. They'll come right down from Belfast and take you away."

"What are you talking about?" Molly turns her head toward Olive, and Olive can smell the woman's breath from those false teeth she's had for years.

"They don't advertise," Olive says. "No frills. I told Henry that's the outfit we'll be using when the time comes."

She pulls out of the parking lot and starts down the road toward the Bonneys' house, which is way down at the end of the point. She has offered to go back with Molly to help lay out the sandwiches, avoiding, that way, the cemetery. The lowering of the casket and all that business—she can do without.

"Well, it's a nice day, anyway," says Molly, as they pass the Bullock place on the corner. "Helps a little bit, I think." And it's true the sun is strong, the sky very blue behind the Bullocks' red barn.

"Is Henry able to understand, then?" Molly asks a few minutes later.

For Olive, this is like someone has swung a lobster buoy and slammed her in the breastbone. But she answers simply, "Some days. I think so, yes." Lying is not what makes her angry. It's the question that has somehow made her angry. And yet, she also has an urge to tell this woman, sitting stupidly beside her, how she took the dog over last week on that day the weather was so warm; how she brought Henry out to the parking lot and the dog licked his hands.

"I don't know how you do it," Molly says quietly. "Going there every day, Olive. You're a saint."

"I'm hardly a saint, and you know it," Olive answers, but she is so angry she could drive right off the road.

"I wonder what Marlene is going to do for money," says Molly. "Do you mind if I open a window? I think you *are* a saint, Olive, but no offense, it smells a little doggy in here."

"Offense is not taken, I assure you," says Olive. "Open any windows you like." She has turned onto Eldridge Road, and this is a mistake because now she will have to drive by the house where her son, Christopher, used to live. She almost always makes a point of going the other way, taking the old route down to the bay, but here she is, and now she prepares herself to turn her head away, feigning nonchalance.

"Life insurance," Molly is saying. "Cousin Kerry—she told someone there was life insurance, and I guess Marlene's also thinking of selling the store. Apparently Kerry's the one who's been running the business this year."

Olive's eye has caught the clutter of cars in the front yard, and she turns her head as though to glance through the spruce trees out to the water, but the afterimage of the junky front yard remains in her eye; and oh, it had been a beautiful place! The lilac by the back door would have its tight little buds now, the forsythia at the kitchen window probably ready to burst—if those beastly people haven't knocked it down, living there like pigs. Why buy a beautiful house and junk it up with broken cars and tricycles and plastic swimming pools and swing sets? Why do a thing like that?

As they come over the crest where only juniper bushes and blueberry bushes grow, the sun is so bright above the water that Olive has to put the sun visor down. They pass by Moody's Marina, down into the little gully where the Bonney house is. "Hope I haven't lost the key she gave me," says Molly Collins, fishing through her handbag. She holds up a key as the car stops. "Pull up a little farther there, Olive. There'll be a lot of cars here when they get back from the cemetery." Years ago, Molly Collins taught home ec at the same school where Olive taught math, and even back then she was a bossy thing. But Olive pulls the car up farther.

"She probably ought to sell the store," says Molly as they walk around to the side door of the Bonneys' big old house. "Why bother with the headache of all that, if she doesn't need to?"

Inside, standing in the kitchen looking around, Molly muses, "Maybe she ought to sell this place, too."

Olive, having never been inside before, thinks the place looks tired. It's not just because some tiles are missing from the floor by the stove, or that part of the counter has bubbled up along the edge. The place simply has an air of exhaustion. Dying. Not dying. Either way, it tires you out. Olive peeks into the living room, where a large window looks over the ocean. It is a lot to take care of. On the other hand, it's Marlene's home. Of course, if Marlene sells the place, then Kerry, who lives in the room above the garage, will have to move out as well. Too bad, Olive thinks, closing the closet door with their coats hung up, heading back into the kitchen. Kerry Monroe had her eye on Christopher a few years back, smelled some money in that practice of his. Even Henry felt compelled to tell him to watch out. Don't worry, Christopher said, she's not my type. Which is pretty funny to think of now. "You could laugh your head off with that one, ha-ha thud," says Olive to no one, as she comes into the kitchen, knocks her knuckles a few times on the table. "Put me to work, Molly."

"See if there's any milk in the refrigerator, and pour it into these creamers." Molly is wearing a bib apron that she must have found here in the kitchen somewhere. Or maybe she brought it along. One way or another, she appears to have made herself at home. "Now, Olive, tell me. I've been wanting to ask. How is Christopher these days?"

Molly sets out plates on the table as quick as playing cards.

"He's fine," says Olive. "Now, what else do you want me to do?"

"Arrange these brownies on this. He likes it out there in California?"

"He's very happy out there. Got a nice practice going." Little tiny brownies. What was wrong with making a brownie big enough to sink your teeth into?

"How can people in California have problems with their feet?" asks

Molly, moving around Olive with a plate of sandwiches. "Don't they drive everywhere?"

Olive has to actually look at the wall and roll her eyes because of how stupid this woman can be. "But feet they have. And Chris has a very nice practice."

"Any grandchildren on the way?" Molly draws the words out with a kind of coyness, while she shakes sugar cubes into a little bowl.

"Haven't heard," says Olive. "And I don't believe in asking." She takes one of the little brownies and puts it into her mouth, making her eyes big at Molly. Olive and Henry had told no one except their old friends Bill and Bunny Newton, who lived two hours away, that Christopher was now divorced. Why tell anyone that? It was nobody's business, and Christopher living so far away—who needed to know that his new wife had walked out after moving him across the country? And that he didn't want to come home? No wonder Henry had a stroke! How unbelievable it was! Never, in a hundred years, would Olive tell Molly Collins, or anyone else, how terrible it was when Christopher came back to visit his father in the nursing home, how terse he was with her, how he went back early—this man who was her dearly loved son. A woman, even Marlene Bonney's age, could expect one day to outlive her husband. A woman could even expect her husband to get old and have a stroke and stay slumped in a chair at a nursing home. But a woman did not expect to raise a son, help him build a lovely house nearby, get started in a steady podiatry business, then have him marry and move across the country and never move home again, even when he found himself deserted by a beast of a wife. No woman, no mother, expected that. To have a son stolen away.

"Leave enough for others, Olive," says Molly Collins, and then, "Well, at least Marlene has her kids. Wonderful kids they are, too."

Olive takes another brownie and puts it into her mouth, but then—here they are, the kids themselves, coming through the back door with Marlene, moving through the kitchen as the sound of cars pulling into the gravel alongside the driveway can be heard, and then doors slamming shut. And Marlene Bonney herself, standing now in the hallway, holding her pocketbook slightly up and away from her body, as though the pocketbook belongs to someone else, standing there until someone leads her into the living room, where she sits down politely on her own couch.

"We were just saying," Molly Collins says to her, "that honestly, Marlene, you and Ed turned out the three best kids in town." And it's true they are something to be proud of: Eddie Junior in the coast guard, smart the way his father was (although he is not as outgoing; there is a wariness in his dark eyes), Lee Ann studying to be a nurse, Cheryl about to graduate from high school; you never heard about any trouble they were in.

But Marlene says, "Oh, there's lots of nice kids around," taking the coffee that Molly hands her. Marlene's brown eyes seem a little out of focus, the flesh of her cheeks a little more droopy. Olive sits down in a chair across from her.

"That cemetery stuff's bad business," Olive says, and Marlene smiles, her dimples twinkling like tiny imprints of stars high up on her cheeks.

"Oh, hello, Olive," she says. It has taken Marlene years to stop calling her Mrs. Kitteridge, which is what happens when you have people in school. And of course the opposite is true, which is that Olive continues to see half the town as kids, as she can still see Ed Bonney and Marlene Monroe as young schoolkids, falling in love, walking home day after day from school. When they reached the Crossbow Corners, they would stand and talk, and sometimes Olive would see them there as late as five o'clock, because Marlene had to go one way and Ed the other.

Tears have appeared in Marlene's eyes, and she blinks fast. She leans toward Olive and whispers, "Kerry says nobody likes a crybaby."

"Hells bells," answers Olive.

But Marlene sits back as Kerry appears, stick-thin and high-heeled, thrusting out that black-suited pelvic bone as soon as she stops walking, and it crosses Olive's mind suddenly that maybe Kerry was bullied when she was very young, skinny little kid. Kerry asks, "You want a beer, Marlene? Instead of that coffee?" She is holding a beer herself, her elbow tucked to her waist, and her dark eyes are keen, taking it in, the still-full cup of coffee in Marlene's hand, and the presence of Olive Kitteridge, too, who years ago sent Kerry to the principal's office more than once, before Kerry got shipped off to live with relatives some-where. "Or would you like a little whiskey?"

Henry might have remembered why they sent the girl away. Olive has never been one for remembering things.

"A drop of whiskey sounds good," says Marlene. "You want any, Olive?"

"Nope. Thanks." If she drank, she'd be a guzzler. She stays away from it, always has. She wonders if Christopher's ex-wife might have been a secret guzzler, out there drinking all that California wine.

The house is filling up. People move down the hallway and out onto the front porch. Some of the fishermen have come over from Sabbatus Cove, all scrubbed-looking. Their big shoulders slumped, they seem sheepish, apologetic, as they move into the living room, taking the tiny brownies with their big hands. Soon the living room is so full that Olive can no longer see out to the water. People's skirts, belt buckles move past her. "I just wanted to say, Marlene"—and here, in a sudden clear-ing of people, is Susie Bradford, pushing herself between the coffee table and the couch—"that he was so brave during his sickness. I never saw him complain."

"No," says Marlene. "He didn't complain." And then: "He had his basket of trips." At least that's what Olive thinks she's heard. Whatever Marlene has said seems to embarrass her. Olive sees the woman's cheeks flush, as though she has just divulged some private, very inti-mate secret that she shared with her husband. But Susie Bradford has spilled jelly from one of the cookies down her front, and now Marlene is saying, "Oh, Susie, go into the bathroom down the hall. Such a pretty blouse, what a shame."

"No ashtrays in this house," says a woman on her way past Olive, and because of a little crush of people, the woman has to stand there in front of Olive for a moment; she takes a deep drag from her cigarette, squinting her eyes against the smoke. Some tiny ping of recognition, of knowledge, takes place in Olive, but she could not tell you who this woman is—she knows only that she doesn't like the looks of her, with her long, stringy hair that contains a lot of unflattering gray. Olive thinks when your hair gets gray, it's time to chop it off, or pin it up on top of your head, no point in thinking you're still a schoolgirl. "I can't find an ashtray in this house," the woman says, tilting her face up quickly as she breathes out a stream of smoke.

"Well," says Olive, "I guess that's too bad." And the woman moves away.

The couch comes into view again. Kerry Monroe is drinking a tumbler of brown stuff—the whiskey she was offering earlier, Olive suspects—and while Kerry's lipstick remains bright, her cheekbones and jawline still impressively proportioned, it's as though inside her black clothes her joints have become loosened. Her crossed leg swings, a foot bobs, some inner wobbliness is there. "Nice service, Marlene," Kerry says, leaning forward to pick up a meatball with a toothpick. "Really nice service; you've done him proud." And Olive nods, because she would like Marlene to be comforted by this.

But Marlene doesn't see Kerry, she is smiling upward, taking hold of someone's hand, and says, "The kids planned it all." And the hand belongs to Marlene's youngest girl, who in her blue velour jersey and navy-blue skirt squeezes between Marlene and Kerry, putting her head on Marlene's shoulder, nestling her big-girl's body close.

"Everyone's saying how nice the service was," Marlene says, smoothing the girl's long bangs away from her eyes. "You did a real nice job."

The girl nods, her head pressed against her mother's arm.

"Great job," says Kerry, tossing back the rest of the whiskey in her glass as though it were merely iced tea.

And Olive, watching all this, feels—what? Jealousy? No, you don't feel jealous of a woman whose husband has been lost. But an unreachability, that's how she'd put it. This plump, kind-natured woman sitting on the couch surrounded by children, her cousin, friends—she is unreachable to Olive. Olive is aware of the disappointment this brings.

Because why, after all, did she come here today? Not just because Henry would have said to go to Ed Bonney's funeral. No, she came here hoping that in the presence of someone else's sorrow, a tiny crack of light would somehow come through her own dark encasement. But it remains separate from her, this old house filled with people, except one voice is beginning to rise above the others.

Kerry Monroe is drunk. In her black suit she stands by the couch and raises an arm. "Cop Kerry," she says, loudly. "Yep. That should have been me." Laughing, she sways. People say, "Watch it, Kerry," "Careful there," and Kerry ends up sitting on the arm of the couch, slips a black high heel off and flips up and down her black-stockinged foot. "Up against the wall, buster!"

It's disgusting. Olive rises from her chair. Time to leave; goodbyes aren't necessary. No one will miss her.

The tide is going out. Near the shore the water is flat, metal-colored, although out past Longway Rock, it's starting to get choppy; there's even a whitecap or two. Lobster buoys down in the cove bob slightly, and seagulls circle the wharf near the marina. The sky is still blue, but off to the northeast, the horizon is lined with a rising cloud bank, and the tops of the pine trees are bending, over there on Diamond Island.

Olive is not able to leave after all. Her car is blocked in the driveway by other cars, and she would have to ask around and make a fuss, and she doesn't want to do that. So she has found herself a nice private spot, a wooden chair right below the deck, off to one corner, in which to sit and watch the clouds move in slowly over the bay.

Eddie Junior walks by on his way down to the shore with some of his cousins. They don't notice her sitting there, and they disappear down the skinny path between the bayberry bushes and the rugosa, and then reappear again on the shore, Eddie Junior lagging behind the rest. Olive watches as he picks up stones and skips them through the water.

Above her on the deck she hears footsteps, big men's boot-shoes *clump, clump*. Matt Grearson's voice says in a long drawl, "Be a real high tide later tonight."

"Yep," says someone else—Donny Madden.

"Marlene's going to get lonesome out here this winter," says Matt Grearson after a while.

Godfrey, thinks Olive from her chair below—run like hell, Marlene. Big flub-dub Matt Grearson.

"I guess she'll manage," answers Donny, eventually. "People do."

In another few minutes their boots clump back inside, Olive hears the door close. People manage, she thinks. It's true. But she takes a deep breath and has to shift her weight on this wooden chair, because it's not true, too. She pictures Henry, not even a year ago, measuring what was needed for the mopboards in their new room, down on his hands and knees with the measuring tape, telling her the numbers while she wrote them down. Then Henry standing up, a tall man. "Okay, Ollie. Let's widdle the dogs and go into town." The car ride—what did they talk about? Oh, how she wants to remember, but she can't remember. In town, in the parking lot of Shop 'n Save, because they needed milk and juice after they went to the lumber store, she said she would stay in the car. And that was the end of their life. Henry got out of the car and fell down. Never stood up again, never walked down the pebble path to the house again, never said an intelligible word again; only sometimes, those huge blue-green eyes would look at her from the hospital bed.

Then he went blind; now he will never see her again. "Not much to look at these days," she's told him, when she has gone to sit with him. "Lost a little weight now we don't have our crackers and cheese every night. But I guess I look like hell." He would say that wasn't true. He would say, "Oh no, Ollie. You look wonderful to me." He doesn't say anything. Some days in his wheelchair he doesn't even turn his head. She makes the drive every day and sits with him. You're a saint, says Molly Collins. God, how stupid can you be? A scared old woman is what she is; all she knows these days is that when the sun goes down, it's time to go to bed. People manage. She is not so sure. The tide is still out on that one, she thinks.

Eddie Junior has stayed down there on the shore, skipping stones. His cousins are gone; just Eddie Junior down there on the rocks alone. Hurling those flat stones. Olive feels pleased by how good he is at this, skip-skip, skip-skip; even though the water is no longer flat. She likes the way he immediately bends down, finding another, hurling that.

But there's Kerry, and where did she come from? She must have gone down to the shore from around the other side of the house, because there she is in her stockinged feet on the rocks, veering over the barnacled rocks, calling out to Eddie. Whatever she's saying, he doesn't like. Olive can tell that from here. He keeps on skipping stones, but finally he turns to her and speaks. Kerry opens her arms in a kind of pleading gesture, and Eddie Junior just shakes his head, and a few minutes later, Kerry comes back up from the shore, crawling up the rocks, clearly drunk. She could break her neck out there, Olive thinks. Not that Eddie Junior seems to care. He throws a stone, real hard this time, too hard—it doesn't skip, just smashes into the water.

For a long time Olive sits there. She looks out over the water, and on the far edge of her mind she can hear people getting into their cars, driving away, but she is thinking of Marlene Monroe, a young girl, so shy, walking home with her sweetheart Ed Bonney, how happy a girl she must have been, standing at Crossbow Corners while the birds chirped and Ed Bonney perhaps said, "Gee, I hate to say goodbye." They lived right here in this house with Ed's mother for the first years of their marriage, until the old lady died. If Christopher had stayed married, his wife wouldn't have let Olive live with them for five minutes. And now Christopher was so different he might not let her live with him either—should Henry die and she find herself in trouble. Christopher might stick her in the attic, except he'd mentioned his

California house didn't have an attic. Tie her to a flagpole, but he didn't have one of those either. *So fascist,* is what Christopher said, the last time he was here, as they drove past the Bullocks' house with the flag out front. Whoever went around saying things like that?

A stumbling sound on the deck above her, and then a slurred voice, "I'm sorry, Marlene. Really, you have to believe me." And then the murmuring sounds of Marlene herself, telling Kerry it's time to go sleep it off, and after that, clumping sounds down the deck stairs; more silence.

Back inside the house, Olive puts a brownie into her mouth and goes off to find the bathroom. Coming out, she runs into the woman with the long gray hair, who is right now sticking a cigarette butt into a potted plant that sits on a table in the hallway. "Who *are* you?" Olive says, and the woman stares at her. "Who are *you*?" the woman answers, and Olive walks past her. That is the woman who bought Christopher's house, Olive realizes with an inner lurch, that woman who hasn't the decency to respect even a poor potted plant, let alone everything Olive and Henry worked for, their son's beautiful house, where their grandchildren were going to grow up.

"Where's Marlene gone to?" Olive asks Molly Collins, who still has Marlene's apron on, and is walking around the living room officiously collecting plates, balled-up paper napkins. Molly looks over her shoulder and says vaguely, "Gee, I'm not sure."

"Where's Marlene gone?" Olive asks Susie Bradford, who comes by next, and Susie says, "Around."

It's Eddie Junior who tells her. "Kerry got drunk and Mom's gone to put her in bed." He says this with a dark look at the back of Susie Bradford, and Olive likes the boy a good deal. She did not have this young fellow in school. She left teaching years before to tend to her own family. Christopher out in California. Henry over in Hasham, at the home. Gone, gone. Gone to hell.

"Thank you," she says to Eddie Junior, who, in his young eyes, seems to have some awareness of hell himself.

———

It is no longer a lovely April day. The northeast wind that blows against the side of the Bonney house has also brought the clouds in, and now a sky as gray as November hangs over the bay, and against the dark rocks the water slaps ceaselessly, swirling seaweed around, leaving it bumpily combed out along the higher rocks. Right down to the point the rocky coastline looks barren, almost wintry, only the skinny spruce and pines show dark green, for it is far too early for any leaves to come out; even close to the house the forsythia is only budded.

Olive Kitteridge, on her way to find Marlene, steps over a smashed-looking crocus by the garage's side door. Last week, after the day that was warm enough to take the dog to Henry in the parking lot, it snowed, one of those April dumpings of pure white that all melted the very next day, but the ground in places is still soggy from the assault, and certainly this crushed yellow crocus has been done in. The side door of the garage opens directly to stairs, and Olive walks up them cautiously, stands on the landing; two sweatshirts are hanging on hooks, a pair of muddied yellow rubber boots stand side by side, toes facing in opposite directions.

Olive knocks on the door, looking at the boots. She bends over and places one boot on the other side of its mate, so they look like they go together, could walk off together, and she knocks again. No answer, so she turns the knob, pushes the door open slowly, walks in.

"Hello, Olive."

Across the room, facing her, Marlene sits like an obedient schoolgirl in a straight-backed chair by Kerry's double bed, her hands folded in her lap, her plump ankles crossed neatly. On the bed sprawls Kerry. She lies on her stomach with the abandonment of a sunbather, her face turned toward the wall, elbows out, but her hips are turned slightly, so that the black outline of her suit seems to accentuate the rise of her rear end, and her black-stockinged legs are sleek, in spite of the fact that the stockings are shredded in a series of tiny runs at her feet.

"Is she asleep?" Olive asks, walking farther into the room.

"Passed out," Marlene answers. "Upchucked first in Eddie's room, then fell asleep here."

"I see. Well, it's a nice place you've given her here." Olive walks over toward the little dining alcove and brings back a chair, sits down by Marlene.

For a while neither woman speaks, then Marlene says pleasantly, "I've been thinking about killing Kerry." She raises a hand from her lap and exposes a small paring knife lying on her green flowered dress.

"Oh," says Olive.

Marlene bends over the sleeping Kerry and touches the woman's bare neck. "Isn't this some major vein?" she asks, and puts the knife flat against Kerry's neck, even poking slightly at the vague throbbing of the pulse there.

"Yuh. Okay. Might want to be a little careful there." Olive sits forward.

In a moment Marlene sighs, sits back. "Okay, here." And she hands the paring knife to Olive.

"Do better with a pillow," Olive tells her. "Cut her throat, there's going to be a lot of blood."

A sudden, soft, deep eruption of a giggle comes from Marlene. "Never thought of a pillow."

"I've had some time to think about pillows," Olive says, but Marlene nods vacantly, like she's really not listening.

"Mrs. Kitteridge, did you know?"

"Know what?" says Olive, but she feels her stomach turn choppy, whitecaps in her stomach.

"What Kerry told me today? She said it happened with her and Ed only once. Just one time. But I don't believe that—it had to be more. The summer after Ed Junior graduated from high school." Marlene has started to cry, is shaking her head. Olive looks away; a woman needs her privacy. She holds the paring knife in her lap and gazes out through the window above the bed, only gray sky and gray ocean; too high up to see any shoreline, only gray water and sky out there, far as the eye can see.

"I never heard anything," says Olive. "Why would she choose today to tell you?"

"Thought I knew." Marlene has pulled a Kleenex from somewhere, from inside her sleeve maybe, and she dabs at her face, blows her nose. "She thought I knew all along, and I was just punishing her by keeping on being nice to her. She got drunk today and started saying how good I got her, killing her and Ed with kindness that way."

"Jesum Crow," is all Olive can think to say.

"Isn't that funny, Olive?" Again, out of nowhere comes Marlene's deep giggle.

"Well," says Olive. "I guess it's not the funniest thing I ever heard."

Olive looks at the black-suited body of Kerry sprawled there on the bed and wishes there were a door to close or a curtain to draw so they didn't have to see the rise of this girl's rear end, her black stockings outlining the slim calves of her legs. "Does Eddie Junior know?"

"Yuh. Seems she told him yesterday. Thought he knew, too, but he says he didn't. He says he doesn't believe it's true."

"It may not be."

"Shit," says Marlene, shaking her head, crying again. "Mrs. Kitteridge, if you don't mind, I'd like to just say *shit*."

"Say *shit*," says Olive, who never uses the word herself.

"Shit," says Marlene. "Shit, shit, shit."

"I guess so." Olive breathes in deeply. "I guess so," she says again, slowly. She looks around her with little interest—a picture of a cat is on one wall—and her glance comes back to Marlene, who is squeezing her nose. "Quite a day, kiddo. Vomit upstairs, and cigarette butts downstairs." The woman with the long gray hair has really shaken Olive up: *Seismic* spells itself across her fog-colored mind. She says, "That creature who bought Christopher's house, she's walking around putting her cigarettes out in your plants."

"Oh, her," says Marlene. "She's a piece of shit, too."

"I guess so." She's going to tell this to Henry tomorrow. She'll tell him the whole thing; only he won't like hearing the word *shit*.

"Olive, could I ask you to do me a favor?"

"I wish you would."

"Could you, please—" And here the poor woman looks so bereft, dazed, in her green flowered dress, her brown hair coming loose from its pins. "Before you leave, could you go upstairs in the bedroom? Turn right at the top of the stairs. In the closet you'll find pamphlets, you know, of different places to go. Could you take them with you? Just take them with you, and throw them all away. The basket they're in, too."

"Of course."

Marlene has tears running down past her nose. She wipes her face with a bare hand. "I don't want to open that closet door, knowing it's there."

"Yes," says Olive. "I can do that." She brought Henry's shoes home from the hospital, put them in a bag in the garage, and they are still there. They were new, bought just a few days before the last time they pulled into the parking lot of Shop 'n Save.

"Any other stuff, if you want, Marlene."

"No. No, Olive. It's that we sat there and made believe we'd go places together." Marlene shakes her head. "Even after Dr. Stanley told us what the situation was, we'd go through these pamphlets, talking about the trips we'd take when he got well." She rubs her face with both hands. "Gosh, Olive." Marlene stops and looks at the knife Olive is holding. "Oh, gosh, Olive. I'm so embarrassed." And it seems she really is; her cheeks are flushing a deep pink, now a deep red.

"No need to be," Olive tells her. "We all want to kill someone at some point." Olive's ready right now to say, if Marlene wants to hear, the different people she might like to kill.

But Marlene says, "No, not that. Not that. That I sat there with him and we planned those trips." She tears at the Kleenex, which is pretty well shredded. "Gosh, Olive, it was like we believed it. And there he was, losing weight, so weak—'Marlene, bring over the basket of trips,' he'd say, and I would. It makes me so embarrassed now, Olive."

An innocent, Olive thinks, gazing at this woman. A real one. You don't find them anymore. Boy, you do not.

Olive stands up and walks to the window over the little sink, looking down onto the driveway. People are leaving now, the last of them; Matt Grearson gets into his truck, backs out, drives away. And here comes Molly Collins with her husband, walking over the gravel in her low pumps; she put in a full day's work, Molly did, just trying to do her best, Olive thinks. Just a woman with false teeth and an old husband—who in two shakes will be dead like the rest of them, or worse, sitting next to Henry in a wheelchair.

She wants to tell Marlene how she and Henry talked about the grandchildren they would have, the happy Christmases with their nice daughter-in-law. How only a little more than a year ago they would go to Christopher's house for dinner and the tension would be so thick, you could put your hand against it, and they'd still come home and say to each other what a nice girl she was, how glad they were that Christopher had this nice wife.

Who, who, does not have their basket of trips? It isn't right. Molly Collins said that today, standing out by the church. *It isn't right.* Well. It isn't.

She would like to rest a hand on Marlene's head, but this is not the kind of thing Olive is especially able to do. So she goes and stands near the chair Marlene sits on, gazing out that side window there, looking down at the shoreline, which is wide now that the tide's almost gone out. She thinks of Eddie Junior down there skipping stones, and she can only just remember that feeling herself, being young enough to pick up a rock, throw it out to sea with force, still young enough to do that, throw that damn stone.

Ship in a Bottle

"You'll have to organize your days," Anita Harwood was saying, wiping at the kitchen counter. "Julie, I mean this. People go crazy in prisons and the army because of this exactly."

Winnie Harwood, who at eleven years old was younger by ten years than her sister, Julie, watched Julie, who was looking at the floor and leaning against the doorway, wearing the red hooded sweatshirt and jeans that she'd slept in. Julie's hands were jammed into her pockets, and Winnie, whose adolescent feelings for her sister amounted these days to almost a crush, tried unobtrusively to put her own hands into her own pockets, and lean against the table with the indifference that Julie appeared to have at what was being said.

"For example," continued their mother. "What are your plans for today?" She stopped wiping the counter and looked over at Julie. Julie did not look up. Only recently had Winnie's feelings teetered from her mother to her sister. Her mother had won beauty pageants before Julie was born, and she still looked pretty to Winnie. It was like having more candy than other people, or getting stars on homework papers—to have the mother who looked the best. A lot of them were fat, or had stupid hair, or wore their husbands' woolen shirts over jeans with elastic waistbands. Anita never left the house without lipstick and high heels and her fake pearl earrings. Only lately had Winnie started to have the uncomfortable sense that something was wrong, or *might* be wrong, with her mother; that others talked about her in a certain eye-rolling way. She'd have given anything for this not to be the case, and maybe it wasn't—she just didn't know.

"Because of *this exactly*?" Julie asked, looking up. "In prisons and the army? Mom, I'm dying, and you're saying stuff that makes no sense."

"Don't be casual about the word *dying*, honey. Some people really are dying right now, and terrible deaths, too. They'd be glad to be in your shoes—getting rejected by a fiancé would be like a big mosquito bite to them. Look. Your father's home," Anita said. "That's sweet. Coming home in the middle of a workday to make sure you're okay."

"To make sure *you're* okay," Julie said. Adding, "And it's not accurate to say he rejected me." Winnie took her hands out of her pockets.

"How's everyone? Everyone doing good?" Jim Harwood was a slightly built man, with a nature of relentless congeniality. He was a recovered alcoholic, going three times a week to AA meetings. He was not Julie's father—who had run off with another woman when Julie was a kid—but he treated her kindly, as he treated everyone. Whether or not their mother had married him while he was still a drunk, Winnie didn't know. All of Winnie's life, he had worked as a janitor at the school. "Maintenance supervisor," their mother had said once, to Julie. "And don't you ever forget it."

"We're fine, Jim," said Anita now, holding the door as he brought in a bag of groceries. "Look at this, girls. Your father's done the shopping. Julie, why don't you make pancakes?"

It was a family custom to have pancakes on Sunday nights; this was Friday noontime.

"I don't want to make pancakes," said Julie. She had started to cry, soundlessly, and was wiping her face with her hands.

"Well, I'm afraid that's too bad," said their mother. "Julie, sweetheart. If you keep on with this crying, I'm going right through the roof." Anita tossed the sponge into the sink. "Right through the roof, understand?"

"Mom, my God."

"And stop with the swearing, sweetheart. God has his hands full without you calling upon him in vain. Routine, Julie. Routine is what makes prisons and armies work."

Winnie said, "I'll make the pancakes." She wanted her mother to stop talking about prisons and armies. Her mother had been talking about prisons and armies ever since those pictures had come out with the hooded prisoners overseas, and American soldiers leading them around on leashes like dogs.

"We deserve everything we get," her mother had said a few months ago in the grocery store, talking loudly to Marlene Bonney. And Cliff Mott, who had a big yellow ribbon decal on his truck because of his grandson, had come around from behind the cereal aisle and said, "Be careful with your crazy talk, Anita."

"All right, Winnie," said her mother. "You make the pancakes."

"Want some help?" asked her father. He had taken some eggs from the grocery bag, and leaned to switch on the radio.

"No," Winnie said. "I'll do it."

"Yes," said her mother. "Jim, get the bowl out."

He got the mixing bowl from the cupboard while Frank Sinatra's voice rose, fell, then rose again, "Myyyy waaayy."

"Oh, please," Julie said. "Please, please, please turn that off."

"Jim," Anita said. "Turn the radio off."

Winnie was the one to lean over and turn the radio off. She wanted Julie to see that she was the one who had done it, but Julie wasn't looking.

"Julie, sweetheart," said their mother, "this can't go on forever. The family has the right to listen to the radio. You know, eventually."

"It's been four days," Julie said. She wiped her nose on the sleeve of her sweatshirt. "Come on."

"Six," said her mother. "Today is day six."

"Mom, please. Just give me a break."

Winnie thought someone should give her a tranquilizer. Uncle Kyle had brought some over, but their mother only doled them out at night now, breaking them in half. Winnie woke up sometimes and could tell Julie was awake. Last night the moon had been full and their bedroom had had white all through it. "Julie," Winnie had whispered. "Are you awake?"

Julie hadn't answered.

Winnie had turned over and looked through the window at the moon. It had been huge, hanging over the water like something swollen. If there'd been a curtain, Winnie would have closed it, but they didn't have curtains in their house. They lived on the end of a long dirt road and their mother had said there was no need for curtains, although a year ago she had hung fishnet up around the edges of the windows in the living room for decoration. She'd sent Winnie and Julie down to the shore to get starfish, all different sizes, so she could dry them out and stick them on the fishnet curtains. Julie and Winnie had walked over the seaweed, flipping back rocks, stacking up a pile of bumpy-skinned starfish.

"This has to do with her father—and mine," Julie had said. Julie was the only person who told Winnie stuff like that. "She misses both of them. Her father used to bring her starfish at the end of the day when she was a kid. And then she wanted Ted to do that, too, and he did for a while."

"That was a long time ago," Winnie had said, peeling a starfish off a rock, a little one; its leg ripped as she pulled. She put the starfish back onto the rock. They grew new legs if they lost them.

"Doesn't matter," Julie had said. "Missing someone doesn't stop."

Their grandfather had been a fisherman whose boat had gotten stuck on a ledge out at sea. The newspaper clipping was in the same scrapbook showing the picture of Anita as Miss Potato Queen. "People used to call her Tater Tits," Julie told Winnie. "Don't tell her I told you she told me." Anita had married Ted, a carpenter, because she was pregnant with Julie, but Ted had never wanted to stay with anyone for long. Julie said he had made that clear from the beginning. "So she lost both of them in just a couple of years." Julie peered into the pail of starfish. "We have enough. Let's go." Walking back over the rocks, Julie added, "Bruce told me most fishermen can't swim. It's funny I didn't know that."

Winnie was surprised Bruce knew that; he wasn't from around here. He'd come up from Boston and rented a cottage for a month with his brothers, and Winnie didn't know how he would know if fishermen could swim.

"Could *he* swim?" Winnie asked Julie. She meant their grandfather, but she didn't have a name to call him, since he was never mentioned.

"Nope. He had to just sit on that boat with the other guy, watching the tide come in. He'd have known he was going to drown. That's the part that makes Mom nuts, I think."

After their mother put the starfish in the fishnet curtains, they began to smell because they hadn't been dried out enough first, and Anita threw them out. Winnie watched while her mother stood on the porch leaning over the rail, throwing the starfish back into the ocean one by one. She wore a pale green dress that the wind moved so it showed her figure, her breasts, her tiny waist, her long bare legs, her feet arched as she lifted up onto her toes to throw the starfish out. Winnie heard a sound, like a little scream, come from her mother as she threw the last one.

"Honey," Anita said to Julie now, "take a shower, you'll feel a whole lot better."

"I don't want to take a shower," said Julie, still leaning in the doorway, wiping her sleeve across her mouth.

"Now, why not?" asked her mother. "What's the difference between crying in the kitchen and crying in the shower?" She put a hand on her hip, and Winnie saw the pink fingernail polish, perfectly done on her mother's fingertips.

"Because I don't want to take my clothes off. I don't want to see my body."

Anita's jaw got hard, and she nodded her head in tiny nods. "Winnifred, watch your sleeve near that flame. Another catastrophe right now and I'm liable to kill someone."

Their house didn't have a shower and a bathroom the way most houses did. There was a shower stall off the hallway, and across from that was a closet with a chemical toilet, a barrel-shaped plastic thing that made a whirring sound when you pushed a button to flush it. There wasn't any door for this closet, just a curtain to pull. Sometimes if Anita walked by, she'd say, "Whew! Who just had a movement?" If you wanted to take a shower, you told people to stay out of the hallway, otherwise you had to get undressed inside the metal shower stall and toss your clothes out into the hall, then wait for the water to warm up, as you pressed against the stall's metal side.

Julie left the kitchen and soon there was the sound of the shower spraying. "I'm taking a shower," Julie called loudly. "So please stay out."

"No intention of bothering you," Anita called back. Winnie set the table and poured some juice. When the shower turned off, they could all hear the sound of Julie's crying.

"I don't know if I can stand this another minute," said Anita, drumming her nails against the counter.

"Give it time," said Jim. He poured pancake batter into the frying pan.

"Time?" said Anita, pointing toward the hall. "Jimmy, I have given that girl half my life."

"Well," said Jim, winking at Winnie.

"Well? Well, hell. I'm really, really getting tired of this."

"Your hair looks good, Mom," Winnie said.

"It should," said Anita. "It cost two months of groceries."

Julie came back into the kitchen, her wet hair stuck to her head, the ends dripping onto her red sweatshirt, making it dark on the shoulders. Winnie saw her father flip a pancake made in the wobbly shape of a J. "A J for my jewel," he said to Julie, and that made Winnie wonder what had happened to the wedding rings.

———

The limousine had caused some tension. At first the driver refused to come to the house; he said they should have mentioned the dirt road, that the branches would scratch the paint. "Julie's not walking down a dirt road in her damn wedding dress," Anita said to her husband. "You make that driver drive the foolish car up here." The limousine had been Anita's idea.

Jim, looking all scrubbed and pink in his rented tuxedo, stepped outside and talked to the driver. In a few minutes, he went into the cellar and came back up with some hedge clippers. Then he and the driver disappeared down the driveway, and a few minutes later the limousine drove up, Jim waving from the front seat.

Bruce arrived at the house looking sick.

"You can't see the bride before the wedding," Anita called through the window. "Bruce, dear God!" She started to run to the door, but Bruce had already stepped inside, and when Anita saw his face, she stopped what she was saying. Julie, coming right up behind her, didn't say anything either.

Julie and Bruce went out onto the back lawn, which wasn't so much a lawn as a kind of clearing of roots and pine needles. Winnie watched through the window with her mother. Jim got out of the limousine and came inside and watched with them. Julie looked like an ad from a magazine, standing there next to a bayberry bush in her gown, the white train folded on itself, but still flowing behind her, six feet long.

"Jimmy," Anita said, "people are at the *church*."

But he didn't answer. The three of them kept standing there watching through the window. Julie and Bruce hardly moved. They didn't touch each other, or even move their arms, and then Bruce stepped through the bayberry bushes and headed to the road.

Julie came back to the house like a walking Barbie doll, and the three of them were at the screen door when she came in. "Mommy," said Julie, quietly. Her eyes weren't quite right. "This isn't happening, is it?"

———

Uncle Kyle showed up with pills. Jim spoke to the limousine driver and then went off to the church. The limousine drove away, catching the leaves of a poplar tree in its back fender above the tire, and Winnie sat on the steps in her bridesmaid dress. After a while her father came back. "Guess you can take that off, Winnie-doodle," he said, but Winnie just kept sitting there. Her father went inside, and when he came back out, he said, "Julie's resting on our bed along with your mother." Winnie figured that meant Uncle Kyle had drugged them both.

She sat on the steps until she had to go to the bathroom. She didn't like going to the bathroom in the house anymore, behind the curtain like that, when everyone was home. But no one was around when she went inside. She could hear her father downstairs in the cellar, and her parents' bedroom door was closed. In a few minutes, though, the door opened and her mother walked out. She had on her old blue skirt, with a pink sweater, and she didn't look the least bit drugged.

Jim Harwood had been building a boat for years. It was going to be a big boat—the frame took up a lot of the cellar. For almost a year he hadn't done anything more than spread the blueprints out onto the living room floor and look at them each night. But finally he went into the cellar and set up two sawhorses. Every night the family could hear the electric saw buzzing, and sometimes the sound of hammering, and very slowly the curved-out skeleton of a boat began to appear. The boat stayed in its skeleton shape for a long time. Jim kept going down there night after night to work on it. "It's at the slow point now, Winnie-doodle," he said. He had to press pieces of wood in clamps to get them to arch the right way, and then he'd varnish the wood carefully and put over each nail gummy cement that took four days to dry.

"How're you going to get it out of here when it's done?" Winnie asked him one night, as she sat watching on the cellar stairs.

"Good question, isn't it?" he said. He explained how he'd figured it out beforehand, mathematically, measuring the cellar door, and the circumference of the hull, and that theoretically if he turned it at a certain angle, it should be able to get through the door when the time came. "But I'm beginning to wonder," he said.

Winnie wondered, too. The boat was looking awfully big. "Well, then it will be like a ship in a bottle," she said, "like the ones at Moody's store."

"That's right," said her father. "It'll be kind of like that, I guess."

When Winnie was smaller, she used to play in the cellar with Julie. Sometimes Julie would play store with her, with the canned food their mother bought, pushing it across a table pretending to ring it up. Now the cellar was pretty much taken over by the boat and her father's tools. He had built shelves along the wall; up on top was an old rifle that had been around for years, and on the shelves below were wooden boxes filled with cords and nails and bolts, separated according to size.

Sun streamed through the window over the kitchen sink. Winnie could see dust particles floating through the air. "Now," said her mother, putting down her coffee cup, "let's get the day figured out. Daddy's going back to the school for a bit, I'm going to feed my roses, and what are you girls up to?" She raised her eyebrows and tapped her painted fingernails on the table.

Julie and Winnie didn't say anything. Winnie put her finger on the top of the syrup and then into her mouth.

"Winnie, please, don't be a pig," her mother said, standing up, putting her coffee cup into the sink. "Julie, you'll be a lot better off when you figure out what to *do.*"

One thing Anita had found to do the day there wasn't a wedding was write Bruce a letter. She told him she would shoot him if she ever saw him again, if he ever came close to her daughter. "That's a federal crime, I think," Jim had told her quietly. "Putting a threat in the mail."

"Federal crime be damned," Anita said. "He's the one who did a federal crime."

Winnie remembered Cliff Mott telling her mother in the grocery store to stop her crazy talk. It was a strange feeling—to go from being proud of your pretty mother to wondering what people said about her, if maybe she was nuts; and Winnie suddenly thought how her mother didn't have close friends the way other mothers did. She didn't talk on the phone or go shopping with anyone.

Now Winnie sat with Julie at the kitchen table, and saw through the window her mother walking around to the rosebushes, a trowel in her hand. "You know what this is all about, don't you?" Julie said quietly. "Sex."

Winnie nodded, but she didn't know, exactly. The sun, bright in the kitchen, was giving her a headache.

"She can't stand that I had sex with him."

Winnie got up and dried a plate and put it away. Julie was staring straight in front of her, blankly, like she wasn't really looking at anything. Winnie had seen her mother looking that way sometimes. "Winnie," Julie said, still staring, "always lie to Mom. Remember I said that to you. Just lie. Lie your head off."

Winnie dried another plate.

The gist of it was that Bruce had gotten scared. He didn't want to break up with Julie, he just didn't want to marry her. He wanted to live with her instead. Anita had told Julie that if she wanted to live like a common slut with a man who had left her so publicly at the altar, she could expect to never come home again.

"She doesn't mean it," Winnie had said to Julie. "People live with each other all over the place."

"You want to bet? You want to bet she doesn't mean it?" Julie had said. And Winnie had felt something almost like car sickness; she guessed she didn't want to bet on anything where their mother was concerned.

"Paint a picture. Read a book. Hook a rug." Anita's hand slapped the table with each suggestion. Julie wasn't answering. She sat nibbling a cracker while Anita and Winnie had soup; they had made it through another day—it was Saturday lunch. "Clean the windows," Anita said. "Winnie, don't drink from the bowl like a pig." Anita wiped her mouth with a paper towel, which is what they used for napkins. "What you *should* do is call Beth Marden and see about having your job back at the nursery school this fall." Anita stood and put her bowl into the sink.

"No," said Julie.

"Say, *I* know." Her mother was pleased about this one, Winnie could tell. When her mother's eyes got shiny like that, it made Winnie want to hug her, the way you'd want to hug some child who'd gotten confused about something.

"Oatmeal cookie dough," Anita said. She nodded at Julie, then at Winnie. "We'll make a batch and we won't bake *any*. We'll just eat it all as dough."

Julie didn't say anything. She started picking at her nail.

"So, what do you say?" Anita asked.

"I don't think so," Julie said, glancing up at her. "I mean, thank you, though—it was a nice idea."

Anita's face got blank, like she couldn't find the expression to put on it. "Julie," Winnie said. "Come on, it'll be fun." She got up and brought out a bowl and a spoon and the measuring cups.

Anita walked out of the kitchen and they heard the front door open and close. Anita was supposed to be working today at her job as a cashier at the hospital's coffee shop. She had called in sick. Through the window Winnie saw their mother move past the bayberry bushes and head down the road to where her goldfish pool was. The first year Anita made the goldfish pool, she let the fish freeze in the ice for the winter; she said she'd heard you could do that, that they'd thaw out in the spring. Winnie used to scrape the snow off sometimes to look at the blurry orange spots in the ice.

"I guess I blew that, huh," Julie said. She sat with her chin in her hands.

Winnie didn't know if she should start the cookie dough or not. She took some butter out of the refrigerator and the telephone began to ring. "Get that," Julie said, sitting up straight. "Quick." She was in the chair by the corner, and she started pushing at the other chairs that were in her way. The phone rang another ring.

"Are you home?" Winnie asked. "You know, if it's Bruce or something?"

"Winnie, just *get* it," Julie said. "Before Mom hears it. Hurry. Yes, of *course* I'm home."

"Hello?" Winnie said.

"Who," Julie mouthed. "Whoo?"

"Hello," said Jim. "How's everything?"

"Hi, Daddy," Winnie said.

Julie turned and left the kitchen.

"I'm just checking in," said Jim. "Checking in."

When Winnie hung up, the phone started to ring again. "Hello?" she said. No one said anything. "Hello?" she said again. Through the phone she heard the sound of a tiny bell.

"Winnie," said Bruce. "I want to talk to Julie without your mother around."

"Here I am," said Anita, coming through the back door. "What's the story with the cookie dough? You kids decide to make it or not?"

"I don't know," Winnie said, still holding the phone.

"Who's that?" her mother asked.

"Okay, goodbye," Winnie said into the phone, and hung up.

"Who was that?" her mother said. "Was that Bruce? Winnifred, tell me, was that Bruce?"

Winnie turned around. "It was Daddy," she said, not looking at her mother. "He'll be home pretty soon."

"Oh," said her mother. "Well."

Winnie put a stick of butter in the bowl and tried to smoosh it with a spoon. Moody's store, she thought. The bell she'd heard when Bruce called was the little bell on the screen door at Moody's.

Anita said, "One of the fish has that fungus again."

Julie was down on the shore, sitting on a rock not much bigger than her bottom, staring out at the water. She turned her head slightly when

Winnie's feet made a sound on the seaweed, then she looked back at the water. Winnie turned over rocks, looking for white periwinkles. She used to collect them when she was little, watching the way their muscly foot would cling to the rock, and then close up tight when she touched it with her hand. But today Winnie left them alone. The desire to collect them was gone, it was only habit that made her look. A lobster boat passed by, and Winnie waved. It was good manners to wave to someone in a boat.

"Bruce called," she said. Julie turned her head. "And it wasn't from Boston either, I think. I think he was up at Moody's." A loud bang sounded from up by the road.

"He called?" Julie said. There was another bang.

"What is that?" Winnie said. "Fireworks?"

"Oh, Jesus," Julie said, scrambling up over the rocks. "Winnie, that was a gun."

Anita was in the driveway holding the rifle with both her hands, but carefully, sort of, not aiming it at anything. "Hi there," she said. Her eyes were shiny, and there were drops of sweat in the pale pockets of skin right below them.

"What are you *doing*?" Julie said. Anita looked back at the rifle in her hands, looking down at the end of it. "Mom," Julie said.

"He's all right," said Anita. She kept looking at the gun, peering at the trigger. "He drove up and drove away—that's all." Her finger was on the trigger. "This hasn't been used in years," she said. "I think it got jammed. Don't these things sometimes get jammed?"

"Mom," said Winnie, and there was this sharp, short crack of a sound and the gravel in the driveway sprayed out. Julie screamed and Anita screamed, only hers was a surprised shout really, but Julie's scream kept on going.

Anita held the gun away from herself. "Goodness," she said. Julie ran to the house yelling. Anita was rubbing her arm.

"Mommy," Winnie said. "Are you all right?"

"Oh, sweetie," she answered, brushing a hand across her forehead. "It's kind of hard to say."

This time Anita did take a pill, Winnie saw her take it, obediently at the kitchen sink when Uncle Kyle asked her to, and then she went to bed. Uncle Kyle asked Julie if Bruce was the type to press charges, and Julie and Jim both said no, and then Julie asked Jim if she could call Bruce on his cell phone later just to make sure, and Jim said yes, she could do that, that Anita would probably sleep right through until morning.

Winnie went out the back door and around to the side of the house where there were ferns and lily leaves pressed against the foundation, and she looked into her mother's bedroom window. Anita lay on her side with her hands tucked under her cheeks, her eyes closed, her mouth partly open. She seemed bigger than usual; the tops of her arms and her bare ankles were pale and fleshier than Winnie had noticed before. There was something deeply uncomfortable about the sight, as though Winnie had come across her mother naked. She went down to the shore and gathered up some starfish and laid them out on a big rock above the tide line to dry.

The sun was setting over the water. Winnie watched it through the bedroom window. It looked like the postcards they sold at Moody's. On her bed, Julie sat painting her fingernails. She had spoken to Bruce, who was on his way back to Boston, and no, he wouldn't press charges. But he had said he thought Anita—and Julie whispered this, leaning forward—*was a fucking nut.*

"That's not nice," Winnie said. She felt herself blush.

"Oh, baby girl." Julie sat back. "When you get out of here," she said, "if you ever do get out of here, you'll find out not everyone lives like this."

"Like what?" Winnie said, sitting down on the foot of her bed. "Lives like what?"

Julie smiled at her. "Let's start with toilets," she said. She held up a pink fingernail and blew on it gently. "People have toilets, you know, Winnie, flush toilets. And let's move on to shooting people. Most mothers don't shoot their daughter's boyfriends in the driveway."

"I know that," Winnie said. "I don't have to go away to know that. We'd have a flush toilet, too, except Daddy says a septic tank—"

"I know what Daddy says," Julie told her, twisting the cap to the nail polish carefully, her fingers splayed out. "But it's Mom. She wants to stay in this house because her poor now-lost-and-legendary father bought it when she got pregnant with me, and Ted didn't have a nickel to spare. Daddy'd move out of here tomorrow, he'd move into town."

"There's nothing wrong with living here," Winnie said.

Julie smiled calmly. "Mommy's little girl."

"I am not."

"Oh, Winnie," Julie said. But she was squinting at her baby finger, and then she unscrewed the nail polish again. "You know what Mrs. Kitteridge said in class one day?" Julie asked.

Winnie waited.

"I always remember she said one day, 'Don't be scared of your hunger. If you're scared of your hunger, you'll just be one more ninny like everyone else.' "

Winnie waited, watching Julie do her baby fingernail once more with the perfect pink polish. "Nobody knew what she meant," Julie said, holding her nail up, looking at it.

"What *did* she mean?" Winnie asked.

"Well, that's just it. At first I think most of us thought she was talking about food. I mean, we were just seventh graders—sorry, Doodle— but as time went by, I think I understand it more."

"She teaches math," Winnie said.

"I know that, dopey. But she'd say these weird things, very powerfully. That's partly why kids were scared of her. You don't have to be scared of her—if she's still teaching next year."

"I am, though. Scared of her."

Julie looked at her sideways. "Lot scarier stuff right here in this house."

Winnie frowned, pushed her hand into the pillow near her on her bed.

"Oh, Winnie," Julie said. "Come here." She held out her arms. Winnie stayed where she was. "Oh, poor Winnie-doodle," Julie said, and she moved down the bed to where Winnie was, put her arms around her awkwardly, holding her hands out to keep the nail polish from smudging. Julie kissed the side of Winnie's head, and then she let her go.

In the morning, Anita's eyes were puffy, as though all that sleep had exhausted her. But she sipped her coffee, and said brightly, "Whew, that was some sleep I had."

"I don't want to go to church this morning," Julie said. "I'm not ready to have everyone look at me yet."

Winnie thought there might be a fight about that, but there wasn't. "Okay," said Anita, after she had considered for a minute. "All right, honey. Just don't sit around and mope while we're gone."

Julie piled the breakfast dishes into the sink, her pink nails shining. "I won't," she said.

In the hallway, Jim said to Winnie, "Doodle-bug, give your old father a hug," but Winnie brushed past him, patting his arm that he held out, before going to put on her church clothes. In church she sat with her dress sticking to the pew. It was a hot summer day; the church windows were open but there wasn't any breeze. Through the window Winnie saw in the distance a few dark clouds. Next to her, she heard her father's stomach growl. He looked at her and winked, but Winnie looked out the window again. She thought how she had passed by him when he'd asked for a hug, how she had seen her mother do that to him, too, only sometimes Anita would touch his shoulders and kiss the air beside his cheek. Maybe Julie was right, she was Mommy's girl, and maybe Winnie was going to turn out to be like her, someone who brushed past people even when she was smiling; maybe she'd grow up and shoot people in the driveway with a rifle.

Tiredly, she stood up for the hymn. Her mother reached to straighten a wrinkle in the back of Winnie's dress.

On Winnie's pillow was a folded note. "PLEASE make them think I'm out taking a walk. I've gone to Moody's to catch the bus. My life depends on this. I love you, Doodle, I do." Hot tingles shot through Winnie's arms and fingers; even her nose and chin tingled.

"Winnifred," her mother called. "Come peel some potatoes, please."

The bus to Boston stopped at Moody's at eleven thirty. Julie would still be there, probably trying to stay out of sight, maybe sitting in the grass behind the store. They could go get her in the car. She'd cry and there'd be a big fight and someone might have to give her a pill, but they could still do it, she was still here.

"Winnifred?" Anita called again.

Winnie took her church clothes off, took her hair out of its ponytail, so the hair would fall in front of her face.

"You all right?" Anita asked.

"I have a headache." Winnie scooched down and took some potatoes from the bin in the bottom cupboard.

"You need some food in your stomach," her mother said. "Where's your sister? You'd think she could have started the potatoes." Anita put the Sunday steak into the broiling pan.

Winnie washed the potatoes and started to peel them. She filled a pot with water and cut the potatoes; they plopped into the water. She looked at the clock above the stove.

"Where *is* she?" Anita asked again.

"Gone for a walk, I think," Winnie said.

"Well, we're about to eat," her mother said, and then Winnie almost cried.

Uncle Kyle had told a story once about being on a train that hit and killed a teenage girl. He said he would never forget how he sat there looking out the window of the train as they waited for the police, thinking about the girl's parents, how they would still be in their house watching TV or doing the dishes, not even knowing that their daughter was dead, while he sat on the train and knew.

"I'll go look for her," Winnie said. She rinsed her hands and dried them.

Anita glanced at the clock and turned over the steak. "Just give a holler," she said. "Out by the back woods."

Winnie opened the back door and stepped outside. The clouds were moving in. The air had gotten chilly and smelled like the ocean. Her father stepped out onto the back porch. "About to eat, Winnie." Winnie pulled at the leaves of a bayberry bush. "Look kind of lonesome out there," he said.

The phone rang in the kitchen. Her father went back inside and Winnie followed, watching from the hall.

"Yes, hello, Kyle," her mother said.

In the afternoon it started to rain. The house got dark and the rain beat down on the roof and against the big windowpane in the living room. Winnie sat in a chair and watched the ocean, choppy and gray. Uncle Kyle had gone to Moody's for a paper, and he had seen Julie up near the back of the bus as it pulled away. Anita had rushed into the girls' bedroom, tearing things apart. Julie's duffel bag was gone, and most of her underwear, and her makeup, too. Anita found Julie's note to Winnie. "You *knew*," she said to Winnie, and Winnie understood that something had changed for good, something more than Julie's running away. Uncle Kyle had come over, but now he was gone.

Winnie sat in the living room with her father. She kept thinking of Julie on the bus riding through the rain, staring out the window at the turnpike going by. She thought her father was probably picturing this too, maybe imagining the sound of the bus's windshield wipers going back and forth.

"What're you going to do when you finish the boat?" Winnie asked.

Her father looked surprised. "Well," he said. "Dunno. Go for a ride, I guess."

Winnie smiled to be nice, because she didn't think he'd be going anywhere. "That'll be fun," she said.

Toward evening the rain stopped. Anita hadn't come out of her room. Winnie tried to figure out if Julie was there yet; she didn't know how long it took to get to Boston, but it took a long time.

"I wonder if she's got some money with her," her father said, but Winnie didn't answer—she didn't know.

Rain dripped from the side of the roof and off the trees. She thought of all the starfish she had laid out on the rock, all of them drenched from the rain. After a while her father stood up and went to the window. "Didn't plan on things working out like this," he said, and Winnie had a sudden thought of him on his own wedding day. Unlike Anita, he had not been married before. Anita had not worn a white dress, because of Julie. "You only wear white once," Anita had said. There were no wedding pictures—that Winnie knew of, anyway—of her parents' wedding day.

Her father turned around. "Pancakes?" he asked her.

Winnie didn't want pancakes. "Sure," she said.

Security

It was May, and Olive Kitteridge was going to New York. She had never, in her seventy-two years, set foot in the city, although she had on two occasions many years ago sat in a car and ridden past it—Henry at the wheel, worried about this exit and that—and seen from a distance the skyline, buildings against buildings, gray against a gray sky. Like a science-fiction city, it had seemed, built on a moon. It held no appeal, not then, not now—although back when those planes ripped through the towers, Olive had sat in her bedroom and wept like a baby, not so much for this country but for the city itself, which had seemed to her to become suddenly no longer a foreign, hardened place, but as fragile as a class of kindergarten children, brave in their terror. Jumping from the windows—it clutched her heart, and she had felt a private, sickening shame to know that two of the dark-haired hijackers, silently thrilled with their self-righteousness, had come down through Canada and walked through the airport in Portland on their way to such hellacious destruction. (She might have driven right by them that morning, who knows?)

Time passed, though, as it does, and the city—at least from Olive's faraway vantage—seemed eventually itself again, no place she cared to go, in spite of the fact that her only son had moved there recently, acquired a second wife and two children not his. The new wife, Ann—if you were to believe the one photograph that took ages to download—was as tall and big as a man; pregnant now with Christopher's child, and according to a characteristically cryptic e-mail from Chris, with no attention paid to punctuation or any use of capital letters, Ann was tired and "had pukes." In addition, it seemed Theodore turned into a hellion each morning before going off to preschool. Olive had been summoned to help.

The request had not been put this way. After sending the note, Christopher had called from his office and said, "Ann and I've been hoping you'll come visit for a couple of weeks." To Olive, this meant they needed help. It had been years since she'd been in the company of her son for a couple of weeks.

"Three days," she said. "After that I stink like fish."

"A week, then," Chris had countered, adding, "You could walk Theodore to school. It's around the corner one block."

Like hell, she thought. Her tulips, seen right there through her dining room window, jubilant cups of yellow and red, would be dead by the time she got back. "Give me a few days to make the arrangements," she said. The arrangements took twenty minutes. She called Emily Buck at the post office and told her to hold her mail.

"Oh, this'll be good for you, Olive," said Emily.

"Ay-yuh," said Olive. "I'm sure."

Then she called Daisy up the road and asked her to water the garden. Daisy, who'd had fantasies—Olive was certain of this—of living out her widowhood with Henry Kitteridge if only Olive could have died early on, said she would be glad to water the garden. "Henry was always so good about watering mine when I went to see Mother," Daisy said. Daisy added, "This will be good for you, Olive. You'll have a good time."

A good time was not something Olive expected to have again.

That afternoon she drove to the nursing home and explained to

Henry what she was up to, while he sat motionless in his wheelchair, the expression on his face one he frequently wore—that of confused politeness, as though something had been placed on his lap that he could not comprehend, but which he felt required a polite expression of thanks. Whether or not he was deaf, there was still some question. Olive did not believe he was, nor did Cindy, the one nice nurse. Olive gave Cindy the number in New York.

"She a good person, this new one?" Cindy counted pills into Dixie cups.

"Haven't a clue," Olive said.

"Fertile, though, I guess," Cindy said, picking up the tray of meds.

Olive had never been in a plane by herself. Not that she was by herself now, of course; there were four other passengers with her in this plane, which was half the size of a Greyhound bus. All of them had gone through security with the complacency of cows; Olive seeming the only one with trepidation. She'd had to remove her suede sandals and the big Timex watch of Henry's that she wore on her large wrist. Perhaps it was the queer intimacy of standing there in her panty-hosed feet, worried that the watch might not work after it went through the machine, that made her, for one half a second, fall in love with the big security fellow, who said kindly, "There you go, ma'am," handing her the plastic bowl that had rolled toward her with the watch in it. The pilots, as well—both looking twelve years old with their unworried brows—had been kind, in the easy way they'd asked Olive if she'd mind sitting toward the back for weight distribution, before they climbed into the cockpit, closing the steel door. A thought unfolded before her—their mothers should be proud.

And then as the little plane climbed higher and Olive saw spread out below them fields of bright and tender green in this morning sun, farther out the coastline, the ocean shiny and almost flat, tiny white wakes behind a few lobster boats—then Olive felt something she had not expected to feel again: a sudden surging greediness for life. She leaned forward, peering out the window: sweet pale clouds, the sky as blue as your hat, the new green of the fields, the broad expanse of water—seen from up here it all appeared wondrous, amazing. She remembered what hope was, and this was it. That inner churning that moves you forward, plows you through life the way the boats below plowed the shiny water, the way the plane was plowing forward to a place new, and where she was needed. She had been asked to be part of her son's life.

But at the airport Christopher seemed furious. She had forgotten that, because of security, he would not be able to meet her at the gate, and apparently it hadn't occurred to him to remind her. Why this should make him so angry, Olive couldn't figure out. She was the one who had wandered around the luggage area with panic bubbling through her, her face hot as fire by the time Christopher found her lumbering back up the stairs. "Godfrey," he said, not even reaching to take her bag. "Why can't you just get a cell phone like everyone else?"

It was not until later, hurtling down an expressway with four lanes and more cars than Olive had ever seen moving together, that Christopher said, "So, how is he?"

"The same," she answered, and said nothing more until they had taken an exit and were moving through streets lined with uneven buildings, Christopher lurching the car around double-parked trucks. "How's Ann?" Olive asked then, shifting her feet for the first time since she'd gotten into the car, and Christopher said, "Uncomfortable." Adding, in a didactic, doctor-ish tone, "It gets very uncomfortable," as though entirely ignorant of the fact that Olive herself had once been pregnant, uncomfortable. "And Annabelle's waking up in the night again."

"Ducky," said Olive. "Duck soup." The buildings were lower now, all with steep stoops in the front. She said, "You indicated little Teddy's become quite a handful."

"Theodore," said Christopher. "God, whatever you do, don't call him Teddy." He pulled the car up sharply, and backed into a space near the sidewalk. "Honestly, Mom?" Christopher ducked his head, his blue eyes looking straight into hers, the way he would do years ago. He said softly, "Theodore has always been a little piece of crap."

Confusion, which had started the moment she had stepped off the plane and not found anyone waiting for her, and which had then grown into an active panic on the airport's escalator, changing into a stunned block of perfect oddness the whole drive in, now, as Olive stepped from the car onto the sidewalk, seemed to cause everything to sway around her, so that reaching to get her bag from the backseat, she actually stumbled and fell against the car. "Easy, Mom," said Christopher. "I'll get the bag. Just watch where you step."

"Oh, goodness," she said, for already her foot had landed on a crusty roll of dog mess there on the sidewalk. "Oh, hell."

"I hate that," Christopher said. He took her arm. "It's the guy who works on the subway and comes home early in the mornings. I've seen him out here while his dog takes a shit, looking around to see no one'll catch him, just leaving it there."

"My goodness," said Olive, because adding to her confusion was the additional factor of her son's loquaciousness. She had seldom heard him speak so passionately or so long, and she was quite certain she had never heard him use the word *shit*. She laughed, a false, hard sound. The earlier clarity of the young pilots' faces came to her as something she had dreamed.

Christopher unlocked a grated gate beneath a large brown stoop of stairs, and stepped back to let her enter. "So, this is your house," she said, and gave that laugh again, because she could have wept at the darkness, the smell of old dog hair and soiled laundry, a sourness that seemed to come from the walls. The house she and Henry had built for Chris back home in Maine had been beautiful—filled with light, the windows large to show the lawns, and lilies, and fir trees.

She stepped on a plastic toy and almost broke her neck. "Where is everyone?" she asked. "Christopher, I've got to take off that shoe before I track dog mess all through the house."

"Just leave it here," he said, stepping past her, and so she slipped off the one suede sandal, and walking through a dark hallway, she thought how she had forgotten to bring another pair of panty hose.

"They're out back in the garden," said her son, and she followed him through a capacious, dark living room, into a small kitchen that was cluttered with toys, a high chair, pots spread over the counter, open boxes of cereal and Minute Rice. A grimy white sock lay on the table. And suddenly it seemed to Olive that every house she had ever gone into depressed her, except for her own, and the one they had built for Christopher. It was as though she had never outgrown that feeling she must have had as a child—that hypersensitivity to the foreign smell of someone else's home, the fear that coated the unfamiliar way a bathroom door closed, the creak in a staircase worn by footsteps not one's own.

She emerged, blinking, into a small outdoor area—this could not possibly be what he meant as a garden. She stood on a square of concrete. Around her was a chicken wire fence that had been knocked into by something large enough to leave a whole section gaping and broken. A child's plastic swimming pool was before her. In it, a naked baby sat, staring at her, while a small, dark-haired boy stood nearby, his wet swim trunks sticking to his skinny thighs. He stared at her as well. Behind him, a black dog lay on an old dog bed.

Not far from Olive, a wooden staircase rose, leading to a wooden deck above her head. From the shadow beneath the stairs came the word, "Olive." A woman appeared, holding a barbecue spatula. "Gosh, there you are. What a sight for sore eyes. I am so *glad* to meet you, Olive." Briefly Olive had the image of a huge walking girl-doll; the hair was black and cut straight above the shoulders, the face as open and guileless as a simpleton's.

"You must be Ann," said Olive, but the words were lost in a hug the large girl wrapped her in, the spatula falling to the ground, causing the dog to groan and stand up; Olive could see this from just a sliver of vision left to her. Taller than Olive, and with a stomach huge and hard, this Ann held her long arms around her and kissed the side of Olive's head. Olive did not kiss people. And to be held in the arms of a woman taller than she was—well, Olive was positive this had never happened before.

"Do you mind if I call you Mom?" asked the girl, stepping back but holding Olive by her elbows. "I'm so dying to call you Mom."

"Call me anything you want," Olive replied. "I guess I'll call you Ann."

The boy moved like a slithery animal to grab hold of his mother's ample thigh.

"You're Thaddeus, I suppose," said Olive.

The boy began to cry.

"Theodore," said Ann. "Honey, that's all right. People make mistakes. We've talked about that, right?"

A rash stood out high on Ann's cheek, and ran down the side of her neck, where it disappeared under a huge black T-shirt worn over black leggings. Her feet were bare; bits of a pink polish were on her toenails.

"Perhaps I'd better sit down," Olive said.

"Oh, absolutely," Ann said. "Honey, pull that chair over here for your mother."

In the midst of the aluminum beach chair scraping across the cement and the boy crying and Ann saying, "God, Theodore, what *is* it?"—in the midst of all this, one shoe off and one shoe on, sinking back into the beach chair, Olive distinctly heard the words *Praise Jesus.*

"Theodore, honey, please, please, please stop crying."

In the plastic pool the baby slapped the water and shrieked. "Jesus, Annabelle," said Christopher. "Keep it down."

Praise the Lord, came distinctly from somewhere above.

"What in God's name—" said Olive, putting her head back, squinting upward.

"We rent the top floor to a Christian," Ann said in a whisper, rolling her eyes. "I mean, who would think here in this neighborhood we'd get stuck with a tenant who's a Christian?"

"Christian?" said Olive, looking back at her daughter-in-law, thoroughly confused. "Are you a Muslim, Ann? Is there a problem?"

"Muslim?" The girl's plain, big face looked pleasantly at Olive while she bent to pick up the baby from the pool. "I'm not a Muslim." Quizzi-cally: "Wait, *you're* not a Muslim, are you? Christopher never—"

"Oh, godfrey," said Olive.

"What she means," Christopher explained to his mother, fiddling with a large barbecue grill near the staircase, "is that most people in this neighborhood don't go to church. We live in the *cool* part of Brook-lyn, hippity hop as hell, Mother dear, where people are either too artsy-fartsy to believe in God, or too busy making money. So it's somewhat unusual to have a tenant who's a real so-called Christian."

"You mean like a fundamentalist," said Olive, amazed once again at how talkative her son had become.

"Right," said Ann. "That's what he is. You know, fundamentally Christian."

The boy had stopped his crying and, still holding his mother's leg, said to Olive in a high, earnest voice, "Whenever we swear, the parrot says 'Praise Jesus' or 'God is king.'"

And to Olive's horror and amazement, the child looked skyward and yelled, "Shit!"

"Honey," said Ann, and smoothed his hair.

Praise God, came the response from above.

"That's a parrot?" asked Olive. "Good Lord, it sounds like my Aunt Ora."

"Yeah, a parrot," said Ann. "Weird, huh."

"You couldn't have said no pets allowed?"

"Oh, we'd never do that. We love pets. Dog-Face is part of our fam-ily." Ann nodded in the direction of the black dog, who, having re-turned to his ratty bed, now had his long face resting on his paws, his eyes closed.

Olive could barely eat her dinner. She had thought Christopher was going to grill hamburgers. But he had grilled tofu hot dogs, and for the grown-ups had, of all things, diced up a can of oysters and poked them into these so-called hot dogs.

"Are you okay, Mom?" It was Ann who asked.

"Fine," said Olive. "When I travel, I sometimes find I'm not hungry. I think I'll just eat this hot dog roll."

"Sure. Help yourself. Theodore, isn't it nice to have Grandma come and stay?"

Olive put the roll back onto her plate. Not once had it occurred to her that she was "Grandma" to Ann's children, who had been, she only recently discovered as the hot dogs had been set before her, fathered by two different men. Theodore did not respond to his mother's question but gazed at Olive while he ate with his mouth open, making appalling chewing sounds.

Less than ten minutes, and the meal was over. Olive told Chris that she'd like to help clean up but that she didn't know where anything went. "Nowhere," Chris said. "Can't you tell? In this house nothing goes anywhere."

"Mom, you go make yourself comfortable," Ann said.

So Olive went down into the basement, where they had brought her earlier with her little suitcase, and she lay down on the double bed. The fact was, the basement was the nicest place Olive had seen in the house. It was "finished" and painted all white, and even had, next to the washing machine, a white telephone.

She wanted to cry. She wanted to wail like a child. She sat up and dialed the phone.

"Put him on," she said, and waited until she could hear only silence. "Smack, Henry," she said, and she waited a while longer until she thought she heard a tiny grunt.

"Well. She's a *big* girl," said Olive. "Your new daughter-in-law. Graceful as a truck driver. A little dumb, I think. Something I can't put my finger on. But nice. You'd like her. You two would get along fine."

Olive looked around the basement room she was in, and thought she heard Henry grunt again. "No, she's not going to hightail it up the coast anytime soon. Got her hands full here. Belly full, too. They've got me down in the basement. It's kind of nice, Henry. Painted white." She tried to think what else to say, what Henry would want to hear. "Chris seems good," she said. She paused for a long time after that. "Talkative," she added. "Okay, Henry," she finally said, and hung up.

Back upstairs, no one was around. Thinking they must be putting the children to bed, Olive stepped through the kitchen and out onto the concrete yard, where twilight was gathering.

"Caught me," said Ann, and Olive's heart banged.

"Godfrey. You caught me. I didn't see you sitting there."

Ann was holding a cigarette in one hand, balancing a beer on her high belly with the other, her legs apart as she sat on a stool by the barbecue. "Have a seat," Ann said, gesturing toward the beach chair Olive had been sitting in earlier. "Unless it makes you crazy to see a pregnant woman drink and smoke. Which I totally understand if it does. But it's just one cigarette and one beer a day. You know, when the kids finally get put down. I call it my meditation time."

"I see," Olive said. "Well, meditate away. I can go back inside."

"Oh, no. I'd love your company."

In the dusk she saw the girl smile at her. Say what you might about judging a book by its cover, Olive always found faces revealing. Still— the bovine nature of this girl was baffling. *Was* Ann a bit stupid? Olive had taught school enough years to know that large amounts of insecurity could take the form of stupidity. She lowered herself into her chair, and looked away. She didn't want to guess what might be seen in her own face.

Cigarette smoke wafted in front of her. It amazed her that anyone would smoke these days, and she couldn't help but feel it as a kind of assault. "Say," Olive said, "that doesn't make you feel sick?"

"What, smoking this?"

"Yes. I shouldn't think that would help the nausea."

"What nausea?"

"I thought you had the pukes."

"The pukes?" Ann dropped the cigarette into the bottle of beer. She looked over at Olive, her dark eyebrows raised.

"You haven't been sick with the pregnancy?"

"Oh, no. I'm a horse." Ann patted her belly. "I just keep spittin' these things out with no problem."

"Apparently." Olive wondered if the girl was tipsy from the beer. "Where's your newest husband?"

"He's reading Theodore a story. It's nice to have them bonding."

Olive opened her mouth to ask what kind of bond Theodore had with his real father, but she stopped. Maybe you weren't supposed to say "real father" these days.

"How old are you, Mom?" Ann was scratching at her cheek.

"I'm seventy-two," Olive said, "and I wear a size ten shoe."

"Hey, cool. I wear a size ten. I've always had big feet. You look good for seventy-two," Ann added. "My mother's sixty-three and she—"

"She what?"

"Oh." Ann shrugged. "You know, she just doesn't look so good." Ann hoisted herself up, leaned toward the grill, where she picked up a box of kitchen matches. "If you don't mind, Mom, I'm just going to have one more cigarette."

Olive did mind. This was Christopher's baby in there, trying to develop its own respiratory system right about now, and what kind of woman would jeopardize such a thing? But she said loudly, "Do whatever you want. I don't give a damn."

Praise God, came from above them.

"Oh, for heaven's sake," said Olive. "How can you stand that?"

"Sometimes I can't," Ann said, sitting down again, hugely.

"Well," Olive said, looking at her lap, smoothing her skirt. "It's temporary, I guess." She felt a need to look away as the girl lit a fresh cigarette.

Ann didn't respond. Olive heard her inhale, then exhale, as the smoke drifted back toward Olive. A realization flowered within her. The girl was panicking. How did Olive know this, never in seventy-two years having put a cigarette to her own lips? But the truth of it filled her. A light went on in the kitchen, and Olive watched through the grated windows as Christopher walked to the kitchen sink.

Sometimes, like now, Olive had a sense of just how desperately hard every person in the world was working to get what they needed. For most, it was a sense of safety, in the sea of terror that life increasingly became. People thought love would do it, and maybe it did. But even if, thinking of the smoking Ann, it took three different kids with three different fathers, it was never enough, was it? And Christopher—why had he been so foolhardy as to take all this on and not even, until *after the fact,* bother to tell his mother? In the near darkness, she saw Ann lean forward and put out her cigarette by sticking the tip into the baby pool. A tiny *phisst* of a sound, then the girl tossed the rest over toward the chicken wire fence.

A horse.

Christopher had not been truthful when he'd e-mailed that Ann had the pukes. Olive put her hand to her cheek, which had grown warm: Her son, being Christopher, would never be able to say, "Mom, I miss you." He had said his wife had the pukes.

Christopher stepped through the door, and her heart rose toward him. "Come join us," she said. "Come. Sit down."

He stood, his hands loosely on his hips, and then he took one hand and rubbed the back of his head slowly. Ann stood. "Sit here, Chris. If they're asleep I'm going to take a bath."

He didn't sit on the stool, but pulled up a chair next to Olive, and sat in the same sprawled-out way that he used to sit on the couch at home. She wanted to say, "It's awful good to see you, kid." But she didn't say anything, and he didn't either. For a long while they sat together like that. She would have sat on a patch of cement anywhere to have this—her son; a bright buoy bobbing in the bay of her own quiet terror.

"So, you're a landlord," she finally said, because the oddity of that struck her now.

"Yup."

"Are they a nuisance?"

"No. It's just the guy and his religious parrot."

"What's the fellow's name?"

"Sean O'Casey."

"Really? How old is he?" she asked, pulling herself up in her chair so her breath could move through.

"Let's see." Christopher sighed, shifting his weight. He was familiar to her now, slow moving, slow talking. " 'Bout my age, I think. Little younger."

"He's not related to Jim O'Casey, is he? The fellow that drove us to school? They had a shoe full of children. His wife had to move, once Jim went off the road that night. Remember that? She took the kids and went back to her mother. Is this guy upstairs one of those?"

"Haven't a clue," Christopher said. He sounded like Henry, the absentminded way Henry used to respond sometimes: Haven't a clue.

"It's a common enough name," Olive admitted. "Still, you might ask him if he's any relation to Jim O'Casey."

Christopher shook his head. "Don't care to." He yawned, stretching out farther, his head thrown back.

She had first seen him at a town meeting, held in the high school gym. She and Henry were sitting on folding chairs near the back, and this man stood near the bleachers, close to the door. He was tall, his eyes set back under that brow, his lips thin—a certain kind of Irish face. The eyes not brooding exactly, but very serious, looking at her with seriousness. She had felt a pulse of recognition, although she knew she'd never seen him before. Throughout the evening they had glanced at each other a number of times.

On their way out, someone introduced them, and she found he had come to town from West Annett, where he taught at the academy. He had moved with his family because they needed more room, living out there now by the Robinsons' farm. Six kids. Catholic. Such a tall man he was, Jim O'Casey, and during the introductions there seemed a whiff of shyness to him, a slight deferential ducking of his head, particularly as he shook Henry's hand, as though already apologizing for absconding with the affections of this man's wife. Henry, who didn't have a clue.

As she stepped out of the school that night, into the wintry air, walking with the talking Henry to their car in the far parking lot, she had the sensation that she had been seen. And she had not even known she'd felt invisible.

The next fall Jim O'Casey gave up his job at the academy and started teaching at the same junior high school Olive taught at, the one Christopher went to, and every morning, because it was on the way, he drove them both there, and then back home again. She was forty-four, he was fifty-three. She had thought of herself as practically old, but of course she hadn't been. She was tall, and the weight that came with menopause had only begun its foreshadowing, so at forty-four she had been a tall, full-figured woman, and without one *sound* of warning, like a huge silent truck that suddenly came from behind as she strolled down a country road, Olive Kitteridge had been swept off her feet.

"If I asked you to leave with me, would you do it?" He spoke quietly, as they ate their lunch in his office.

"Yes," she said.

He watched her as he ate the apple he always had for lunch, nothing else. "You would go home tonight and tell Henry?"

"Yes," she said. It was like planning a murder.

"Perhaps it's a good thing I haven't asked you."

"Yes."

They had never kissed, nor even touched, only passed by each other closely as they went into his office, a tiny cubicle off the library—they avoided the teachers' room. But after he said that that day, she lived with a kind of terror, and a longing that felt at times unendurable. But people endure things.

There were nights she didn't fall asleep until morning; when the sky lightened and the birds sang, and her body lay on the bed loosened, and she could not—for all the fear and dread that filled her—stop the foolish happiness. After such a night, a Saturday, she had been awake and restless and then had fallen asleep with suddenness; a sleep so heavy that when the phone beside the bed rang, she didn't know where she was. And then hearing the phone picked up, and Henry's soft voice, "Ollie, the saddest thing happened. Jim O'Casey drove off the road last night right into a tree. He's in intensive care down in Hanover. They don't know if he'll make it."

He died later that afternoon, and she supposed his wife was at his side, maybe some of the kids.

She didn't believe it. "I don't believe it," she kept saying to Henry. "What happened?"

"They say he lost control of the car." Henry shook his head. "Terrible," he said.

Oh, she was a crazy woman, privately. Absolutely nuts. She was so mad at Jim O'Casey. She was so mad, she went into the woods and hit a tree hard enough to make her hand bleed. She cried down by the creek until she gagged. And she fixed supper for Henry. Taught school all day, and came home and fixed supper for Henry. Or some nights he fixed it for her because she said she was tired, and he'd open a can of spaghetti, and God, that stuff made her sick. She lost weight, looked better than ever for a while, which lacerated her heart with the irony. Henry reached for her often those nights. She was certain he'd had no idea. He would have said something, because Henry was that way, he did not keep things to himself. But in Jim O'Casey there had been a wariness, a quiet anger, and she had seen herself in him, had said to him once, We're both cut from the same piece of bad cloth. He had just watched her, eating his apple.

"Oh, wait a minute," Christopher said, sitting up straight. "Maybe I did ask him. Yeah. He said his father was the one who drove into a tree in Crosby, Maine, one night."

"What?" Olive looked at her son through the darkness.

"That's when he got really religious."

"Are you serious?"

"Thus, the parrot." Christopher extended an arm upward.

"Oh, my goodness," said Olive.

Christopher dropped his arm with an exaggerated gesture of defeat, or disgust. "Mom, I'm kidding you, for crying out loud. I have no idea who the guy is."

Through the kitchen window Ann appeared, wearing a bathrobe and a towel around her head.

"Never liked that guy," Christopher said, musingly.

"Who, the tenant? Keep your voice down."

"No, what's his name. Mr. Jim O'Casey. So stupid to drive into a tree."

There were fingernail clippings and soggy Cheerios on the table when Olive sat down with her cup of coffee in the morning. Ann was in the next room getting Theodore ready, and called out, "Good morning, Mom. Did you sleep?"

"Fine." Olive raised a hand in a brief wave. She had slept better than she had in four years—since Henry's stroke. The same hopefulness she had felt on the plane seemed to return as she fell into sleep, holding her on a pillow of soft joy. Ann had no morning sickness; Christopher missed his mother. She was with her son, he needed her. Whatever rupture had occurred, starting years ago, as innocuously as the rash on Ann's cheek, spreading downward till it had split her from her son—it could be healed. It would be leaving its scar, but one accumulated these scars, and went on, as she would now go on with her son.

"Help yourself, Mom," Ann called. "To anything."

"Right-o," Olive called back. She got up and wiped the table with a sponge, though touching other people's nail clippings was hardly her thing. She washed her hands thoroughly.

Other people's kids weren't her thing either. Theodore came and stood in the doorway, a knapsack on his back, so big that even while the child faced Olive, you could see the knapsack on both sides of him. She picked a doughnut from a box she had seen high on the counter and sat down again with her coffee. "You shouldn't have a doughnut before you have your growing food," the boy told her, in a tone amazingly sanctimonious for a child.

"I'd say I'd grown enough, wouldn't you?" Olive replied, taking a big bite.

Ann appeared behind Theodore. " 'Scuse me, honey pie," she said as she stepped past him to the refrigerator. She was holding the baby girl on her hip, the baby's head turning around to stare at Olive. "Theodore, you need two juice boxes today.

"It's field trip day," she said to Olive, who was tempted to stick her tongue out at that damn little staring baby. "The school takes them to the beach and I get worried about him getting dehydrated."

"I don't blame you," said Olive, finishing her doughnut. "Chris ever tell you about the sunstroke he got when we went to Greece? He was twelve. A witch doctor came over and did some swoopy arm motions in front of him."

"Really?" said Ann. "Theodore, do you want grape or orange?"

"Grape."

"I *think*," Ann said, "grape makes you more thirsty. What do you think, Mom? Doesn't grape make you more thirsty than orange?"

"Haven't a clue."

"Orange, honey." And Theodore began to cry. Ann gave Olive a hesitant look. "I was going to ask you to walk him to school, just a block—"

"No," Theodore cried. "I don't want her walking me to school. . . . I don't want her walking me to school. . . ."

Shut the hell up, Olive thought. Chris was right, you are a little piece of crap.

Ann said, "Oh, Theodore, pleeeease don't cry."

Olive pushed back her chair. "How about I take Dog-Face to the park?"

"You don't mind picking up his poops in the bag?"

"No," said Olive. "I certainly don't. Having stepped in one myself."

———

She was, to be truthful, uneasy about walking the dog to the park. But the dog was a good boy. He sat while they waited for the light to change. She walked him past picnic tables and big garbage bins overloaded with food and newspapers and tinfoil streaked with barbecue sauce, and he did strain a bit on the leash toward all that, but when they got to the meadow, she let him run free, as Ann had said she could do. "Now stay nearby," she said. He sniffed around, not running off.

She noticed a man watching her. He was young, and wore a leather jacket, even though it was warm enough that you didn't need to wear a leather jacket. He stood beside the trunk of a huge oak, and called to his dog, a short-haired white dog with a sharp pink nose. The man made his way over to her. "Are you Olive?" he finally asked.

Her face got hot. "Olive who?" she said.

"Christopher's mother. Ann said you were coming to visit."

"I see," said Olive, reaching into her pocket and finding her sunglasses. "Well, here I am." She put on her sunglasses and turned to watch for Dog-Face.

"You staying at the house?" the man asked eventually, and Olive didn't really think it was any of his business.

"I am," said Olive. "The basement's very nice."

"Your son stuck you in the basement?" the man said, and Olive especially didn't think that was nice.

"It's a very pleasant basement," Olive said. "It suits me quite well." She looked straight ahead but she could feel him looking at her. She wanted to say: "Haven't you ever seen an old lady before?"

She watched her son's dog sniff the rear end of a passing golden retriever, whose heavy-breasted young owner held a metal mug in one hand, the leash in the other.

"Some of these old brownstones have rats and mice in their basements," the man said.

"No rats," said Olive. "A nice daddy longlegs went by. Didn't bother me a bit."

"Your son's practice must do well. These places cost a fortune now."

Olive didn't answer. That he should say this was vulgar.

"Blanche!" called the man, starting after his dog. "Blanche, come here *now*."

Blanche had no intention of coming, Olive noted. Blanche had found an old, dead pigeon, and the man went berserk. "Drop it, Blanche, drop it!" Blanche had the mess in her pointed mouth, and slunk away from her approaching owner.

"Jesus Christ," said the big-breasted woman with the golden retriever, because the bloodied insides of the pigeon's body were right there, sliding out of Blanche's mouth.

Praise God, came a voice from the oak tree.

Olive called to Dog-Face, clicked the leash onto his collar, then turned and walked home. Right before she got to the house, she glanced behind her and saw the man crossing the street with Blanche on a leash, and a parrot on his shoulder. A sense of disorientation came over her. Was that the *tenant*? That pretentious leather jacket, a manner that seemed—to Olive—confrontational. Unlocking the grated gate, she felt as though by eight o'clock in the morning a small battle had been fought. She didn't think her son should be living in this city. He was not a fighter.

The kitchen was empty. Upstairs she heard a shower running. She sat down heavily in a wooden chair. She had once known each of their six names. Now she could remember nothing but the wife's name, Rose, and one girl—Andrea? Sean could very possibly have been one of the youngest. But how many thousands of Sean O'Caseys were wandering around, and did it even matter? As though remembering something heard about a distant relative, Olive sat in the dark kitchen and remembered a person—herself—who had once thought that if she left Henry for Jim, she'd have done anything for Jim's children—her love had felt that huge.

"Christopher," she said. He had stepped into the kitchen, his hair wet, dressed for work. "I think I met your tenant in the park. I didn't know he had a dog as well as a Christian parrot."

Chris nodded, drank from a coffee mug as he stood by the sink.

"I didn't care for him."

Christopher raised one eyebrow. "How surprising."

"Didn't think he was a bit nice. I thought Christians were supposed to be nice."

Her son turned to put his mug into the sink. "If I had more energy, I'd laugh. But Annabelle was up again and I'm tired."

"Christopher, what's the story with Ann's mother?"

He wiped a kitchen towel across the counter in one swipe. "She's an alcoholic."

"Oh, dear God."

"Yeah, she's a mess. And the father, dead now—praise God, as the parrot would say—was in the army. Made them do push-ups each morning."

"Push-ups. Well, I can see you two have a great deal in common."

"What do you mean?" His face seemed to flush slightly.

"I was being sarcastic. Imagine your father making you do push-ups."

That he had no response unsettled her slightly. "Your tenant wanted to know how you afforded this place," she said.

Chris scowled, familiar to her again. "None of his damn business."

"No, that's exactly what I thought."

Christopher glanced at his watch, and she had a sudden fear of his leaving, of being left alone with Ann and those kids all day in this dark house. "How long does it take you to get to work?" she asked.

"Half hour. The subway's packed at rush hour."

Olive had never been on a subway. "Chris, do you worry about another attack?"

"Attack? Terrorist attack?"

Olive nodded.

"No. Sort of. Not really. I mean, it's going to happen, so you can't just sit around waiting."

"No, I can see that."

Chris ran his fingers through his wet hair, gave his head a quick shake. "There was a store on the corner here, run by guys from Pakistan. Hardly anything in the store. A few cupcakes, a bottle of Coke. Clearly some kind of front. But I'd stop in to buy the paper each morning, and the guy would be real nice. 'How you doing today,' he'd say, with his long yellow teeth showing. He'd give me this smile, and I'd smile back, and it was sort of understood that he had nothing against me, but if he knew which subway was going to blow, he'd smile and watch me walk to get on it." Chris shrugged.

"How do you know that?"

"I don't. But I do. The store closed, the guy said he had to go back to Pakistan. It was in his eyes, Mom, that's all I'm saying."

Olive nodded, looking at the big wooden table. "Still, you like it here?"

"Pretty much."

But the day passed okay, and then another day passed. She took the dog to the park earlier, so as to avoid Sean. And while everything remained strange, like a foreign country, she could not let go of a certain happiness inside her; she was with her son. At times he was talkative, at times he was silent, and he was most familiar to her then. She did not understand his new life, or Ann, who said things that seemed to come from a Hallmark card, but she did not see in Chris any signs of moroseness, and that's what mattered—that, and simply being with him again. When Theodore called her "Grandma," she answered. And while she really couldn't stand the child, she put up with him, reading him a story one night. (Though when she left out a word and he corrected her, she could have swatted his dark head.) He was her son's family, and so was she. When she tired of the child, or when the baby cried, she retired to the basement and lay on the bed, thinking how glad she was that she had never left Henry for Jim. Not that she would have, although she remembered that she felt she would have—and what would have happened to Christopher then?

On the third morning, when Ann returned from taking Theodore to school, and Christopher was off at work, the baby splashed in the pool out back while Olive sat in the beach chair. "Can you watch her, Mom, while I collect some laundry?" Ann asked, and Olive said, "Of course."

Annabelle fretted, but Olive tossed her a twig from nearby, and Annabelle slapped it against the water. Olive gazed up at the deck, looking for any sign of the parrot, who would sometimes say, unprovoked, *God is king.* "Hells bells," Olive said, then said it again, louder, and *Praise God* came from upstairs. She slipped off her sandals, scratched her feet, settled back in her chair, pleased to have maneuvered the response. It did sound just like her Aunt Ora. She got up, went into the kitchen to get a doughnut, and as she stood munching it by the sink, she suddenly remembered the baby.

"Oh, good God," she whispered, and hurried outside. Annabelle was trying to stand up. Olive bent to steady the toddler, and Annabelle slipped; Olive moved around the edge of the pool, attempting to lift the child and keep her face out of the water. Annabelle got more and more agitated, slipping and crying, turning away from Olive. "For the love of God, stop it now!" Olive said, and the baby stared at her, and then cried again.

Our father who art in heaven, shrieked the parrot.

"That's a new one," said Ann, stepping into the backyard with a dish towel.

"She's trying to stand up," Olive explained. "And I couldn't quite get hold of her."

"Yeah, she's about ready to walk any day now." Ann, in spite of her large belly, picked the child up easily.

Olive returned to her chair, shaken with the effort of grappling with the baby. Her panty hose were shredded from running around on this cement.

"Today's our wedding anniversary," Ann said, putting the dish towel around the shoulders of the baby.

"It is?"

"It is." Ann smiled, as though remembering something private. "Let's warm you up, little goose." Annabelle had spread her small legs on each side of Ann's bulbous belly, laid her wet head across Ann's big chest, and was sucking her thumb, shivering.

So easily, Olive could have said: "Well, it'd have been nice of you to tell me you were getting married, to begin with. It's a ghastly thing for a mother to find out later." But she only said, "Happy anniversary, then." That the baby had not drowned while she ate a doughnut had left her so relieved, that the anniversary seemed—while a painful reminder of how left out she had been—nothing to quibble about.

"Did Chris tell you how we met?"

"Not exactly. Not specifically." He had told her nothing.

"In a singles group for divorced people. I'd just found out I was pregnant with Annabelle—you know how when you get divorced, you do crazy things—and Annabelle was the result of a crazy thing—weren't you, chicken pie?" She kissed the top of the child's head.

This was the twenty-first century, thought Olive. It's not as though one had to rely on foam for birth control. But the still-relieved Olive said, with feigned generosity, "That's a nice idea, a singles group for divorced people." She nodded. "You all have that experience in common." She herself had gone to one meeting of a "support group" at the nursing home, and found it absolutely foolish, with foolish people saying foolish things—including the social worker who ran it, and said repeatedly in a sweet, calm voice, "To be angry about the event is normal." Olive never went back. Angry, she thought with disdain. Why be angry about a natural event, for God's sake? She couldn't stand the stupid social worker, or the grown man who sat next to her and wept openly for his stroked-out mother. Absolutely foolish. "Bad things happen," she wanted to say. "Where have you been?"

"It was a therapy group," Ann said. "So we could learn our own responsibility, accept our accountability, you know."

Olive didn't know. She said, "Christopher married the wrong woman, is what he did."

"But the question is why," Ann said in a solicitous way, shifting the baby. "If we learn why we do things, we won't make the same mistakes."

"I see," said Olive. She stretched her feet and felt the soft opening of another big run in her panty hose. She needed to go to a drugstore.

"It was just wonderful. Chris and I became very committed to the process, and committed to each other."

"That's nice," Olive finally said.

"The therapist is this amazing guy, Arthur. You just wouldn't believe how much we've learned." Ann rubbed the dish towel against the baby's back, looked over at Olive. She said, "Anxiety is anger, Mom."

"Is it?" Olive thought of the girl's cigarettes.

"Uh-huh. Almost always. When Arthur moved to New York, we did, too."

"You moved here because of a therapist?" Olive sat up straight in her beach chair. "Is this a cult?"

"No, no. We wanted to move here anyway, but it's great—because we still get to work with Arthur. Always plenty of issues to work on, you know."

"I bet."

Olive made, right then, a decision to accept all this. The first time around, Christopher married someone mean and pushy, and now he'd married someone dumb and nice. Well, it was none of her business. It was his life.

Olive went down into the basement and dialed the white telephone. Cindy said, "How's it going?"

"Fine. Different country down here. Can you put him on?" She held the phone between her neck and shoulder, started to peel her panty hose off, and remembered she had no other. "Henry," she said. "Today's their wedding anniversary. They're okay, but she's dumb, just like I thought. They're in therapy." She hesitated, looked around. "You're not to worry about that, Henry. In therapy they go straight after the mother. You come out smelling like a rose, I'm sure." Olive drummed her fingers on the washing machine. "I have to go, she's doing some laundry down here. I'm fine, Henry. I'll be back in a week."

Upstairs, Ann was feeding the baby part of a baked sweet potato. Olive sat and watched her, remembering how one year for their anniversary, Henry gave her a key chain with a four-leaf clover pressed inside a piece of thick clear plastic. "I called Henry and told him it was your anniversary."

"Oh, sweet," said Ann. Adding, "Anniversaries are nice. A little moment to reflect."

"I liked getting the presents," Olive said.

Walking behind her son and his large wife, and the big double stroller pushed ahead of them, Olive thought of her husband, in bed already perhaps; they tried putting them to bed earlier than small children were put to bed. "Spoke to your father today," she said, but Christopher apparently did not hear her. He and Ann were speaking intently, their heads tilted toward each other as they pushed the stroller along. Oh God, yes, she was glad she'd never left Henry. She'd never had a friend as loyal, as kind, as her husband.

And yet, standing behind her son, waiting for the traffic light to change, she remembered how in the midst of it all there had been times when she'd felt a loneliness so deep that once, not so many years ago, having a cavity filled, the dentist's gentle turning of her chin with his soft fingers had felt to her like a tender kindness of almost excruciating depth, and she had swallowed with a groan of longing, tears springing to her eyes. ("Are you all right, Mrs. Kitteridge?" the dentist had said.)

Her son turned to glance at her, and his lucid face was enough to keep her going, because she really was fatigued. Young people had no idea that you got to a stage where you couldn't just gallivant around, morning, noon, and night. Seven stages of life? Is that what Shakespeare said? Why, old age alone had seven stages! In between you prayed to die in your sleep. But she was glad she had not died; here was her family—and here was the ice cream shop, with an empty booth right up front. Olive sank gratefully onto the red cushioned seat.

"Praise God," she said. But they didn't hear her. They were busy un-buckling the kids, arranging the baby in a high chair, Theodore in his own chair pulled up to the edge. Ann's stomach was too big to get her into the booth, so she had to trade places with Theodore, make him sit in the booth, which he did only when Christopher took the child's small wrists in one hand, leaned forward, and said quietly, "Sit."

Something vaguely discomfiting moved in Olive. But the child sat. Politely, he said he wanted vanilla ice cream. "Christopher was always so polite," she said to him. "People used to compliment me on how po-lite my little son was." Did Christopher and Ann exchange a glance? No, they were just getting ready to order. It seemed impossible to Olive that Ann carried within her the grandchild of Henry, but there you were.

She ordered a butterscotch sundae.

"No fair," said Theodore. "I want a sundae."

"Well, okay, I guess," said Ann. "What kind?"

The kid looked distressed, as if the answer were beyond his com-prehension. Finally he said, putting his head down onto his arms, "I'll have a vanilla cone."

"Your father would have ordered a root beer float," said Olive to Christopher.

"No," said Christopher. "He would have ordered a dish of straw-berry ice cream."

"Nope," said Olive. "A root beer float."

"I want that—I want a root beer float," said Theodore, picking his head up. "What is it?"

Ann said, "They put lots of root beer in a glass, and then they float vanilla ice cream in it."

"I want it."

"He's not going to like it," said Christopher.

And he didn't. Theodore began to cry halfway through, and said it wasn't what he thought it would be. Olive, on the other hand, enjoyed her butterscotch sundae immensely, eating every spoonful, while Ann and Christopher talked about whether Theodore should be allowed to order again. Ann was for it, Christopher against. Olive stayed out of it but noticed that Christopher won.

Walking home, she had more energy, undoubtedly from her ice cream. And also because Chris walked with her, while Ann pushed the stroller ahead of them, the children, thank God, quiet. Chris's podiatry practice was going well. "People in New York take their feet very seriously," he said. Often, he saw twenty people a day.

"Good heavens, Chris. That seems a lot."

"I have a lot of bills to pay," he said. "And soon I'll have even more."

"I guess. Well, your father would be proud." It was getting dark. Through the lighted windows they passed, she could see people reading, watching television. She saw one man who appeared to be tickling his little son. A feeling of benevolence swept through her; she wished the best for everyone. In fact, saying good night once they got through the door, Olive felt she could have kissed them—her son, Ann, even the children, if she'd had to. But there was a feeling of distraction, and Chris and Ann said only, "Good night, Mom."

Downstairs she went, into the white basement. Stepping into the little closet of a bathroom, she flicked on the light, and saw in the mirror that across her blue cotton blouse was a long and prominent strip of sticky dark butterscotch sauce. A small feeling of distress took hold. They had seen this and not told her. She had become the old lady her Aunt Ora had been, when years ago she and Henry would take the old lady out for a drive, stopping some nights to get an ice cream, and Olive had watched as Aunt Ora had spilled melted ice cream down her front; she had felt repulsion at the sight of it. In fact, she was glad when Ora died, and Olive didn't have to continue to witness the pathetic sight.

And now she had become Ora. But she *wasn't* Aunt Ora, and her son should have pointed this out the minute it happened, as she would have to him, had he spilled something down his front! Did they think she was just one more baby they were carting around? She took the blouse off, ran hot water in the little sink, then decided not to wash it. She wrapped it in a plastic bag and stuck it into her suitcase.

The morning was hot. She sat in the backyard, on the beach chair. She had dressed before the sun came up, and had climbed the stairs cautiously, not daring to turn on any lights. Her panty hose had caught on something in the basement and she had felt the little series of runs in them. She crossed her legs, bobbing a foot, and as it got light, she saw the runs had spread up over her thick ankles. Ann appeared first, seen through the kitchen window, holding the baby on her hip. Christopher came up behind, touched Ann lightly on the shoulder as he reached past her. Olive heard Ann say, "Your mom'll take Dog-Face to the park, and I'll get Theodore ready, but I'm letting him sleep a little later."

"Isn't it wonderful when he sleeps those extra minutes?" Chris had turned around and was running his fingers through Ann's hair.

Olive was not taking Dog-Face to the park. She waited until they were both close enough to the window, and she said, "Time for me to go."

Christopher ducked his head. "I didn't know you were out there. What did you say?"

"I said," Olive responded loudly, "that it's time for the damned old lady to go."

Praise Jesus, came from the upstairs deck.

"What do you mean?" asked Ann, sticking her neck toward the window, at the same time the baby's foot kicked over a carton of milk on the counter.

"Shit," said Christopher.

"He said, 'Shit'!" Olive called up to the deck, and nodded quickly when the parrot squawked, *God is king.* "Yes, indeed," Olive said. "He is indeed."

Christopher walked out to the backyard, closing the screen door behind him carefully. "Mom, stop it. What's happening?"

"It's time for me to go home. I stink like fish."

Christopher shook his head slowly. "I knew this was going to happen. I knew something would trigger things off."

"What are you talking about?" Olive said. "I'm simply telling you it's time for me to go home."

"Then come inside," Christopher said.

"I guess I don't need my son telling me what to do," Olive said, but when Chris went back inside, murmuring to Ann, she got up and joined them in the kitchen. She sat in a chair by the table; she had hardly slept, and felt shaky.

"Did something happen, Mom?" Ann asked. "You weren't going to leave for a few more days."

She'd be damned if she was going to tell them how they'd let her sit there and dribble stuff down herself; they'd have treated their own kids better than that, wiped the mess off. But *her* they let just sit there with butterscotch sauce all down her front. "I told Christopher when he first asked me here that I'd stay for three days. After that I stink like fish."

Ann and Christopher looked at each other. "You said you'd stay a week," Chris said, warily.

"Right. Because you needed help, but you weren't even honest enough to say that." A fury was rumbling up through her, ignited further by their sense of conspiracy; how Chris had stroked Ann's hair, the look they had exchanged. "God, I hate a liar. No one brought you up to lie, Christopher Kitteridge." From Ann's hip, the baby stared at her.

"I asked you to come visit," Christopher said slowly, "because I wanted to see you. Ann wanted to meet you. We were hoping we could just have a nice time. I was hoping that things had changed, that *this* wouldn't happen. But, Mom, I'm not going to take responsibility for the extreme capriciousness of your moods. If something happened to upset you, you should tell me. That way we can talk."

"You've never talked your whole damn life. Why are you starting now?" It was the therapist, she realized suddenly. Of course. That foolish Arthur fellow. She ought to be careful, this would get repeated in a therapy group. *Extreme capriciousness of your moods.* That was not Christopher's voice. Good God, they'd discussed her to pieces already. The thought caused her whole body to shudder. "And what are you talking about, the capriciousness of my moods? What in hell is that all about?"

Ann was mopping at the milk with a sponge, still holding the baby. Christopher stood calmly in front of her. "You kind of behave like a paranoid, Mom," he said. "You always have. At least a lot, anyway. And I never see you taking any responsibility for it. One minute you're one way, the next—you're furious. It's tiring, very wearing for those around you."

Beneath the table, Olive's foot bounced like the devil. Quietly, she said, "I don't need to sit here and be called a schizoid. I've never heard of such a thing in all my life. A son turning around and calling his mother schizoid. God knows, I didn't like my mother, but I never—"

"Olive," said Ann. "Please, please stay calm. No one called you any names. Chris was only trying to tell you that your moods change kind of fast sometimes, and it's been hard. For him growing up, you know. Never knowing."

"What in God's name would you know about it? Were you there?" Olive's head was all twirly inside. Her eyesight didn't seem right. "I suppose both of you now have degrees in family psychology."

"Olive," Ann said.

"No, let her go. Go, Mom. That's fine. I'll call you a car service to get you to the airport."

"You're going to send me out there alone? For God's sake!"

"In one hour I have to go to work, and Ann has the kids to take care of. We can't drive you to the airport. The car service will be fine. Ann, why don't you call them? You'll have to go to the ticket counter, Mom, to get your ticket changed. But there shouldn't be a problem."

Amazingly, her son started to collect dirty dishes from the counter and load the dishwasher.

"You're kicking me out, just like that?" Olive said, her heart pumping ferociously.

"See, there's an example," Chris answered, calmly. Loading the dishwasher, calmly. "You say you want to leave, then accuse me of kicking you out. In the past, it would make me feel terrible, but I'm not going to feel terrible now. Because this is not my doing. You just don't seem to notice that your actions bring reactions."

She got up, holding the edge of the table, and made her way to the basement, where her bag was already packed. She had packed it in the night. She brought it back up the stairs, panting.

"The car will be here in twenty minutes," Ann said to Christopher, and he nodded, still loading the dishwasher.

"I can't believe this," Olive said.

"I shouldn't wonder." Christopher had started scrubbing a pot now. "I always found it unbelievable myself. But I just don't want to put up with it anymore."

"You haven't put up with me for years!" Olive shouted. "You have treated me poorly for years!"

"No," said her son, quietly. "I think if you think about it, you'll see that the story is quite different. You have a bad temper. At least I think it's a temper, I don't really know what it is. But you can make people feel terrible. You made Daddy feel terrible."

"Chris," said Ann, in a warning kind of way.

But Christopher shook his head. "I'm not going to be ruled by my fear of you, Mom."

Fear of her? How could anyone be afraid of her? She was the one who was afraid! He kept scrubbing the pots, the pans, wiping down the counters, all the while answering her calmly. Whatever she said, he answered calmly. Calm as the Muslim who sold him a newspaper each morning, before sending him off on a subway to blow up. (Wasn't *that* paranoid? Her son was the one who was paranoid!)

She heard Theodore call from the top of the stairs, "Mummy, come here. Mummy!" Olive started to cry.

Everything became blurry, not just her eyes. She said things, with more and more fury—and Christopher answered, calmly, still washing kitchen things calmly. She kept crying. Christopher was saying something about Jim O'Casey. Something about him being a drunk, driving into a tree. "You'd scream at Daddy like Jim's death was his fault. How could you do that, Mom? I don't know what I hated more—when you went after him and sided with me, or when you went after me." Christopher was tilting his head, as though really considering this.

"What are you talking about?" Olive cried. "You, with your new wife. She's so *nice*, Christopher, it makes me puke. Well, I hope you have a damn nice life, since you've got it all figured out."

Back and forth, Olive crying, Christopher calm. Until he said quietly, "Okay, get your bags. Here's the car."

The line to get to the gate—the security line—was so long it went around a corner. A black woman, wearing a red airport vest, kept saying in the same plangent tone, "People, move around to the corner and against the wall. Move around to the corner and against the wall."

Twice Olive approached her. "Where do I go?" Olive asked her, thrusting forward her ticket.

"This line right here," the woman said, raising an arm toward the long line. Her hair had been straightened and seemed like a badly fitting bathing cap with whiskers around its back rim.

"Are you sure?" Olive said.

"The line right here." Raising her arm again. Her indifference was impenetrable.

(*You were the scariest teacher at the school, Mom.*)

Standing in line, she looked to those near her for some confirmation that this was ridiculous, standing in a line this long, that something must be wrong. But people who met her eye looked away with no expression. Olive put her sunglasses on, blinking. Everywhere she looked, people seemed removed and unfriendly. As she got closer, she didn't understand—the line spread into one mass of people who all seemed to know what she didn't—where to go, what to do.

"I need to call my son," she said to a man standing near her. What she meant was that she had to leave the line to get to a pay phone because surely if she called Christopher, he would come get her—she would beg, she would bawl, anything it took to be saved from this hell.

It had just gone terribly wrong, that's all. Sometimes things went terribly wrong. But looking around, she could see there were no pay phones anywhere; everyone had a cell phone stuck to their ear, talking, talking; they all had someone to talk to.

(His utter calm as he washed those dishes while she wept! Even Ann had had to leave the room. *Do you have no memory of these things at all? These days, they'd send a social worker right to the home, if a kid showed up that way.*

Why are you torturing me? she had cried. What are you talking about? All your life I have loved you. And this is what you feel?

He'd stopped washing the dishes. Said just as calmly: *Okay. Now I don't have anything left to say.*)

The man she had told she had to call her son looked at her, then looked away. She couldn't call her son. He was cruel. And his wife was cruel.

Olive was moved along with the small sea of people: Move along, handbag on the rollers, move along, have your boarding pass out. A man, not nicely, motioning for her to step through the security arc. Glancing down, saying without expression, "Take off your shoes, ma'am. Take off your shoes."

She pictured standing before him, her shredded panty hose exposed like some crazy lady. "I will not take off my shoes," she heard herself say. She said, "I don't give a damn if the plane blows up, do you understand? I don't give one good goddamn if any of you are blown sky-high." She saw the security man give the slightest gesture of his hand, and two people were beside her. They were men, and in half a second a woman was there, too. Security officials in their white shirts and special stripes above the pockets.

In voices of great gentleness, they said, "Come this way, ma'am."

She nodded, blinking behind her sunglasses, and said, "I'd be glad to."

Criminal

That morning Rebecca Brown stole a magazine, even though Rebecca was not, ordinarily, the type of person who stole things. Ordinarily, Rebecca wouldn't take the soap from a motel bathroom on Route 1; she'd never even think to take the towels. It was the way she had been raised. In truth, Rebecca had been raised not to do a lot of things, and she'd done a great many of them anyway, except for stealing—she had never done that. But in the bleak white of a doctor's office in the town of Maisy Mills, Rebecca stole a magazine. There was a story in it that she wanted to finish, and she thought: This is only a doctor's office, and only a magazine, so really this is no big deal.

The story was about an ordinary, balding, kind of out-of-shape man who came home for lunch every day and sat at the kitchen table with his wife, eating sandwiches and talking about things like getting the lawn mower fixed. It gave Rebecca the same hopeful feeling that she got sometimes when she walked down a side street at night and saw through the window some kid playing in his pajamas, with a father ruffling the kid's hair.

So when the nurse opened her glass window and called out a name,

Rebecca rolled up the magazine and slipped it into her knapsack. She didn't feel bad about it. She felt pleased when she got on the bus and knew she could finish the story.

But the man's wife wanted more from life than Saturday trips to the hardware store and eating sandwiches every day just because lunchtime had rolled around, and by the end of the story, the wife had packed up and left, and the man stopped coming home for lunch. He just stayed in his office at lunchtime, not eating anything. Rebecca felt sick when she finished the story; she was not a person who should read on a bus. The bus went around a corner and the magazine fell, and when Rebecca picked it up, it was open to a picture of an ad for a man's shirt. The shirt looked like a painter's smock, gathered across the chest and kind of billowy. Rebecca turned the magazine, looked at it more. By the time she stepped off the bus, she had decided to order the shirt for David.

"You'll love it," the woman said over the telephone. "It's all hand sewn and all. A beautiful shirt." The number had been an 800 number, and this woman taking the order had a Southern accent. Rebecca thought her voice was like stepping into one of those television commercials for laundry soap where sunlight streams through a window across a shiny floor.

"Now, let's see," the woman said. "These come in small, medium, and large. Oh, honey, I've got to put you on hold."

"That's all right," Rebecca said. On the bus ride home, her stomach had started to feel like a wet balloon was in there, with its insides stuck together, so she put the phone between her neck and shoulder and reached across the counter for the Maalox spoon. Maalox sticks to everything. You can't put the spoon in the dishwasher because even the glasses come out flecked with white. They had a serving spoon David called the Maalox spoon, and it stayed right there by the corner of the sink. Rebecca was standing there licking the Maalox spoon when her father's voice came into her head. It was in her head, but it was clear as a bell. *I hate a person who steals,* he said.

The day her father died, Rebecca read in a magazine about a psychic woman who helped police solve murders. The woman said she did it by reading the thoughts of the dead people, that dead people still had thoughts even after they were dead.

"I'm sorry about that," said the woman with her Southern accent.

"It's okay," Rebecca said.

"Now," said the woman. "Is your husband's width more in his shoulders or in his stomach region?"

"He's not my husband," Rebecca said. "Not exactly. I mean, he's my boyfriend."

"Well, sure," the woman said. "And is your boyfriend's width in his shoulders, or his stomach region?"

"Shoulders," Rebecca said. "He runs a health club and he always works out."

"Okay," said the woman slowly, like she was writing this down. "Now, I'm just wondering if a large would be too loose around the waist."

"We probably *will* get married," Rebecca said. "You know, someday."

"Well, of course," the woman said. "What size suit does he wear? That might help us out."

"I don't know if I've ever seen him in a suit."

"Why don't we go with the large," the woman said.

"I don't usually order things like this," Rebecca told her. "To get sent to me, I mean. And I've never ordered anything online. I'd never give my credit card number online."

"No?" the woman asked. "Some people feel that way. Some people don't like to order things anyway. You prefer to do your shopping right there in the store. I'm like that myself."

"Things get lost," Rebecca told her. "There's a lot of billing clerks and truck drivers out there. You know, all those people who could have a bad night's sleep or a fight with their boss." As she spoke, she flipped through the magazine, found the first page of the story—when the man had still been happy—and ripped it out slowly. Using the cigarette lighter she kept in her back pocket, Rebecca set the page on fire in the sink.

"I suppose if you think about it like that," the woman said, agreeably. "But we guarantee delivery."

"Oh, I trust you," Rebecca said, and she did. What a voice that woman had—Rebecca could have told her anything. "It's just that I'm the kind of person," Rebecca continued, "that thinks if you took a map of the whole world and put a pin in it for every person, there wouldn't be a pin for me."

The woman didn't say anything.

"Do you ever think that?" Rebecca asked. She watched the small flame, like a little living spirit, flare up for a moment in the sink.

"No," the woman said. "I never do."

"Oh, I'm sorry," Rebecca said.

"Don't be sorry," said the woman. "It's a pleasure. We'll do this. We'll go with the large, and if it's too big, you just send it on back."

Rebecca ran water over the flakes of ashes in the sink. "Can I just ask you something?" she said to the woman.

"Well, sure," the woman said.

"Are you a Scientologist?"

"Am I—" There was a pause. "No, I'm not," the woman said, in her easy Southern accent.

"Me either. It's just I happened to be reading an article about Scientology, and, boy, it sounds like pretty weird stuff."

"I guess to each his own. Now—"

"I always talk too much," Rebecca explained to the woman. "My boyfriend tells me that. And now I've given myself this headache."

"It's a pleasure doing business with a friendly person," the woman said. "A cold facecloth pressed right against the eyeballs should help. And don't be afraid to really press either."

"Thank you," Rebecca said. "I guess large will do."

"Obviously you've got to lie right back," the woman said. "Put the facecloth in the freezer first."

———

Rebecca Brown came from a line of Congregational ministers. Her grandfather had been a much-loved pastor of a large church in Shirley Falls, and her mother had been the daughter of this Reverend Tyler Caskey's second marriage, his first wife dying and leaving him with two small girls. By the time he had married again, and had Rebecca's mother, the other girls were old enough to not pay much attention to her, and it wasn't until Rebecca's mother married a minister herself, and then left very suddenly to go to California to be an actress, that Rebecca's aunt Katherine got involved. "It is unthinkable that a mother would take off like that," she said, with tears in her eyes. Except it wasn't unthinkable at all—Rebecca's mother had done it, and had not even put up a fight when Rebecca's father, Reverend Brown of a tiny church in Crosby, Maine, had gone to court for custody. "This is sick," said Aunt Katherine. "He'll spousify you. Let's hope he gets married again soon."

Aunt Katherine had had a lot of therapy, and Rebecca was nervous around her. In any event, her father did not remarry, and Rebecca had grown up in a solitary house owned by the church, and had known quietly and secretly, the way that children know things, that her father was not the minister her grandfather had been. "It breaks my heart," Aunt Katherine said once, on a visit, and Rebecca hoped she wouldn't come again. Her mother, in California, sent a postcard once in a while, but when it was discovered that she had joined the church of Scientology, even Aunt Katherine said it was better not to have much to do with her. That wasn't hard—the postcards stopped coming.

Rebecca sent a whole bunch of letters, one after another, to her mother at the last address she had for her—in a town called Tarzana. Rebecca never put on a return address, because she didn't want her father to find the letters if they got returned. And most likely they would have been returned. The address was four years old, and when Rebecca called directory assistance for a telephone number in Tarzana, and all the towns nearby, there was no listing for Charlotte Brown, or Charlotte Caskey either. Where did the letters go?

Rebecca had gone to the library to read about Scientology. She read how they wanted to clear the world of body titans, aliens who they believed inhabited the earth after a nuclear explosion seventy-five million years ago. She read how members were required to "disconnect" from family members who were critical of Scientology. Which is why her mother didn't write to her anymore. Maybe writing to Rebecca had been a "suppressive act"—and her mother had been required to go before the Rehabilitation Project Force. Rebecca read about one member who was told that, with the right training and discipline, he could learn to read people's thoughts. *Come get me,* Rebecca thought—hard—to her mother. *Come get me, please.* Later on, she thought, *Fuck you.*

She stopped reading about Scientology and started reading books about being a minister's wife. You were supposed to have a can of fruit cocktail in the pantry in case some parishioner came to call. For a number of years Rebecca made sure to have fruit cocktail in the cupboard, though it was very seldom that anyone came to call.

When she graduated from high school and knew she'd be going two hours away to the university, *living somewhere else,* Rebecca was so dazed to think such good fortune had finally arrived that she worried she'd be hit by a car and become paralyzed and have to live in the rectory forever. But once she was at the university, she sometimes missed her father, and she tried not to think of him alone in that house. When people spoke of their mothers, she would say quietly that her own mother had "passed away," which made people uncomfortable, because Rebecca had a way of looking down after she said this, as though to indicate she could not bear to say any more about it. She thought, in a very technical way, what she said was true. She didn't say her mother was dead, which, as far as she knew, wasn't true. Her mother had passed (as in an airplane far above) away (to a different land), and Rebecca was quite used to the phases she went through when she thought a great deal about her mother, and then when she did not think about her at all. She did not know anyone else whose mother had run off and never looked back, and she thought her own thoughts about it must be natural, given the circumstances.

It was during her father's funeral that Rebecca had the kind of thoughts she knew couldn't be natural. Certainly not during a funeral, anyway. A shaft of sunlight had come through a window of the church, bouncing off the wooden pew and slanting across the carpet, and the sun like that had made Rebecca want someone. She was nineteen years old, and had learned some things in college about men. The minister doing the funeral was a friend of her father's; they had gone to seminary together years ago, and watching him up there with his hand raised in a blessing, Rebecca started thinking about things she could do to him under his robe, things he'd have to pray about later. "Carleton's spirit remains here with us," the minister said, and goose bumps started all over Rebecca's head. She thought about the psychic woman reading dead people's thoughts, and she got the feeling that her father was right behind her eyeballs, seeing what she was imagining doing to his friend.

Then she thought about her mother—that maybe her mother had been taught to read people's thoughts, and was reading Rebecca's thoughts right now. Rebecca closed her eyes as though she were praying. *Fuck you,* she said to her mother. *Sorry,* she said to her father. Then she opened her eyes, looked at the people in the church, as dull-looking as dry sticks. She pictured lighting little piles of papers in the woods; she had always liked the sudden small burst of a flame.

"What've you got there, Bicka-Beck?" David asked. He was sitting on the floor aiming the remote control at the television, switching channels every time a commercial came on. Above him on the windowpane were reflections from the television screen, jerking and dancing across the glass.

"A dental assistant," Rebecca said, from where she sat at the table.

She circled the ad with her pen. "Experience preferred, but they'll train if they have to."

"Oh, sweetie," said David, looking at the television. "People's *mouths*?"

There was no way around it, jobs were a problem for her. The only job Rebecca had ever enjoyed was a job she had one summer at the Dreambeam Ice Cream Machine. The manager was drunk every day by two o'clock and he let his help eat all the ice cream they wanted. They'd give the kids who came in huge ice cream cones and watch their eyes get big. " 'S okay," the manager would say, weaving between the ice cream freezers. "Run the place broke, I don't give a shit."

Right before Rebecca had moved in with David, she'd been a secretary at a big firm of lawyers. Some of the lawyers would buzz her on the phone and tell her to bring them coffee. Even the women lawyers did this. She kept wondering if she had the right to tell them no. But it didn't matter—within a few weeks, they'd sent a woman over to tell her that she worked too slow.

"Remember, sweetie pie," David said, switching channels again. "Confidence is the name of the game."

"Okay," said Rebecca. She kept on circling the ad for the dental assistant until the circle took up almost half the page.

"Go in with the attitude they're lucky to get you."

"Okay."

"In a nonthreatening way, of course."

"Okay."

"And be friendly but don't talk too much." David pointed the remote control and the television switched off. The end of the living room was dark. "Poor old sweetie pie," said David, standing up and walking to her. He put his arm around her neck and squeezed playfully. "We should just take you out to the pasture and shoot you, poor old thing."

David always fell asleep right afterward, but a lot of nights Rebecca lay awake. That night she got up and walked into the kitchen. There was a bar across the street that you could see from the window, a noisy place—you could hear everything that happened in the parking lot, but Rebecca liked having the bar there. On nights when she couldn't sleep, she liked knowing there were other people awake. She stood there thinking of the man in the story, the ordinary, balding man sitting alone in his office at lunchtime. And she thought of her father's voice, how she had heard it in her head. She remembered how one time he had said to her, years ago, There are some men in the world that when they lie down beside a woman, they are no different from dogs. She remembered how once, a few years after her mother left, Rebecca announced she was going to go live with her. You can't, her father said, without looking up from his reading. She gave you up. I've gone to court. I have sole custody.

For a long time, Rebecca had thought it was spelled *s-o-u-l*.

She watched a police car pull into the parking lot. Two policemen got out and the flashing lights stayed on, the edge of them zinging blue through the window, across the sink and the Maalox spoon. There had probably been a fight—a lot of nights there were fights in the bar. Rebecca, standing at the window, felt a tiny smile inside her getting larger—how delicious it would be: that one moment of perfect joy, propped up and righteous with booze, to let that first punch fly.

"Feel this," said David, flexing his muscle. "Really."

Rebecca leaned over her cereal bowl and touched his arm. It was like touching frozen earth. "That's amazing," she said. "That really is."

David stood and looked at himself in the toaster. He flexed both arms together, like a boxer showing off before a crowd. Then he turned side-to and looked at himself that way. He nodded. "Okay," he said. "Not bad."

The only mirror Rebecca's father had in their house was the one that hung over the bathroom sink. If she wasn't brushing her teeth or washing her face, she wasn't supposed to be near that mirror; vanity was a sin. "Your mother ran away from one cult just to join another," her aunt Katherine had said. "For God's sake, no Congregationalist lives like this." Except Rebecca did. She wished her aunt would stop it, just go away and stop saying those things. "Do you want to come live with us?" her aunt asked her once, and Rebecca shook her head. She didn't want to mention the soul custody. Besides, her Aunt Katherine made her anxious, the same way her math teacher, Mrs. Kitteridge, did. Mrs. Kitteridge would look at her hard sometimes, when the class was supposed to be working. Once she had said to Rebecca in the hall-way, "If you ever want to talk to me about anything, you can."

Rebecca hadn't answered, had just moved past her with her books.

"All right, I'm out of here," David said, zipping his workout bag closed. "You got the number for the dental assisant?"

"Yes," Rebecca said.

"Good luck, Bicka-Beck," said David. He went to the refrigerator and drank from the orange juice carton. Then he picked up the keys and kissed her goodbye. "Remember," he said. "Be confident, and don't talk too much."

"Right, got it," Rebecca said, nodding. "Goodbye." She sat at the table with the dirty cereal bowls in front of her, and thought about her urge to talk. It had come over her soon after her father died, and it had not gone away. It was a physical thing, really; she wanted to give it up the way people gave up smoking.

Her father'd had a rule—no talking at the table. It was a strange rule, when you thought about it, because there had been only the two of them sitting in the little dining room of the rectory each night. It could be that her father was tired at the end of his day after visiting the sick and the dying—it was a small town, but there was usually some-one sick, and quite frequently someone dying—and he wanted it quiet so that he could rest. At any rate, they had sat there night after night, the only sounds being silverware touching a plate, or a water glass being put back on the table, and the soft, too-intimate sounds of their chewing. Sometimes Rebecca would look up and see how her father had a piece of food caught on his chin, and she wouldn't be able to swallow, she'd feel such a sudden love for him. But other times, especially as she got older, she was glad to see all the butter he used. It was his love for butter she was counting on, hoping that would do him in.

She stood now and washed out the cereal bowls. Then she wiped the counter and straightened the chairs. A pinprick of heat started up in her stomach, so she got the Maalox bottle and the Maalox spoon, and as she was shaking the bottle, she got an image of David leaning toward her, reminding her not to talk too much, and it came to her then that of course the large would be too big.

"No problem," the woman said. "I'll just check and see if the order's gone out."

Even scraping with her fingernail, there was a layer of dried Maalox that wouldn't come off the spoon. Rebecca put the spoon back onto the counter. "I thought I probably wouldn't get the same person again," she said. "Wow. Or maybe you're just a small outfit." There was no answer. "I mean, being a small outfit's just fine," said Rebecca, ripping two pages of the story out of the magazine. There was still no answer, and finally Rebecca understood she'd been put on hold. She watched the pages go up in flames—the section where the wife just left. The flame was higher than the sink. A thrill of anxiety rose in Rebecca; she waited—her hands on the faucet—but the flame dipped down.

"Never mind," the woman said, back on the phone. "The order's already gone out. Just send it back if it's too big, and we'll send out a medium. Tell me, how's your headache today?"

"You *remember*?" Rebecca said.

"Well, of course I remember," the woman said.

"No headache today," Rebecca said. "But I have a problem. I have to get a job."

"You don't have a job?" the woman asked, with her lovely Southern voice.

"No, I have to get one."

"Well, sure," the woman said, "a job is real important. What kind of job are you looking for?"

"Something low stress," Rebecca said. "It's not that I'm lazy or anything," she said, and then she said, "Well, maybe I am, maybe that's true."

"Don't say that," the woman said. "I'm sure that's not true."

She was a wonderful woman. Rebecca thought about the man in the story—he should meet this woman.

"Thank you," Rebecca said. "That's really nice."

"Now, you send it back if it's too big. It's no problem," the woman assured her. "No problem at all."

The death of Rebecca's father was not the saddest thing. Nor was the absence of her mother. The saddest thing was when she fell in love with Jace Burke at the university and he broke up with her. Jace was a piano player, and one time when her father went to a conference, she brought Jace back to Crosby for the night. Jace looked around the rectory and said, "Baby, this is one strange place." He looked at her with a tenderness that was like a sweet erasure of all the darkness in her past. Later, they went to the Warehouse Bar and Grill, where the kind-of-crazy Angela O'Meara still played the piano in the bar. "Oh, man, she's great," Jace said.

"My father always lets her come to the church to play whenever she feels like it. She doesn't have a piano," Rebecca explained. "She never did."

"She's great," Jace repeated softly, and Rebecca felt a delicious warmth toward her father then, as though her father had seen some greatness in poor half-soused Angie, too, that Rebecca had never known. When they left, Jace slipped a twenty-dollar bill into Angela's tip jar. Angela made a kiss in their direction and played "Hello, Young Lovers" as they left the bar.

When Jace left the university, he played in bars all over Boston. Sometimes the bars were fancy places with thick carpets and leather chairs, and sometimes there'd be a poster out front with Jace's picture on it. But a lot of times his luck was bad and he'd have to play the electric organ in strip joints just to earn some money.

Every weekend, Rebecca took a Greyhound bus and stayed with him in his dirty apartment, where there were cockroaches in the silverware drawer. On Sunday evenings when she got back, she'd call her father and tell him how hard she was studying. Later on, when she was living with David, she'd sometimes let herself remember those weekends with Jace. The dirty sheets against her skin, the way Jace's metal chairs felt, sitting on them naked while they ate English muffins by the open window, grime all around the window casing. She'd remember standing at the dirty sink in the bathroom, naked, Jace standing behind her, naked too, seeing themselves in the mirror. There was no voice of her father's in her head, no thoughts of men behaving like dogs. All of it was easy as pie.

One night in the bathtub, Jace told her about a blond woman he'd met. Rebecca sat with the facecloth in her hand, staring at the cracked caulking around the edge of the tub, at the dirt wedged into the cracks. These things happen, is what Jace said.

Later that week, her father called. Even now, Rebecca didn't understand exactly what had been wrong with her father's heart; he hadn't said, exactly. Only that there was nothing the doctors could do. "But they can do all sorts of things, Daddy," she said. "I mean, I hear about all kinds of heart procedures and stuff."

"Not my heart," he answered, and there was fear in his voice. The fear made Rebecca wonder if perhaps her father hadn't believed all those things he'd preached for years. But even when she heard the fear in his voice, and felt the fear herself, she knew what she felt most badly about was Jace and the blonde.

"Tell me," David said. "What's a facecloth doing in the freezer?"

"I didn't get the job," Rebecca said.

"No?" David closed the freezer door. "I'm kind of surprised. I thought you would. What do they want, a Ph.D.?" He tore the end off a loaf of bread that was on the counter and stuck it into a jar of spaghetti sauce. "Poor Bicka-Beck," he said, and shook his head.

"Maybe it's because I talked about the barium enema I had," Rebecca said, with a shrug. She turned the heat down so the spaghetti wouldn't boil over. "I talked a lot," she admitted. "I probably talked too much."

David sat down at the table and looked at her. "See, that might not be a good idea. See, Bicka, maybe nobody ever told you this, but people don't really want to hear about other people's barium enemas."

Rebecca took the facecloth out of the freezer. She folded it into a strip and sat down across from David, holding the facecloth over her eyes. "If a person's *had* one," she said, "I don't think they would mind."

David didn't answer.

"Evidently the dentist never had one," Rebecca added.

"Man," said David. "Where in the world did you come from? Can I just ask how the subject came up? Wouldn't it make more sense to be talking about teeth?"

"We'd already talked about teeth by then." Rebecca pressed on the facecloth. "I was telling him why I wanted the job. How important it is for all these helpers dressed in white to be nice to scared people."

"Okay, okay," David said. Rebecca peeled back the facecloth and looked at him with one eye. "Tomorrow you'll get a job," he said.

And she did. She got a job in Augusta, typing traffic reports for a fat man who scowled and never said *please*. The man was the head of an agency that studied the flow of traffic in and around different cities in the state, so the cities would know where to build ramps and put up lights. Rebecca hadn't thought of anyone doing that before, studying traffic, and it was interesting the first morning, but by afternoon it was not so interesting anymore, and after a few weeks, she knew she would probably quit. One afternoon as she was typing, her hand began to shake. When she held up her other hand, it was shaking, too. She felt the way she had on the Greyhound bus that weekend Jace had told her about the blonde, when she kept thinking: This can't be my life. And then she thought that most of her life she had been thinking: This can't be my life.

In the lobby near the mailboxes was a brown padded envelope addressed to Rebecca. The shirt had made its way from Kentucky to Maine. Rebecca carried it upstairs to the apartment, and pulled the tab across the top of the envelope, while pieces of gray stuffing sprayed across the table. The woman was right, it was a beautiful shirt. Rebecca spread it out over the couch, arranging the full sleeves over the cushions, and then stepped back to look. This was not a shirt David would wear. Never in the world would David wear this shirt. This was a shirt for Jace.

"It happens," the woman said cheerfully. "Just send it on back."

"All right," Rebecca said.

"You sound discouraged," the woman said. "But you'll get your money back, honey. It'll take a few weeks, but you'll get it back."

"All right," Rebecca said again.

"No problem, honey. It's no problem at all."

The next day, Rebecca looked around the doctor's office for something to steal. Other than magazines, there wasn't much. It was like they'd planned it that way, even the coat hangers were the kind that couldn't come off the rack. But there was a small glass vase on the windowsill, plain and ordinary, with the pale remnants of a brown stain around the bottom.

"The doctor will see you now," said the nurse. Rebecca followed her down the hallway into the examining room. She rolled up her sleeve for the blood pressure check. "How's the stomach feel?" the nurse asked, and glanced at the chart.

"Good," Rebecca said. "Well, not good. The Maalox doesn't really work."

The nurse unpeeled the Velcro strip from Rebecca's arm. "Tell the doctor," she said.

But the doctor, Rebecca could see right away, was irritated with her. He folded his arms across his white-coated chest and pressed his lips together, gazing at her without blinking.

"It still hurts," Rebecca said. "And—"

"And what?"

She had been planning on telling him how her hands were shaking, how she felt that something was deeply wrong. "And I just wondered why it still hurt." She looked down at her feet.

"Rebecca, we've run upper and lower GI's on you, done the blood work. And what you have to accept is that you're fine. You have a sensitive stomach. A lot of people do."

Back in the waiting room, Rebecca put her coat on, standing near the window and gazing out, as if she were interested in the parking lot below. For a moment, her head didn't ache, her stomach didn't ache, there was nothing in her except a thrill as clean as fresh water. Like she was the pure flame her lighter became. Nearby, a man read a magazine. A woman filed her nails. Rebecca put the vase into her knapsack and left.

That night they sat on the floor watching an old movie on television. Anyone looking through the window would have seen Rebecca sitting, leaning against the couch, David next to her, holding a bottle of seltzer water, as ordinary-looking as a couple could be.

"I never shoplifted when I was a kid," Rebecca said.

"I did," said David, still watching the movie. "I stole a watch from the drugstore I worked in. I stole a lot of things."

"I never did it, because I was scared I'd get caught," Rebecca said. "Not because it was wrong. I mean, I knew it was wrong, but that's not why I didn't do it."

"I even stole a present for my mother's birthday," David said, and he chuckled. "Some kind of pin."

"Most kids probably do it at some point," Rebecca said. "I guess. I don't know. When I was little, I never went over to other kids' houses and they never came to mine." David didn't say anything. "My father said it didn't look good," Rebecca explained. "For a minister's kids to show favorites. In a small town like that."

David kept looking at the television. "That stinks," he said. "Watch this. I love this part. The guy's going to get chopped up by that boat propeller."

She looked out the window at the dark. "Then I got to ninth grade," she said, "and my father decided the church shouldn't be spending money on a housekeeper for us anymore, so after that I cooked. I used to cook special meals for him practically soaked in butter. God," she said.

David hooted. "There he goes. Gross."

"I bet legally that makes me some kind of criminal."

"What's that, honey pie?" David said. But Rebecca didn't say it again. David patted her foot. "We'll bring our kids up differently. Don't you worry."

Rebecca still didn't say anything.

"This is a great movie," David said, settling back against her legs. "This is just great. In a minute, they cut off that cat's head."

Something was going on at the bar. Three police cars pulled into the parking lot and the lights were left flashing while the police went inside. Rebecca waited by the kitchen window, the lights zinging across her arm, across the kitchen floor. Two of the policemen came out of the bar holding a man between them with his hands behind his back. They stood the man against one of the cars, and then one of the policemen said to him, "You have the right to remain silent. Anything you say can be used against you in a court of law." The policeman's voice was not kind or unkind, just steady and clear. "You have the right to an attorney. If you cannot afford an attorney, you have the right to have an attorney appointed to you." It was like poetry, the way the Bible was like poetry if you heard it read the right way.

The other policemen came out of the bar, and pretty soon they put

250 | Olive Kitteridge

the man in the backseat, and then all three cars drove away. The kitchen seemed dark without their flashing lights. She could make out the Maalox spoon by the corner of the sink, a few glinting white specks on it. For a long time, Rebecca sat at the kitchen table in the dark. She pictured the doctor's office, the streets the bus took to get there. In Maisy Mills no buses ran at night. She thought it might take her almost half an hour to walk. If you can't figure out something, Jace had once told her, don't watch what you think, watch what you do.

She watched herself take the barbecue starter stuff from beneath the sink, put it into her knapsack. She watched herself quietly slip from her underwear drawer the old postcards from her mother. In the kitchen she ripped them in half—and when she did, a tiny sound came from her. She put them into the knapsack. Then she put in the shirt she'd bought for David, and also the rest of the magazine where the ad had come from. She put two cigarette lighters into her coat pocket.

Moving carefully down the hall stairway, the words repeated in her head. *You have the right to remain silent. You have the right—You have the right—You have the right.*

It would be worth the arrest if they put it like that.

River

The day before, she almost backed into him in the parking lot of the library, and though he didn't shout, he raised an arm as though to ward off the coming car, or perhaps just out of surprise. In either case, Olive had stepped on the brake in time, and Jack Kennison did not look at her, just kept walking to his own car—a small, shiny red one, parked a few feet away.

Old horror, Olive thought. He was a tall man with a big belly, slouching shoulders, and—in her mind—a kind of arrogant furtiveness in the way he held his head thrust forward and didn't look at people. He had gone to Harvard, had lived in New Jersey—whether teaching at Princeton or somewhere else, Olive didn't know—but a number of years ago he had retired with his wife to a house they'd built on the edge of a small field here in Crosby, Maine. At the time, Olive had said to her husband, "Stupid to pour all that money into a place not even on the water," and Henry had agreed. The reason she knew Jack Kennison had gone to Harvard was because the waitress at the marina told Olive that he let everyone know.

"How obnoxious," Henry had said, with real disgust. They had never had a conversation with the Kennisons, had only passed them sometimes in town, or had seen them at the marina for breakfast. Henry always said hello, and Mrs. Kennison said hello back. She was a small woman, with a quick smile.

"I expect she's spent her life making up for his boorishness," said Olive, and Henry nodded. Henry did not always warm up to summer people or retirees, those who came up the coast to live out their last days in a setting of slanting light. They were apt to have money, and, often, a grating sense of entitlement. For example, one man felt entitled to write an article in the local paper, poking fun at the natives, saying they were cold and aloof. And there was the woman who'd been overheard at Moody's store, asking her husband, "Why is everyone in this state fat, and why do they all look retarded?" She was, according to whoever had told the story, a Jew from New York, and so there was that. Even now, there were people who'd have preferred a Muslim family to move in rather than be insulted by a Jew from New York. Jack Kennison was neither, but he was not a native, and he had an arrogant look.

When the waitress at the marina reported that the Kennisons had a daughter who was gay, living in Oregon, and that it was Mr. Kennison who wouldn't accept it, Henry said, "Oh, that's wrong. You need to accept your children either way."

Henry had never been tested, of course; Christopher was not gay. Henry had lived long enough to see his son divorced; but a massive stroke soon after—and Olive would never be convinced the divorce hadn't done it—had kept Henry paralyzed and unknowing when Christopher married again. Henry died in the nursing home before the baby was born.

One and a half years later, this still squeezed Olive so hard she felt like a package of vacuum-packed coffee, as she clutched the steering wheel, leaning forward in the dawn's light to peer through the windshield. She had left the house while it was still dark—she often did—and it would grow light on the winding tree-lined road into town, a twenty-minute drive. Every morning was the same: the long drive, the stop at Dunkin' Donuts, where the Filipino waitress knew she liked extra milk in her coffee, and Olive would take the newspaper and some doughnut holes—she'd ask for three, but the girl would always toss in extra—and go back into the car to read the paper, feeding a few dough-nut holes to the dog in the backseat. By six o'clock, she felt it was safe enough to walk by the river, though she'd never heard of any trouble on the asphalt path. At six, it was mostly the old folks, and you could walk a good mile before seeing anyone.

Olive parked in the gravelly parking lot, took her walking shoes out of the trunk, tied them on, and took off. It was the best, and only bear-able, part of the day. Three miles in one direction, three miles back. Her one concern was that such daily exercise might make her live longer. *Let it be quick,* she thought now, meaning her death—a thought she had several times a day.

She squinted. A body was slumped on the path not far from the first mile's stone bench. Olive stopped walking. It was an old man—she could see that much, as she walked tentatively closer—a balding head, a big belly. God in heaven. She walked with faster steps. Jack Kennison lay on his side, his knees bent, almost like he'd decided to take a nap. She leaned down and saw his eyes were open. His eyes were very blue. "Are you dead?" she asked loudly.

His eyes moved, looked into hers. "Apparently not," he said.

She looked at his chest, his big stomach bulging out beneath his L.L.Bean jacket. Then she looked in both directions, up and down the path. No one was in sight. "Have you been stabbed or shot?" She leaned closer to him.

"No," he said. Then he added, "Not that I remember."

"Can you move?"

"I don't know. I haven't tried." His big stomach was moving, though, slowly up and down.

"Well, try." She touched her sneaker to his black walking shoe. "Try to move this leg."

The leg moved.

"Good," said Olive. "Try an arm."

Slowly, the man's arm moved onto his stomach.

"I don't have one of those cell phone things," Olive said. "My son keeps saying he'll buy me one, but he hasn't. I'm going back to the car and drive to call someone."

"Don't," said Jack Kennison. "Don't leave me alone."

Olive stood, uncertain. It was a mile away, her car. She looked at him, lying there, his blue eyes watching hers. "What happened?" she asked.

"I don't know."

"Then you ought to get to a doctor."

"Okay."

"I'm Olive Kitteridge, by the way. Don't believe we've ever formally met. If you can't get up, I think I should go find you a doctor. I hate them, myself. But you can't just lie there," she said. "You might die."

"I don't care," he said. A small smile seemed to come to his eyes.

"What?" Olive asked loudly, bending way down toward him.

"I don't care if I die," the man said. "Just don't leave me here alone."

Olive sat down on the bench nearby. The river was calm, barely seemed to be moving. She bent toward him again. "Are you cold?" she asked.

"Not really."

"It's nippy out." Now that she had stopped walking, she felt a chill herself. "Do you hurt?"

"No."

"Is it your heart, do you think?"

"I don't know." He began to stir. Olive stood and put a hand beneath his arm, though he was much too heavy for her to do any good. Still, after a great deal of struggling, he managed to get himself up, and settled on the bench.

"All right," said Olive, sitting down beside him. "This is better. Now we wait for someone to come along with a phone." She added suddenly, "I don't care if I die either. I'd like to, in fact. Long as it's quick."

He turned his balding head toward her, studied her tiredly with his blue eyes. "I don't want to die alone," he said.

"Hell. We're always alone. Born alone. Die alone. What difference does it make? Long as you don't shrivel for years in a nursing home like my poor husband did. That's *my* fear." She pulled at her sweater, clutched it closed with a fist. She turned to look at him carefully. "Your color seems all right. You don't have any idea what happened?"

Jack Kennison stared out at the river. "I was walking. I saw the bench and felt tired. I don't sleep well. So I sat down and started to feel dizzy. I put my head between my legs, and next thing I knew I was lying on the ground, with some woman squawking at me, 'Are you dead?'"

Olive's face became warm. "You seem less dead every minute," she said. "Do you think you can walk?"

"In a moment, I'll try. I'd like to sit here a moment."

Olive glanced at him quickly. He was crying. She looked away, and from the corner of her eye, she saw him reach into his pocket, heard him blow his nose, a real honk.

"My wife died in December," he said.

Olive watched the river. "Then, you're in hell," she said.

"Then, I'm in hell."

In the doctor's waiting room she sat, reading a magazine. After an hour, the nurse came out and said, "Mr. Kennison's worried about you waiting so long."

"Well, tell him to stop it. I'm perfectly comfortable." And she was. In fact, it had been a long time since she'd been this comfortable. She wouldn't have minded if it took all day. It was a newsmagazine she was reading, something she hadn't done for quite a while—she turned one page quickly, because she couldn't stand to look at the president's face: His close-set eyes, the jut of his chin, the sight offended her viscerally. She had lived through a lot of things with this country, but she had never lived through the mess they were in now. *Here* was a man who looked retarded, Olive thought, remembering the remark made by the woman in Moody's store. You could see it in his stupid little eyes. And the country had voted him in! A born-again Christian with a cocaine addiction. So they deserved to go to hell, and would. It was only her son, Christopher, she worried about. And his baby boy. She wasn't sure there would be a world left for him.

Olive set the magazine aside and leaned back comfortably. The outer door opened, and Jane Houlton walked in, took a seat in the waiting area not far from Olive. "Say, that's a pretty skirt you're wearing," said Olive, although she had never cared for Jane Houlton one way or another, Jane being a kind of timorous thing.

"Do you know, I got this on sale at a store that was closing in Augusta." Jane smoothed her hand down over the green tweed.

"Oh, wonderful," said Olive. "Every woman loves a bargain." She nodded appreciatively. "Very good."

She drove Jack Kennison back to the parking lot by the river so he could get his car, and then she followed him home. In the driveway of his house on the edge of the field, he said, "Would you like to come in and have some lunch? I might find an egg, or a can of baked beans."

"No," said Olive, "I think you should rest. You've had enough excitement for one day." The doctor had taken a whole bunch of tests, and so far nothing had been found to be wrong with him. *Stress fatigue,* is what the doctor, for the moment, had diagnosed. "And the dog's been cooped up in the car all morning," Olive added.

"All right, then," Jack said. He raised a hand. "Thanks very much."

Driving home, Olive felt bereft. The dog whined, and she told him to stop it, and he lay down on the backseat, as though exhausted from the morning himself. She telephoned her friend Bunny and told her the story of finding Jack Kennison on the path by the river. "Oh, the poor man," said Bunny, whose husband was still alive. A husband who had driven her nuts for most of her married life, arguing about how to raise their daughter, wearing a baseball hat when he sat down to lunch—all this had driven Bunny batty. But now it was as though she'd won a lottery, because he was still alive, and Olive thought Bunny could see what it was like, her friends losing their husbands and drowning in the emptiness. In fact, Bunny—Olive sometimes thought—didn't really want to be around Olive too much, as though Olive's widowhood was like a contagious disease. She'd talk to Olive on the phone, though. "How lucky you came by and found him," Bunny said. "Imagine, lying there."

"Somebody else would have ambled along." Olive added, "I might just give him a call later to make sure he's all right."

"Oh, do," said Bunny.

At five o'clock, Olive looked up his number in the phone book. She started to dial, then stopped. At seven o'clock, she called. "You all right?" she asked, not introducing herself.

"Hi, Olive," he said. "I seem to be. Thanks."

"Did you call your daughter?" Olive asked.

"No," he said, with what Olive thought was a small sound of puzzlement.

"She might want to know you weren't feeling well."

"I don't see any reason to bother her," he said.

"All right, then." Olive looked around the kitchen, its emptiness and silence. "Goodbye." She went into the next room and lay down, holding her transistor radio to her ear.

A week passed. Olive was aware on her early-morning walks by the river that the time spent in the waiting room while Jack Kennison saw the doctor had, for one brief moment, put her back into life. And now she was out of life again. It was a conundrum. In the time since Henry had died, she had tried many things. She had become a docent at the art museum in Portland, but after a few months, she found she could hardly endure the four hours required for her to be in one place. She had volunteered at the hospital, but she could not bear wearing the pink coat and arranging dead flowers while the nurses brushed past her. She had volunteered to speak English to young foreigners at the college, who needed simple practice with the language. That had been the best, but it was not enough.

Back and forth she went each morning by the river, spring arriving once again; foolish, foolish spring, breaking open its tiny buds, and what she couldn't stand was how—for many years, really—she had been made happy by such a thing. She had not thought she would ever become immune to the beauty of the physical world, but there you were. The river sparkled with the sun that rose, enough that she needed her sunglasses.

Around the little bend in the path, there was the stone bench. Jack Kennison sat on it, watching her approach.

"Hello," said Olive. "Trying again?"

"All the tests came back," said Jack. He shrugged. "Nothing wrong with me, so I thought I'd get back on the horse, as they say. Yes, I'm trying again."

"Admirable. Are you coming or going?" The idea of walking two miles with him, and then three miles back to the car, unnerved her.

"Going. Going back."

She hadn't noticed his red, shiny car in the parking lot when she'd started out.

"Did you drive here?" she asked.

"Yes, of course. I've not yet learned to fly."

He was not wearing dark glasses, and she saw how his eyes searched for hers. She did not take her sunglasses off.

"That was a joke," he said.

"I understand that," she responded. "Fly away, fly away, fly away home."

With his open palm, he touched the stone slab he sat on. "You don't rest?"

"Nope, I just keep on going."

He nodded. "All right, then. Enjoy your walk."

She started to move past him, and turned. "Do you feel all right? Did you sit down because you got tired?"

"I sat down because I felt like it."

She waved a hand above her head, and kept going. She noticed nothing on the rest of the walk, not the sun, not the river, not the asphalt path, not any opening buds. She walked and thought of Jack Kennison without the wife, who'd been the friendly one. He'd said he was in hell, and of course he would be.

When she got back to the house, she telephoned him. "Would you like to go to lunch one day?"

"I'd like to go to dinner," he said. "It would give me something to look forward to. If I go to lunch, then I still have the rest of the day."

"All right." She didn't tell him she went to bed with the sun, that to have an actual dinner in a restaurant would be, for her, like staying up way past midnight.

"Oh, that's lovely," said Bunny. "Olive, you've got a date."

"Why would you say something so foolish?" Olive asked, really annoyed. "We're two lonely people having supper."

"Exactly," said Bunny. "That's a date."

Funny how much that irritated Olive. And she didn't have Bunny to tell it to, since Bunny was the one who'd said it. She called her son, who lived in New York. She asked how the baby was.

"He's great," Christopher said. "He's walking."

"You didn't tell me he was walking."

"Yuh, he's walking."

Immediately a sweat broke out on her—she felt it on her face, beneath her arms. It was almost like being told Henry had died, how the nursing home hadn't called her till morning. And now a little relative of hers and Henry's, down there in the foreign land of New York City, was walking through the dark living room of a big old brownstone. She doubted she would be asked to visit, as the last visit had not gone well, to put it mildly. "Chris, maybe you can come up here this summer for a bit."

"Maybe. We'll see. Got our hands full, but sure, we'd like to. We'll see."

"How long has he been walking?"

"Since last week. Held on to the couch, smiled, then took right off. Three full steps before he fell down."

You would think a child had never walked before any place on the earth, to hear Christopher's voice.

"How are you, Mom?" His happiness had made him nicer.

"You know. The same. Do you remember Jack Kennison?"

"No."

"Oh, he's a big flub-dub whose wife died in December. Sad. We're having supper next week and Bunny called it a date. What a *stupid* thing to say. Honestly, that irritated me."

"Have dinner with him. Consider it volunteer work or something."

"Yes," Olive said. "You're exactly right."

The evenings were long this time of year, and Jack suggested they meet at the Painted Rudder at six thirty. "Should be a nice time of day, right there on the water," he said, and Olive agreed, although she was distressed about the time. For most of her life, she had eaten supper at five o'clock, and that he didn't (apparently) reminded her he was someone about whom she knew nothing, and probably didn't care to either. She had never liked him from the start, and it was foolish to have agreed to dinner.

He ordered a vodka and tonic, and she didn't like that. "Water, please," she said firmly to the waitress, who nodded and backed away. They were sitting kitty-corner to each other, at a table for four, so that they could both see the cove with the sailboats and the lobster boats, and the buoys bobbing just slightly in the evening's breeze. He seemed much too close to her, his big hairy arm draping down to his drink. "I know Henry was in the nursing home for a long time, Olive." He looked at her with his very blue eyes. "That had to be hard."

So they talked like that, and it was kind of nice. They both needed someone to talk to, someone to listen, and they did that. They listened.

Talked. Listened more. He never mentioned Harvard. The sun was setting behind the boats as they sat with their decaf coffees.

The next week they met for lunch at a small place near the river. Maybe because it was daytime, the spring sunshine full on the grass outside, the parked cars seen through the window reflecting shards of brightness—maybe the midday-ness of it made it not as lovely as the time before. Jack seemed tired, his shirt pressed and expensive-looking; Olive felt big and baggy inside her long vest that she had made from an old set of curtains. "Did your wife sew?" she asked.

"Sew?" As though he didn't know what the word meant.

"Sew. Make things from cloth."

"Oh. No."

But when she said that she and Henry had built their house themselves, he said he'd like to see it. "Fine," she said. "Follow along behind." She watched in the rearview mirror as his red car moved along behind hers; he parked so poorly he almost ruined a young birch tree. She heard his steps behind her on the steep walkway. She felt like a whale, imagining her large back from his eyes.

"It's nice, Olive," he said, ducking his head, although there was plenty of room for him to stand up straight. She showed him the "bump-out room," where you could lie and see the side garden through all the glass. She showed him the library built the year before Henry's stroke, with its cathedral ceiling and skylights. He looked at the books, and she wanted to say, "Stop that," as though he were reading her diary.

"He's like a child," she told Bunny. "He touches everything. Honest to God, he picked up my wooden seagull, turned it around, put it back in the wrong place, then picked up the clay vase Christopher gave us one year, and turned *that* over. What was he looking for, a price?"

Bunny said, "I think you're being a little hard on him, Olive."

So she didn't talk to Bunny about him anymore. She didn't tell

Bunny how they had supper again the next week, how he kissed her on her cheek when she said good night, how they went to Portland to go to a concert, and that night he lightly kissed her mouth! No, these were not things to be spoken of; it was nobody's business. And certainly nobody's business that she lay awake at the age of seventy-four and thought about his arms around her, pictured what she had not pictured or done in years.

At the same time, in her head, she criticized him. He's afraid to be alone, she thought. He's weak. Men were. Probably wants somebody to cook his meals, pick up after him. In which case, he was barking up the wrong tree. He spoke of his mother with such frequency, and in such glowing terms—something had to be wrong there. If he wanted a mother, he'd better go looking elsewhere.

For five days it rained. Harsh and heavy—so much for spring. This rain was cold and autumnal, and even Olive, with her need to walk by the river, saw no point in heading out in the mornings. She was not one to carry an umbrella. She had to wait it out, in the car outside Dunkin' Donuts with the dog in the backseat. Hellish days. Jack Kennison didn't call, and she didn't call him. She thought he'd probably found someone else to listen to his sorrows. She pictured him sitting beside some woman at a concert in Portland, and thought she could put a bullet right through his head. Once again she thought about her own death, *Let it be quick.* She called Christopher in New York. "How are you?" she said, angry because he never called.

"Fine," he said. "How are you?"

"Hellish," she answered. "How's Ann and the kids?" Christopher had married a woman with two children, and now there was his. "Everyone still walking?"

"Still walking," Chris said. "Crazy, hectic."

She almost hated him then. Her life had once been crazy and hectic, too. You just wait, she thought. Everyone thinks they know everything, and no one knows a damn thing.

"How was your date?"

"What date?" she asked.

"With that guy you couldn't stand."

"That wasn't a date, for crying out loud."

"Okay, but how was it?"

"Just fine," she said. "He's a nitwit, and your father always knew it."

"Daddy knew him?" Chris said. "You never told me that."

"Not *knew* him knew him," Olive retorted. "Just knew him from afar. Enough to know he was a nitwit."

"Theodore's crying," Christopher said. "I have to go."

And then—like a rainbow—Jack Kennison called. "It's supposed to clear off by tomorrow. Shall we meet on the river path?"

"Don't see why not," Olive said. "Six o'clock I take off."

In the morning, when she drove into the gravelly lot by the river, Jack Kennison leaned against his red car, and nodded, his hands staying in his pockets. He had on a Windbreaker she'd not seen before, blue—it matched his eyes. She had to get her walking shoes from the trunk and put them on in front of him, which annoyed her. Her walking shoes had been bought in the men's department, right after Henry died. Broad, and beige, they still laced up, they still "walked." She stood up, her breathing heavy. "Let's go," she said.

"I might want to rest on the one-mile bench. I know you like to keep going."

She looked at him. His wife had died five months ago. "I'll rest whenever you want to rest," she said.

The river was to their left, broadening at one point, the small island seen, some of the bushes on it already a bright, bright green.

"My ancestors paddled their canoes up this river," Olive said.

Jack didn't answer.

"I thought I'd have grandchildren that would paddle up the river, too. But my grandson's growing up in New York City. I guess it's the way of the world. Hurts, though. Have that DNA flung all over like so much dandelion fuzz." Olive had to walk slower, to match Jack's ambling stride. It was hard, like not drinking water fast if you were thirsty.

"At least you have DNA to get tossed," he said, his hands still in his pockets. "I won't be having any grandchildren. Or not really."

"What do you mean 'not really'? How can you *not really* have grand-children?"

It took him a while to answer, as she suspected it would. She glanced at him and thought he did not look his best; something un-pleasant sat on his face, his head thrust forward from his sloping shoulders. "My daughter has chosen to live an alternative lifestyle. Out in California."

"I guess California's still the place for that. Alternative lifestyles."

"She lives with a woman," Jack said. "She lives with a woman the way others would live with a man."

"I see," Olive said. There, in the shade, was the first-mile-marker granite bench. "Want to sit?"

Jack sat. She sat. They looked out over the river. An elderly couple walked by holding hands, nodded to them, as though they were a couple, too. When the couple was out of earshot, Olive said, "So I take it you don't like that, about your daughter?"

"I don't like it at all," Jack said. He raised his chin. "Perhaps I'm shallow," he said.

"Oh, you're sophisticated," Olive answered, adding, "Though I guess in my opinion, that can mean the same thing."

He looked at her, his old eyebrows shooting up.

"However, I'm not the least bit sophisticated. I'm essentially a peasant. And I have the strong passions and prejudices of a peasant."

"What does that mean?" Jack asked.

Olive reached into her pocket, found her sunglasses, put them on.

After a while, Jack said, "Be honest. If your son told you he wanted to sleep with men, did sleep with men, was in love with a man, lived with him, slept with him, made a home with him—do you think, really, you wouldn't mind?"

"I wouldn't mind," Olive retorted. "I would love him with all my heart."

"You're being sentimental," Jack said. "You don't know how you'd feel because you haven't been presented with it."

Olive's cheeks grew warm. There was the prick of perspiration beneath one arm. "I've been presented with plenty."

"Like what?"

"Like the fact that my son married a hellion who moved him to California, then walked out on him."

"Statistically, Olive, that happens all the time. Fifty percent of the time."

"So what?" It struck her as a stupid, unfeeling response. "And what are the statistics of having a gay child?" she asked. Her feet looked enormous, stuck out there at the end of her legs. She pulled them in under the bench.

"It changes. Every study they do says something new. But obviously, fifty percent of one's offspring do not turn out to be gay."

"Maybe she's not gay," said Olive. "Maybe she just hates men."

Jack Kennison folded his arms against his blue Windbreaker, stared straight ahead. "I'm not sure that's very nice, Olive. I haven't offered a theory on why your son married a hellion."

It took Olive a moment to absorb this. "Ducky," she said. "A ducky thing to say." She stood up, and didn't wait to see if he stood, too. But she heard him behind her, and she slowed enough to walk with him; she was heading back to the car.

"I still don't know what you mean by saying you're a peasant. In this country I don't think it's peasantry. Perhaps you mean you're a cowboy." She glanced at him, was surprised to see he was smiling at her good-naturedly. "I can see you as a cowboy," he said.

"Fine, I'm a cowboy."

"A Republican, then?" Jack asked, after a moment.

"Oh, for God's sake." Olive stopped walking, looked at him through her sunglasses. "I didn't say *moron*. You mean because we have a cowboy for a president? Or before that an actor who *played* a cowboy? Let me tell you, that idiot ex-cocaine-addict was never a cowboy. He can wear all the cowboy hats he wants. He's a spoiled brat to the manor born. And he makes me puke."

She was really riled, and it took her a moment to see that he was looking away, his expression closed off, as though inside his head he had backed away, was just waiting for her to finish.

"God," she said finally. "You didn't."

"Didn't what?"

"You voted for him."

Jack Kennison looked tired.

"You voted for him. You, Mr. Harvard, Mr. Brains. You voted for that stinker."

He gave a small bark of a laugh. "My God, you do have the passions and the prejudices of a peasant."

"That's it," said Olive. She began walking, at her pace now. She said over her shoulder, "At least I'm not prejudiced against homosexuals."

"No," he called. "Just white men with money."

Damn right, she thought.

She called Bunny, and Bunny—Olive couldn't believe this—actually *laughed*. "Oh, Olive," she said. "Does it really matter?"

"Matter that someone voted for a man who is lying to the country? Bunny, for God's sake, this world is a mess."

"That's true enough," Bunny said. "But the world has always been a mess. I think if you enjoy his company, you should just let it go."

"I don't enjoy his company," Olive said, and hung up. She'd never realized Bunny was an idiot, but there you were.

It was terrible, though, when you couldn't tell people things. Olive felt this keenly as the days went by. She called Christopher. "He's a Republican," she said.

"Well, that's gross," Christopher answered. Then: "I thought you were calling to see how your grandson is."

"Of course I wonder how he is. I wish you'd call *me* to tell me how he is." Where and how, exactly, this rupture with her son had taken place, Olive couldn't have said.

"I do call you, Mom." A long pause. "But—"

"But what?"

"Well, it's a little hard to converse with you."

"I see. Everything is my fault."

"No. Everything is someone else's fault; that's my point."

It had to be her son's therapist who was responsible for all this. Who would ever have expected this? She said into the phone, "Not I, said the Little Red Hen."

"What?"

She hung up.

Two weeks passed by. She walked along the river earlier than six, so she wouldn't bump into Jack, and because she woke after just a few hours' sleep. The spring was gorgeous, and seemed an assault. Star-flowers popped through the pine needles, clusters of purple violets were there by the granite seat. She passed the elderly couple, who were holding hands again. After that, she stopped her walking. For a few days she stayed in bed, which—to her memory—she had never done before. She was not a lie-er downer.

Christopher didn't call, Bunny didn't call. Jack Kennison didn't call.

One night she woke at midnight. She turned on her computer, and typed in Jack's e-mail address, which she had gotten back when they were having lunch and going into Portland for concerts.

"Does your daughter hate you?" she wrote.

In the morning was the simple "Yes."

She waited two days. The she wrote: "My son hates me, too."

An hour later came the response. "Does it kill you? It kills me that my daughter hates me. But I know it's my fault."

She wrote immediately. "It kills me. Like the devil. And it must be my fault, too, though I don't understand it. I don't remember things the way he seems to remember them. He sees a psychiatrist named Arthur, and I think Arthur has done this." She paused a long time, clicked on Send, then immediately wrote, "P.S. But it has to be my fault, too. Henry said I never apologized for anything, ever, and maybe he was right." She clicked on Send. Then she wrote: "P.S. AGAIN. He was right."

There was no reply to this, and she felt like a schoolgirl whose crush had walked off with a different girl. In fact, Jack probably did have a different girl, or woman. Old woman. Plenty of them around— Republicans, too. She lay on the bed in the little bump-out room and listened to the transistor radio she held to her ear. Then she got up and went outside, taking the dog for a walk on a leash, because if he was loose, he'd eat one of the Moodys' cats; this had happened before.

When she came back, the sun was just past its peak, and it was a bad time of day for her; it'd be better when it got dark. How she had loved the long evenings of spring when she was young, and all of life stretched before her. She was looking through the cupboard for a Milk-Bone for the dog when she heard her phone message machine beep. It was ludicrous, how hopeful she was that Bunny or Chris had called. Jack Kennison's voice said, "Olive. Could you come over?"

She brushed her teeth, left the dog in his pen.

His shiny red car was in his small driveway. When she knocked on the door, there was no answer. She pushed the door open. "Hello?"

"Hello, Olive. I'm back here. I'm lying down, I'll be right there."

"No," she sang out, "stay put. I'll come find you." She found him on the bed in the downstairs guest room. He was lying on his back, one hand beneath his head.

"I'm glad you came over," he said.

"Are you feeling poorly again?"

He smiled that tiny smile. "Only soul poor. The body bangs on."

She nodded.

He moved his legs aside. "Come," he said, patting the bed. "Sit down. I may be a rich Republican, though I'm not that rich, in case you were secretly hoping. Anyway—" He sighed and shook his head, the sunlight from the windows catching his eyes, making them very blue. "Anyway, Olive, you can tell me anything, that you beat your son black and blue, and I won't hold it against you. I don't think I will. I've beaten my daughter emotionally. I didn't speak to her for two years, can you imagine such a thing?"

"I did hit my son," Olive said. "Sometimes when he was little. Not just spanked. Hit."

Jack Kennison nodded one nod.

She stepped into the room, put her handbag on the floor. He didn't sit up, just stayed there, lying on the bed, an old man, his stomach bulging like a sack of sunflower seeds. His blue eyes watched her as she walked to him, and the room was filled with the quietness of afternoon sunlight. It fell through the window, across the rocking chair, hit broadside the wallpaper with its brightness. The mahogany bed knobs shone. Through the curved-out window was the blue of the sky, the bayberry bush, the stone wall. The silence of this sunshine, of the world, seemed to fold over Olive with a shiver of ghastliness, as she stood feeling the sun on her bare wrist. She watched him, looked away, looked at him again. To sit down beside him would be to close her eyes to the gaping loneliness of this sunlit world.

"God, I'm scared," he said, quietly.

She almost said, "Oh, stop. I hate scared people." She would have said that to Henry, to just about anyone. Maybe because she hated the scared part of herself—this was just a fleeting thought; there was a contest within her, revulsion and tentative desire. It was the sudden memory of Jane Houlton in the waiting room that caused Olive to walk to the bed—the freedom of that ordinary banter, because Jack, in the doctor's office, had needed her, had given her a place in the world.

His blue eyes were watching her now; she saw in them the vulnerability, the invitation, the fear, as she sat down quietly, placed her open hand on his chest, felt the thump, thump of his heart, which would someday stop, as all hearts do. But there was no someday now, there was only the silence of this sunny room. They were here, and her body—old, big, sagging—felt straight-out desire for his. That she had not loved Henry this way for many years before he died saddened her enough to make her close her eyes.

What young people didn't know, she thought, lying down beside this man, his hand on her shoulder, her arm; oh, what young people did not know. They did not know that lumpy, aged, and wrinkled bodies were as needy as their own young, firm ones, that love was not to be tossed away carelessly, as if it were a tart on a platter with others that got passed around again. No, if love was available, one chose it, or didn't choose it. And if her platter had been full with the goodness of Henry and she had found it burdensome, had flicked it off crumbs at a time, it was because she had not known what one should know: that day after day was unconsciously squandered.

And so, if this man next to her now was not a man she would have chosen before this time, what did it matter? He most likely wouldn't have chosen her either. But here they were, and Olive pictured two slices of Swiss cheese pressed together, such holes they brought to this union—what pieces life took out of you.

Her eyes were closed, and throughout her tired self swept waves of gratitude—and regret. She pictured the sunny room, the sun-washed wall, the bayberry outside. It baffled her, the world. She did not want to leave it yet.

SIMON &
SCHUSTER

Elizabeth Strout

Amy & Isabelle

Shortlisted for the Orange Prize for Fiction

Amy Goodrow wants a new mother. Isabelle Goodrow never
expected to be one, and has struggled for the last sixteen years
to do it properly. When Amy is discovered in the throes of an
intense affair with her maths teacher, mother and daughter
engage in a battle of wills that threatens to break down the
brittle construct of their existence in Shirley Falls, and reveal to
all the hidden grief and shame that dominates their lives.

'A complex and moving account of growing up, which depicts
the powerful emotions of adolescence – and, indeed, of later
life – with humour and sympathy'
The Times

'A novel of shining integrity and humour, about the bravery
and hard choices of what is called ordinary life'
Alice Munro

ISBN 978-1-84983-304-2
PRICE £7.99

SIMON &
SCHUSTER

Elizabeth Strout

Abide with Me

When five-year-old Katherine is struck dumb with grief at her mother's death, it is down to her father, minister Tyler Caskey, to bring his daughter out of her silence.

But Tyler is barely surviving himself. His cold, church-assigned home is colder still since his wife's death, and he struggles to find the right words for his sermons; struggles to be a leader to his congregation when he himself is lost.

As the small town rumour-mill goes into overdrive, Tyler's darkest hour approaches. Soon, a startling discovery will test his congregation's humanity – and his own will to endure the kinds of trials that sooner or later test us all.

From the Orange Prize-shortlisted author of *Amy & Isabelle*, this is a startlingly beautiful novel about love and abandon-ment, faith and hypocrisy; and the peril of family secrets.

ISBN 978-0-7434-6228-0
PRICE £7.99

SIMON &
SCHUSTER

Elizabeth Strout

The Burgess Boys

Haunted by the freak accident that killed their father when they were children, Jim and Bob Burgess escaped from their Maine hometown of Shirley Falls for New York City as soon as they possibly could. Jim, a sleek, successful corporate lawyer, has belittled his bighearted brother their whole lives; and Bob, a legal aid attorney who idolises Jim, has always taken it in his stride. But their long-standing dynamic is upended when their sister, Susan – the sibling who stayed behind – urgently calls them home. Her teenage son, Zach, has landed himself in a world of trouble, and Susan needs their help. And so the Burgess brothers return to the landscape of their childhood, where long-buried tensions begin to surface in unexpected ways that will change them forever.

ISBN 978-1-4711-2738-0
PRICE £7.99